yours

JASINDA WILDER

This book is dedicated to nurses the world over: you are the unsung heroes of the medical profession. Thank you, each of you, for all you do.

Special thanks as well to Russel, Parker, and Casey for writing "Yours":

I heard a single line in a song— "You put a new heartbeat inside of me" —and felt this story unfold in my mind, cut from whole cloth. Just goes to show the power of good music.

Just lost in the sky wondering why

Pacific Coast Highway,
just north of Los Angeles, California

"No—" It comes out as a sob.

"NO." A denial.

"NO!" A plea.

The sun beats down on me, pounding on the back of my head, burning the back of my neck. Heat radiates in visible, palpable waves from the blacktop and it burns under my shins as I kneel on the side of the highway. Sweat trickles down my temples, slides like a warm, tickling finger between my breasts.

I shake my head. Damp, tangled ringlets of brown hair stick to my cheek and against my lips. I lean forward and shake his inert body.

I pull my hands away. Sticky. Red.

"Ollie. Talk to me. Please. You're going to be

fine. Please."

I know it's futile, but still I plead. "Come back to me, Ollie. Don't leave me." I beg, but I know only a ghost will hear me.

I look around and see a slow procession of cars inching past us in a slowly moving river of steel and glass, morbid curiosity slowing them. I hear snippets of conversation.

"Mommy, why is that woman crying?"

"Because the man is hurt, sweetie."

No one stops. No one pulls over. Then I hear sirens, somewhere far away. I collapse onto Ollie, and feel something wet and warm and sticky against my cheek. Oliver's blood. I taste it in my mouth.

"Ma'am?" A woman's voice. Small hands on my shoulder, pulling me away. Calm and professional. "Can you sit up, please, ma'am?"

I shake my head and clutch Ollie's cooling arms.

"I need to take a look at him, ma'am. I need you to come with me, okay?"

"He's dead. You don't need to look at him, because he's dead." I don't bother opening my eyes; I just lie on top of Oliver and cling to futility and misery.

Insistent hands, now. Two pairs. Three. Pulling me away forcefully. Something drips from my chin.

"You're hurt, ma'am. We need to look at your

arm." The same voice, the same woman.

I twist, and look at her. She's young, blonde, beautiful. Dressed in dark blue paramedic gear, hair in a fishtail braid over her left shoulder. She gently takes hold of my left arm near my elbow and near my wrist. I look down and see that my arm is broken. Very badly, and in more than one place. White bone protrudes from the skin near the middle of my forearm. Her touch reminds me that I am in excruciating agony. I scream.

I scream more for Oliver than because of my own physical pain.

I glance up and see two paramedics placing Oliver in a body bag, closing the zipper, and then lifting him onto the gurney.

"No, no..." I pull away, lurching toward Oliver. "Let me say goodbye, let me—let me say goodbye, please."

The female paramedic moves with me, somehow anticipating my movements and managing to keep hold of my injured arm with both hands. I use my one good hand to shove her away. I bang my injured arm on the stretcher, but the pain is nothing compared to the ocean of grief, the sea of shock boiling just beneath the surface of my psyche, waiting to yank me under like a riptide.

I know this feeling all too well.

The paramedic lowers the zipper so I can see Ollie's face. It's battered, bruised, cut. Part of his face is missing. He was so beautiful, but now…death has made him ugly. But I don't care. I kiss his forehead, the only part that is strangely untouched.

"I love you, Ollie. I love you. God, I'm sorry. I'm so sorry." My legs shake and give out, and then I'm on the ground. "I'm so sorry."

Hands are there to help me up. I breathe deeply, because now my own training kicks in, and I force myself to my feet, force myself to remain upright. I shudder, brushing away a lock of Oliver's hair, black with strands of premature gray. I used to call him Pep, short for Pepper, joking that when the gray took over completely, I'd start calling him Salty.

So much skill, so much bravery. All of it gone. Snatched in an instant. His life over in milliseconds.

I bend over once more, kissing his forehead. "Goodbye, Oliver."

The men glance at me, and I nod. Then I watch as they close the body bag once more.

Orange cones, strobing lights, sirens, flares. Police officers direct traffic, a fire truck and an EMS rig park at angles around the accident scene to block it off from rubber-neckers and gawkers. A few feet away is what remains of our car, overturned, smoking, totalled. Further down the freeway is the tipped-over semi that slammed into us. I see other cars, more ambulances and police cruisers, more flares and cones, another team of medics is tending to someone else.

The scene is a mess, a fucking mess.

I'm led to the back of an ambulance, helped up and in, and I sit on the bench. The blonde EMS woman is examining my arm. "Can you tell me your name?"

"Niall Emory James." Here comes the shock. I feel it rolling through me, but I don't fight it.

"How old are you, Niall?"

"Thirty-two. My husband's name is Oliver Michael James—was...was Oliver Michael James. He is—he was a surgeon with Doctors Without Borders. And I'm in shock, I believe."

"That's understandable. Does anything else hurt besides your arm?" She's very good, this medic. Keeping me talking while she works on my arm. Immobilizing it until we get to the hospital. It's too badly broken to be set here.

"No. Just my arm." I speak, but it feels like my lips are thick and frozen, as if the words are tumbling out of my mouth unbidden.

Her voice is distant. "Can you tell me what happened?"

"A semi. Somebody cut us off, clipped our front end, and I overcorrected. I was driving. I wasn't paying attention. We were arguing. Something stupid. Not a real argument, just…one of those tiffs you get into when you're both stressed, you know? He wanted the radio on The Highway, I wanted it on Hits One. *So stupid*. I wasn't paying attention. The semi smashed into us, and we just went—flying. Hit another car. That one up there." I point, and my finger shakes. "I don't know. We rolled. When we stopped, we were both conscious. I tried to get him out. I knew I shouldn't move him, but he was bleeding and I had to save him, I had to—I tried to—I had to save him, and I couldn't. His femoral artery was nicked, and he had severe cranial trauma, and—and internal bleeding too, I think. I tried. I tried…But I couldn't save him."

I look down at my hands. They're red. Coated in crimson. There is a layer of thick dark red under my fingernails. Crusted blood has dried red around my cuticles. The wrinkles on my wrist are white creases in the layer of effluvia. I touch my face, tracing the tacky gore on my cheek, and in the strands of my hair.

"You couldn't have saved him, Niall. I saw him. Okay? There was nothing you could have done. There's nothing anyone could have done. Even if you'd had him in a hospital, I don't think he would have made it." She's done with my arm for the moment, and now she has a towel and she's wiping my face. Cleaning away the worst of Oliver's blood.

"Emily—you guys ready?" The gruff male voice of the paramedic looking in through the open back doors of the rig.

"Yeah, take us out."

I know I'll cry rivers of tears. But right now, I can't. I can only sit and feel the sting of tears behind my eyes waiting to be released, and feel the raging inferno of pain that's still distant somehow.

It's not real. It's still not real. I know it will become real eventually, but right now Oliver is just somewhere else. I'll be waiting for him to come home, but he won't. He's not dead, yet. Not in my head.

"Oliver, he's...he's a donor. An organ donor."

"Saving lives even when he's gone," she says.

She understands.

"He had the most beautiful soul. His heart...he lived to help other people. Every beat of his heart was...for someone else. I hope his heart goes to someone good."

I was a boat stuck in a bottle

The British Virgin Islands

I SHOULDN'T DO THIS. I *REALLY* SHOULD NOT BE DOING THIS. My doctors, an army of lawyers, shit, even Leanne would tell me not to fucking do this.

Which, of course, is why I'm going to do it anyway.

I've been standing on this rock cliff for the past ten minutes, timing the swell, watching the angry, roiling, spraying surf gush and rise and fill the tidal pool below, watch it drain back out, revealing a keyhole archway leading out of the pool and into the open ocean beyond. It's goddamned suicide, this jump. The surf is going to be mad, the undertow murder. The open archway is *maybe* six or seven feet across, with unscalable walls of vicious rock on every side. If I mistime the jump, I'll get churned into toothpaste. If I can't hold my breath long enough, I'll get churned into toothpaste. If I can't swim hard enough to get through the keyhole, I'll get sucked under and churned into toothpaste. It's no fucking wonder I shouldn't be doing this.

My nerves are jangling.

My heart is thumping dangerously hard.

I watch the swell rise and fall twice more. Then I take three deep breaths, hold the fourth, and jump as the swell reaches its apex. I kick as hard as I can, straining my arms with everything I've got, diving deeper so I don't crack my skull on the arch. I feel the undertow pulling me forward, through the opening. I feel the water churning all around; I hear the muffled echoing thunder of the surf crashing above me. The water is white, nearly opaque, and I can't see more than a few feet in any direction.

I'm swimming for all I'm worth, feeling my heartbeat ratcheting to dangerously high levels. I have to surface. I have to breathe. The longer I go without oxygen, the harder my heart has to work, and making my heart work any harder than necessary is complete foolishness.

Or, at least, that's what the lab coats tell me.

But fuck 'em.

I keep swimming until the churning fades, until the crashing thunder of the surf quietens, until the undertow is lessened. I let myself drift upward, let my head break the surface and then blink the brine out of my eyes. I twist, tread water, and look back.

I howl my victory; pump my fist in the air as my companions jump and cheer on the cliff top.

Yay! I did it! And I didn't fucking die!

Again.

Go me.

I swim lazily around the opposite side of the rock formation that creates the pool and archway to where the *Vagabond* is anchored. I watch the other tourists I've been partying with the last few days, my "friends of the day"—my term for the temporary, single-serving friends I make wherever I go—run across the rocks on bare feet, making for my boat.

I swim up to the boat and climb up the ladder onto the deck, flopping over onto my back, still trying to get my heartbeat under control.

"You jumped?" Leanne says, pissed.

"Shit, yeah!" I hop to my feet, jubilant, flush with adrenaline. "I jumped, and I made it. I told you I'd be fine."

She crosses her arms over her breasts, snarling at me. "But what if you hadn't made it, Lock?"

I grab her by the arms, and jerk her up against me. "Then I'd be dead, and it wouldn't fucking matter."

"Yeah, it kind of would." She's sniffling now, trying to play my emotions.

Good luck with that, sweetheart.

I shut her up with a short, hard kiss. "Lee, seriously. You gotta quit worrying about me, babe. I'll be fine. I'm always fine."

"One of these days you *won't* be fine." She turns away, no trace of the sniffles remaining as we both watch the FODs scramble down the rock, jump into the water, swim for the boat, and then hop onto the deck, chattering to each other, and to me, and to Leanne.

There are six of them today. Hell if I can keep them all straight, but I know the big burly one is Carlos, the tall, stacked, black chick with the dreadlocks is Mel, and the short, smarmy dude is Victor. The other three are newer—they just showed up yesterday when they saw the party raging on deck, and invited themselves over. Fine by me because, hell, the more the merrier. Carlos, Mel, and Vic are all tourists, down in the BVIs for a week of fun in the sun that includes lots of booze and sex. I think Carlos is from Spain, Mel is from the UK somewhere, and Vic is Italian. That's all I know, that's all I care to know.

Once everyone's aboard, I pull anchor and catch the wind. Carlos knows his way around the sails, so he's immediately on the lines, helping me get us underway. The beauty of the *Vagabond*'s design is that I'm completely capable of running her all by myself, but obviously it's easier with more hands to help.

Once the sails are set and the lines are cleated where I want them, I break out the good stuff: Lagavulin 16. After making that jump I feel I deserve a reward. We're headed for Tortola—Road Town, to be specific—and it won't take but an hour or so to get there, which means we've got plenty of time to party. I pour healthy measures of the fine-ass sixteen-year-old single malt over ice for the guys, and hand Leanne and Mel each a beer. Lee will drink whisky when it's just the two of us, but in company she sticks to beer.

There's a lively debate going on between Carlos and Vic about soccer, of course. *Football*, I should say. Those two will argue football from dawn till dusk, and if you add in some booze, it'll get heated. All in good fun, though. Leanne and Mel are off by themselves, talking…about what I don't know. My other FOD guests are a couple from Connecticut, John and Lacey, down here on their honeymoon, and the last person is a single girl. A sexy as hell single girl, too. Platinum hair, perfect skin, a bangin' body, and a cute little Scandinavian accent. Astrid, her name is.

I offer her a beer, but she simply cocks an eyebrow at me. "Can I not have the whisky? Or is that only for the men?"

"You want whisky?"

"Beer is for pussies and those already drunk."

I laugh. "Well, all right then. Neat or on the rocks?"

"On the rocks, please."

"Coming right up." I pour a glass over ice and hand it to her.

"So, Astrid. What brings you down this way?"

A laconic shrug. "I have just finish my degree at university. I am on holiday before I start doctorate work."

"Doctorate, huh? In what?"

She sips the Lagavulin, swallows it without so much as a wince. "Medical research. Cancer research, more specifically."

"Damn. That's impressive."

A smile, not quite shy, not quite proud, somewhere in between. "I suppose. What is it you do, Lachlan?"

"Call me Lock—only my mom calls me Lachlan." I gesture at the boat with my tumbler of whisky. "This. Sail wherever I want to go, drink with friends. The occasional adventure, when the mood strikes me."

A speculative glance, then. "So you do nothing?"

"Not all of us can be cancer researchers, Astrid." I shake my glass to stir the ice.

"Don't mistake me, please. It sounds wonderful." She leans back against the railing, squints behind her sunglasses at the brilliant sunlight bathing her face. "To go wherever you wish, do whatever you wish? That is your whole life?"

"Pretty much."

"How do you afford it?"

My turn to shrug. "The answer to that will only irritate you even more."

"I am not irritated. Only jealous, a little."

"It's a good life. A little jealousy is natural."

She lifts her glass, and I clink mine against hers. "To a good life, then."

"To a good life," I agree.

There's a lot I'm not mentioning, of course. Things I'd never tell anyone, even Leanne. She has been sailing with me since South Africa, four and a half months ago, and there's things even she doesn't know. There's no sense burdening anyone with bullshit that can't be changed.

"I do not think I could do it, though," Astrid says. She sips, and tugs at the strap of her halter bikini top, lifting her breasts up, then tugs the elastic beneath them, snugging those big, pale melons into place.

I can't help but watch, and I know Astrid is watching me watch.

"Do what?" I ask.

She gestures with her tumbler, the way I did. "Your life. I am driven to work. I have to feel productive. And besides, I did not choose cancer research for the excitement of it."

"No? Why did you, then?"

"My father died of cancer. So did my aunt. It is a nasty thing, to watch someone die of cancer. I want to do my part to find a cure."

"Admirable."

I can sense her cornflower blue eyes cut to mine, sharp and speculative. "Admirable? Why does that sound like an insult?"

"It's not, I swear. It really *is* admirable. I respect you for having that goal, and for working as hard at it as I suspect you do."

"I do work hard. I am twenty-three, and I have completed my undergraduate and graduate university work. I will have my doctorate by the time I am twenty-five. By thirty, I will be the most sought-after research doctor in Europe. You watch, you will see."

"Damn, girl. You do have goals." I really do respect the hell out of her for it, too. I'm not just paying lip service.

She nods. "Of course. Without goals, how do you know where you want to go in your life? You would only drift, aimless, like a ship without a keel." She looks at me as she says this. It's a dig. Subtle, but a dig.

"Not everything is as it seems, Astrid," I murmur. I don't owe her any explanations. "I have goals."

"Such as what?"

Live to see thirty-one, or die trying? I don't say this, though. "My goals aren't the kind of thing you'd recognize as such. I don't mean that as an insult, either. A person's life, a person's worth can't be summed up by what they've done, what they've accomplished. It's not that easy, to just…" I wave my hand in circles, "boil it all down to something that neat and simple."

"Perhaps not."

Astrid and I talk for the rest of the trip to Tortola, the topics shifting from philosophy to religion, politics, even to exes.

We arrive at the marina and I gently pull us into a slip and tie us off. The Lagavulin is gone by this point—that bottle, at least—and the party sort of naturally breaks up. Mel and Vic and the couple from Connecticut head off to find another party. Carlos has Leanne enthralled with an unlikely sounding story about hang gliding in Brazil. Leanne cuts me a glance, and I acknowledge it with a nod; she subtly starts moving off the *Vagabond* and Carlos goes as well, helping her onto the dock. I watch them vanish into the crowds, Carlos still gesticulating with typical Latin ebullience.

Astrid is on her third glass of whisky, and looking loose and happy. I take a seat beside her on the long, cushion-lined bench in the galley, sliding my arm behind her.

She leans into me. "I thought you and Leanne were…" She circles a hand. "A thing."

"Not really. Sort of, but not really."

"What does this mean?"

"It means we have an understanding."

"You are a thing when it is convenient for you both?"

"Pretty much." I twist so my back is against the cushion, pulling her closer. "It just means we're not exclusive. She went with Carlos. She'll come back in the morning, or if she decides she wants to hang here in Tortola with him for a while, then…whatever. I'm heading for St. Thomas tomorrow afternoon and she knows it. If she's staying here in Tortola, she'll drop by to get her things."

"And you wouldn't miss her?" Astrid rests her sweating, mostly empty tumbler on my chest, peering at me curiously. "You seem to know each other well."

I shrug. "I'd miss her. We've sailed together for several months now. She made the Atlantic crossing with me. We've had some good times, and she's a great companion. Smart, fun, easy to talk to, good looking, and a good sailor. But if she stays here, that's her decision. I'd miss her, but it'd be her decision."

"And you've slept together, you and Leanne?"

I nod. "Yeah. She's a great lay."

This gets me a frown. "It's a strange relationship. You speak of it so openly."

"It is what it is. She knows how it works as well as I do. We've talked about it. It was just her and me for a good month, from when we left South Africa to when we made landfall after the crossing. Just recently, Carlos, Mel, and Vic joined us. So Lee and I had a lot of time to just talk."

"And this?" Astrid's eyes penetrate mine, her palm on my chest, near my neck. She's referring to her and me. She's tipsy, but lucid, sharp. She wants to know the score. "What is *this*?"

"Whatever you want it to be, honey." I take her glass from her and set it aside. I pull her up against my body, cup her ass and move in for a kiss, but stop short. I don't take the kiss just yet. "It can be for tonight, or it can be for longer. You want to come to St. Thomas with me?"

"But it is not a thing?"

"If you want it to be a thing, it can be a thing."

"Until someone else comes along, you mean."

"Nope. If you and me are a thing, then we're a thing. There wouldn't be anyone else until we decided to go our separate ways."

"But it's not a forever thing."

"Nothing is forever."

"Some things are."

"You're headed back to Sweden for your doctorate, yeah?"

"Yes."

"You looking for forever?"

"Not really, but—"

"Then why are you asking about it?"

She shrugs; it's a cute, endearing gesture. "Good point. I tend to get philosophical when I've been drinking."

"My philosophy is, when a good thing comes along, enjoy it for as long as you can."

"And what does this mean for me?" This comes out sultry, her hips bumping against mine.

Oh man, she's game; hell, yeah. "It means you're a really good thing, and I'd like to enjoy you for as long as you want it to last."

"That was a good line." Her lips brush mine, but she's holding back.

I go in for the kiss, and she responds eagerly. Knowing this kiss is just the beginning, I take her hand and lead her to my cabin. Neither of us are wearing much, so it doesn't take long to shed the little we have on, and then she's moving on top of me and I've got a handful of her slippery Slavic blonde locks, showing her how I like her to move. She takes what she wants, shows me how she likes it. She moves hard and fast, using her fingers to get herself there faster. Takes my breath away, when she gets there. When I find my own release, my heart hammers hard, and I get dizzy.

My heart is thumping so hard it hurts, and that's a really bad thing.

Astrid is limp on top of me, and normally I'd welcome it, but I can't breathe. I don't want to worry her, so I try to make it casual, the way I roll her off. Then I tug her against my side so she's in the nook, close, but no longer lying on my chest, not pressing against my lungs. She's on the right side, so she can't feel how mad my heartbeat is. I hold her, and focus on square breathing.

Square breathing is a technique I learned years ago to slow my heartbeat: deep breath in through my nose, hold it for four seconds, deep breath out, hold it for four seconds. Repeat until my heartbeat evens out.

It doesn't take long for me to realize that Astrid is out, the combo of whisky and an orgasm taking her under. I slip my arm out from underneath her, go to my collection of stupid little orange fucking bottles. It's a sizable collection, most of which shouldn't be mixed with booze, but fuck it.

That's my real philosophy: Fuck it.

I take the pill I need, pour another drink, down it, and get back in bed with Astrid.

It's only late evening, but it's been a long day, so I let myself slide under the veil of sleep.

At some point, Astrid wakes me up, and we go another round.

When I wake up again, it's dawn, and she's gone.

She left a note: *You are wrong about one thing, Lock: the only true measure of a person is what they do with their life.*

Ouch, that's a little rough, Astrid.

But goddamn if she isn't right. The problem is, it takes time to accomplish anything worthwhile.

And time is the one luxury I do not possess.

Rio de Janeiro, Brazil
Four weeks later

Funny how things work out. Leanne and Carlos are, as Astrid would have put it, a thing. And they're both aboard the *Vagabond* with me. Astrid left after that first night and I haven't seen her since. Leanne is now with Carlos. Which leaves me…with Mel.

We hit St. Thomas for a while, but that played

out pretty quick, so we decided to head for Rio to see if we could find a good berth for Carnival. I'm not exactly jealous of Carlos and Leanne, but it's not what I expected. I'd thought things with Astrid would run their course, and the thing with Leanne and Carlos would do the same, and then things would go back to the way they were: me and Leanne, sailing and fucking.

It was a good system.

But, like I told Astrid, I can't be jealous since Leanne and I had agreed we didn't have a thing going, that we had an understanding.

I'm not jealous, because we didn't have a thing, and now she and Carlos do.

They have a really good thing, actually. And that's what pisses me off.

Leanne told me, back in South Africa, that she was running away from her old life, from everyone, from a good thing gone bad. She didn't want to take anything seriously. Just take me wherever you go, she'd said. We'll have a good time and eventually I'll find somewhere to be, or I'll head back to Jo-burg.

Leanne is a hell of a bartender, so she can find work anywhere. Carlos is—I don't know. Someone with his own money and plenty of time to kill. He's cool, he's suave, and he's got good stories.

And shit, man, that was my role.

But I ain't mad at the guy. Apparently he's got good game, landing a running-wild chick like Leanne. They're talking about staying in Rio after Carnival, since *of course* Carlos has a line on a good place for lease right near the beach, close to all the bars where Leanne can get a job, and he can work from anywhere.

I can only watch them make plans, watch them solidify the good-thing status of what they've got going on.

Mel and I aren't really a thing. We kick it, but she's only in it for the temporary pleasure. Once the golden sheen of fresh sex fades to a patina, she'll go her own way.

And I'll be alone.

Which is cool.

Totally cool.

Right now, we're hiking in the rain forest outside Rio. Not a real hike, just sort of walking around. Carlos knows the area well enough to not get lost, so he's in the lead, Lee tagging behind him. Mel is with me and we are a few paces behind them. It's slow going for me. Hiking is hard with my condition. I can do it, but I have to be careful. If I'm going to buy the farm, I don't want it to be all sweaty and gasping on a hillside. If it's gonna happen, I want to be doing something cool and badass, like on top of a mountain, or cliff diving, or in bed with a hot chick. You gotta make the risks worth taking; that's the secret to living the way I do. Go big or don't do it. Hiking? Meh. I'd rather sit on the beach, drink whisky, and watch the honeys sashay on the Copacabana.

Or…

"Hey, Carlos." I jog to catch up. "You said you went hang gliding around here, didn't you?"

He pauses, wiping the sweat off his forehead. "Yeah, it was a long time ago but, yes, I did."

"That sounds like fun. You want to try it again?"

He hesitates long enough that I wonder about the veracity of the story. "Sure. Why not?"

Leanne shoots me a look. "Hang gliding? Isn't that dangerous?"

"A little, sure. But that's the fun of it." I wink at her—why does she care?

She's watched me do some crazy shit in the months we've been sailing together, so she knows my penchant for adrenaline-rush activities. She watched me jump off cliffs, watched me swim with sharks, watched me windsurf in some crazy-ass weather—if it's crazy and dangerous, I've done it. And she's hated it every single time. She doesn't get my addiction to the thrill, and I've never bothered to explain to her. She'd just try to mother me, worry about me, tell me to take it easy and remind me to take my pills and not drink so much. She's got the worry-gene, and I don't need that shit. We do not have an exclusive, committed thing. We're friends, sometimes with benefits, and nothing more. So I keep her in the dark as much as I can.

She knows something's up, though, and I let her wonder. I don't need the pity, don't need the compassion, and don't need the added worry.

The next day I talk Carlos into taking me somewhere where they rent hang gliders. We get set up and then it's a long drive up a fucking massive hill, hang gliders strapped to the roof of the ancient SUV. Lee and Mel are with us in the SUV, but they're not flying with us. The driver will take them back down the mountain, and we'll all meet back at the condo Carlos and Lee are renting.

The drive takes a long-ass time, but we finally reach the summit where the hang gliding company has a sort of runway set up on a cliff overlooking the rain forest. The forest is a wide green rolling crescent spreading in every direction, huge hills jutting up around us, the city itself perched on the edge of the beach, inching up into the hills and following the curve of the bay. I'm only half-listening to the safety instructions—I'm fixated on the sights below.

The view is glorious, and that's what this is all about. It's what my entire life is about. Take it in. Memorize the beauty, absorb it. Let it fill the spaces in my heart, let it coat the cracks in my soul.

Behind me, Carlos is hemming and hawing at the pointed questioning of the driver.

"You've never been hang gliding have you?" I say, not looking at him.

He grins sheepishly. "I did, but it scared me shit-less."

"That's when you know you're alive," I say.

The driver pulls into the parking area and helps us get the gliders off the SUV. He does a credibly thorough safety check and then he gestures to me and Carlos, indicating he's ready when we are.

We get strapped in and I squeeze the handle hard with both hands. Then I run to the edge of the cliff and jump off like someone with something to prove. I kick off hard and immediately feel the wind catch the wings of the hang glider, lifting me up, up, up. The ground falls away, and I see the forest way down below, hundreds of feet beneath me, and I'm howling at the sky like a fucking wolf, feeling the wind in my face and freedom all around. I push one side of the handle a little to angle downward, and my stomach lurches into my throat as I dip and soar. I bring it around, lift up, catch the wind and rise. Rise. Rise.

The bright sun is blinding, but once in a while I can see people like dots way down below. No one around me up here. No condition. No mountain of pills. No deadlines. Just me, the hang glider, the wind, the sun…freedom. The fear in my veins reminds me I'm alive. Knowing the wind could smash me down into the forest tells me this is crazy, this is dangerous. I could die any second. But fuck it, I'd rather die happy, soaring wild and free like a hawk, like an eagle, soaring above everything.

This is everything to me. The rush. The freedom. Nothing else matters in this moment.

I'm *alive*, at this moment.

I skipped the meet-up at the condo and went back to the *Vagabond*.

Alone.

Shit with Mel had run its course anyway and we both knew it. It had been a short course, and not all that great to begin with, since our chemistry was only marginal at best.

My plan now is to go for a swim, get wasted, and then head south in the morning. Maybe see if I can hit the Straits of Magellan, make the long as fuck trip north to Cali. I'll pick up a temporary crew somewhere along the way.

I shower after my swim and then hop out, toweling off.

I go to take my pills and there she is, just sitting on my bed, staring at me, watching me pop one pill after another, washing them down with Perrier.

"Lee—Jesus, you scared the shit out of me." I take the last pill; cinch the towel around my waist.

Not out of modesty, since Leanne and I have spent plenty of time together naked; it's more because I sense she wants to *talk*. Which is hard to do with any seriousness when one is buck-ass naked.

"What's up, buttercup?" I run my hands through my short blond hair so it's spiked up and messy.

"You're an idiot."

"Well, let's not beat around the bush, shall we?" I sit beside her and offer her the green glass bottle of sparkling water. "That's not really news, babe. Hate to break it to you."

She takes a sip, hands it back. "Not like that. I mean, yeah, you're an idiot. You take too many risks. You obviously have a death wish. That's not new, and that's not what I'm talking about."

"Then what kind of idiot am I this time?"

She ducks her head and picks at a loose thread on the quilt. "You know I'm staying here, in Rio? With Carlos."

"Yeah, I know."

"And you're fine with it?"

I sigh. "This is about Astrid, isn't it?"

Leanne groans in frustration. "No, you douche. It's not about fucking *Astrid*. Or the fact that you fucked Astrid. I fucked Carlos that night—we have an agreement. So no, that's not it."

"Then what is it? If you want to stay in Rio, stay in Rio. That was always the reality, Lee: you'd find somewhere that called to you, and sail with me until you found it. Seems you've found it. Carlos is a good dude."

"You won't even miss me? You don't even care?"

"Fuck." Now it's my turn to give in to frustration—I drop the towel and reach into the closet where I find a pair of board shorts and step into them. "Just come out and say it."

I turn around and Lee's there. Right there. Inches away, staring up at me. God, she's gorgeous. Medium height, hair dyed ombre, blonde near the roots and brunette at the bottom, cut shoulder-length to frame her heart-shaped face. Bright brown eyes. Skin tanned caramel by hours in the sun on a deck wearing nothing but a bikini—or nothing at all. Nice full hips, a juicy ass taut from plenty of yoga. Not overly big tits, but a decent handful each. She's in shape, lithe, lovely. Sweet. Smart. She's a lot of things.

I *am* an idiot.

Especially when she says her next piece. She says it facing me, looking up at me, hands on my chest.

Eyes wide. Full of emotion, letting it all hang out. "I could have loved you, Lock."

My heart squeezes. Aches. Fuck, I hate myself, my life, and the shitty goddamn hand Fate has dealt me. But she can't know that.

Better that she think I'm a cold-hearted asshole.

I grab her wrists; keep my eyes hard and focused, keep my emotions caged way down deep, chained up where they belong. I force her hands off me. "I know you could have, Lee. I may be an idiot, but I'm not blind. That's just…it's not where I'm at."

Anger suffuses her features. "Not where you're at?" She slaps my chest, hard enough to leave a red handprint. "What the *fuck* does that mean? Is that the new asshole way of saying 'it's not you, it's me'?"

I'm careful to keep cool, to keep my gaze steady, my expression neutral. "Basically, yeah. But it has the additional benefit of being true. I'm doing this for you, Leanne. Carlos is better for you than I am for more reasons than I care to go into. Please believe me when I tell you I'm doing you a favor."

She's disgusted, now. "God, you're full of bullshit lines, aren't you?"

"Pretty much."

She blinks back tears. "Any other lines you want to feed me?"

I think for a moment. "You're gonna make some

guy really happy. I just wish that guy could be me."

A nod. "That one is nice and traditional. Any more?"

"I think that's it."

She takes a deep breath and I'm asshole enough to enjoy the way her breasts swell. "You're unbeliev-able." She turns away, takes a few steps across the room to the doorway leading to the rear deck. But then she stops. "You know, I really thought there was more to you than the rich adrenaline-junkie playboy. I really did. I hoped there was. Guess I was wrong."

"Guess you were."

I let her get off the boat and onto the pier before I stop her. "Lee?" She turns back, and fucking dammit if there isn't still a glimmer of hope in those brown eyes. "You know what sucks?"

"That I always seem to fall for the asshole?"

"Well, yeah, that too. But no."

"Then what?"

"They weren't just lines. Every single word was true."

She shakes her head, rolls her eyes, huffs, turns on a heel and flounces away. "Yeah, sure. I fucking bet they were."

No point arguing. I let her go, and once she's gone I throw myself onto the couch running along the outside of the stern deck. I crack open a brand new bottle of Lagavulin, and work on blacking out.

I'm not man enough to face the ghosts of all the things I regret.

Two weeks later

All the wisdom I've gathered in the two weeks I've been kicking it in the islands around Cape Horn tells me it's a fool's errand to try this passage, no matter which route I take—there's the Straits of Magellan itself between the mainland and Tierra del Fuego, or Beagle Channel between Tierra del Fuego and Isla Navarino, as well as numerous other routes between the Wollaston Islands and Hermite Island. The problem is—as those in the know tell me—all of them are dangerous. They're all narrow, fraught with wicked, unpredictable winds, strong currents, and are dotted with icebergs and outcroppings of rock. The Drake Passage is the safest, being the widest, though the most southerly, but it's still no cakewalk by any stretch of the imagination.

So, of course I pick the hardest: Beagle Channel. I hire experienced sailors to crew for me—there will be no eye candy on this trip.

We bomb it, hard and fast. The water is jade

green, choppy, tossing us up and down and side to side. It's fucking cold as balls, and the wind whips and howls nonstop, cutting like a knife, driving us to dangerous speeds, even without trimming the sails too tight. Mountains rise on every side, snow-capped and cloud-crowned. Despite the danger, it is thrillingly beautiful.

I let the sails belly in the driving wind, haul them taut, ignoring the wise advice of my crew to slow down. We tip as we tack, the wind nearly pushing us over—it's only a rush if it's dangerous. I only feel alive if I'm encroaching on death, if I'm toeing the bleeding edge of insanity.

Santiago, Chile
A month and a half later

After the harrowing trip around Cape Horn I take a while to rest up and to get the *Vagabond* checked out and re-stocked. The crew I hired for the passage takes their leave of me in Santiago with hefty bonuses all around, considering the risks I took with our lives on that passage. I take on a month's worth of food and water and spend a bunch of money on new fenders and lines and such, although, all things considered, the boat is in great shape.

I haven't climbed a mountain in a while, and Santiago seems to be as good a place as any to put that to rights. So I get kitted out and locate a group heading up into the wild highlands. It starts out as a fairly relaxing day hike out of Cerro Providencia, but quickly gets more challenging as we begin the ascent. I'm no novice at climbing, having summited Everest twice, so this climb is child's play compared to that.

For me, the climb proves to be too easy, not really providing any thrills, aside from the one time my grip on my ice axe slips and I have to scramble for stability while hanging onto the edge of a cliff using my crampons and a second axe.

As we hike back to town at the end of the day I know I need more of a challenge. I'm approaching my thirtieth birthday and I want to feel something, a buzz, anything that will give me the adrenaline rush I crave.

The next day I hitch a ride north to Copiaopaó and find a group with a decent guide who are headed up the *Ojos del Salado* volcano. None of my companions on this climb speak much English, and I only speak a smattering of Spanish—which I don't think these fellas speak, either. I used a translator to make the arrangements, and they made it clear I had to keep up or be left behind; they weren't going to haul my ass up the peak or wait around for me.

Fine by me. I've never asked for help. I've never accepted a handout in anything, with the single, notable exception of living off dear old Dad's money. I'm pretty goddamned sure I can handle this volcano. Of course, I didn't say that to them. I just agreed, signed the waiver, smiled, and bought a couple rounds.

As we finally approach the marshalling area I look around...and up. *This* is what I'm talking about. It's barren land—wind-swept and cold. A true wasteland—no greenery, no vegetation. The highlands are an endless wilderness strewn with rocks and boulders.

Merely getting close to the base camp area of the volcano was an adventure requiring an experienced, daring driver who provided us with some intense white-knuckle moments. But then we arrive and the mammoth volcano—the second highest peak on the continent—rises like a massive monument to an unknown god. Made principally of volcanic stone and rock, *Ojos del Salado* reaches into the dizzying blue bowl of the sky.

We quickly grab our packs and listen to some last-minute instructions delivered in broken English. I'm positioned in the middle of the hiking group, three ahead of me, three behind. The translator is immediately behind me. Everyone is chattering to each other, shouting jokes back and forth, laughing, and scampering up the incline like fucking mountain goats. I don't understand a damn word they're saying, but it doesn't matter. I'm focused on the climb, focused on the sky above, and focused on this massive mountain under me, above me, and all around me. I'm focused on soaking up and storing each moment.

Remembering each moment.

Savoring each second.

Live every minute as if it could be the last, because for me, it very well might be.

I am so focused on the climb, head down, putting one foot in front of the other, that I almost miss the moment when we summit.

Which is a fucking joke, of course, because that's the theme of my whole goddamn life: Focus on the journey, don't think about the destination.

I feel a slap on my shoulder. "Hey. American. Look up."

I straighten, and look around. "Jesus Christ."

"Is very something, no?" He's a little younger than me, German, maybe, with shaggy black hair, a sparse beard, burly, wearing expensive gear and lived-in boots.

I can only nod and soak in the vista of the world spread out around me, a wide endless expanse of rock and sky. Even at daylight, this high up, the stars are visible in their countless millions. Breathing is hard in the thin air, and my heart is knocking so hard I have to sit down.

I could cry.

This is it.

This is why I live.

My chest is tight, my heart—the metaphysical one—is full. I'm *alive*. Today is my thirtieth birthday, and I'm alive. I'm not just alive, but I'm literally on top of the world.

I could die; my heart is pounding so hard. I'm dizzy.

Lightheaded.

My heart is failing.

I lay back and rest my head on the knife-sharp shale and rock. I stare up at the stars in the indigo sky.

It's a good time to die.

I feel a tap on my shoulder. "Climb down now." The same dude, gesturing at the descent.

I shake my head. "I'll—I'll catch…catch up."

A weathered South American—Ecuadorean? Chilean? Brazilian? I don't know. He peers down at me, eyes hidden behind mirrored UV goggles, his neck gaiter pulled down. "You sick." It's not a question.

I blink. Try to breathe. Chest fucking aches like an elephant is sitting on me. I feel each heartbeat, focus on each one, and count each one. When your heart could give out without warning at any moment, you sort of become attuned to each flutter, each irregularity, and each thumping beat, attuned to the rhythm.

No shit I shouldn't be climbing mountains. It's the very last thing, literally, the actual *last* thing I should ever do. But statistically, it's virtually impossible that I'll ever find a match for my heart, and I'm a terrible candidate for a transplant, so I gave up on that idea a long time ago. My only goal in life is to see thirty-one, and to do and see everything I can imagine in the meantime.

Dad died at thirty-eight.

Grandpa died at forty-five.

Great-Grandpa at sixty.

Me?

Thirty-one is a pipe dream. Always has been.

Fuck.

And now I'm goddamned dying. Here on a mountain. In the middle of nowhere. With a bunch of strangers.

My meds are all back in Valparaiso, on the boat. There was no fucking way I was hauling around a backpack full of my meds on this trip. Because fuck it. Because I'm an idiot with a death wish.

I'm basically already dead, living on borrowed time and have been doing so for some time. I don't really have a death wish, not really. I love life. I love each moment my heart continues to beat, but I know that each beat is one less I'll ever have. Each thump of my heart is one less in the countdown to the day I die. To the day my heart ceases to beat. The sky is narrowing above me—tunnel vision. The stars wheel above me, like those time-lapse montages in movies where the mountain is the static image and the sky is pinking and blueing and going black and then gray and pink and bright and the stars spin and stir and wheel and fade and prick and poke and brighten.

I don't see my life flash before my eyes, which is weird, and unfortunate, because there have been a lot of really fine sets of tits I'd like to see again.

God, I'm such an asshole. Thinking about tits while dying.

What? I'm supposed to be all sappy and philosophical about this shit? Fine.

Women are the greatest part of life. They make it worth living. More than the adrenaline rush, more than the thrill, women are what I live for. And unlike most one-and-done playboys, I fully appreciate every single moment I get with each one. I remember them all.

Liv. Lisa. Ali. Astrid. Toni. Michaela. Vivian. Mimi. Tanya. Mel. Leanne. Jesus, Leanne; I regret having to send her on. Anya. Heidi. Heidi again, a different one. Another Lisa. Michelle. Jen, four different ones.

Yeah, there have been a lot of women. But I know all their names. I remember each face vividly.

I remember where I spent the night—or morning, or afternoon, or weekend, or entire week, or month—with each one.

Rome. Constantinople. Moscow. Various points and ports by the dozen in the Caribbean and Mediterranean. A hundred places in Indonesia. Hong Kong. Prague. Paris. London.

God, what a life.

I've been everywhere. I've seen both the Aurora Borealis and the Aurora Polaris. I've walked in the footsteps of Jesus himself, in Israel and Palestine.

And you know what marks each place I've been? Not the adventure, not the myriad ways I've found to nearly kill myself. Not the skydiving, or free-climbing cliff faces, not the scuba diving and pearl diving and racing motorcycles and drag racing muscle cars and nearly wrecking a borrowed two and a half million-dollar Bugatti in Monaco, or....

Shit, I can't list all the adventures I've had.

No, it's none of that.

It's the women.

The way their hair would fall across their faces. Watching Leanne undress in the starlight on the deck of my boat, nothing but ocean for hundreds and thousands of miles in each direction. Pale breasts wet as we tumble naked in the warm midnight surf of a deserted Saint John beach. Waking up in the middle of the night on the Argentinian pampas in a tiny little pup tent and making Luisa scream so loud the fucking wolves answered her. Moonlight on auburn hair and blonde and red and purple—god, Viv was a wildcat, hair dyed purple and white for an upcoming college football game—pale skin and tan and golden and brown and every shade in between. Blue eyes and green and gray and brown.

A good way to die, indeed, reliving the best parts of my life, on top of a mountain.

Except…the pain fades.

The dizziness subsides.

I can breathe again, sort of.

Maybe I'm not going to die here, after all.

It takes a few more minutes, but I manage to sit up.

At which point I realize my companions did indeed keep their word, having gone back down without me.

This was a real mountaintop experience, let me tell you.

Hah, I'm so fucking funny.

But for real, though. It was.

But now I've got to haul ass and climb down

alone and hopefully not die in the process.

Beverly Hills, California
Ten months later

I didn't die descending *Ojos del Salado*. I made it down and managed to hitch a ride with one of the last vehicles leaving the area for the day. The weather was changing fast, so I was lucky I got out in time.

I spent the rest of the following year making my way slowly up the western coast of South America, then along Central America, and finally North America. I'm home in Beverly Hills two months shy of my thirty-first birthday.

I'm only here because I made Mom a promise that I'd be back home for this one, and I do keep my promises.

It's boring as fuck.

I find myself in the "garden", which is a quaint term for the thousand-square-foot courtyard in the middle of the west wing. The space is exploding with greenery and flowers and palm trees and exotic plants of all sorts. There are benches and little wrought iron tables and chairs dotted here and there in cute little still life scenes.

I hate it.

But it's where Mom "receives me", like she's some goddamn queen or something.

"Your mother will receive you in the garden," Javier says.

Javier is the butler.

Yes, the butler.

This is why I live alone on a boat, and why I'm usually thousands of miles away. Mom is so fucking pretentious. Cold and iron-hearted since Dad's death, and I don't know what she was like before that because I was six when he died. I do remember her smiling more and possibly drinking less, but my memory of childhood before Dad died is negligible.

She runs his companies with a fist of steel and a mind like a bear-trap lined with razors. Nothing escapes her notice, or her ire. For me, she conjures up a thin façade of sympathy, because of my "condition", which is yet another reason I live alone on a boat thousands of miles from this fucking estate.

I'm sitting here, sipping on some ridiculously expensive scotch—which isn't much better than my beloved Lagavulin, despite costing triple. Waiting. She always makes you wait…because she can.

I hear her heels on the flagstones behind me. I stand up, preparing to greet her. I endure her stupid faux-European air cheek kisses—*muah*—*muah*. Like it means something. Who *does* that? Everyone in this goddamn city, that's who.

"Hello, darling. So good to see you." *Muah... muah.*

"Hey, Mom." I endure the kisses, don't return them, instead opting to give her a too-rough man hug, just to piss her off.

"Not good to see me too, Lachlan?"

"You know I hate it in Beverly Hills, Mom. Always have, always will. I'm only here because I promised you I'd come back for my thirty-first."

"Your thirty-first...you know, I have quite a to-do planned. It's going to be marvelous. I've invited pretty much everyone I know, which means it will be rather something."

I slam the scotch down and attempt, badly, to tamp down my irritation. "Mom. I told you. No fucking parties."

"I'm your mother. It's your thirty-first birthday. It's important."

"Only to me. I never expected to make it this far."

"But you did, despite your best efforts."

"Yes, I did, despite my best efforts." I pour more scotch, because I made Javier leave the bottle. "Thirty-one isn't an important milestone to anyone but me, so the idea of a big party is just...stupid. And please note the fact that I did say *no fucking parties.*"

"If it's important to you, Lachlan, it's important to me."

"Oh, come on. You just want an excuse to have one of your fancy soirees. All your friends, dripping diamonds and stiff with plastic surgery and Botox. No one is even capable of smiling!" I take a deep breath, because it wouldn't do to get so worked up I have to take a pill, certainly not because of the froufrou bullshit denizens of Beverly Hills, California.

I'm a simple man. Give me a boat, some whisky, and some women. That's all I need. It's all I've ever needed.

"Lachlan, dear. Let's get back to the basics, shall we? The reason your thirty-first birthday is so important."

"I wasn't supposed to live this long. I never expected to, and no else did either. Not even you."

"And I'm happy you have! Thus…a party."

I sigh. "Which I understand. I really do. But your idea of a party and mine…are rather different."

Mom makes a sour face. "Yes. Indeed. Your idea of a party is booze and strippers. Mine is slightly more sophisticated."

"I'm insulted, Mom." I sip some scotch; god, the burn is so beautiful. "I'd never pay a woman to get naked. When you're this good looking, you don't have to." I grin, a broad, cheesy grin.

It's supposed to be a joke.

Sort of.

I mean, it's true. But it was a joke.

Mom doesn't get it. "Do you hear yourself, Lachlan Montgomery? You're a pig."

"It was a joke, Mom."

"No, it wasn't."

I tip my head side to side. "It is true that I've never had to pay a woman to take her clothes off—or do anything else, for that matter. But nonetheless, it was a joke."

"Not a funny one."

"That's just because you don't have a goddamned sense of humor. You're just as cold and stuffy and stuck-up as all your friends." I stand up. "I've got to go. I've got things to do."

"You've never worked a day in your life, Lachlan. What could you possibly have to do?"

"Didn't I mention? I'm picking up some hookers. I'm having a kegger up at the Trinidad property."

"Lachlan."

I shake my head. "Mom. Seriously. Learn to take a joke."

"You have to at least make an appearance at your party, Lachlan. Please. It's important to me."

I finish the glass of scotch; crunch an ice cube—just to piss Mom off, again. "Fine. I'll make an appearance. But that's it. Don't expect much from me past showing up for a drink or two." I set the glass down, hesitate, and then take the bottle. "And then I'm gone. I've got a berth on an ice-breaker headed up past the Arctic Circle."

"You're kidding."

"I never kid about travel, Mother. It's the one thing I take seriously." I lift the bottle in salute. "That, and women."

"You could have done something worthwhile with your life, Lachlan." Trust Mom to get the last word in, and to make it a scathing parting shot.

"Probably," I say. "But I didn't. I wasted it enjoying the limited time available to me."

Two months later

The party is everything I imagined it would be, and worse: Massive. Elaborate. Sophisticated. Expensive. There are fireworks, and some famous pop band with fancy hair and great teeth and shitty singing voices. Swans. Fragile globes of light on delicate strands of silver wire strung across wrought iron pergolas. Cloth-covered tables. Open bar, top-shelf liquor and wine. Men in tuxedos and women in evening gowns.

Lots of fake tits and expensive noses.

I show up in ripped jeans and a Bullet For My Valentine T-shirt. Mom loves it, of course, and praises my exquisite fashion taste.

Hah. Right.

She scolds me for dressing like a degenerate, and then tries to take the bottle of whiskey from me; it's a limited edition Michter's Celebration Sour Mash, worth over four grand, with a label made from 18k gold. And I'm drinking it straight out of the bottle. I thought about taking the Dalmore 64 from Dad's collection, but I couldn't bring myself to do it; that's a whisky that deserves fucking respect and proper treatment, thus I leave it where it is.

When I make it clear I'm not giving up my prize, which is my birthday present to myself, she tries to introduce me to the well-heeled, well-groomed so-cialite daughters of her friends.

Don't get me wrong, I'm not above a tumble with a rich bitch or four, but they're annoying when they're not naked and their mouths otherwise occu-pied. The trick with chicks like them is to keep them busy so they can't talk. Know what I mean?

Flirting is fun, though. They're all pretty, of course, and they all like me.

I'm dangerous. I'm a bad boy, a real rebel. I mean, I sold off my 50% share of Dad's company to the highest bidder the day I turned eighteen. And, believe me, I got the *highest* bidder because I'm no idiot. I could have been a hell of a businessman had I chosen to do so. I used the proceeds to build the *Vagabond,* and had enough left over to fund my adventures for the past twelve years.

Yeah, Dad's company was worth a mint. And I sold it off to sail the world and live in idle luxury. Real Prodigal Son, I am.

I get bored, though. I cap the bottle and carry it with me to the helipad on the far end of the east wing, a ditzy heiress named Lana under one arm, and a rowdy communications major named Morgan under the other. I have the family pilot, Robby, take us to a deserted beach I know about, a good forty minutes by air north of LA. Robby brings us down right on the beach, and I help the girls get out, and then I signal to Robby to be back in two hours.

We waste no time in getting naked and, for once, I let myself be pleasured without giving back.

Usually, I'm adamant about making sure whoever I'm with gets theirs first, usually more than once, before I get mine.

But tonight it's all about me, and only me.

I'm thirty-one, motherfuckers. I made it to thirty-one.

I let them touch and kiss and go wild, let them

show me that, yes, if I gave them enough high-end whiskey, they'll do things to each other, and to me, that…well…are best left to the imagination, and my memory.

Moonlight, whiskey, breasts, mouths all over me, the ocean crashing and the surf licking at my toes—and…what's her name? Oh yeah, Morgan. She's licking me elsewhere…it's a good way to turn thirty-one.

Until shit conspires against me.

Too much whiskey, and too much vigorous sex doesn't mix well with a congenital heart defect. Who knew?

Combine that with being in the middle of nowhere without any meds, and spotty cell coverage?

It started with finishing my third climax in—well, mostly in, partly on—Lana's mouth. Your heart hammers pretty hard after a wicked awesome orgasm, but it's supposed to calm down after a minute, unless you're in terrible shape, and I'm not. I'm in fucking fantastic shape, heart condition be damned.

I'm naked and drunk with a pair of clueless heiress socialite blondes climbing all over me. Not that there aren't smart blondes out there—hey, Astrid!—but there are reasons stereotypes exist.

This is like Chile all over again.

But this time, my heart doesn't slow down. It hammers even harder.

I do square breathing; focus on the beats, count-
ing them, slowing them.

Eventually I have to move away from the girls
and sit in the sand, head in my hands, and breathe.
Hope. Beg to make it just another day.

One more day.

I mean, to die on my thirty-first birthday?

Jesus, what a laugh.

But it's real.

Not on the mountain in Chile, no.

At home, in Cali.

On a beach, naked, with a couple of pretty girls.

Again, there are worse ways to go.

But deep down, the truth is I don't want to go
at all.

I've resigned myself to it. I've kept everyone at
bay my whole life because I knew it was coming,
sooner rather than later.

I just...I've always hoped that maybe I could
cheat it, day by day, and somehow it wouldn't catch
up.

But it caught up all right.

"Hey, Lock? You okay?" Morgan, this is.

I think it's her, anyway. It's hard to tell, because I
can't hear, and it's hard to make things out. I'm seeing
double, and it's not from the whiskey. I've got the tunnel vision again. Chest aching. That fucking elephant

is sitting on my chest again.

Here we go again.

I get reflective, because this kind of dying takes time. It feels like it to me, at least. I have time to stare at the waves and wish I were out there on the sea, riding the waves, hauling at the *Vagabond*'s lines, trimming the sails, reefing the jib.

"Lock?" This is Lana. I can tell because she's in front of me, and she's got a cool birthmark on her left tit. Looks like Italy, right on the slope, sort of near the outside. "Lachlan?"

I wave. "I…it'll pass."

"Are you sure you're all right?"

I shake my head. "No."

But this time the feeling is not passing.

I'm on my back, and I don't remember lying down. I hear rustling, and thudding. The helicopter, Robby is landing. Sand stings my eyes. I see skirts around me, which is what the rustling noise was—the girls putting on their dresses. Someone laboriously and with great difficulty gets my pants on me.

I feel Robby throw me over his burly shoulder, and set me in the back of the chopper.

"Yo, Lock, you good, man?"

I squeak out a breath. My heart…I'm not sure if it's beating too hard or not hard enough. I stare up at Robby. "Hosp…" I can't get it out. "Hosp—hospital."

"You got your meds?" With effort, I shake my head no. "Shit, man. We're a good thirty minutes from a hospital, and that's by air. You gotta hold on. Girls, sit down and buckle up. We're gonna haul ass and it ain't gonna be pretty." Robby is an ex-military pilot, and I got him to show me some tricks once. Dude can fucking fly.

Which is good, because it's hard to think. Hard to see. Hard to breathe. Hard to do anything except stare at the ceiling and hope.

I hear sniffling.

Lana is crying.

"Quit...that...shit," I snarl. Okay, not a snarl, more of a gasp and a whimper. "Had it...coming. Whole...life."

Robby was right. It's not pretty. He keeps low and hauls ass, breaking a lot of laws, probably.

I realize my head is on Morgan's lap.

There's a theme, here: not a bad way to go, head on the lap of a pretty girl.

Blackness is winning.

I'm holding on, but there's not much to hold on to at this point.

Everything is faint.

I feel...thin.

Darkness.

I succumb.

Head looking down

Los Roboles Hospital and Medical Center
Los Angeles, California
Six years earlier

"TWELVE YEAR-OLD MALE, MULTIPLE GUNSHOT wounds." This is from Delaney, the ER resident on duty this morning, shouting as she runs beside a stretcher. "Pulse is thready and fading. Blood type O-neg."

I'm running beside the stretcher, visually assessing the victim. Young, black, adorable. Innocent. Terrified. His eyes roam and flick and flit everywhere, seeking something to fix on. He's in agony. Knows he's dying.

"Hi, sweetie," I say, getting his attention. "What's your name?"

"Mal—Malcolm." He's gasping; there's a whistle

to it. Shitshitshit. "Am I—am I going to die?" His voice
is barely audible.

Probably. I just smile down at him, calm and
sweet. "No, honey. Of course not. We're gonna take
super great care of you. Okay? You're going to be
fine."

"Promise? Mama...Mama needs me."

"Is your mama here?" I ask.

"No." He groans, arching off the stretcher as
pain ravages him.

We get the gurney into a room and really get to
work. The paramedics who brought him in are assisting. Delaney is calling the shots as the senior nurse on
duty, and I'm hooking up Malcolm to the monitors.

He's gushing blood from at least four different
entry wounds, despite the triage efforts by the paramedics to slow the bleeding. One to the chest, two to
the stomach, a fourth in the thigh. It's a miracle he's
even conscious, let alone lucid. Little fighter.

"Do you know where she is?" I have to keep him
talking, keep him awake. "Malcolm? Does your mama
know you're here?"

He cries out as Delaney stabs a local anesthetic
into his chest around the sucking wound there. He
cries out again as she probes into the wound, digging
in before the medicine has a chance to take effect.

"No, no—Mama...Mama's at work. I was s'posed

to be at school." He's trying like fuck to be a man, I can see it. Refusing to cry, refusing to scream. God, if I had half the courage of this little guy. "She's gonna be so—so mad at me."

"No, honey, no. She won't be mad. She'll just be glad you're okay, all right? I promise, your mama won't be mad."

Delaney glances at me, and I really don't like the look in her eyes. Nor do I like the slowing beeps of the heart monitor. His eyes roll back into his head. The godawful whistling from his chest wound can be heard over the ambient noise. But it's the stomach wounds that are killing him. Stomach acid is leaking into his body.

"I'm dying, ain't I?" He looks up at me, and even after three years of ER triage, it never gets easier, the lying to patients.

"No, Malcolm, baby. Delaney is fixing you up, okay? We're gonna take care of you. I promise." I'm working like crazy, trying to stop the bleeding in his thigh. It's not stopping. The paramedics slowed it, but it's not stopping. I'm in his thigh, hunting for the severed artery that's spouting blood like a fountain. "Where were you, Malcolm? If you weren't at school, where were you?"

He's fading. My heart squeezes. Going to have nightmares about this tonight. His eyes, scared, beg me to save him.

"Playing—ball." He blinks hard, sucks in a breath. Finds my eyes. "It hurts. I'm cold. I don't want to die. I don't…Mama?"

He's got brand new Jordans on. The pristine white leather is dotted with blood. Basketball shorts. A little big. Why do I notice these things? He's tied his shoes in a big fat triple knot, to keep the laces up out of the way. There's a big perfectly round drop of blood right on the tip of his left shoe. I watch his toe flex in the shoe, flexing the leather.

"Malcolm? Stay awake for me, baby." I've found the artery. I pinch it off with hemostats, but it's not gonna save him. Delaney is still working on his chest. "Malcolm? Who's your favorite basketball player, Malcolm?"

He's not responding. He sees me, but he looks confused. Blinks become flutters. Then a long unfocused stare, his eyelids fluttering. Breath slowing.

We keep working.

You don't ever stop, not even when you know it's hopeless.

Delaney watches the monitor as it flatlines. She shouts for the paddles, calls out the charge setting. *Clear!* We all back away. *Pop!* Nothing. *Pop!* Nothing. A few more times, but we all know he's gone.

Finally, Delaney has to back away, panting from

the exertion. It's over.

Delaney wipes the sweat off her forehead with the back of her wrist. Checks her watch, the face of which is on the underside of her wrist. "Time of death—eleven twenty-three a.m."

I've only cried at work two other times. Once when it was a girl I knew, a good friend from nursing school. Suicide. Slit her wrists. Nobody had any clue she was struggling. The other time was when there was a fifteen-car pileup on the 210. Dozens of injuries, six fatalities, two of which were little babies.

Whom I treated.

And lost.

Something about losing Malcolm...I can't handle it.

Delaney sees it. "Take ten, Niall." I hesitate, and she makes the face that says *don't argue, bitch*. "Go. *Now*. Ten minutes."

"All right, all right. Ten minutes." I'm just repeating it, because I'm dizzy and it's what you do, repeat orders. Make sure you've got it right.

I'm almost outside when an orderly grabs me. "Ummm...Niall?" I pause, try to focus on her. Blink back tears. A young woman, green scrubs, Asian, gesturing at my hands. "Maybe give me those, huh? I'll take care of them."

I don't know what she's talking about. I glance

down and see that I'm still wearing the bloody latex gloves, the hemostats in a death grip. I turn around and see that I've dripped a trail of blood all the way here. I let her take the hemostats, duck into a bathroom and strip off the gloves, wrap them in a brown paper towel and discard them. I wash my shaking, trembling hands.

I always get the shakes after surgery or an emergency. Never during.

Finally outside, I wander aimlessly. Looking for somewhere quiet. I want to be alone. Away from the ambulances arriving at the ER entrance. Away from the patients and visitors at the main entrance. Finally, I just collapse on the curb underneath a towering palm tree. I bury my face in my hands and try to keep from actually sobbing. I try to banish the vision of Malcolm fading, confused, afraid.

I become aware of the sound of soles scuffing on the concrete, and I blink through my salt haze to see a big pair of tan combat boots, and the faded, torn cuffs of blue jeans. The guy sits down beside me. I clear my throat. Blink away tears, rub at them quickly.

"Here." Smooth, attractive male voice. Not deep, but smooth.

I glance, and see a large masculine hand, hair and scars on the knuckles, proffering a cigarette.

"I don't smoke."

"Neither do I." He reaches over, bold as you please, and places the filter between my lips. Sparks plume, and it's lit. "But you need it at times like this."

I take it between my index and middle fingers, like I've seen Delaney do on countless occasions, and pull it away from my mouth. Finally I take a look at my companion.

Oh. Whoa. Okay. He looks like McDreamy from *Grey's Anatomy*. Early thirties, thick black hair swept back, streaks of silver at his temples. Ten-day scruff, not quite a beard, also salted with silver. Brown eyes, the corners wrinkled from smiles and the sun.

"Puff." He commands it. Soft, but insistent. "Trust me."

I take a puff.

"Now inhale. You'll cough, but it'll be worth it."

I inhale. Taste mint…menthol. Then I cough like I've got emphysema, but the subsequent rush is… worth it. Just like he said. I extend the cigarette to him, but he shakes his head.

"I only smoke after an operation, and then only after the really gnarly ones." He rubs at the corner of his mouth with a big thumb. "That's the trick to not getting addicted. You only have one when you're cracking up."

"You're a doctor?"

He nods. Watches me take another hit, and hack

again. "A surgeon with MSF."

"MSF?" It sounds like something I should know.

"*Médecins Sans Frontières*," he clarifies, in a flaw-less French accent. "Doctors Without Borders."

"I've heard of it for sure, but I don't know much about it."

"Non-profit, international humanitarian aid. We put together teams of medical personnel from all over the world, and we go into nasty situations, pro-vide medical treatment. Civil wars, natural disasters, disease outbreaks."

"Where have you been?"

His eyes reflect the fact that he's seen hell. "South Sudan, Uganda, Cambodia, the quake in Haiti. I was stationed in Côte d'Ivoire for a couple of years." He points at my still-shaking hands. "I get those, too. The shakes, after it's all over."

"Lost a patient." It's all I can get out.

He nods, squinting as the sun peeks out from be-hind a cloud to shine in our faces. It's L.A. hot. "Never gets easier. Harder, if anything."

"He was twelve. Shot four times. Just…bled out."

"And you promised him you'd save him." I can only nod, and he manages to be a little closer to me without moving, somehow. Nudges me with his shoulder. "Never stop making that promise. They need the lie, and so do you. We have to lie to ourselves, just so we'll keep trying even when it's hopeless. We lie, and work so that maybe it won't be a lie after all."

"I hate that lie."

"Me too." He extends his hand to me. "I'm Oliver James."

I take his hand. Don't really shake, just hold it. Like a needy dumbass. "Niall Mackenzie."

A silence, then. Comfortable. I don't really smoke the cigarette, just hold it. Take a puff now and again, but the act is soothing. Comforting. The pretense is... necessary. I see what he means.

Oliver stands up after a few minutes. "Got to go back inside, check on my dad."

I stand up too. "Is he a patient?"

A nod. "Yeah. Bypass. Second one. Stubborn old goat won't quit the Big Macs, y'know?"

"Thank you, Oliver."

He grins, and god, is that smile gorgeous. McDreamy, even.

He turns serious, then. "You make a difference. Every patient, save 'em or lose 'em, you make a difference."

That doesn't help my still-roiling emotions. "Thanks. That means a lot."

He waves, an easy toss of his hand. Only makes it a few steps before he turns back around. "I don't suppose you speak French, do you?"

I frown. "Um, actually, I do. Not perfectly, but pretty well. Took it all through middle school, high school, and college. My roommate in nursing school was from Quebec, so I'm conversational to a certain degree."

"My MSF team, we're short-staffed and shipping out for the Central African Republic in a couple months. We desperately need French-speaking nurses trained in emergency triage." He strides over to me, hands me a card, and scribbles a phone number on the back. "Call this number tomorrow morning if you're interested, ask for Dominique. I'll put in a word for you tonight."

I consider his offer. "Is the work like that?" I gesture at the hospital.

He shakes his head. "Worse. You're there when the guns are going off. When the mines are exploding. When the endemic is sweeping like wildfire through entire towns. What's going in Africa right now? It's gonna be gnarly. But if you can do that—" he jerks his head at the ER entrance, "—you can do it. Plus, I'll be there and we'll be on the same team. I'll always be right beside you, if you ship out with us."

He doesn't give me a chance to respond, he simply strides away. Not quite a swagger, but close. A sexy walk, a man who is utterly self-confident, but not arrogant.

I tuck his card into the back pocket of my scrubs and go back to work.

And the next morning, over a cup of coffee, I stare at that card. I've got my cell phone in hand, thinking hard. Then I dial the number.

"'Allo?" Strong French accent.

"Hi, is this Dominque?"

"Oui, c'est moi."

I start the conversation by speaking in English, hoping she can understand me, "My name is Niall Mackenzie. I, um, I met Dr. Oliver James yesterday. He said he'd talk to you and, um, I'm a nurse. An ER nurse. He said you needed—"

"Ollie did indeed speak to me," Dominque replies in rapid French. "What are your qualifications?"

I have to switch mentally into a French-speaking headspace. It takes a second to translate my thoughts. "I'm an RN, received my degree from UCLA. I have three years experience in the ER at Los Robles." The fact that I say this in passable—if not flawless—French is evidence of my qualification in that language, so I don't mention it.

"Why do you want to work for MSF?"

Why *do* I? I don't answer right away; take a moment to formulate my thoughts.

"I want to make a difference. Save lives. Help as

many people as I can. It's why I became a nurse." I say this in English. Saying that I also want to go because I want to be close to Oliver probably isn't a good idea.

What I've said is true, but there's more...I haven't mentioned the down-deep reason for wanting a change like this. And it doesn't have anything to do with Oliver at all, to be honest. I mean, yeah, he's hot, sexy, and who wouldn't want him? But...I have this need. I don't know how to fully explain it to myself other than to say it's a need to take things farther, a drive to push myself to my limits.

Being an ER nurse in an LA hospital is pretty damn close to working in a war zone. You see all sorts of horrible shit. But as much as I sometimes hate it, there is something in me that needs the rush. The adrenaline. The frenzy to fix a patient. To save a life. To try my damnedest, even if I fail. To know that I've helped. To make a difference, as Oliver put it.

There's a pause on the other end of the line. "If Ollie tells me I should bring you on, it is reason enough for me," Dominique says, in English now. "He is never wrong. Not about people." She rattles off an address, tells me to bring my resumé and prepare for a more in-depth interview, but then reassures me it's a formality, and that I'll have the position if I want it, on the strength of Oliver's recommendation.

When I report for my next shift at work, I have

to break the news to Delaney and hand in my notice.

She hugs me, with a teary-eyed smile. "You're too talented a nurse to be stuck here. I knew someone would lure you away someday." She holds me by the arms and looks at me. "Just be sure it's what you want. MSF, it's...hardcore. And very dangerous."

"I know. Maybe it's crazy, but...that's part of why I'm going, if I'm being honest."

Delaney grins. "You're at your best when things get hairy. You'll be great. Just...stay safe, okay?"

"I'm not leaving for another two months, Delaney."

A sniff. "But still. I'm not going to say goodbye. When you go, just go. And know I'll miss you."

Delaney is my best friend. She was enrolled in nursing school at UCLA, a year older than me. She got the job here first and rose up the ranks. She'll be unit head before long. I can't imagine not being with her. We work almost every single shift together. Side by side, every day, for twelve or fourteen hours a day. We drink a bottle or three of wine together after work, and watch Real Housewives, talk about boys and never about work.

Now I'm leaving her.

We drop the subject and prep for a night shift of incoming patients. A weekend midnight shift always hits hard and heavy with multiple GSWs, stab wounds, concussions and contusions, car accidents and cardiac arrests.

Through it all, we stay calm, because that's what we do.

As the shift finally comes to an end, I spare a thought for the future. I wonder what it'll be like, in Africa.

Bangui, Central African Republic
Six months later

"Niall! Get your ass over here!" Oliver shouts from the other side of the tent.

"I'm kinda busy, Ollie!" I shout back.

"I'll take over," François says in French, stepping in, taking over my suturing job. "He needs you. It's bad."

I strip off my gloves, toss them in a garbage can, and tug a new pair out of a box on my way over to Oliver's table.

Fuck.

He's working on an adult male, late forties. Entire stomach is blown open, intestines pulled out of the cavity to reveal a rupture, blood gushing like something out of a Tarantino film. One leg is missing from the knee down, the stump blackened and oozing.

Mine, or a car bomb.

Oliver is covered in blood up to his elbows, and from his hips to his chest. His face is covered in a mask, but I can see his eyes are laser-focused on the job at hand.

He feels me come up beside him, and doesn't have to tell me what he needs. One glance, and I'm on it. I take the forceps from him and hold them, then blot away the blood so Ollie can see what he's doing. We manage to stop the internal bleeding, then Ollie dumps the intestines back in the cavity and we both watch as they rearrange themselves. He pulls the edges of the gaping stomach wound back together, and then Ollie leaves me to do the sutures while he tends to the leg. Remove shrapnel, clean it, cauterize it, and bandage it.

Finally done, Ollie steps away and lets someone else move the patient to a recovery tent. We strip off our blood-soaked gear, step out of the tent and into the blazing African sun. Walk together in silence, both of us pretending our hands aren't shaking.

"You can't fucking hesitate, Niall," he says, his voice tired, a little angry.

"I didn't *hesitate*. I was stitching somebody's arm back on, okay?" I'm defensive.

"If I need you, I need you right away. Get someone to take over and get where I need you. You have to trust me to know what's a priority."

"I'm sorry." I want to think I know better, but he's the surgeon, and I'm the nurse.

He's got lots of experience on me. My job is to trust him.

"How're you holding up?" He leans up against a two-ton truck, rubbing his eyes.

"Fine," I sigh. "You?"

"Well, aside from having been awake for thirty hours, I'm just dandy."

I'm about to say something else, but a truck rumbles into the station, and the air is filled with shouts in English, French, and several African dialects. There's a swarm of activity, crimson-soaked bodies being hauled out of the back of the truck and carried to the triage tent.

"Ollie!" Dominique, shouting, urgent. "Need you, *now!*"

A sigh. "Hello, another thirty hours." Ollie pinches the back of my neck and rubs it. "You're doing great, Niall. But trust me, yeah?"

"I will. I mean...I do." I glance up at him. Our eyes meet, and the sparks are there.

We've been too busy for anything to happen between us, but we both know it's on the horizon. If we ever get a break. If the fighting ever dies down. The UN has nearly evacuated us a few times, it's gotten so bad. But Dominique refuses to leave, and so do the rest of us. When the fighting is at its worst, that's when we're needed the most. They'll have to tie us up and drag us away to get us out of here. This is what we do.

Namely, run back to the triage tent, tug on gloves, pull on new aprons, and assess incoming. Sort the dying from the ones who'll make it with immediate treatment, get Ollie working on the worst cases, me beside him, assisting. We don't need words, Ollie and me. We just know. I know how he works, and what he needs. He knows I won't flinch, won't fail. Won't hesitate, won't get sick, won't get tired. You don't get to do any of that until after it's over. Then you can have your meltdown.

And we all have them.

The next eleven hours are a frenzy of blood and stitches and severed limbs. There's a skirmish going on between sects to the north of us, dozens are wounded, and all of them coming our way. By far, it's the worst it's ever been. Since I've been here, at least.

Of the thirty-eight victims that come through our tent, five die and seven more probably won't last the night.

Finally, in the smallest hours of the night, Dominique sends us away. My feet drag, and I stumble. Oliver is barely functioning. He's been awake and working for forty-eight hours straight. Not stopping for anything, not until the last patient has been given the best possible care. I hang onto him, and he onto me. We're leaning on each other, supporting each other.

We find a spot to lie down, in the bed of an old, battered Nissan pickup used to transport supplies across the station. We lie down side by side in the bed, staring up at the stars. Just breathing. I have that dizzy feeling you get when you finally stop moving after being in motion for endless hours. Like after a day at a theme park, when you close your eyes and it feels like you're still on a rollercoaster. Like that, but infinitely worse. Your hands want to stitch, compress, apply pressure, wrap bandages. Your eyes see wounds, pleading eyes, you hear whimpers. You see it, feel it, hear it even after you're done.

Ollie lifts a hip, digs in his back pocket, comes up with a flattened soft-pack of Camel Lights, and a blue lighter. Puts one to his lips, lights it, drags.

That's when I know he's struggling. So far, Ollie hasn't had to light up, yet.

He breathes out the smoke, and it's a shuddery, frail sound. "Jesus Christ, that was bad."

"Yeah."

He hands me the cigarette, and we share it in silence.

When he lights a second, I know he's working up to something.

"Nights like this, I hate it here. I hate people. I hate what we do. I hate that people can hate each other for no reason, hate each other so badly they'll just... butcher one another like that. Over what? I don't even know. Beliefs? Traditions? Politics?" I watch him put the cigarette to his lips, watch the orange cherry tremble in the darkness. I see his fingers shake in the dim glow as he drags on it.

"It's so senseless." I don't know what else to say. I'm only good at comfort when I'm in the thick of things. Otherwise, I get...tongue-tied.

He gives me a drag, takes the butt back, and flicks it away. Lifts up on an elbow. Starlight illuminates his beautiful face, gorgeous even when haggard, exhausted, done in.

My heart thumps wildly as he looks down at me.

"I'm gonna kiss you now. Okay?" His eyes are intense, piercing.

I just nod, reach for him. Pull him down to me, and we kiss.

That kiss, that's when I know.

He's it.

He's my only.

When he pulls away, breaking the kiss, I can see

he felt that, too.

"I really, *really* like kissing you." There's a twang to his voice I've never noticed until now.

"Probably because you're so damn good at it," I say.

"Lots of practice."

"Not supposed to admit that, I don't think." I grin up at him, though, because I like this banter. It takes my mind off things.

"Oops."

"Where are you from, Ollie?"

He lies back down beside me. Twines his fingers in mine. "Heard that twang, did you?"

"I caught a little something, yeah."

"Ardmore, Oklahoma. It's right on the border of Texas." He pretends to tip an imaginary hat. "I'm a real-deal cowboy, I'll have you know."

"For real?"

He laughs. "For really real. Grew up on a six-thousand-acre ranch, roping steer and breaking broncs. My dad kicked a fit when I moved to LA to go to med school. Had to give the ranch to my kid brother who, I have to say, can't ride half as good as me."

"How did your dad end up in Los Roboles?"

"Long story. Marcus still has the ranch down in Ardmore, but Mom and Dad retired a few years ago, moved to the middle of nowhere up in northern Cali.

Humboldt County, somewhere. Deserted and rugged, the way they like it. I'm still not quite sure how he ended up in that hospital, actually. I just know I got the call from Mom, so I went. That's when I met you. Dad's a stubborn, taciturn old fucker. It's hard to get two words in a row out of him."

"So how'd you end up so loquacious?"

This gets me a big old grin. "I get that from Mom. She's the opposite of Dad. It's hard to get him to talk at all, harder yet to get her to ever shut up. I'm sort of in between."

"Sounds like they're quite a match." I know I sound plaintive, a little jealous.

"What are your folks like?" He's asking, but I think he knows it's a loaded question.

I can't help a sigh. "My dad took off with the nanny when I was eleven, left Mom with me, my brother, and a pile of debt. Mom wasn't exactly…up to the task of being a single mother of two while struggling under crushing financial debt. So I finished junior high and high school living with my mom's folks, my grandparents. They passed when I was in nursing school, and I don't talk to Mom, seeing as she abandoned me just like Dad did. Nate, my brother, is a problem child, always has been. In and out of jail, off and on drugs. No one can do anything for him and, believe me, I've tried.

"I grew up in San Francisco, moved to LA for nursing school when I was eighteen and never looked back. Don't know where Mom is, don't know where Dad is, and don't know where Nate is. Delaney is my best friend and she's really my only family."

"Jesus, babe. That's rough."

"It is what it is." I shrug. "And now I'm here."

"And now you're here," he agrees. Touches my chin with a thumb, kisses me softly, sweetly, quietly. "And now you have me. Always will."

We kiss again, and that leads to more…a lot more.

Which leads to us getting married when we ship back to the States after doing a year together in Africa.

And that leads to six glorious years with Ollie. Six years of love, sex, and arguments. Six years of war zones, earthquakes, disease outbreaks, hurricanes, typhoons, and even a tsunami.

Six years.

And I'd never trade a single moment of any of those years, not for all the treasure in the world.

Just live for the spin and hope for the win

Mayo Clinic
Rochester, New York

I REMEMBER A LIGHT. A WHITE LIGHT. BULLSHIT, I ALWAYS thought. But it's fucking real. There was a white goddamn light, and I went into it. I remember peace. I remember floating. I remember this…nothingness, a beautiful, all-encompassing, soothing nothingness.

That's something I'll never forget, that peace.

I didn't die. I don't know why, but I didn't. Robby got me to the hospital in time, and they kept me alive. I don't remember any of that, because I was kept alive via machines. I was in an induced coma, just waiting.

It was futile.

I'd never get a transplant.

They could keep me alive on the machines indefinitely, as long as that machine was plugged in. But without a transplant, I'd never leave the bed.

And fuck that.

I signed the DNR form a long time ago; if I die, let me die. Don't put me on the heart-lung machines; don't keep me alive and tethered to fucking pumps and shit. But Mom, I guess, circumvented my wishes, and had me kept alive.

"Alive", though, is a relative term. My brain was on, but my heart was a useless lump in my chest. I was unconscious. If they switched off the machine, I'd die.

Which is what should have happened.

I should have died at the hospital in LA.

So why the *fuck* am I awake, in a hospital bed?

Because I am. It's taking me some time to sort through things, to wake up, to take stock of reality.

And reality is, I'm alive. There's a catheter—fuck those things, and the indignity of them. A bunch of wires trailing to monitors, keeping track of HR, BP, pulse-ox, all that. But no heart-lung machine. No pumps whirring and sucking and plunging. No mask over my face, no tubes down my throat. I mean, there's a cannula in my nose, but that's typical for post-op care.

It's hard to move.

There's a cockload of pain, not localized to anything in particular, just…everything hurts.

Wait.

Post-op care?

No.

Fucking no.

I can barely get my finger to slide across the bed and hit the call button.

In less than a minute a middle-aged woman with brunette hair done up in a tight bun bustles in; all nurse efficiency and sharp friendliness.

"Mr. Montgomery. Good to see you awake. How are you feeling?"

My voice, when I speak, is a rough, sandpapery rasp. "A…alive."

"And isn't it wonderful?"

"No."

She looks up from checking my charts. "No? What do you mean, no? It's a miracle you're alive. That they found a heart to match you, and that your system has accepted the new organ…it's a miracle. You are truly fortunate, Mr. Montgomery."

"I signed a fucking DNR."

"Your mother argued, successfully it would seem, that you signed the DNR under mental and emotional duress, and that you weren't in a position to make such decisions for yourself."

"It was *my* goddamn decision."

"You'll have to take that up with God, and your mother."

"Fuck God, fuck my mother, and fuck you."

"Well now, that's not very nice. I'm just doing my job, Mr. Montgomery, and my job is to help you get well so you can get out of here. So you can get mad at me for situations I had nothing to do with, and we can be at odds, or you can realize that I'm just the nurse and that I'm here to help, and we can get along famously."

"I don't want to be here."

"That much is obvious. So it's in your best interest to cooperate with me. Then we can get you out of here and you can get on with your life."

"I don't have a life to get back to."

"Then you get to start one." She smiles at me, and the smile is warm, bright, and—like everything about this woman—sharp. "You have a new lease on life, Lachlan Montgomery. It's a cliché phrase, but it's grounded in a very real truth. You were supposed to die. You should have died. You *did* die. And now you're alive. You have a strong, healthy new heart in your chest, and your whole life in front of you."

I swallow hard. Nothing makes sense. My emotions are all haywire. Wild, manic, frenetic, a hurricane of so much bullshit I can't grasp at any one thing. Everything hurts, but it's not a physical pain.

It's emotional pain.

I'm alive. And I don't know how to fathom that.

I duck my head, stare at the thin white blanket covering my lap, and blink back the bizarre tears that burn my eyes and blur my vision. The nurse bustles around me, checking charts and paperwork and monitor leads, not looking at me. Giving me privacy to deal with my embarrassing emotions. God, I'm fucking crying? What the fuck? I don't cry. I never cry.

What the hell am I crying for? I'm alive. I should be glad.

I spent my whole life expecting to die. Waiting to die. Knowing I'd die.

And now I'm alive, and…

Now what?

Trinidad, California
Three and a half months later

I refused to see Mom through the entire post-op care process.

I refused to let her into my room. When she came in anyway, I refused to speak to her.

Immature? Yeah.

But I don't know how to deal with any of this. I

don't know how to deal with the fact that she kept me alive when I specifically indicated the opposite.

I don't know how to deal with being alive.

I don't know how to fucking deal.

After the transplant, I remained in the hospital for two weeks and then spent the following three months in transitional care at the Mayo Clinic, enduring biopsies, lung function tests, EKGs, and echocardiograms. When it was all over, the team of doctors told me my body had successfully accepted the new heart. On hearing that news, I went back to Mom's house in LA, packed my shit and headed north.

Dad kept a property in Humboldt County, way north. A tiny little house, comparatively speaking. Only three thousand square feet, worth maybe five mil, in a remote little town called Trinidad. Compared to the castle in Beverly Hills and the sprawling estate in Franklin, it's nothing. But when Dad died, he left it to me. I think he knew I'd need this place someday. Maybe he meant for me to come up here to die.

It's mine, but I haven't been up here in years. I spent a week or so up here after I graduated high school, while I was waiting for the *Vagabond* to be finished, but I haven't been back since. There's a caretaker, of course, a local old guy with not much to do but swing by and check on things. His wife dusts from time to time and keeps the place clean and the cupboards stocked with non-perishable food. I called him after I left the Mayo Clinic, had him open it up, stock the fridge, shit like that.

God, it's gorgeous up here. The house is on a bluff overlooking the ocean and there are views from every room. There's a forest behind and the village of Trinidad spread out below. Eureka is even visible in the distance on a clear day. I park my brand-new truck in the driveway, step out and stand on the running board, stare at the house and look over at the rippling, winking blue ocean in the distance. I inhale the clean, clear air.

I say new truck, because I sold the *Vagabond*. I also sold the Pagani.

Jesus, I sold the Pagani. That car was Dad's baby, and the *Vagabond* was mine. I packed all my shit—clothes, a couple cases of Lagavulin, a kayak, a stand-up paddleboard, and my climbing gear. That's my life, and it all fits in the back of a tricked-out F-250 King Ranch.

I figured, I'm starting over. I'm moving up here to Humboldt County, for one thing, and Humboldt is rugged and wild, which means a Pagani Zonda isn't exactly practical. I brought everything with me, because I don't know what I'm doing, where I'm going, where I'll end up. I'll probably stay here in Trinidad for a while, but I don't think I'll be here forever.

Truth is, I don't know what to do with myself.

I've lived my entire life certain I'd never make it past thirty-one. Well, here I am, thirty-one, and alive. With everything in front of me.

And I'm scared shitless.

Confused.

Paralyzed, really.

Gregor, the caretaker, is in the backyard, putting a coat of finish on the deck railing. He hears me come around the corner, turns, can of finish in one hand, brush in the other. Gray hair, blue eyes, and wrinkled, weathered skin. Friendly smile. "Mr. Montgomery. So glad to see you, sir."

"Call me Lock. Things all set, Gregor?"

He nods, goes back to applying the finish. "Sure is. Just putting some of this on the deck, since the paint was peeling a little. The missus got everything cleaned for you, and we stocked up the fridge. Lots of fresh produce, steaks and fish, all of it local. You should be all set, but you got my number if you need anything."

"Thanks, Gregor. I think I'll be good."

He swipes the paintbrush a few more times, then pauses, and glances at me. "Gotta say, Lock, it's good to see you. Real good. I never thought—" he cuts off, unsure how to finish.

I take mercy on him. "I never did, either. That's

why I'm up here."

He nods. "Your dad, he came up here, right near the end. I think he bought this place for…" a vague wave, "—to get ready. He knew it was coming and… he needed to—to get ready."

"He gave it to me so I could do the same."

Another nod. "Well, now…you're here for the exact opposite reason. That's…that's a damn good thing."

"You knew Dad?"

A shake of his head. "Not well. You get tourists and the occasional newcomer, folks up for summer vacation every year, things like that, and they keep to themselves, mostly. But your dad was…different. You all got money, and a lot of it, but he acted like a local. Friendly with everybody, generous, liked to drink at the local watering holes. Everybody liked him, round these parts."

"He spend a lot of time up here?"

A nod. "Sure did. Toward the end, he was up here more than anywhere else. I think he wanted to…to pass on up here, but your mother talked him out of it. I think maybe—well, that's conjecture, and it don't do to speak on it. You're here, and that's all that matters. Does my old heart good, is all I'm saying."

I unpack, put all my clothes on hangers and in the drawers, pile my gear in the garage. It's weird, unpacking, being on solid ground and in one place after so long. The floor doesn't roll. There's nowhere to go. No Friends of the Day. No new adventure to go looking for.

Once I'm unpacked, I—

I have no idea what to do next. Mom said she would be coming up for the weekend. I did everything in my power to dissuade her, but she's not a woman to take no for an answer. I sure don't need or want a babysitter, but sometimes it's just easier to give in to her.

Gregor has left, and the house is utterly silent. Onboard the *Vagabond*, there was always sound of some kind. The caw of gulls, the chuck of waves, the ever-present wind, the clink of metal on the mast, the snap of bellied sails. And, usually, music, women laughing, men tossing playful insults at each other. Now…there's nothing. The doors and windows are all closed, there's no music, no voices. Just…complete silence.

And I don't know what to do.

I'm rarely alone.

Rarely enveloped in silence.

Rarely left to my own thoughts, left to let my emotions boil up and over.

And fuck, are there a lot of thoughts and emotions to deal with.

I slide open the windows, pull open the back door and move out onto the deck. And that's not helping, because the ocean is there. The sea has always been my siren, calling me. And there she is, right there. Wide and blue, whispering to me. *Come*, she says. *Follow my currents. Ride my winds*.

I can't, though. That was my old life. This is my new one. If I go out there, if I follow the sea, I'll never come back. I'll fall into my old patterns. And now, that just…it feels wasteful.

It feels like running away.

I put my hand over my chest, feel my heart beating. The thud under my ribcage is steady, strong, reassuring. No defect. No end in sight. I reached the deadline, and I'm past it. I'm alive.

In the back of my mind I know I will only have a few hours to myself before dear old mom arrives so, somehow, I'm off the deck, but I don't remember leaving. I'm barefoot, stumbling through scrub to the wooden staircase leading down to the sea. It's a long way down, hundreds of stairs. I start the descent, and my pulse remains steady and slow. My old heart would have been pounding by this time, reminding me, reminding me.

Eventually I reach the beach, sand cool underfoot, and the ocean azure and endless. Surf crashes. Gulls caw. Wind soughs through my hair, touches my

cheekbones, ruffles my hair. I scuff through the sand
to the water's edge, and the lap of Pacific against my
toes is cutting and cold. There's no one, not in either
direction. No boats, no neighbors. Just me, and the
sea, and my thoughts.

The temptation to crack a bottle of Lagavulin is
strong. My mouth waters. I want that drowning feeling. I don't have to think, or feel. I don't have to decide. All I'd have to do is drink, and drink, and drink.

Wake up, and repeat.

Shit, the need to escape the chaotic welter in my
mind is so strong I'm tempted to wade out into the
frigid sea and swim until my arms and legs and lungs
give out.

Great-Grandpa didn't get this chance.

Grandpa didn't.

Dad didn't.

Why did I?

Why do I get to live?

Why couldn't Dad have gotten a transplant? Why
couldn't I have grown up with a father?

I have no one. No one expects anything of me.
No one is waiting for me. No one cares whether I
come or go.

No one cares.

I made sure of that.

Jesus fuck—I can't handle that line of thought for

long. I head back up the stairs, amazed at how easy it is, jogging up those steps, feeling my heart beat harder and harder without hurting, without worrying, without getting dizzy or faint.

I wonder whose heart is in my chest?

I sit on the deck with a bottle of Lagavulin tucked between my legs. I'm weak. I'm so fucking weak. I shouldn't be drinking. At all. That was, like, number one on the list of injunctions from the doctors. Yet here I am, on the deck, pounding it back like a fool.

I hear a door open, but it's too late to hide the evidence, so I kick my feet up on the railing, cap the bottle, and sip from the glass as Mom comes out onto the deck.

She's dressed in her "casual" clothes, which means she's only wearing like ten or fifteen grand worth of designer clothes rather than twenty or more. She's got her hair—naturally blonde like mine—piled on top of her head, and a pair of Chanel sunglasses wedged into her thick locks. Diamonds on her wrist, fingers, neck, and ears. She's wearing heels, even out here. Just a casual day at the beach.

She takes one look at me, and goes into full freakout mode. "Lachlan Thomas Michael Montgomery! You're *drinking*?!" She snatches the bottle and, before I can stop her, upends it over the railing. "That has *got* to stop. You know this is the one thing you're not supposed to be doing. The doctors were all very clear on that fact, Lachlan. Your liver has been through enough, and now it has to work even harder to break down the Cyclosporine and all the other medications." She pauses to take a breath. "Speaking of which, have you taken your meds today?"

"Jesus, Mom. It's a couple drinks. What's the big deal?" I attempt to stand up and immediately regret it, because it belies my claim.

She's got tears in her eyes. "Because it could kill you. You're *alive*, Lachlan." She grabs my face, looks me in the eyes and whispers, her voice broken. "I lost you. You died. I was there—I watched you—I watched…I watched you die. But then we got the call to say that an organ donor had been identified, a perfect match for you. Because of that, you're alive. Don't waste it, Lachlan. *Please*…don't waste it."

"I don't know how not to, Mom." I feel the words tumble out, unbidden. "It's all I know how to do."

"Well, it's time to learn." She turns away, placing the sunglasses over her eyes, hiding her own emotions. We're a lot alike, in that way. "You're the only man in our entire family to survive the defect. You owe it to *them*, if nothing else. You owe it to Thom-

as—to your dad. To Grandpa Michael. You owe it to
me."

"To *you*? To YOU?" I'm shouting. "You took away
my choice! I signed a DNR. I wanted to die. I didn't
want to be brought back. Or to be kept alive."

"I wanted you to have a chance." Again, her voice
is a whisper, now barely audible. Her voice is smaller
and quieter than it's ever been, I think.

"It was *my* choice, Mom."

"I couldn't lose you, Lachlan! I only had thirteen
years with your father. I deserved more. I thought I'd
only have maybe thirty years with you. And then I
did lose you. They barely brought you back, and then
there was no guarantee we'd ever get a match.

"Do you have any idea what it was like for me,
Lachlan? Sitting in that room for two months, watching you lie there, unconscious, kept alive by a machine, knowing I'd have to be the one to tell them to
pull the plug? I knew you didn't want to be kept alive
like that. And I'd—I'd made a deal with myself. We'd
wait for three months, maybe four, and if there wasn't
a donor in that time, I'd—I'd have to let you go. And
I would have. But…can you even fathom what it was
like? Knowing—thinking I'd have to watch you die a
second time?"

She's standing closer than I think she's ever gotten to me. Inches away, so I can smell her perfume

and see the makeup under her eyelids and on her eye-lashes, and see the lipstick on her lips. "Don't—don't waste this, Lock. Please…please don't. I know you're mad at me. I get it. I deserve it, maybe. That's fine. But don't…don't waste this."

She leaves me then, going back into the house, shutting the door quietly behind her.

And I stay out on the deck, watching the sun go down, sobering up, and repeating her words over and over and over.

Don't waste this.

Going nowhere with no one but me

Ardmore, Oklahoma

I SLIDE THE TIP OF THE THERMOMETER UNDER THE LITTLE girl's tongue. "Okay, now just hold still for a few seconds for me. All right, good job, Eva. Now I need to look in your ears, okay?"

I go through the motions. Temp, ears, reflexes, nose, the works. Routine checkup. The next patient is the same. And the one after that. Then a young guy arrives with a sprained wrist and a concussion—he got tossed off a mule and landed the wrong way. All the usual stuff you'd expect to see as a physician's assistant in a small rural town. The whole day goes that way. A summer cold. Some stitches in a forehead. Prescription refill. An annual physical.

As the PA, I take ninety percent of the patients. Dr. Amos Beardsley is going on eighty-five, and he really only sees the patients who've been with the practice for several generations, so I get the rest, the walk-ins, the checkups, the refills, the sutures and fractures and concussions and "is this rash normal" sort of questions.

It's work.

It keeps me busy, and that's all I need.

By the time the last walk-in has been seen, everyone else has cleaned up and shut down. Just as I prepare to close up for the day, a teenage girl arrives, too embarrassed and scared to ask her parents for contraceptives.

Finally, I grab my purse and head out to my vehicle. I'm tired, ready for bed. It's seven o'clock, and I was at the office before seven this morning, and I didn't have time for lunch. I'm still in my lab coat; still have my stethoscope draped over my neck.

I climb up into the cab of the truck and slam the door closed. I lower both windows to let the heat of the Oklahoma summer billow out. I'm already sweating, and I've only been in the truck for two seconds. It's only going to get worse, too, because this old wreck doesn't have AC.

I could afford a new truck, of course—I make decent money. But this was Ollie's truck. He fixed it up himself, back in high school. When I first moved down here, after the accident, I visited Marcus, Ollie's younger brother. We didn't click, Marcus and I. He was country, and I'm…not. We just don't see the world the same way, and I think the grief of losing Ollie was too much for both of us.

But Marcus was sympathetic to my grief, and realized my need to have something to connect me to Ollie. So he gave me this truck. I paid to have it looked over, anything broken got fixed. I spent more on it than it's worth, probably, and it still breaks down all the time. The AC went at the beginning of the summer, and I just haven't gotten around to getting it fixed. It's not a big deal, though, since I work six days a week, sunup to sundown, and thus I'm rarely in it during the real heat of the day.

I'll drive this old heap until it quits on me, because I can smell Ollie in it. See him in it. I've got his picture wedged into a gap in the dashboard, a candid photo I took in Africa. He's blood-spattered, in the middle of stripping off his gloves. He's exhausted; you can see it in the bags under his eyes. But he's happy. I'd just told him I loved him, out of the blue. He'd needed to hear it, and I knew it, so I shouted it out across the tent: "Hey, Pep! I love you!" And he'd looked up, grinned, and I'd snapped the shot. I got him grinning, a moment of happiness amid all the hell.

I turn the engine over and it coughs, rattles, and then catches with a rumble. The radio is on—it's always on—and the cab is filled with country music, Ollie's favorite. It's a traditional station, the same station where he'd had it tuned. Hank Williams, Johnny Cash, Waylon Jennings, Randy Travis, Alan Jackson, maybe some older Tim McGraw and that crowd. Nothing new. It's the soundtrack of this town of Ardmore—slides on steel strings and songs about love lost and taillights in the dust.

I hate it.

But the old radio has never been changed. Not once, not ever, and I'll never change it.

We used to sit in that old Nissan pickup at the MSF compound, and Ollie would pull out his trusty iPod, filled to max capacity with every country song he could think of, tuck the left ear bud in my ear, the right in his, and we'd listen to country music and catch a breath or two between incoming two-tons full of bloody refugees.

I'll always hate country music.

But I listen to it anyway.

Home is a good twenty minutes away on the outskirts of town. *Outskirts* may be pushing it. It's a tiny one-room shotgun shack at the end of a long dirt road, sitting on a half-acre pocket in the midst of hundreds of acres of grass and hay in every direction. No neighbors but the Jensens half a mile down, who own all those acres, and the dozen or so horses grazing on them. It's a lonely little place, dead silent at night except for the hooting of the occasional owl, and the crickets, and the humming of the light fixed to the power line pole at the edge of my property. It's not much, but it's mine.

I've got a couch, a TV, a few overflowing book-shelves, a bed, and a dresser; that's all that'd fit any-way. It's all I need, all I'll ever want.

I toss my lab coat and purse on the couch, strip out of my scrubs, toss them in the hamper. Throw my sports bra and panties after them, step in the shower and rinse off the day. I towel off, brush my hair and slip on an old T-shirt of Ollie's. It used to smell like him, but the smell has faded now even though I don't wash it much; I'm trying to preserve the last shreds of his scent on it.

Pep, my cat and only friend, waits until I'm sitting on the couch with a book before saying hello. He's a little black and white tom, so of course I named him Pep. I adopted him as my first official act after mov-ing down here, because you can leave a cat in a house alone all day, and I needed *something*.

And god, does Pep come through for me. He's a snuggly little fella; I like to sit cross-legged on the couch, and he likes to curl up like a comma in the space between my legs. Purrs like a little engine for as long as I stroke his back and the little strip of fur between his ears. He sleeps on the pillow next to mine at night, and takes my warm spot after I get up in the morning.

I read until my eyes blur, until my head spins. And then I climb into bed, set Pep on his pillow, and go to sleep.

Then, I wake up in the morning, and do it all over again.

Same as I've done every day since I came down here.

I had to go somewhere, and Ollie's hometown seemed as good a place as any, especially since his parents didn't live here anymore. They were up in northern California somewhere, and I couldn't stand to be near them. Ollie sounded like his father and looked like his mother, and both of them tore my heart to shreds.

Being in Ardmore was another way of holding on to him, of being alone with him. Another way of keeping him as close as I could. Feeling him. Seeing him. He'd gotten milkshakes at the diner, bought his first pair of Tony Lomas at the outfitter a few blocks down. Took his first girlfriend to the movies at the theater across from the town square. He's all over this town, and that's equal parts comforting and cutting.

I don't cry myself to sleep at night.

I stopped doing that months ago.

I don't whisper his name when I'm lonely, because I'm lonely all the time.

I don't get the shakes anymore, because I don't do anything more dangerous or traumatic than stitching up the occasional boo-boo. I quit MSF, of course. I couldn't go back, not after losing Ollie. I couldn't face any of them. I couldn't face Africa again, not without him.

I can't face *life* without Ollie.

I don't know how.

I know what I'm doing is unhealthy. I'm not moving on. I'm not healing. I've grieved, but I just can't seem to *stop* grieving. I can't stop needing him. I can't breathe without him, and he's gone, so I can't breathe.

So here I am, in Ardmore, Oklahoma.

Alone.

The only thing I know how to be.

At least I've got Pep.

Wandering the city streets

Trinidad, California

"**I**'M SORRY, BUT I CAN'T SHARE THAT INFORMATION with you." The voice on the other end is quiet but firm, and the call ends with a click.

"Goddammit!" I toss the phone across the room where it lands on the bed.

I've been trying like hell to find out whose heart I've got in my chest. I don't know why, but I've got to know.

I've *got* to know.

And no one will tell me.

So as much as I hate to do it, there's only one person left to call. So I call him.

"Hello?"

"Howdy, Larry."

"Lachlan. To what do I owe this pleasure?" Larry

Carter, family attorney, and well-paid bulldog.

"I need a favor, Larry."

"Well I can't make any promises, but tell me what you need and I'll see what I can do. Usual rates apply, of course."

"No shit." I hesitate, blow out a breath. "I need to know who my organ donor was."

"I—what?" This is the first time I've ever heard Larry caught off-guard. As the go-to attorney for several ultra-wealthy clients, he's used to all sorts of requests.

"The heart in my chest. I need to know who the donor was. No one will tell me, and if anyone can get the information it's you."

"I'll see what I can do. It can't be that hard to get that kind of information. I'll get back to you."

"Thanks."

"Sure thing." A pause. "How have you been—?"

"I'm fine, Larry. Just find out who the donor was, yeah?"

"Yes, sir. Shouldn't take long."

"Good." I hang up, and go out on the deck.

I'm drinking Perrier. I'm drinking a lot of Perrier these days. I gave Gregor all my Lagavulin, and Mom watched me do it. She searched the house herself, made sure I was really giving it all away. I'm not sure what to think about this, because I never thought of myself as an alcoholic. I didn't drink all day every day, and rarely to wild excess.

Okay…maybe that's a lie.

I did drink a lot, now that I think about it.

Most days.

By noon, most days.

To blackout, some days.

I never saw a reason to quit, though, you know? I was gonna die anyway, so what did it matter if it was liver failure or heart failure? Something was going to give out, and it was gonna be my heart. So might as well drink up while I could.

But now that it matters, now that I'm aware of the importance of not drinking, it's really, *really* fucking hard to quit. I want a drink every single goddamn moment of every single goddamn day. I'm a fucking mess. I don't smoke, never have. Don't drink, now, because I can't. I might be able to handle a drink or two. *Maybe*. But what if I can't? What if I'm a real-deal alkie, like I take a drink and somehow I'm wasted, with no in between? The *what if*, that's the fucking worst.

No, not having any outlet is the worst.

I don't actually *do* anything. I'm not skilled at anything except sailing, drinking, and fucking. And the problem is, if I set out to do the first, I'll end up doing the second. And right now, as odd as it feels to realize this, I'm not in any place to be doing the third.

I'm lonely as hell, of course. I've never been alone before—I don't know how. But here I am, alone, all day, every day.

I run a lot. Up the beach a few miles and back. Swim in the frigid water. I read a lot of books—I'm catching up on the classics I never read by not going to college.

I don't have a talent.

I don't have a trade.

I don't have a skill.

I don't have…anything worthwhile.

I am no one.

Goddamn you, Astrid, for putting the thought in my head: *You are wrong about one thing, Lock: the only true measure of a person is what they do with their life.*

Now I can't forget that shit, and I can't stop realizing, time and again, over and over, that it's the truth, and the truth in this case inculpates me.

What have I done with my life? Not a goddamn thing.

What am I worth? Not a goddamn thing.

I mean, financially I'm worth a lot. Mom wrangled back the shares I sold all those years ago, and recently signed them back to me. So now I'm worth a fuck-ton of money again.

Super cool.

But…what do I do with it?

Funny how life works. Live like I'm dying, because I am, and enjoy every moment, knowing it's coming to an end all too soon. But now that I have a future in front of me I hate myself, I hate every moment of my life. Legit, I have zero self-esteem.

No direction.

No plan.

No reason for existing.

Before, I had a reason: live like I'm dying, as that old Tim McGraw song goes.

Now—alive and not dying, I have no reason.

"Lachlan, Larry here." There's a rustling of paper on the other end of the line. "I have some information for you."

"Great. Let's hear it."

"The donor was a man named Oliver James. A doctor, specifically a surgeon who worked for Doctors Without Borders. Died in a car accident on the PCH. He was thirty-six. Married, no children. His parents are listed as his next of kin, and they're actually in your area. Down in Kneeland, or thereabouts."

He gives me an address, and tells me to give him a call if I need anything else. I don't know what I'll find. I don't even know what I'm looking for. I just know I can't stay here anymore. I need…I don't even know. But if I can find something out about this Oliver James, whose heart beats in my chest, maybe I'll…

Maybe I'll what? I don't even know.

I don't question the need to leave, though. I toss a backpack and some camping gear into the back of my truck and head down to Kneeland.

Damn…this is backwoods. Real backwoods. Not much here but ranches, farms, and old houses on rolling hills tucked back into quiet old-growth forests.

Even after I find the correct county road, it takes me another thirty minutes of driving before I spot the mailbox with the right house number. I pull into a long, winding, dusty driveway, which in turn leads me way, way back into the wooded hills. Rolling fields behind, hundred-foot-tall trees towering ahead, swaying in a gentle breeze. I've got the windows open so I can smell the air, taste the fine grit of the dirt road, and hear the crunch of my tires.

The house itself is a tiny little place, ramshackle, probably a good hundred years old, maybe more. Smoke curls up from the chimney, even in the summer. Little screened-in porch, an old white Silverado with a rusted rear bumper parked at an angle on the grass near the front door. Pole barn out back, off to the right, and a stable with an attached split-rail corral on the left. A couple of splotchy horses graze quietly along one corner, the kind that are white with big brown or red spots. Paints, maybe? I don't know much about horses.

I park behind the Silverado and hop out. Of course, in these parts you can hear visitors coming from a mile away and by the time they pull up you're waiting for them at the front door.

He's old. Seventies, eighties maybe. Tall, straight, strong-looking, the kind of man who'd once cut a hell of a figure and still does, even now. White hair combed straight back, piercing, deep-set brown eyes. Hand on a knobby, gnarled walking stick.

I approach slowly. "Hey."

"Help you, son? Ain't likely you're lost, around here."

"No, sir. I'm not lost."

"Then what'cha want? I ain't buyin' nothin', and I got plenty of Jesus."

I rub my hand through my hair; it's grown out, as have my whiskers. No point in looking fine since no one's looking at me but me and, lately, I don't give a shit. "There's no good way to come at this, sir, so I'll just say it straight—"

"Always best, I figger. Beat around the bush,

you're likely to scare out a snake."

"My name is Lachlan Montgomery."

"Fancy name."

"Yeah, I guess. I was born with a congenital heart defect, and I was told I would likely not live past thirty because of it."

"Sorry to hear that. What's it got to do with me?"

I sigh. Ornery old bastard, ain't he? "It caught up with me, about six months ago. I died, and they brought me back to life on the table. I wasn't likely to last long, because I've got a really rare blood type which made it nearly impossible for me to get a transplant."

His gaze narrows; he's starting to suss out where I'm going with this. "Son, get to it."

"Your son, Oliver—"

I don't get another syllable out. He's on me, shoving me backward, pressing the thick walking stick across my throat, pinning me against the hood of his truck. "No, son. You don't want to come up on my property talking about my son. You just don't wanna do it."

"Sir, I just—"

He lets me up, grabs me by the shirtsleeve and shoves me toward my truck. "No. I know where you're going, and I don't wanna fuckin' hear it. He's gone and that's that. You best get the hell out of here before my wife comes out. You upset her, there'll be hell to pay. Hear me? Get gone."

"I just wanted to know what he was like."

"He was a goddamn hero, that's what he was like. Wasn't a better man this side of heaven. Saved lives every single damn day. That's what my Oliver was like. Now go."

I slide into my truck. Start the engine, let the diesel knock around for a minute. Breathe, keep it together. I hear knuckles on my window.

The old man, rubbing an arthritic knuckle against his forehead. "I may have gone off a bit, and I do apologize."

I shake my head. "No, sir. It was unexpected and unwelcome. I'm the one who should be apologizing. It's just...since the transplant, I—" I stop, shake my head again. "I'm sorry, sir. I'll go."

He scratches at a lined, weathered cheek, eyes me sidelong. "You're looking for something."

"Yeah."

"Ain't gonna find it here. He never lived here." A pause, a thoughtful look. "Keep looking, son. Never know what you might find out there, you look hard enough."

I don't know what that means.

"Thanks, Mr. James," I say. "Have a nice day."

"You too, son."

I wave as I swing the truck around and head out of Kneeland.

I don't know where I'm going next, but it's not back north, back to Trinidad.

Once my cell shows enough reception to make a call, I dial Gregor. He answers on the third ring. "Lock, how can I help you today?"

"I'm leaving, Gregor. I need you to close the place up for me."

A long silence. "Sorry to see you go, but I get it. I'll take care of it for you."

"Thanks, Gregor."

"No problem."

Click.

I drive for a few hours, heading steadily south.

A thought strikes me, and I use bluetooth to dial Larry.

"Lachlan."

"Hey, Larry. Oliver James's parents didn't want to talk. So I need something else. You said he was married?"

"Yeah. To...um..." papers shuffling— "Niall James. Thirty-three. Worked with Oliver in MSF."

"MSF?"

"Yeah, *Médicins sans Frontières*. It's a French organization, the name translates to what we call it, Doctors Without Borders."

"Where is she?"

"Looks like…" more papers shuffling, "Ardmore, Oklahoma."

"Oklahoma. All right. Thanks, Larry."

"What are you hoping to—?"

"Hell if I know, Larry." I hang up.

I pull over and put Ardmore, Oklahoma into the GPS. Turns out Ardmore is on the border with Texas, a long, long way from here.

Good. A road trip sounds perfect.

Fuck road trips. Two days in and the monotony of the endless blacktop is getting to me.

Long driving trips can be the loneliest damn thing on the planet. At least on a boat, you have the sea to keep you company; you're busy all the time trimming the sails, and watching the wind, and keeping an eye on the wheel and the currents and the skies. Maybe spot a pod of dolphins or a whale now and again. But driving? It's boring and hypnotic. Nothing but the radio, nothing but the endless yellow and white lines, the blacktop, farms and desert and prairie and a whole bunch of nothing ahead, and even more nothing behind.

There's nothing to do but think.

Which leads nowhere good, just endless mental forays into the Land of Regret. I relive the last twelve or thirteen years of my life; there are some good memories, of course. I don't really regret any of it, per se. I just…I don't know.

What did any of it mean?

You face death, and you tend to get a dose of perspective. Could I have done anything different? What if I'd taken the approaching end of my life as a motivation to accomplish something, to becoming something, to doing something worthwhile? Where would I have ended up?

No way to know.

I think of Astrid a lot, actually, of her sense of purpose, and her thinly disguised disapproval of my privileged life of idle luxury and ridiculous excess. I didn't *do* anything, and that was anathema to someone like her. She used me for a good time, and she wouldn't have spared me another thought under any other circumstances. Surprisingly, it hurts more than I'd expect it to, knowing Astrid wouldn't have bothered with me, except to get the O out of me. I was a night of feeling good for her and nothing more.

Funny how that feels, now that the tables are turned.

I thought we had a decent connection, had some good conversation throughout the evening. I may not have gone to college, but I am well read. Out on the high seas, there's not much to do except read, so I read a lot, and I've always had varied interests. I've read biographies, histories, books on psychology and philosophy and anthropology, as well as fiction of all genres. It was a haphazard self-education, but it means I can converse on a wide range of topics with just about anyone.

But Astrid? She was highly educated, highly sophisticated. We only had a few hours together, but our conversation is still stuck in my head. *She* is stuck in my head. What she said, in that note she left. I mean, she didn't even bother to say goodbye, or have breakfast, or some wake-up nookie. Nothing. Just a note left in the wee hours of the morning.

That's all I was worth to her. Why?

Because to her, your calling, or whatever it was that you did, defined who you were. But me? I didn't really do anything but party and do dangerous and irresponsible shit, so I wasn't really anyone in her eyes.

Fuck of it all is, she was right.

And these are the things I think about on the long drive southeast to Oklahoma.

The first hint of change for Lachlan Montgomery

comes in the form of a near miss on the highway.

I'm tired, still driving after a good thirteen hours non-stop. Hungry, seeing double. Past midnight, windows down, blasting heavy metal on the XM radio to try to stay awake.

It's a two-lane highway through a whole lot of wild nowhere, miles of emptiness on every side, miles of farm fields, nothing to see but hints of corn or wheat or soy or whatever reflected in the headlights through the pitch dark. Occasionally, I'd cross another smaller highway or dirt road, or see a farmhouse in the distance with the light over the barn shining white-yellow.

I blink, and the road is empty.

Blink again, and there's a huge brown shape in the middle of the road, eyes illuminated by my headlights. I shout a curse and jam on the brake pedal, fishtail, swerve, and narrowly miss whatever it is in the road. A small deer, or a large dog. Coyote, maybe? I don't know. It all happened in an instant.

I'm sideways in the middle of the road, my headlights blazing, a pool of light spearing across the road.

Something large and dark cowers in the shadows just outside the smear of light from my headlights. I get out of the truck and approach cautiously.

There's a growl, low and vicious.

I back up, crouch, ready to run for my open truck

door.

But then the shape slinks forward, into the light…

It's a dog, all right. An Irish wolfhound, unless I miss my guess. Huge, and I mean absolutely massive. Shaggy gray-brown fur that looks matted and dirty. It's thin, though. A stray?

I kneel down, click my tongue. "Come here, boy. It's all right."

Is it a boy, though? I can't tell, yet. The dog crouches down, head between its paws, tail tucked, slinking fearfully toward me, whimpering.

I pat my thigh, try to sound soothing. "Come on, now. I won't hurt you. Come on. That's good."

It takes a lot of cajoling to get the gargantuan yet timid beast to finally reach me, and then it immediately rolls over, paws in the air, tail wiggling crazily; it's a female.

"Hey, girl." I pat her belly, gently, and then her chin, her ears.

She rolls over, sits on her haunches, and god, she's *huge*; sitting on her haunches she's taller than I am kneeling on my knees. She'd be taller than me, standing on her hind legs. Standing on all fours, her shoulders will easily reach my hips, if not higher. I search her neck for a collar, and that's when my heart clenches. No collar, just an old length of rope with a torn, frayed end where it looks as though she broke free; the rope is so tight around her throat it's a wonder she can even breathe. Jesus.

I have a multi-tool in my pocket so I take it out, and carefully unfold the blade, murmuring to the dog in low, comforting tones as I slide the blade between her skin and the rope, sawing gently until the rope pops apart. I have to sort of peel it off of her, which gets me a whimper and a growl, but then the rope is off, and she shakes herself vigorously, gives me a doggy grin and a yip.

"Well, girl. Now what?" I look around, but obviously there's nothing and no one anywhere. "Want to come with me? I don't know where I'll end up."

She cocks her head as if she's listening, and then trots over to the truck, sits again. Smart pup, huh? I've got an old wool blanket in the backseat, which I unfold onto the rear bench for her, then pat the blanket. She hops in easily, lies down on the blanket, chin on paws. Her tail thumps slowly as she watches me climb up into the driver's seat.

I glance back at her. "Guess we're friends now, huh, girl? What should I call you?"

A soft little whine, wide brown eyes staring at me.

I glance at the GPS; I'm in Utah, so... "Hey girl, whassup?" I laugh at my own stupid joke—quoting a country song to a dog, and I don't even really like country music all that much. I'm slap-happy, is what I am. "How 'bout I call you Utah?"

This gets me a full-on bark, ears perking, head tipping to one side.

"Utah?"

Another yip.

Either this dog understands me, or I'm crazy.

Probably both are true.

"All right then, Utah it is. Howdy, Utah. My name is Lock. Ready to go?"

She lays her head down on her front paws again, and her eyes flutter and close. Guess she's ready, huh?

I drive until I find one of those tiny highway towns, the kind of place that has a couple of fast food restaurants, a Quality Inn or something like that, a ratty supermarket, two or three gas stations, and a strip mall.

It's very late, but I manage to find a motel and pay cash for a first-floor room. I park in front of my room's door, crack a truck window for Utah, go inside and fill the ice bucket with some water and let her drink some. Once she's settled I go inside and catch a couple hours of sleep. In the morning, I head to the nearest store to buy some supplies for my new buddy.

I question, as I peruse the pet supplies section, what I am doing? Why am I taking on the responsibility of a dog? It's stupid. A dog is the last thing I need.

But, somehow, it feels like Utah is *exactly* what I need.

I buy a leash, collar, a bag of large breed dog food, a couple of bowls for food and water, a couple gallons of water, a couple toys, a ball, doggie snacks, and a brush. I take Utah back to the motel and sneak her inside. Technically, the place doesn't allow pets, but I'm guessing they probably don't allow hookers either, and there's one turning tricks a couple doors down, so I figure I'm fine. I lead Utah into the bathroom and into the tub with the promise of a treat.

Fortunately, the shower has one of those removable head things, so I can give her a decent bath. I expect trouble, shaking, running, a freak-out of some kind. But sweet old Utah? She just stands there, massive and wet, a doggy grin on her face as I massage glob after glob of the complimentary shampoo into her thick, matted, shaggy fur. It takes the entire bottle to get her clean. Even when I've got the worst of the dirt and twigs and leaves washed away there are still several mats in her coat, so I dry her off—using all the towels in the bathroom—and then I use the brush on her. After a good twenty minutes of brushing, and judicious use of the scissors on my multi-tool, I manage to get most of the mats out of her fur.

Okay, so I'm not gonna be a professional dog groomer, but she's clean and mat-free. It's a step in the right direction, and she looks a hundred percent less like a stray.

She eats two full bowls of food and slurps more water, and then indicates she's done by going over to the front door and sitting down, swiveling her head to look at me. I swear she's got a look on her face that says, "You coming or what?"

"All right, all right," I say, gathering up my stuff, "I'm coming. You're ready to get out of here, huh?"

She gives that yip again, her tail thumping the floor.

I let her out, and she hauls across the parking lot to the scrub vegetation taking over the vacant lot next door. She trots around, sniffing erratically while I pack up the gear under the tonneau cover. Eventually she does her business—both kinds—and trots back on her own to sit by the rear passenger door.

I stare at her, amazed. "You are, like, the smartest dog there is, aint'cha?"

YIP!

I laugh, and open the door for her. As this is happening, though, the day clerk is watching as he checks the room next to mine. "Was she in the room with you?"

I see no point in lying—especially since I could probably buy this place with a couple of phone calls. "I gave her a bath."

"There's a strict no-pets policy, sir. I'm afraid I'll have to charge you a room-cleaning fine."

Two doors down, a door opens. An older guy with a belly stretching the confines of a stained wife-beater and greasy, baggy khakis leaves the motel room, digging in his hip pocket. He peels a few bills off a roll, and extends it. A woman of indeterminate age—probably middle to late thirties, if I was forced to guess—accepts the cash. She doesn't stuff it into a pocket or a bra, because she doesn't have either. She's got a thin silk robe on, hanging from her shoulders, loosely tied, which means it's sagging open and thus covering precisely zero percent of her naughty bits.

I look at her, she looks at me, and the day clerk looks from her to me and back again.

I smirk at him. "I assume there's a strict no-hookers policy, too?"

The woman just glares. "Fuck you."

"*You'd* have to pay *me*, sweetheart," I say.

She turns a little, facing us both, and lets the robe fall open even more, lifting a knee in a pose meant to be provocative, probably. "There's a policy, all right." A wink. "But Ricky likes to live on the wild side, don't you Ricky?"

I laugh. "Ah, I see." I punch good old Ricky in the arm, not exactly gently. "She gives it to you for free, and you turn a blind eye to the tricks."

"She pays rent," Ricky mumbles, rubbing his arm.

"I bet she does." I jerk open the door of my truck. "You won't be charging me cleaning fees or anything else."

Ricky turns away, but I can tell his attention is on the hooker. Anticipating the turn-a-blind-eye BJ he's probably about to get. "No…nothing extra."

"Didn't think so."

I drive away, but in the rearview mirror I can see the hooker dragging the clerk into her room while undoing his belt. Not a bad gig, if you don't mind stinky hooker-poon.

Not my thing, personally. I like it fresh and wild, not…*that*. Whatever the hell that is.

I don't have any nice words to describe it, and in the name of turning over a new leaf, I'll keep the unkind ones to myself.

Just…yuck. I'll leave it at that.

I've never owned a dog before, and I have to admit that having a dog is fun.

She sleeps for a while as I drive, and then hops into the front seat beside me. I lower the window for her and she sticks her head out, enjoying the wind in her face. I like watching her have fun, shaking her head, drool spattering the side of the truck and the back window.

When I feel like stopping, I pull over onto the shoulder. There's nothing but brown in every direction, so I let Utah hop down and I toss the ball for her, hurling it as far as I can. She hauls after it, finds it, and brings it to me, dropping the slobbery tennis ball at my feet, barking for me to throw it again. So I do, and thus I spend a good half an hour, throwing a damp, gritty tennis ball for a big wolfhound, and having more fun than I've had in a long time. Feeling good. Feeling…okay.

She accepts me without question. Doesn't need to know anything about me, doesn't care about anything except that I've taken care of her, fed her, cleaned her, and I give her attention.

Back on the road, she somehow curls her absurdly mammoth body onto the front bucket seat, her head on the console between us, and I get to rest my hand on her head and scratch her ears while I drive.

Windows down, music up, sun in my face, a dog beside me.

I'll take this.

GPS says I should make it from Humboldt County, California to Ardmore, Oklahoma in around thirty-two, thirty-three hours. But I'm in no hurry, so I make it in just shy of three days.

Ardmore, Oklahoma is flat, dry, and hot. The downtown area, though, is cute and quaint, a throwback to when this area was the real-deal Wild West. You can see it in the layout, the way the downtown streets are narrow with the buildings fronting right up to the street and cars parked in an angled row. Most of the buildings still have the original brick façade, actually, and they're all connected, one to the other.

This ain't Humboldt County, that's for sure.

I park in front of a coffee shop, clip a leash to Utah's collar, and walk the sidewalks.

People are friendly, welcoming. More than once I'm stopped by perfect strangers who just seem to want to pass the time, scratch Utah's ears and remark on how big she is, and saying isn't she the sweetest thing.

More than once, too, I'm asked what I'm doing in these parts, which makes it obvious this is a small town, the kind of place where folks all know each other and strangers stick out. I tell them, truthfully enough, that I'm just passing through.

Also, I probably look about as California as I feel. Never realized before how much I look like what I am:

a rich, spoiled Beverly Hills asshole. Never worked a day in my life. Went where I wanted, did what I wanted. Thrived on adventure and danger. That kind of insouciance is hard to miss.

I've been all over the world. I consider myself cultured, well traveled, and interesting. Most people I've met seemed to think so, too.

'Round here? I'm just a fancy-Dan big city boy. That's my impression, and I don't even know anyone.

Larry didn't give me an address, or any way to locate this Niall James, so I find a cafe with an outdoor seating area where Utah can hang out, and I call him again.

"Lachlan, how are you? *Where* are you?"

"Good, Larry, I'm good. I'm in Ardmore, but I have no idea how to find this girl."

Larry sighs. "I looked into it a little more, figuring you'd probably be calling again. Trouble is, it doesn't feel like she wants to be found. I don't get the sense she's running, exactly...like she's not in any kind of trouble, not trying to stay off the grid or anything. But she very clearly doesn't want to be found. No phone number, no home address. Her last address is in LA, but that was over seven years ago, now. She was with MSF for six years, and when her husband died, she just...vanished. No forwarding address, just a PO box for mail, which is how I found her in the first place.

"Now, I could hire a PI if you're determined enough. The PO box is all I could find from a cursory search. So…you'll have to tell me how you want to proceed. A private investigator could find her easily enough but…honestly, Lachlan, that seems a little excessive, if not invasive. I'm not trying to tell you what to do, but I feel I should try to advise you. She's lost her husband. She probably won't welcome anyone poking their nose into her business, if you know what I mean. So if you really want to just…talk to her, find whatever peace it is you're looking for down there, I'd say you're going to have to do this the old-fashioned way: with charm and determination."

"I'm long on the first and short on the second, Larry."

"Not sure I can help you with that."

"So I'm learning," I say with a sigh.

"I'll say this: she's a nurse. So chances are, she'll have returned to what she knew, which would be a hospital, an ER, a doctor's office, something like that. Ask around. A name like Niall…down in that place? Someone is bound to know her, or *of* her, at least. Can't be too many women named Niall James in the world, know what I mean?"

"I gotcha. Thanks, Larry."

"My pleasure, Lachlan."

He hangs up and I pocket the phone, absent-mindedly scratch Utah's ears.

How do I proceed?

No, hiring a PI isn't the best idea. It'll spook her for sure, if she gets a whiff of it. And if I do find her, how do I tell her how I found her? *Oh, by the way, Niall, I had a private investigator hunt you down.* Bad enough I'm doing this at all, but to sic a PI on her? No way.

I'll have to, as Larry said, look for her myself, the old-fashioned way.

I was one in a hundred billion

BUSIEST DAY AT WORK I'VE HAD IN A LONG, LONG TIME. Horrible day, actually. Two nurses are out sick, and Dr. Beardsley is out hunting, which means I'm covering for three people, as well as trying to keep on top of my own responsibilities. I'm running ragged, is what I am.

I got the call first thing this morning asking me to come in, the prepaid cell phone I keep for emergencies waking me out of a dead sleep…a very rare dead sleep, because I don't sleep well anymore. I was supposed to have the morning off, be able to sleep in and go in at noon. But then Lindsey, the office manager, calls me, tells me Naomi and Michelle are both down sick. Mary is out of town on a pre-approved vacation, and Amy is on maternity leave, so there's no one else left to cover. Plus, oh yeah, Dr. Beardsley is hunting and out of reach. So, could I please, *please* come in early and help cover some of the slack?

Sure.

Cover ALL the slack, she means. And that's what I do.

Doesn't help that we're double-booked for most of the day and there's a summer cold going around, so we're busier than usual on top of being short-staffed. By the time the last patient is out the door, I'm dragging my feet. I mean, this is nothing compared to sixty-hour shifts doing triage in Africa with Ollie, but it still sucks. Sucks more, really, because it's boring, there's no adrenaline to keep me rushing, no pressure to keep me sharp. I can barely move, barely keep my eyes open.

I trudge to my truck, hand-crank the windows down, start the old engine.

It coughs, coughs, coughs, wheezes...and refuses to catch.

I'm so tired, and I just want to go home. Curl up in bed with Pep and my Kindle and a mug of tea.

I try again, fighting the urge to just break down and cry.

Finally, the cranky old engine catches and I pull out of the parking lot. I get halfway home when I remember I have no food at home, and will have to pick up something. So I turn around and head to the other side of town to the Chick-fil-A drive-thru, pick up some tasty but bad for me fast food.

And, of course, a few miles from home, my truck starts coughing again. I'm in the process of making a left turn, and halfway through the intersection the gas pedal goes limp, and the engine quits responding. I floor the pedal, and get nothing. I coast to a stop, right in the middle of the intersection, engine dead.

I try the ignition a few times, horns honking all around me.

Nothing.

I slam my fist onto the steering wheel, fighting tears.

Horns honk. People shout and curse.

I put it neutral, get out of the truck, and with one hand on the doorframe and the other on the steering wheel, I push—*hard*. But this old truck weighs a goddamn ton, literally a metric ton, and I struggle to even get it moving.

And does anyone help me?

Fuck no.

Can't stop the tears now, because I just want to go home. I want to eat my stupid chicken sandwich and my stupid delicious waffle fries.

I feel a presence behind me. "Get in." The voice

is deep, thunderously deep, yet smooth as velvet. A whisky voice, smooth and fiery and potent.

I turn, and the man standing there is…a god.

I'm struck dumb.

Six-four, easily. Wild, loose, long, wind-tangled blond hair, a thick unkempt beard. He looks like a deity of the wilderness, from far and remote places. His eyes are blue-green, vibrant, piercing, the color of the sea. They're wrinkled at the corners, as if he's spent untold hours in the sun.

"I said get in, honey." He gestures at the seat.

Honey? That shakes me out of my daze. "I can handle it."

"Traffic is piling up behind us, and this truck has to be heavier than hell. Just get in and let me help."

I want to be stubborn. No one calls me "honey"—no one. But he's right, and I'm tired. So I get in. He settles in where I was, in the corner of the open door, hands on the frame and the wheel. He pushes, and his muscles bulge. And Jesus, we start to move.

I am not unaffected, and that in itself is odd. It's not like there aren't any men in Ardmore. There are, and some are rather attractive. They're all country bros and cowboys, which is cool. Not really my thing, exactly—were I to have a thing anymore—but cool.

So what's different about this guy?

I don't know, and that makes me even more irritable. I keep my hands on my lap while he pushes my truck out of the intersection and into a nearby parking lot.

When we're out of the way, my rescuer leans against the open door and passes his hand through his hair. "There. You got Triple-A or anything?"

I shrug. "No."

"Someone to call to come get you?"

Another shrug. "No. But I don't live far from here. I'll be fine. Thank you."

I take my keys, slide the strap of my purse over my shoulder, gather the white paper bag with my sandwich and fries, my cup of soda, roll up the windows and close the door. I start walking. When I said it wasn't far, it was a little bit of a lie.

Or a lot of a lie: it's five miles to home, easily, and my feet ache already. But I'm not about to let this perfect stranger take me home. Just because he's gorgeous doesn't mean he's trustworthy.

Or that my suddenly whacked-out hormones can be trusted around him. Honestly, this second issue might be the bigger problem.

"I'm not letting you walk across the town by yourself. It's getting dark." He says this while catching up to me.

"So?"

"So you're a woman alone. It's not safe."

I laugh, gesture around us at the small country town. "Have you looked around?" I keep walking. "I think I'll be okay."

He keeps walking beside me. "Listen—"

I stop, face him. "No, *you* listen. Thank you for your help—I really do appreciate it, but I'll be okay from here. Please leave."

He raises his hands in a gesture of surrender. "All right, fine." He's not offended at all, or doesn't seem to be, anyway. Equanimous, even-keeled, unruffled by my outburst.

I may have snapped at him, unfairly perhaps. He was being a gentleman.

But there's no place in my life for polite, gentlemanly, attractive men.

No place in my life, no place in my heart—shit, who am I kidding? I don't have a heart anymore. I buried it with Ollie.

So I keep walking, and don't look back. At some point I hear the deep diesel rumble of a big pickup, and see a new but dusty black F-250 roll by, windows down, some kind of hard-driving and definitely *not* country music blasting loud. California plates. A huge, shaggy dog hangs its head out the passenger window, tongue lolling in the wind, and I can see my blond god savior at the wheel, bobbing his head to the music, one hand trailing out the window. He glances at me, waves goodbye, a polite, friendly gesture.

I could be in that truck right now, sitting on some nice leather seats, AC blasting, a gorgeous guy beside me, a dog in the back licking my hand, listening to music that isn't country.

But I'm not. I'm on foot, in the drowsing dusk, on aching feet, with five miles or more to walk—alone.

Once you're out of the downtown area, things get dark real quick at nightfall. The little city doesn't give off a lot of light pollution, and the streets out this way are narrow, mostly dirt, and unlit except for the occasional orange-yellow streetlight. Which means, once I get out this far, I don't really feel as brave and fearless as I did back in that nicely lit intersection. Of course, it's plenty safe around here. But...you never can tell, can you?

It takes me over an hour and a half of walking, but I finally make it home.

My feet throb and ache and it feels like I've got knives stabbing into my arches. I'm dusty from the dirt road, have grit in my mouth, and I long since finished my dinner, which means I'm still hungry with nothing to eat except some pasta noodles but no sauce, and some stale bread.

So I make the noodles and eat them without sauce, and save the bread for breakfast.

But I do have plenty of something else.

Wine.

My own version of a sleeping pill.

So I pour a big glass of wine and drink it in bed while trying to read.

It takes me a while, but eventually I'm tipsy enough to fall asleep.

And when I do?

I dream of Ollie.

In the dream, we're lying in the bed of that battered old Nissan, back in Africa. The metal is still hot under our backs—I can feel it. I can smell the dust. I can smell blood, too.

I feel Ollie, but I can't see him. I can sense him, and I know he's beside me. In the way of dreams, I feel this urgency, this driving need, this bone-rattling panic. I have to see him. I don't know why, but I have to see him. But I can't turn my head. If I don't turn my head to look at my beloved Ollie, I'll never see him again.

If I don't look at him, he'll die.

It's the only way to save him.

TURN YOUR HEAD, NIALL! I scream it at myself, in the dream.

I strain and twist.

But it's like my head is caught in salt-water taffy, stretchy, sticky, trapping me. I can't turn my head. I CAN'T—I CAN'T!

OLLIE, please Ollie, don't go.

Don't die, Ollie.

I can't look at him, and somehow time is running out. He's calling me.

NIALL—NIALL—NIALL; I can't actually hear him, his voice isn't audible, but I know he's calling me.

I'm sobbing. I can't see him. I won't make it in time. My head is turning, but it's in slow motion. I can't see him, I need him, and everything is happening in slow motion. Panic has me in its claws, and if I could I'd grip my head in my hands and physically pivot my head with my hands, just to look at Ollie so I can save him, but even my hands are trapped in the slow-sludge of dreaming.

And then, just like that, time unsticks, and I can turn my head.

And there's Ollie, lying in the battered bed of the blue Nissan. His eyes are open, but he doesn't see me. His eyes, those beautiful brown eyes like melted chocolate, they're dead and lifeless. Blood trickles out of his mouth. His forehead is smashed open, and I can see brain matter mingling with his blood on his cheekbone.

There's blood, sticky, tacky, old blood, so dark as to be nearly black, pooling beneath him. His chest is ripped open. He's freshly dead. Still warm. And the blood is now seeping out, trickling down his forehead, and I can hear the gushing whistle of his breath and the gurgle-gasp of blood in his throat, even though he's dead. I'm hot. The heat from the sun is beating down on me, punishing me for letting

*Ollie die. For arguing about stupid music. For not paying
attention to the road, not seeing the semi swerving toward
us, clipping our front end, sending us spinning, tumbling.*

*We're on the PCH, now. In the car. I see the semi, and
I can't do a damned thing. I watch the huge bumper of the
semi smash into our hood, send us twisting, tumbling, flying, rolling. I watch in slow motion the moment Ollie flies
out of the windshield. I see him hurtle through space, and
the car is spinning and smashing against the ground and
rolling and landing upside down. And through the broken
driver's side window, I can see Ollie.*

Limp.

Lifeless.

Bleeding.

Not dead yet.

And I have to get to him.

*My seatbelt is locked, and everything hurts, and I have
to get to Ollie, but I can't.*

I can't.

*I have to look at him, and then I can't look away be-
cause now the slow-sludge of dreaming is back and I can't
look away.*

And Ollie, he's still dead.

*Bu somehow he looks at me. His eyes roll and swivel
and find me. He blinks, once.*

He doesn't say anything, but he judges me.

He hates me.

He blames me for killing him.

In real life, Oliver would never hate me, would never blame me, would never judge me.

But this is dead dream-Oliver.

And I cannot escape the baleful glare in his cold, dead eyes.

He bleeds, and hates me.

When I wake up I'm soaked with sweat, and I'm sobbing. My mouth is caked with thirst-effluvia, I'm so thirsty it hurts to swallow, and my head pounds, and I'm sobbing so hard I can't breathe.

I collapse to the floor, thirst forgotten, and try to conjure up an image of Oliver when he was alive. The way he'd grin at me, knowingly. A grin that said later, after work was done, he'd get me naked in our little room on the MSF compound and he'd make love to me under a sheet, even if we were both dead tired from endless hours on our feet, even if we could barely walk, barely see. He'd make love to me, and his salt-and-pepper hair would fall in front of his eyes while he stared down at me.

"Oh god, honey," he'd whisper to me. "I'm coming. Are you with me?"

"Yes…god, yes," I'd whisper back.

"Niall, oh god, Niall, honey, I'm coming so hard…"

And I'd come with him, and we'd roll over when

we were both finished and he'd wrap an arm around my middle and nestle his sticky, slackening manhood between the globes of my butt and wiggle as close as he could get, and we'd fall asleep like that.

And for some godforsaken reason, I hear a different voice calling me "honey". It was a throwaway term, something thrown out because of habit, the way some guys do.

But the way he growled that term, *honey*—it shook something inside me.

Made me hear it the way my Ollie would murmur it when he came, but now it's a different voice. A new voice. Calling me honey while he comes. And that sends spears of guilt slicing through me, cutting me to ribbons all over again.

I sob on the floor, sob till I shake, till I can't breathe, can't breathe, and I could vomit from the shaking and the sobbing and the lack of oxygen.

Pep finds me. Curls up in front of my face, sitting like a sphinx directly in front of my eyes, and he boops my nose with his little paw.

Somehow, that comforts me.

I pull Pep to my chest and hold him there until I can breathe again.

I think I fall asleep on the floor, because that's where I wake up, on the floor outside my bathroom.

It's early morning. There's bright sunlight bathing the hallway.

I stumble to my feet and into the kitchen, start some coffee—at least I have coffee, and thank god for that. While the coffee maker burbles and glugs, I drink several cups of water from the sink, to slake the demonic thirst of my cheap-wine-hangover.

My kitchen sink has a window over it, which faces the road, and my driveway. I can see anyone coming for a good mile. And if they pass the Jensens' driveway, they're coming here because I'm at the end of the road, with nothing beyond me but grass.

Dust is being kicked around, way up the road. It's been dry as hell lately, so the road has been churned into powdery dust, which means I can't make out the approaching vehicle until it's past the Jensens'.

It's my truck.

What the hell?

Like the sleepy, hungover idiot I am, I stand at my kitchen sink, cup of water in hand, watching my truck approach. I watch as it parks in my driveway, right in front of the slab of concrete that passes for my front porch. And I watch the blond god who rescued me from the intersection unfold his tall frame. That beast of a dog is in the passenger seat of *my* truck.

Once again…what the *hell?*

I watch him approach my front door.

God, he's handsome.

I mean, he's scruffy, unkempt, and wild looking. But he's clean. He's ripped. And his eyes are arresting, blue-green like the deepest sea.

He knocks on my door, and it takes me a few seconds to realize that yes, I do have to answer the door.

I move to the front door and pull it open. There's a screen door, which I don't open, yet.

"What are you doing here?" I demand.

His eyes widen, and his gaze slowly, deliberately rakes down my body. I've never been looked at that way in my entire life, as if I'm something delicious to eat and he's starving. He doesn't just look at me, doesn't just check me out.

He *scours* every inch of my body with his gaze, from toes to hair, up and down. Twice.

He drinks me in, as if he's never seen anything like me in his life. His chest rises and falls, and his fingers tighten into fists at his sides. His eyes narrow. His nostrils flare. I swear the zipper of his faded blue jeans tightens.

And yeah, I'm checking him out too.

But the way he's looking at me, it's...intoxicating. Bizarre, but wild and heated and ravenous.

And that is when I realize what I'm wearing.

Or...not wearing.

I'm in a T-shirt, and that's it. And by T-shirt, I don't mean Ollie's big old UCLA shirt. It's one of mine, and it's old, so it doesn't quite fit me. I never wear it except to bed.

It doesn't quite cover my ass, and it's super tight around my chest.

No bra.

No panties.

Just the T-shirt.

I don't remember undressing, don't remember putting on this T-shirt. I remember watching TV and maybe possibly uncorking a second bottle of wine to go with *Vanderpump Rules*. But clearly, at some point last night, I took off all my clothes and put on this ridiculous shirt.

It's not ridiculous, though. It's my second favorite sleep shirt, after Ollie's UCLA tee. It's comfy. And it's also not ridiculous for me to be basically naked in my own home, not when I have no neighbors, and especially since no one ever has and—I thought—*would ever* visit me, so there's no reason to ever worry about modesty.

Which means I'm standing here, basically naked, oblivious, staring at the most attractive man I've ever seen in my life. My hoo-ha is playing peekaboo, for sure. My tits might as well be bare, because this shirt is so old and has been washed so many times it's basically see-through, and now that I'm aware he's scrutinizing me and that I'm naked, my nipples are pebbling, thickening, going hard and tingling. I see his eyes go to them.

And yeah, his zipper is totally bulging.

I feel a blush creep into my cheeks, fiery.

"Fuck." I murmur this under my breath.

"Yes, please," he growls.

And I swear to god, he puts his hand on the lever of the screen door.

What? No. Don't do that.

I'm frozen, unable to move as he swings open my door. Steps over the threshold, and stands in front of me. Towers over me. I'm not a tall girl—I stand five-five and a quarter when barefoot. So this man, at six-feet and several inches, does indeed tower over me. He stares down at me, those sea-churn eyes flitting over my face, back down my body as if he can't stop looking at me.

And for my part, I can't stop looking either. The bulge in his jeans is *huge*.

I unfreeze then, and back up. Tug the hem of the shirt down in front, which covers my hoo-ha but tightens it around my breasts. Can't win, I don't think.

"You need to leave," I grate out.

"You shouldn't answer the door like that."

"I'm tired. I just woke up." I don't know what's come over me. I should be kicking him out, not talking to him. "And I'm hungover."

"It's past noon, and you just woke up?" He smirks. "That's a hell of a hangover."

"Past—did you say past *noon?*"

"Yeah." He checks the watch on his wrist, an expensive, waterproof-looking thing. "Twelve thirty-four."

"Shit!" I forget him, forget my shirt, forget that I'm naked. "I'm late for work!"

I was supposed to work at eleven again today. I turn and scramble to my bedroom, pull my emergency prepaid cell phone from the bottom of my purse.

Dead.

Where the hell is the charger? My room is kind of a disaster, because I'm not the neatest girl in the world. There are clothes everywhere; half a dozen pairs of scrubs on the floor, more folded in a basket, bras on door handles and on the floor, along with panties and towels.

I can't find my charger anywhere.

"SHIT!"

"Something wrong?" His canyon-deep voice comes from somewhere behind me.

I'm on the floor near the bedside table, rooting through the clothes and old junk mail for the charger. "Yes, there's something wrong. I was supposed to be at work an hour and a half ago." I finally find it, buried. Plug it in, but the phone is old and it takes a while to get enough of a charge to turn on once it's died. "And my phone is dead."

"At least you have your truck, now."

I look at him. He's in the doorway to my bedroom, filling it completely. He's wearing a thin black V-neck T-shirt that hugs his torso and biceps, and the way he's standing, one arm over his head against the door frame, has his shirt hiked up so I can see grooved abdominal definition, and a thick trail of blond body hair leading under his waistband.

"My truck?" I remember how he got here in the first place. "How did you get my truck here?"

"I had it towed, had it fixed, and then drove it here."

"Wait." I stand up, and remember that I'm naked, and sit back down, cover my lap with old clothes. "What are you doing in my house? What are you doing in my *bedroom*? You know what?—Don't answer; you need to leave."

"You want to call your work with my phone?" He digs into his hip pocket, withdraws a sleek smart phone and extends it to me.

Equanimous. How can he be so damn equanimous all the time?

"Stop being so nice." I stretch up from the floor, holding clothes against me to shield me from his gaze, and to hide the evidence that I'm sincerely and severely affected by him. "It's creepy."

"Since when is nice creepy?"

"Since no one is ever nice for no reason," I say, dialing the office.

"I have a reason." More leaning, more smirking, more bulging biceps.

"Oh, yeah?" The line is ringing, ringing, ringing. "What reason?"

"The reason is nice doesn't need a reason."

"That's stupid. Try again."

"Okay." He strokes his beard with long, strong fingers. "Umm…okay, how about this: you're seriously hot, and being nice to you stands to benefit me in some way, at some point, even if it's just more free glances at those big, juicy tits of yours."

I'm struck dumb by this response for a moment, until I recover my wits. "Jesus, you're a pig."

A laconic shrug. "You asked."

"They're not that big." I cross my arms over my chest, not exactly self-conscious, but—okay, plenty self-conscious.

"Big enough, from what I saw, and I'm pretty sure I saw plenty."

I glare at him, sigh in frustration because no one at the office is answering the phone. "Can we stop talking about my breasts?" I say this as someone finally picks up, which means they catch that statement.

"Um, hello?" Lindsey answers, confused.

"Oh, god, Lindsey, hi, it's Niall."

"Niall! Are you okay? We were all worried about you."

"Yeah, I'm—I'm fine. My truck broke down last night, and I slept through my alarm this morning. I'm so sorry, Lindsey. I'll be there as soon as I can. Half an hour, maybe?"

Lindsey confers with someone, the words muffled. "Well, actually Dr. Beardsley is here and he says it's fine, just take the day off."

"Oh, no, I couldn't."

There's the sound of the handset being transferred, then I hear Dr. Beardsley's thick Texas twang. "Niall, darlin', ya'll just stay home today, a'ight? We-all are fine here. Ya'll took care'a things yestiddy, and 'sides, you ain't taken a day off in—well, ever."

"You're sure, Dr. Beardsley? I can be there in less than half an hour."

"I may be old, but I ain't dead yet. I can take care of my own practice for one day."

"If you're sure."

"I'm sure. Now git. I'll see ya'll t'morrah."

"Okay, thanks. And—I'm sorry. I've never done this before in my life."

"Happens to the best of us, I'm afraid. Why, I 'member once I was two hours late to my own surgery."

I laugh, because this is quintessential Amos Beardsley. "Let me guess—you were out hunting?"

"Why Niall, it's like you know me. You are surely right, though. Got a nice eight-point buck that day, and then had my knee replaced." He gives a chesty, rumbling cough, which he's had for as long as I've known him. "Listen to me, rambling on like a fool. I got patients, so I'll let ya'll go. See you t'mrorrah, Niall."

"Bye, Dr. Beardsley."

"G'bye now, sweetheart."

I end the call, toss the phone back into my purse, and then remember it's not mine. Retrieve it, and hand it back to Tall, Blond, and Muscular.

"So you've got the day free?"

I nod. "Looks like it."

"What are you gonna do with it?"

I shrug. "Hell if I know. I haven't had a Wednesday off in...a really long time."

"Might I suggest letting me take you to breakfast? Well, lunch. Brunch. Whatever."

"You may suggest, and I may decline." I don't quite look at him, because if nothing else, real food sounds great. All I've got is stale bread and no toaster.

"I did bring you your truck." Another of those insufferable smirks. "That should earn me brunch, at least."

"Yeah, about that. How'd you do it? I know for a fact I have my keys in my purse."

"Spare key in the magnetic box under the front right wheel well. One of those spare key hideout things." He digs in his hip pocket, withdraws a single key, and extends it to me.

I take it, stare at it. "I didn't even know it was there." I glance up at him. "What was wrong with it?"

"Out of gas." His lips twitch in his beard, as if he's struggling to hold back laughter.

"Out of gas?" I frown, puzzled. "But I just filled it up a few days ago. Shouldn't be empty yet."

"Leaky fuel line. Didn't take them long to fix it."

"How much did it cost, for the tow and the repair?"

"Brunch."

"What?"

"The price of a meal, that's how much the repair cost."

I breathe in and out slowly a few times, trying to gather my thoughts. I should *not* have lunch with this guy.

But why not?

He rescued me last night.

He brought me my truck this morning—this afternoon, rather. He's not asking for repayment.

I don't even know his name, nor he mine, and he's in my bedroom. I'm all but naked, and he's made it clear he likes what he's seen. And, dear lord, he's seen plenty, as he stated himself.

Does that last point go in the pros or cons? I don't know.

He's got me off-kilter.

The dream still lingers in my mind, that image of Ollie's dead eyes swiveling to stare at me. The help-lessness. It's suddenly hard to swallow. If I stay here all day, alone, I'll relive that dream over and over and over again, until I'm crazy.

So, maybe I'm already crazy, but I find myself looking up at him. "All right. Fine. Brunch. But you need to leave so I can get dressed."

"Don't let me stop you."

"You're not watching! Jesus." I shake my head, amazed at his blatant lechery. "You don't even know my name."

"Niall James."

I blink, stunned. "How—how did you know?"

Something dark flickers across his gaze. It's so quick, I almost miss it, and doubt that it was ever there once it's gone. "It was on your registration. I looked in the glove box for the spare key."

"I don't know your name."

"Lock."

I frown up at him. "Lock?"

"It's short for Lachlan, but nobody calls me that except my mother, and that over my repeated protests."

"Lachlan. You have a last name?"

"Nope. I'm an escaped clone from a secret government super-soldier experiment." He manages to say this deadpan.

"Don't be a dick."

He laughs, and god, that sound is sexy as hell. I hate him for it. Or I want to, but I can't quite manage full-on hatred. Annoyance, at best.

"Montgomery," he says. "My name is Lachlan Montgomery."

I stand up, hold a handful of dirty laundry against my belly to hide my crotch, and extend my other hand to him to shake. "Nice to meet you, Lachlan."

He shakes my hand—god his hand is big and rough, the palm callused to the point of feeling like sandpaper. "Please call me Lock." Another of those brief flickers of *something* crosses his features. "It's nice to meet you too, Niall."

"Great, we're introduced. Now. For real. Get the hell out of my house so I can get dressed in privacy."

"Fine, fine." He backs away, as if he can't quite bear the thought of tearing his gaze off of me. Which is weird.

And not unwelcome.

Yes—yes it *is* unwelcome, dammit. What am I thinking?

Did I just agree to have brunch with this guy? Why? Why? Stupid, Niall, so stupid. You're in no position to be going on dates.

But it's not really a date, is it?

I ponder this question as I wait until I hear the front doors close, both the storm door and the entry door. And the answer I come up with, confusingly, is that yes, it is a date.

I agreed to a date with a man whose name I didn't even know at the moment of agreement. A man who barged uninvited into my house, after ogling my mostly naked body.

Well, hell, if it's a date I've agreed to, I can't just throw my hair in a ponytail and wear comfy pants, can I? So I take a shower, depilate all the appropriate areas, and take the time to dry my hair and curl the ends.

Which is a bad idea, because Ollie always loved it when I curled my hair like this. I don't do it often, mainly for special occasions, or the few times in our relationship when we had time alone, together, not working. A day off, a date between assignments with MSF. Our wedding.

And I'm crying, thinking of Ollie while curling

my hair for a date with another man.

God, I'm a mess.

He'd wind the curls around his fingers and tug on them. He'd pull me up against him and twirl my curls and kiss me sweetly, tugging a little. Gently, sweetly, not aggressively, just...sweetly and possessively.

I have to stop and put the curling iron down and breathe. Blink tears away.

Why am I doing this?

Just offer the man some money and get rid of him.

Lock wouldn't take money, though, something tells me. And I already agreed, so I can't back out now, can I?

Of course I could. But it would be rude, especially after he went so far out of his way to help me.

He wants something from me, though. I mean, duh, obviously he wants something from me.

He wants *that* from me, and there's no way in goddamned hell *that's* happening.

So why did I trim my down-under and shave my legs and underarms?

Why am I curling my hair and putting on eyeliner and mascara and lip stain for the first time in over a year?

Why am I stuffing my ass into my smallest pair of shorts, and my tits into a short-sleeve button-down flannel? And why, oh why, oh why am I leaving the top three buttons undone? I button the third button, after re-examining the amount of cleavage being revealed. Two buttons is plenty.

He's already seen more than that, a nefarious little voice whispers, deep down.

I'm fucking lonely, that's why I'm doing all this.

It doesn't mean a damn thing. It's just nice to feel appreciated for more than my ability to take temperatures and suture cuts. It's nice to feel like a *woman*. It's nice to be *wanted*. Doesn't mean I'm going to do anything with it, or about it.

I'm a widow, not a nun. I don't have to be lonely.

Plus, it doesn't hurt that he's sexy as hell. God, those eyes. I never thought I'd like a beard, but that blond mass is hot. It's wild, and makes him look like he's crossed forests and oceans and deserts.

Finally ready, I shoulder my purse, unplug my phone from the charger, make sure I have my keys, and lock the front door.

I find Lock sitting on the tailgate of my truck, using what appears to be half a tree branch to play tug-of-war with that pony-sized dog of his. He gets the stick away, holds it above his head to keep it from the dog. Joke's on him, though, because the dog is so big it can just lift up on its hind legs and snatch it without much effort. Lock laughs, lunges off the tailgate and full-body tackles the dog, wrestles away the stick, and then runs backward a few steps, trying to hold the stick out of reach. But yet again, a single hop covers a good half a dozen feet, and another tiny leap lets the dog latch massive, powerful jaws around the stick and wrench it way.

It's funny, and I can't help laughing. "That is a hell of a big dog."

"She's not small," he agrees, heaving the branch as far away as he can.

"What's her name?"

"Utah." The dog drags the branch to Lock, and then sits on her haunches, expectant. "Utah...go say hi!"

Utah tilts her head, follows Lock's outstretched arm pointing at me, and then she bounds toward me. Which is scary as fuck. Despite the dog's clearly affable nature, having an animal of that size run at you with arm-crushing jaws wide is just plain terrifying. But when she gets to me, Utah skids to a halt, lifts up, and puts her paws on my front shoulders. Standing like this she has to lean *down* to lick my face. I bat at her, try to shove her off, but she's bigger than me in every way, and is clearly determined to lick me to death.

"Utah! Get off me!" I laugh.

And immediately, she pulls her paws off me and

sits at my feet, which puts her head at belly height.

I wipe at my face. "So. What's the plan?"

Lock hefts the tree branch and hurls it into the brush across the road from my yard, and Utah jumps in after it, which in turn scares a rabbit out, Utah in hot pursuit. From initial impressions, I don't think much of the rabbit's chances.

Lock now seems to take note of me for the first time since I emerged from my house. "Damn, girl." He straightens, squares his shoulders. His eyes narrow, and he saunters toward me.

I back up, the intensity and hunger in his gaze rife and powerful and overwhelming. "Stop looking at me like that."

"How am I supposed to not look at you like this when you look like *that?*" He's about a foot away, now, staring down at me, growling.

Well, not growling, really. Purring, more. There's no threat in his voice or his words, only…promise.

I shiver.

Or is it a shudder?

I shove past him. Pretend I can breathe just fine. Pretend my thoughts and emotions aren't in complete juxtapositional turmoil. I jerk open the door of my truck, jam the key in the ignition and start the engine.

And damn me if it doesn't start on the first try.

I hear claws scrabbling on metal, and I twist in place to see Utah in the bed of the truck, prowling in circles three times, and then lying down, chin on paws. And then Lock is in the cab beside me. It's a small cab. Just a single bench seat, no console, just the old ripped cloth and two faded, scuffed plastic and metal seatbelt buckles. He fills the cab. Overfills it, really. Broad, broad shoulders, thick thighs in tight denim, well-worn hiking boots. His hair is brushed this time, but still wild, nearly down to his shoulders, thick and wavy, sticking to his beard in places. And that beard, Jesus. He's brushed it too, and I think I'm catching whiffs of pine and spruce coming from it. Not unpleasant. The opposite, actually.

My truck's engine sounds different. Smoother. Idles more silkily. And then there's the fact that it caught on the first try.

I yank the gearshift down into reverse, back up into the road, jerk it into drive, and then twist to glance at Lock. "What else did you have fixed?"

He's rolling the window down, hanging his arm out, not quite looking at me. Shrugs. "I just told 'em to fix her up. I don't know what all they did."

"Bullshit."

He looks at me, now. "You sound pissed."

"I don't like owing people."

"You don't owe me shit. You'll never owe me

a godddamn thing." He says this vehemently, a little too much so. Off-puttingly so. Curiously so. He
seems to realize this and lets out a slow breath, starts
again more evenly. "Starter. Serpentine belt. The fuel
line, obviously. Brakes...what else? I think that's it.
Oh, no—the spark plugs."

My throat chokes. That's everything the mechanic said it needed to be basically as good as new, en-
gine-wise. I just didn't have the money to fix it then,
and haven't had the time lately. I know how much that
cost him, because I had it quoted for me.

"Lock...that's a lot of money in repairs." I swallow hard. "How'd you get it all done so fast?"

"I had it towed last night. Soon as you walked
away, I called a tow truck and had the mechanic start
right away. Just told him to fix everything that needed
fixing. They must have worked late and started early."

"I'm paying you back. That's too much."

His eyes cut to mine. "The hell you are."

"I'm not a fucking charity case, Lock. I don't
need your help or your money, and I'm not fucking
you just because you've been nice."

"Not because I'm nice, no. But you will." This in
that same low purring growl.

I slam my foot on the brake. "You know what?
Get out of my truck." We skid to a stop, dust skirling
in through the open windows. "Thanks for fixing it,

that was very kind and very unnecessary. Goodbye, Lachlan Montgomery."

"Hey, I was just—"

"You were *not* kidding, so don't try and pull that on me. That may work on bar sluts, that smirk and the purr, but it's not going to work on me. So get the *fuck* out."

"Smirk and purr?" He quirks an eyebrow at me. "You think I purr?"

I groan, burying my face in my hands. "Jesus. You don't take a hint, do you? LEAVE."

He stares at me levelly for a long moment, and god it's hard to resist the siren song in those blue-green eyes. But I do, somehow.

And he gets out. Snaps his fingers. "Utah, c'mon girl. Let's walk."

Happily, the dog bounds out of the bed and walks beside Lock, tail wagging, happy just to be.

God, to be a dog.

I watch them walk.

He totally deserved it.

Bonus reason I kicked him out is because it *was* working and that pisses me off, confuses me, and sends little thrills into my belly all at once.

The road is straight as an arrow for a good couple of miles, so I watch man and dog slowly shrink almost out of view.

But damn it.

Damn it.

I can't let him walk all that way. It's hot as hell out there.

"Goddamn it, Niall. What are you doing?" I ask myself as I throw the truck back into drive and go after them.

What am I doing?

I don't have the slightest clue.

Go all in just to lose again

JESUS, I'M AN ASSHOLE. A COMPLETE AND TOTAL douchebag of the highest order.

I *hit on her.* Multiple times. Openly. Brazenly. Worst of all, clumsily.

Not because you're being nice, no. But you will. Who says shit like that to anyone, much less…*her?* I'm here to explain why I'm here, not to hit on her.

Problem is, I don't really know *why* I'm here.

When I stopped to help her move her car, I obviously had no idea who she was, only that she was a small woman trying to move a large truck. I'm an asshole, a douchebag, a fuckboy, a lazy wastrel, a scoundrel, a playboy, a good-for-nothing, spoiled, rich, trust fund brat. But I *can* be a gentleman. I do have *some* redeeming qualities. She was tiny, in those fucking green scrubs and that goddamn white lab coat, pushing this thirty-year-old pickup, or trying to anyway, and failing. Horns going off, no one helping her. Traffic piling up, as far traffic goes in a podunk shitsville like this.

After she unequivocally sent me on my way I pretended to drive away, then swung around the block and watched her walk away, sipping that soda and popping a waffle fry now and then. Dragging her feet. Obviously exhausted. So I stopped by her truck and noticed the pool of gasoline beneath it, leaned down and saw it dripping from the fuel line.

And hell, why not? I've done little enough for anyone but myself in my life. Might as well begin this whole turn-a-new-leaf part of my life by doing a random act of kindness for the poor woman. She wasn't poor; I don't mean that in a financial sense. She had a Coach purse, and the shoes on her feet were fairly pricey orthopedic footwear for someone who is on their feet all day. Had manicured and painted nails, although she was clearly due for another appointment.

Shut up—spend enough time around rich vacationing tourist bitches, you get to know when a girl is in need of a manicure; she'll tell you, for one thing. Sleep with one too many times in a row; she'll want you to pay for it, too.

Well, not all of them.

Sweeping generalizations are old Lock, so I have to put the kibosh on that kind of thing.

I rub my forehead with a knuckle, regretting the way I acted.

I want to tell myself I couldn't help it; see a hot as fuck woman, try to score. It's ingrained.

And god, Niall James is fine as all hell. Not just "fine" or "hot" or "sexy", though, but genuinely *beautiful*. Audrey Hepburn. Rita Hayworth. Vivien Leigh. Marilyn Monroe. That kind of beautiful. In her scrubs, dark circles under her eyes, so tired she looked ready to drop but still bulldogging on despite it, she was stunning. Thick brunette hair in natural spirals swept to one side and pinned in place. No makeup, loose scrubs...I couldn't look away.

And then, just now, in the house. The way she answered the door? Fuck me running, I nearly had a heart attack. Immediate priapism. I'm still rocking a semi, and getting hard thinking about the vision: thin, old, faded hunter green babydoll tee, the hem riding millimeters above her snatch, creamy thighs I'd love to bury my face between. And that shirt? Jesus. Thin and faded, god, gloriously faded, just enough that I could almost-but-not-quite make out the dark silver-dollar-sized areolae and the buttons of her nipples. C-cup breasts, I'd guess. Big, a little more than a handful—and I've got big hands. Round, firm, taut. And when she turned and ran into her bedroom? The tiny little shirt rode up, baring that ass.

Woman's got ass for days, and I do mean that in the very best possible sense. Juicy, heart-shaped, thick and perfectly round. Slappable. Pale, creamy skin, like she's got all over, but on that ass…oh god. I could slap it and it'd pink up perfectly, slap it hard and there'd be a good jiggle to it.

No makeup, hair a curly, tangled rat's nest. Frizzed, messy, bursting in a halo around her face. Confused expression. Those cheekbones, those cheeks. Those lips? Plump, biteable, kissable. Throat like a delicate ivory carving. Long fluttering eyelashes.

And then she came out of that piece of shit crackerjack box of a house, wearing booty shorts and a thin flannel, unbuttoned just enough, hair brushed and curled to accentuate those natural ringlets, makeup.

I saw my future flash before my eyes.

I've seen my past flash in front of me, a still-frame montage of all the stupid, amazing, crazy, idiotic, daring, incredible things I've done in my life.

But for as many times as I've cheated death, I've never seen my future flash before my eyes.

And that…

That is freaking me right the fuck out.

I was relieved when she kicked me out of her truck.

Because, yeah, she's all curves and classical beauty. She's one hundred percent sophisticated, elegant beauty—if sophisticated elegance wore shorts that cupped a perfect ass, just barely long enough to not be too short. She's perfection in female form, and I'd claim to be a bit of an expert on that subject.

Yet all that being true, what really had me going was her tongue. That acerbic, biting tone, the way she doesn't take any shit whatsoever. Fearless. Bold. A little vulgar. Calling me out on my shit.

Kicked me out of her truck, deservedly so.

I ruffle Utah's head between her ears, and she glances up at me, tongue lolling out, loping beside me without a care in the world. "I messed that right up, didn't I, girl?"

Woof!

"Yeah, I mean, we both know I'm a fuck-up. But that was a fuck-up of the highest order."

Ruff!

"What would I do differently? Everything. Stay on the other side of the door. I mean shit, I don't even remember going in. Who goes into a stranger's house uninvited? Especially when she was very clearly not quite awake yet, and half-naked to boot." I run my hand through my hair, pissed off at myself in the worst way. "I'm such a goddamned idiot, Utah. Remind me to act like I have any manners whatsoever next time, okay?"

Yip!

I laugh, because if I talk to Utah, she always answers.

Makes me feel less alone in the world, which is nice.

But then she stops, cocks her ears, twists her head to look behind us; there's a cloud of dust, Niall's truck at the heart of it. I feel my heart start thumping harder, feel hope burgeon inside me. Maybe I'll get a second chance at this.

What "this" is, I'm still not sure.

I should work on that.

The two-tone, short-bed Chevy—I don't even *like* country music, so why do I keep thinking in terms of country songs?—grumbles to a halt, dust billowing around Utah and me.

Niall leans back in the cab, wrist on the wheel, her other hand out the window. "Get in."

"Listen, Niall, I owe you an apology—"

"Yeah, you do. Get in and do it, though, because I'm hungry and you mentioned brunch."

I glance at my watch. "I think the breakfast portion of brunch is long past, at this point, seeing as it's after one. So let's call it lunch."

"Fine, whatever. Just get in."

I look at Utah, lower the tailgate. "Get up there,

girl. Let's go for a ride." Utah gives a bark, and then leaps up onto the tailgate, which I close behind her.

I get in, work on how to phrase this, because apologies don't come easily to me.

Apparently I wait too long, because Niall shoots me a withering look. "You mentioned an apology?"

I sigh. "Yeah...I was a dick. I'm sorry."

She eyes me expectantly. "And?"

"And what? I'm sorry."

"That's a shitty apology. You should at least say what you're sorry *for*."

"Um." I frown and tug on my beard. "I shouldn't have hit on you like that. And I shouldn't have walked into your house. Or mentioned your tits. Or...well, I apologize for the whole scene, basically," I say, waving back at her house.

"You're not very good at this, are you?" She's laughing at me, I think. That's a good sign.

"No, I'm not. I don't usually apologize."

"Even when you're acting like a mannerless horndog?"

"Especially then, since it's sort of my natural state." I shake my head side to side. "At least, it used to be. I'm trying to...update my operating system, shall we say."

"I don't know what that analogy is supposed to mean."

I wave my hand in circles; I hate this conversation. "Turn over a new leaf. Start fresh, clichés like that."

"Oh." She eyes me, and her eyes are soft green streaked with brown. Unusual, and hypnotic. "Why?"

I hesitate. A little too long, probably. "Uh, well...? That's a long story."

Niall is focused on the road, rather than on me. She taps the steering wheel with a middle finger, then the ring finger of her left hand.

She's still wearing her rings, both of them, the engagement ring and the wedding band.

Jesus.

That cuts me right to the core, to the gut. To the bone. To the heart beating in my chest, the strong, steady, powerful heart that belonged to this woman's husband.

And then, as I'm reflecting on this, she blows out a breath, as if she's let something weighty go. "Well, I do have the whole day off."

Goddamn it.

I need to tell her.

It's why I traveled all the fucking way down here to Ardmore goddamned Oklahoma.

So why does it feel so hard to just...say it?

I came to life when I first kissed you

HIS ENTIRE DEMEANOR SHIFTED THE MOMENT HE SAW my wedding rings. One look, and he went all morose.

I wonder what that's about? Thinking his chances of getting me in bed are worse, now that he thinks I'm married? Shit. Am I still married? I couldn't bear the thought of not wearing the rings. I tried. The day after the funeral I took them off, but then promptly had a panic attack and put them back on. Haven't taken them off since, except for showers. I can't. I just can't.

I flatten my palm against the steering wheel; angle my hand so the sunlight glints off the diamond. It's not a huge diamond, because Ollie was never exactly flush with cash; a half-carat, at most, princess cut and set in white gold. It was a symbol, more than anything. I didn't want a massive diamond anyway, because that wasn't the point. The real treasure was Ollie. His love. Being married to the man who made me complete. Being married to the man who understood me, who accepted me, who pushed me to be a better nurse every single day. The diamond was just the symbol of me being his...so how could I take it off? I'll always belong to Ollie.

But here I am, in Ollie's old truck, with another man.

And I'm thinking about that man, that someone who is not Ollie.

I'm being forced to accept that I want to spend time with him. He's compelling, larger than life, gorgeous, mesmerizing, fascinating. I want to know more. I want to know the meaning of that faraway look he gets in his eyes. What lies behind the fleeting darkness I see in his eyes?

I want to know what the sudden shift in his mood means.

He apologized. He *apologized*. Even when he knew he was wrong, when he knew he'd pissed me off, Ollie never actually apologized. He'd say that he knew he'd fucked up, and he'd try not to do it again, and could I please forgive him? But he'd never actually said the words "I'm sorry" or "I apologize."

I steal glances at my ring as I drive, wondering what I'm doing. What any of this means.

What would Ollie think? What would he tell me, if he could give me any advice in this situation? Jesus, that's stupid. If Ollie could give me advice, he'd be alive and I wouldn't be in this truck with this man.

I notice Lock staring at my ring, too. The look in his eyes is so distant, his thoughts a mile deep, dark as midnight shadows, fathomless as an ocean canyon.

I twist the diamond around my finger with my thumb, and Lock's gaze flits up to mine. "Nice ring."

I swallow hard. "I'm not married." I wince; blow out a sigh, because that's not how I wanted that to come out. Breathe in and start over. "I mean, I *was* married, but I'm not anymore." Shit, that's not any better; now it sounds like I got divorced.

"You don't have to explain," he starts.

I cut in. "Hey, look: we're here." I park in front of a mom-and-pop burger place, switch off the truck and hop out before he can say anything else.

I need to get hold of myself and get a grip on this situation.

I just wish I knew what the situation was. I wish I knew what I wanted.

Well, that's not accurate. I know what I want. And I know what my gut and my heart and my head and my soul and my body are all telling me: different stories, each of them.

Run, part of me says.

Enjoy it while it lasts, another says.

You're betraying your husband, the love of your life, yet a different part claims.

You NEED this.

How dare you think of another man?

God, he's gorgeous. If he'd trim that beard and hair, he'd be…almost too much to look at for long.

I order a bacon cheeseburger and a coke and fries, because I don't often indulge like this. I usually eat fairly healthy—

God, who am I kidding? I don't eat well at all anymore. I should, and part of me wants to, because I see the weight piling on in subtle increments, in my ass, in my thighs, the backs of my upper arms, my belly. But it doesn't matter, does it? Because I'm alone. Ollie died. He's gone. There's no one to see the few extra pounds. And really, it's not that much; enough that I notice, but not enough that I'm worried about it.

Ollie would notice it. And he'd love me anyway. He wouldn't care. He'd tell me to enjoy life, to soak up the good times because they're what get you through the shitty ones.

I'm trying, Ollie. But I've run out of good times to remember, because they're all tied up with you, and you're gone.

What else is there to enjoy? My solitude?

The endless boring work at Beardsley's practice?

It is endless, too, because old Amos isn't getting any younger, and I'm positioned to take over, if I were to bother going back to school to finish my medical degree.

But it's boring work. Stitches and temperatures, and "Here's a prescription for Amoxicillin." There's nothing to enjoy. It's not challenging. It doesn't make my heart pound. It doesn't scare me or require anything of me.

I'm such a mess.

I'm stuffing my face with a greasy burger, shoveling fries into my face, and I'm enjoying the hell out of it, all the while running in mental circles and ignoring my date.

Not a *date*.

Is it a date?

Do I want it to be a date?

Yes, and no.

"Is this a date?" I ask, after swallowing a too-big bite; god, if that isn't apropos. Bite off more than I could chew. I did just that, agreeing to go out with Lock.

"I don't know—is it?" He's not being smarmy, not joking, and I don't think it's a line, either.

Weird.

"That's not what I expected your response to be."

Lock shrugs. "It's an unusual situation. I really

don't know what this is." He doesn't look at me when he says this, and somehow the statement is loaded with meaning I can't quite parse. "My behavior before was unacceptable."

"You said you'd tell me your story." I let my gaze linger on his, try to fathom what's down deep in those blue-green-blue eyes.

"No, *I* said it was a long story, and *you* said you have time."

"Oh." I twist the ring around my finger again, a habit I have when I'm trying not to think about Ollie.

"If you're not married, or not married anymore, why do you still wear the rings?"

"Jeez, going right for the hard stuff, huh?"

He ducks his head. "Sorry. None of my business."

"No, it's fucking not." I take a breath. "Sorry—I'm sorry. That was a little harsh."

"No, I deserved it. I shouldn't have asked."

We eat in silence for a few minutes. The silence isn't companionable; it's rife, thick, and fraught.

"He died." I blurt it out, between bites of French fries. "My husband...he died. And I can't bring myself to take the rings off."

Lock breathes out slowly, almost delicately. Wipes his fingers on a napkin. His eyes meet mine. "You must have loved him a lot."

"He was...everything to me. So, yeah. I loved

him a lot."

Another long silence, as Lock hunts for something to say next. I wish I could help him with that, but I don't know what to say next myself.

"Can I ask how…" He fumbles to a halt. "No, that's—never mind. Too personal."

I wipe my own hands, leave my trash on the table. I'm supposed to pick up after myself, but I'm being ripped apart, and I can't think, can't do anything but walk away, out of the diner. I don't know where I'm going.

I feel a presence: Utah, this time with a leash clipped to her collar, pacing ahead of Lock as he catches up to me on the sidewalk.

He walks beside me in silence a while. And then: "I'm sorry, Niall. I shouldn't have asked." A bitter laugh. "You know, I think I've apologized more to you in the last twenty minutes than I have in my whole life."

"I have that effect, it seems," I say.

I'm crying. Not sobbing, just a few quiet tears slipping down. I didn't even realize until Lock reaches up, gingerly, hesitantly, almost fearfully, and brushes a tear away from the corner of my mouth.

"Fuck," he whispers. "I made you cry."

I shake my head, wipe at my face. "No. No, it wasn't you. It's just…" I laugh, a sound halfway between bitter and rueful. "Actually, it is you. But not *just* you."

We keep walking, Utah ahead of us, sniffing, tail wagging, grinning a doggy grin, greeting every pass-er-by. Lock is right beside me, so close. Too close. I could twitch my wrist and hold his hand. I could lean into him. I do none of these things, I just walk and try to gather myself, try to sort out my thoughts and wade through the jumbled ocean of my emotions.

"His name was Oliver." I don't know who's speaking; surely not me. These words are pouring out, unbidden. "He was a doctor. A surgeon. He could have worked anywhere in the country, opened his own practice, or gotten a top job at any hospital in the world. He was such a talented surgeon; he had these hands that were rock solid, no matter what. Just...steady. *He* was steady, no matter what. Never panicked, never got overwhelmed, always knew ex-actly what to do and always got it done."

"How'd you meet?"

I lift a shoulder, because it's hard to talk past the knot in my throat. It's hard to talk without bursting into sobs. It's hard to do anything but focus on not running away. I haven't spoken Ollie's name since he died, not to anyone. I haven't talked about him, I hav-en't really tried to...remember him.

We're away from the downtown area and into

the neighborhood outside it, now. There's a park just ahead, and I use the time it takes to reach it to suppress the imminent breakdown. We sit on a bench, once again a little too close, his thigh brushing mine, shoulder brushing mine. He unclips Utah, grabs a stick from the grass beside the bench, and throws it. Utah, instead of bringing it back, slumps to the grass where the stick landed and chews on it.

I wipe my cheeks with the heels of my palms, breathe deep. "I was an ER nurse in LA. I'd just—shit, it's *still* hard to talk about, seven years later—I'd just lost a patient. This twelve-year-old kid got shot four times in a drive-by. He cut class to play basketball with his friends, and he caught some stray bullets and died. I couldn't save him. Delaney and I did everything we could, but we lost him. I had to take a break, you know? You can't go through something like that unscathed. I was outside, sitting alone, trying to not completely lose my shit, I guess. Ollie came up, sat beside me, and offered me a cigarette. I was like, no thanks, I don't smoke. And he explained that he didn't either, but when you go through something exceptionally difficult, sometimes you just have to smoke. And then he told me I should leave the hospital and work for MSF, *Médecins Sans Frontières*—Doctors Without Borders. I liked him, and he made it sound exciting and challenging, so I did it. I left LA, left the hospital, left my friends, and joined MSF. Went to Africa and—" I shake my head. "You don't want to hear about Africa. It was...rough. But Ollie and I fell in love, and got married eventually. Had a week's worth of honeymoon in the Bahamas, and then Dominique called, told us there was an earthquake in Haiti. The one in 2010? We were there, ground zero. That was... bad. Real bad. We never really got any time off after that, until we finally got rotated back stateside for some downtime. And then, on the way back down from visiting Ollie's parents up in northern Cali, we got in a car accident. Ollie died."

I can't go on. I can't go there. I just can't.

I'm up again, walking. Running, really, back to my truck. I feel him behind me, but I ignore Lock, ignore Utah, ignore the stares. It's all too much. I'm sobbing openly, running. I reach my truck, throw myself in. Fumble my key into the ignition. Twist it, shove the gearshift into reverse. Back out way too fast, nearly hit Lock, hit the brakes. He slides in, Utah leaping easily into the bed. He's watching me, eyes worried, brows drawn. I hate the look on his face, the pity, the compassion. The understanding.

I'm home and in my driveway without any memory of driving there. Just sitting in the silence, breathing, crying. Windows down, a hot Oklahoma wind blowing dust across my face.

And that's when it hits me: the silence.

The radio is off. The radio is never off.

Lock is in the passenger seat, and Utah is the truck bed.

"God, why can't you leave me alone?" I snarl.

"Because you don't want to be left alone." His voice is low, almost inaudible. Soft, compassionate. Fucking compassion. Makes me shaky, angry, and weak. "You don't run away if you don't want to be chased."

"Oh, yeah? How the hell would you know?"

"Babe, I've made an art form out of running away from problems. You're talking to a bona fide expert."

I jab at the radio. "Did you turn this off?"

"Yeah. I can't stand that twangy, honky-tonk bullshit country. Newer stuff is okay, but that?" He gestures at the radio, which is now blaring an old Hank Williams Jr. song. "I can't stand it. Not my thing."

"Don't touch the radio. Don't ever fucking touch it." I adjust the volume to where it belongs: audible, but not too loud. Where Ollie had it.

"Um, all right. Sorry?" Poor bastard sounds genuinely baffled, and with reason. I'm a volatile disaster.

I breathe out a shaky breath. "I'm sorry, Lock. I'm being a bitch, and you don't deserve it."

"I don't know about that." My left hand is on the steering wheel and he, brazen as you please, reaches up and takes it in his hand, twists the diamond on my finger. "I don't think you've ever really dealt with any of this."

I want to curse him out, want to shout at him, want to hit him. Because he's right, and I hate him for it. He has no business knowing anything about me, about my life, about my emotionally fragile state. So instead of doing any of those things, I shut off the truck and lurch out, walk past my house and into the endless acres of rolling field that is my backyard.

I don't know where I'm going or what I intend to accomplish, and I don't care. I don't know if Lock and Utah are following me, and I don't care. Mainly because he's fucking right again, in that I run because I want to be chased. And I don't *want* to want that. I want to be content alone. I want to be stable and strong and fine, and I'm not.

I'm lonely.

My hormones are a raging, boiling maelstrom. I've always revved high in that area. I hadn't exactly been a nun before I met Ollie, and after we finally admitted our feelings for each other and started getting it on, we went at it *a lot*. Like, crazy rabid bunny fucking, as often as we could. And then one day Ollie died, and I've been alone ever since. Utterly alone. And my emotions have been such a delicate, porcelain thing that even taking care of myself has been hard. I couldn't. It felt like a betrayal of Ollie to touch myself, just to alleviate the pressure of built-up need. Everything is a betrayal, and that's the problem. Breathing, living, existing, wanting, needing—everything is a betrayal of what I had with Ollie.

It's too much.

I can't hold everything in anymore.

I can't tread water anymore, can't flail half-drowning in stagnancy anymore.

I collapse, suddenly.

The grass is knee-high, and when I collapse, it covers me. Buries me. Tickles my neck and my nose, and the stalk-tips wave in the breeze. Blue above me— endless blue dotted with shreds of white.

I feel Lock lie down in the grass beside me, and I hear Utah leaping and prancing around somewhere, barking.

"What do you want from me, Lock?" My voice trembles, because I'm approximately sixty seconds from total meltdown.

"I plead the Fifth."

"You keep following me. And I don't know what you want from me."

A sigh. "I don't know, Niall. I just...I can't leave you alone, not when you're obviously—"

"A fucking disaster?"

"Yeah, basically."

"Thanks," I laugh, bitterly.

But the bitter laugh turns into a hiccup, which turns into a sob, and then the floodgates are opened. And I can't stop it. It's all coming out. The loneliness, the missing Ollie, the self-recrimination. I can't express it except to cry.

When a long arm reaches toward me, I don't even think about it. I roll into him, bury my face against his shirt. "I miss him," I mumble, between sobs. "I miss him so fucking much."

"Hell yeah, you do. How could you not?"

"And I'm lonely. I want him back, but I'm also just…lonely. But I don't know how to do anything but what I'm doing. I can't go back to MSF, and I just—I want to be near him. I moved down here because this is where he grew up. That truck is his truck. I wear his T-shirts to bed, just—just to be closer to him. To feel him. Because…because I *don't*. I don't feel him anymore. And I don't know what to do. I don't know—I don't know anything."

"You don't have to know anything." His words are puffed against my hair.

So close. Too close. Too right.

I'm lying against his left side, and I hear his heart thumping. It's a steady, familiar, reassuring beat, a rhythm down deep in his chest just under my ear.

For a moment, just a moment, I let myself just…

feel it. Pretend this is okay. Pretend I'm allowed to have this, enjoy this.

I even tilt my face up, look into his eyes. He has his other arm propped under his head, and he's looking down at me. There's a kind of shocked expression on his face, as if he can't believe I'm here, in his arms.

I can't believe it either.

It feels right.

It feels okay.

His beard tickles my face, so I move up a little.

And then—Jesus, I don't know what's coming over me, what's devouring me, taking me over. Something hot and more volatile than anything I've ever felt, this sense of need, this hunger, this raw urgency.

I don't know what's wrong with me. I don't know who I am, what fucked up puppeteer is manipulating my strings.

I kiss him.

I lift up, grab a fistful of his thick beard and tug his face down to mine and I kiss him.

And for a split second, less than a heartbeat—my lips on his is the entirety of everything, it's life and breath and the sky above and the earth beneath and the wind all around—but then his palm comes up to cup my cheek, his thumb nudges my chin and his tongue flicks against my lips and his hands grip my hips and bring me up to lay on top of him.

And that breaks the spell.

"Fuck!" I roll off him, crawl away literally on all fours through the grass. "What the hell am I *doing?*"

"Niall, hold on a second—" he says, coming after me.

I whirl on him, slam my fists into his chest. "NO! You need to leave me the fuck alone! Just leave me alone. You mix me up, you confuse me, you make everything—seem too easy. Nothing makes sense when you're around."

He grabs my wrists in gentle fingers. "You mean everything makes too much sense when I'm around."

I rip my hands away and push past him. "Don't follow me. Just leave me alone."

I stalk through the grass back toward home. I can't help looking back, though. To make sure he's not following me, I tell myself. But it's not. Not really.

And when I look back, he's just standing there, watching me. Fingers against his lips, where our lips met. Rubbing, as if—I don't even know.

I feel the tingle of the kiss on my lips, and I have to fight the urge to touch my mouth, where his lips touched mine.

I lock myself in my house. Stand at my sink and resist the need to pour a bottle of wine into a mason jar.

After a few minutes, Utah trots past my window,

her leash leading back to Lock. Tall and gorgeous, one hand in his hip pocket, the other gripping the leash. Not in any hurry, as if he doesn't care it's five-plus miles back to town.

I should give him a ride, but I don't dare.

The tingle on my lips is still too potent.

The need for more is too potent.

And I don't know if I have the will to fight that. I don't even know why I *should* fight that.

It'd be too easy to just give in, to just let myself have it.

Have him.

Have a few moments not being lonely.

I watch him walk away, admiring his ass as he walks. Man's got a nice ass.

A nice everything, really.

Jesus, what's wrong with me?

He kissed me like he meant it, that's what. He kissed me like it meant something to him. Not like some jack-hole hoping for a quick lay from the lonely widow. As if he was kissing me the way I was kissing him: surprised breathless by the wild intensity and wonder of it.

I want more.

That's what's wrong with me.

You make me better
than I was before

FIVE MILES, AND I BARELY REMEMBER WALKING THEM.

I had a hard-on for the first few miles, thinking of Niall's lips on mine, her hips in my hands, her breasts against my chest.

But then I thought of her ear against my chest, listening to my heartbeat. I know she was listening to it, too; I don't think she's aware of it, but she was tapping me with her finger in time with the rhythm— *taptap—taptap—taptap.*

She doesn't know. She doesn't know whose heart thumps in my chest. Whose heart that was slamming a mile a minute after she walked away, whose heart sent my pulse thundering in my ears.

To her, this is all chance. A chance meeting turned into potential romance. She doesn't know I came down here specifically to look for her. It was a chance meeting, though, and that's what's crazy to me.

At some point I reach my truck, unlock it, pat the seat so Utah will hop in. Drive to the pet-friendly hotel I'm staying in, give Utah a bowl of water and some food. I collapse on my bed.

I'm dizzy.

Not from the heat, not from the walk.

She *kissed* me.

She kissed *me.*

I should leave.

She told me to leave.

Only a complete jackass would stay. It's courting disaster, and it's unfair to her. She has no idea who she's getting tangled up with.

But...I *want* her.

Fuck, do I want her. I mean, I'm no stranger to desire, and I'm not used to self-restraint. I'm not used to telling myself no. The problem in this situation is that I shouldn't have her. I shouldn't give in. I owe it to the previous owner of the heart in my chest to walk away and leave this woman to heal on her own terms, not fuck things up for her any more than I already have.

God, the way she cried, it was goddamned heartbreaking.

I couldn't help but pull her close, because when a

woman cries like that, you comfort her. You have to. That's not me, either. I'm not the shoulder to cry on sort. I'm the one you hook up with after your heart's been broken. They say the best way to get over someone is to get under someone else? I'm the one you get under.

I'm good at that. I can help you forget for a while, and then when shit has run its course, you go back to your life.

I don't comfort.

I don't listen compassionately.

I don't just hold you, and let you cry.

But that's what I did.

When she kissed me, then, it was the biggest shock I've ever felt, because everything I've gotten from her so far has been so back and forth, up and down. Curious, intrigued, but cautious. Get too close, she snaps at me, pushes me away.

I'm a jackass.

I'm not going anywhere.

But I *have* to tell her. I have to.

It's eight o'clock the next night, and I've been sitting in the bed of Niall's truck for an hour and a half, waiting.

I've got a plan: I went out and bought an actual picnic basket, filled it with fresh fruit, cheese, crackers, summer sausage, some wine for her and some Perrier for me—I'm hoping she won't ask about that. I've got a blanket. I've got a location picked out. I've got Utah at a boarding place for pets, so she'll have someone to look out for her while I'm gone; I don't dare leave her alone in the hotel room, since she might miss me and tear shit up.

This isn't about trying to woo Niall. It feels like it, but that's honestly not my intention. I'm gonna be dropping a hell of a bomb on her, and I want to be able to…set the scene, I guess.

What will I do if she kisses me again?

Kiss her back, of course.

And then tell her.

Here she comes. Small, graceful, with a juicy body not even scrubs can hide. Fuck, she's hot.

Down, boy.

I kick my feet under the tailgate, hoping I look casual and confident.

I'm not: I'm nervous, shaky, hopeful, fearful. Lots of foreign and difficult emotions for me.

She's moving slow, wiping her face with one hand, swinging her keys on the MSF lanyard with the other. Green scrubs, white lab coat, still has her stethoscope over her neck. It's a hot look, and I never thought I'd say that. I've known a lot of doctors, and I just never, ever thought I'd find the look as sexy as she makes it.

Goddamn it, Lock, get a grip. Stop thinking about her like that. This isn't about that. For once, this isn't about your out-of-control libido.

She sees me, stops a few feet away. Takes a deep breath, lets her head fall backward, lets out the breath. Reaches up, snags her stethoscope off her neck. "What do you want, Lock?"

"Hey. Had dinner?" I hop off the tailgate and move closer to her.

I don't miss the way she tenses, the way she takes a deep preparatory breath. The way her eyes flit over me, searching, seeking. For what, I don't know.

"No, but—"

I take her keys from her, wrap my hand around her back, and lead her to the passenger side of her truck. Open the door, nudge her in. She complies, but resists, turns to look at me as I close the door after her.

"Lock? What are you doing?" She demands this as I slide behind the wheel, gun the engine.

"Taking you to dinner."

She plucks at her lab coat. "I'm not dressed for dinner, for one thing. And I'm not going to dinner with you, for another. Not happening."

"We're not going to a restaurant. Won't be any-one but you and me. I promise."

"I'm not having dinner with you, Lock. Get out and go away."

I turn the radio up, roll the windows down. "It'll be fine."

She laughs. "You can't just go 'it'll be fine—'" she mimics my voice, tries to talk gruff and deep, and it's cute and makes something flip in my chest, "—over me telling you no."

But she doesn't protest any further as I contin-ue to drive until we're already out of town, heading out into the countryside on a little two-lane road. It's summer, so it's not dark yet, but the light is fading, go-ing just past golden. Doesn't take long and we're out in the middle of nowhere, nothing but power lines, barbed wire fences and a whole lot of not much. I just drive, letting the silence breathe around us.

"Where are we going?"

I wave a hand at the road. "Just...this way a ways. Nowhere in particular."

"Lock—Jesus, you're impossible. I'm tired. It's been a long day. I skipped lunch and didn't have much breakfast, and I just—I honestly don't have the energy to deal with you today."

Fuck. That kind of hurts. *Deal with me?*

Some ancient, twangy country song comes on,

something heavy on slide guitar and saccharine sentiment. "Jesus, can we please listen to something else?"
I snarl.

I don't even think about it, I just reach out and
twist the tuner knob until something from this mil-
lennium comes on.

"NO!" The scream from Niall is sharp and sudden and distraught. "I told you! I fucking—I fucking
told you, don't mess with it!"

She twists the knob back, tunes too far back. She's
crazy, desperately twisting and turning the knob, trying to find the station it was on.

"That was his station! It's never been changed,
not once, ever. That's *his* music! Don't you understand? Fuck, I can't fucking FIND IT!" This last comes
out as part scream, part sob.

I pull over, grab her wrist, and pull her hand away
from the radio. "All right, all right. I'll put it back, just
take a breath, okay? Just breathe."

She's hyperventilating, shaking, scrubbing her
face with her palms. I scan the stations, hitting static
and talk and static and hip-hop, then the newer country station I'd initially turned it to.

"Whiskey Lullaby" comes on. Brad Paisley
and…what's her name? Alison Krauss. I've heard this
one before, on the long cruise down here when I had
nothing to do but scan the stations.

I'm about to scan past it, but she grabs my hand, stops me. "Wait."

…Couldn't ever get drunk enough…

That's the phrase that stops her.

We sit there on the side of the road, listening. God, what a fucking sad song. Haunting, gutting.

Niall is trembling all over, hands on her knees, head down, hair coming loose from the braid, wisps sticking to her cheek, the corner of her mouth, her forehead.

"It's so true," she whispers. "You can't ever get drunk enough."

I rub my jaw, realizing I fucked up something sacred to her. "Niall, I'm sorry. I didn't mean to—"

"I couldn't ever bring myself to change it. It's another one of those things I just couldn't bear to part with. Another way to try and hold on to him."

I reach for the knob. "I'll find his station."

She grabs my hand, and somehow neither of us end up letting go. "No, don't. It's done, now." She sighs, a long, shuddery breath that speaks of a vicious battle for composure. "Leave it. Just…drive."

So I drive. Miles and miles. I had a spot in mind, but we passed it. Besides, out here, one spot is as good as another. I don't even know how far we go. But when we stop it's full dark. She's quiet the whole way, staring out the window, wind tousling her hair, blowing more and more strands free. Eventually I spot a little dirt track and pull onto it, trundle and rumble down the rutted path through a stand of trees.

She's still got my hand in hers, and I'm not about to take it away; my heart is in my throat, because this is all so strange and crazy and I don't know what the fuck I'm doing.

The track ends at a gate hinged to a tree on one side and latched to a tree on the other. I park at the gate, kill the lights and the engine.

Niall perks up as if returning to awareness, looks around. It's dark, nothing but the track on the other side of the gate leading off through the fields, the empty highway behind us, fields to either side, and the starry sky above us.

"Where are we?" Niall asks.

I shrug. "No idea."

She laughs, another bitter bark. "Wonderful."

I lever open the door, get out, circle to her side, open the door for her. Extend my hand to her. She sits on the bench, twisting her stethoscope in both hands, staring at me.

"Just come on," I say.

"What is this, Lock?"

I reach into the bed of the truck, haul out the big basket with the food and the blanket, and then take her hand. "It's a picnic. Now come on already,

I'm hungry."

She lets me take her hand, lets me lead her out into the middle of the field. I've got an electric camp lantern in one hand, supplementing the light of the full moon. She watches while I spread out the blanket, set the basket in the corner. I sit down and start pulling food out of the basket.

Niall just watches. "Really?"

I shrug. "Yeah, really."

"If you're hoping for a repeat of the other day, you can think again." She sits beside me, but not too close. Opens the basket of grapes and tears off a branch, pops grapes into her mouth. "That was a mistake."

I try to act like that doesn't sting; that's not working, so I play dumb instead. "Repeat of what?"

She eyes me, probably trying to figure out my game. "The—when we—" she groans in frustration. "God, you're impossible. You know exactly what I'm talking about."

"Why was it a mistake, Niall?" I want to know, because I figured that'd be her response.

"It just was." She's fumbling with the block of cheese, trying to get it open.

I take it from her, pull my multi-tool out of my pocket, cut it open, cut off a slice of cheese for her. Hand it to her. Or, that was my intention, but instead of just taking it from me with her hand, she leans in and takes it out of my hand with her mouth. Automatically, as if that was her natural reaction. But then, once the cheese is in her mouth, she realizes what she's done and freezes. Glances at me, motionless. And then starts chewing again.

"Shut up." She chews some more, hand covering her mouth. "I don't know why I did that."

Me either.

Nor do I know why it made my heart thump like an out of control drum.

It shouldn't have, but it did.

She leans away from me, goes back to the grapes.

"Why was it a mistake, Niall?" I ask again.

She shrugs. "It just was." A pause, a glance at me. "Why are we talking about this?"

"You brought it up."

"You're the one who brought me out here for a picnic like we're sixteen and on our first date."

"Ouch." I let out a breath. "I was just trying to do something nice."

She lets her head droop, tosses the stripped, empty slice of grape vine into the basket. "It's just—I'm tired. I was looking forward to taking a shower and going to bed. A glass of wine, my Kindle, my cat."

"You mean the way you spend every other night?"

"Yeah, and what's wrong with that?" Her voice is

sharp, angry, defensive.

"Nothing, in and of itself. But you can't hide away in there your whole life, just working and going home and reading, getting drunk on cheap wine, hanging out with your cat."

"And you dragging me out on this picnic is supposed to be a remedy or something? Part of your plan to fix poor widow Niall?"

"Yeah, basically."

She lurches to her feet. "Fuck you."

I stand up, realizing belatedly that I shouldn't have said that. "Niall, wait." I grab her by the shoulders, gently, carefully. "I didn't mean it like that."

She whirls in place, fiery. "There's only that one way *to* take it, Lock! I don't want your help. I don't need your fixing. I was getting along just fine on my own, thank you very much."

"Were you?" I don't know why I'm pushing this, but it feels like I'm right.

"Yes!" She stumbles backward, blinking hard. "Yes…" This time she sounds much less sure.

"I'm not trying to fix you, Niall. I just want to—"

"What?" She stabs her finger into my chest. "You want what? 'Cause I can't seem to figure it out."

I sag backward, turn away. "Me neither." I sit on the blanket; pull the wine bottle out of the basket and the one glass. I twist the cap off, pour the glass full, hand it to her. "Here."

She sits down beside me, takes the glass, drinks. "Thanks." A long, long pull, a sigh. "So, if you don't know what you want from me, and I don't know what you want from me, then what are we doing?"

"I don't know that either." I drink from my bottle of Perrier and try not to think about the wine, and how much I want some. I don't even like wine, but right now it sounds good.

She notices, of course. "No wine for you?"

I shrug, shake my head, and try to sound casual. "Nah. Not a big wine drinker. I just figured you'd need some."

"Sure as hell do."

I lie back on the blanket, stare up at the stars, and try to summon the words I need to tell her…what it is I'm supposed to tell her.

"I used to spend a lot of time looking at the stars," I say, just for somewhere to start. "Long, long nights awake, alone, on the deck, nothing around for thousands of miles."

"What do you mean?"

"I lived on a sailboat for—shit, half my life. I've circumnavigated the globe twice."

"Really?" She sounds intrigued.

"Yeah. Name a place, if it has a coast, I've been there. And a lot of the rest of the world besides. Except Russia, I've never—well, actually, that's not true. I sailed up past Alaska through the Bering Strait, just to say I've done it. I got caught in a gnarly storm and had to take shelter in this little fishing village in Russia. Deserted, frigid, lonely little place."

"Where else have you been?" She's sitting beside me, laying waste to the spread I brought.

I tuck my hands behind my head. "Oh man, literally everywhere. India, most of the islands in the South Pacific, Japan, Vietnam, Thailand, South Africa, a few of the ports on the west coast of Africa too. I sailed up through the Bosporus and knocked around the Mediterranean for a while. The Caribbean, Australia, New Zealand, Tasmania."

"That sounds...amazing. And you sailed to all those places alone?"

I shrug. "Not always. I'd take on a crew here and there, and they'd stick with me until they found somewhere else they wanted to be. There's always someone willing to work in exchange for food and passage to somewhere else. The itinerant community is pretty solid, actually, once you delve into it."

"How'd you end up in Oklahoma, then?"

Here we go.

"That's kind of a crazy story." I pause, to gather my courage. "I didn't just end up down here by accident, actually—"

"HEY!" A gruff, loud voice shouts from behind us. I pivot, see a flashlight beam aiming at us. "I see ya'll out here. Ya'll in my field. This here is private property."

I stand up. Wave. "Sorry, we were just—"

He's an older fella, standing in the open door of his truck, a shotgun in hand. "I know what ya'll was fixin' to do. And ya'll ain't doing it in my field. No way, no how. Now get on."

"Let's go, Lock."

I pack up quickly, throw the blanket over my shoulder, and we make our way across the field. The owner has one foot up on the running board of his truck, shotgun dangling from one hand, the other gripping the top of the doorframe. A little portly, graying.

"Ya'll git. Can't just go on other folks' property whenever you want."

"We didn't mean any harm. We were just hanging out," I say, stuffing the blanket into the basket and tying the basket down into the bed. "Sorry to have bothered you."

"Hangin' out my fat old white ass. Only one thing young folks do out in a field at night."

"We're leaving," Niall says, hopping into the driver's seat before I can. "Sorry."

I slide into the passenger seat, and once the owner has backed out and turned around, we're out after him and heading back toward town and Niall's place.

I'm stewing, because I was *this* close to telling her.

I still could.

Still should.

But now the moment has passed, and my heart is pounding.

Why is it so scary to think of telling her?

Because it'll be the end. Once I tell her, that'll be it for whatever we've got going on. And I like what we've got going on.

We talk about my travels on the way back, mostly harmless stories of places I've been, things I've seen, not really delving into any of the crazy stuff, yet.

Before I know it, we're in her driveway. Parked. Engine off, radio on, windows down.

Stars twinkle above us, crickets call. An owl hoots.

Sudden silence between us.

I'm psyching myself up to start over, to get this off my chest.

Niall is picking at her fingernail, staring down. And then her gaze lifts, finding mine. Her eyes search mine, the way she did before. Looking for something. Seeing into me. Maybe if she looks hard enough, she'll see the truth, and I won't have to tell her.

"Fuck it," she whispers. That was to herself, not to me.

And then she kisses me again. Grabs my beard, pulls me close. Buries her fingers in my hair. Reaches down, unbuckles her seatbelt. Fumbles at mine. I hear it *click,* feel it go slack against my arm. I let it go free, spooling back in against the cab frame. Her lips are warm, wet. She tastes like wine. My head is spinning. I'm telling myself to pull away, tell her I can't, tell her I have something to tell her, but I can't. I can't.

I fucking can't.

I'm not strong enough.

All I'm strong enough to do is slide my palm against her neck, brush her hair away, brush my thumb across the corner of her mouth. Slide my touch down her shoulder, to her side, to her waist. Pull her close. Kiss her until I'm reeling.

There's a momentary break, Niall is gasping for breath, pulling back ever so slightly, staring at me as if stunned by the kiss. Eyes searching mine, fingers in my hair, tracing my nape, feeling the muscles in my shoulder.

"Jesus," she whispers. Again, more to herself than me. "So good. I need it—I…"

Instead of finishing, instead of telling me what she needs, she leans into me. Somehow we're going horizontal, me on bottom, my back on the bench,

Niall above me, one knee between my thighs, hands on my face, hands roaming. Touching my pecs, tickle-tracing the lines of my ribs. And kissing me, Jesus, she's kissing the ever-loving fuck out of me, demanding this kiss be the most epic kiss there's ever been. All lips and tongues and teeth, hungry, desperate, devouring kisses. I can't help but kiss her back, can't help but respond to the need I feel in her.

She's fully on top of me, some of her weight braced on her knee, but most is on me. And it feels so good, so perfect. I cup her nape in one hand and let my other find the center of her back, find the hem where her scrub top has ridden up, the lab coat slipped to one side. Soft, warm skin. Firm muscles, soft skin, lush curves. I'm touching her, find the inches of skin one by one. Up, up, to the lower edge of her bra strap. Down. Back down, closer and closer to the tempting swell of her ass.

I slide my hand under the drawstring waistband and palm her ass. She groans, murmurs into my mouth, and breaks the kiss. She rests her forehead against my shoulder. I knead the firm, round globe, and she lets out a breath as if this touch is reaching not just her flesh but also some long-neglected portion of her soul.

She lifts her head, eyes open and on mine. Lips swollen, wet, parted slightly, gleaming in the starlight. And then she slowly, slowly lowers her mouth to mine, and this time it's soft and delicate and sweet, slow as molasses.

I'm getting lost to this.

I want this more than I've ever wanted anything.

But I break the kiss. She's confused. Lifts up, braces her palm on my chest. And Jesus goddamn, I've got a hell of an amazing downblouse view of her perfect cleavage. Hint of nipple, even, the way she's falling out of her bra. God, I'm hard as a rock, and I know she feels it.

We can't do this—that's what should come out of my mouth.

"You are the most beautiful woman I've ever seen." That's what does come out.

Her lip trembles, her eyes close. A tear trickles down.

Now what did I do?

The worst me is just
a long gone memory

HOW COULD HE KNOW? COULD HE SEE HOW BADLY I needed to hear that? I'm ashamed of my tears, of the involuntary way they squeeze from my eyes.

I'm on top of this gorgeous guy, kissing him with all the desperation I possess—which is a lot. And now I'm crying. He's confused, reaching up in that adorably hesitant way he has—as if he's not sure he's doing it right—to wipe away the tear.

"What'd I say?" he asks.

"The right thing, for once."

"Oh. Then why are you crying?"

I shake my head. How do I explain it? I can't. It would take too long, and I don't want to talk.

I want to kiss him again.

I want to get lost in it.

God, I'm already lost in it. I can taste him on my

lips, feel his hand on my butt, feel him tracing my curves. And I want more. So much more. It's been so long and I've been so lonely, so cooped up in this little nowhere town, and I'm desperate enough to just give in. I can't resist it anymore.

It's foolish. I barely know him. He's a vagrant, an itinerant. He'll move on. But I don't care about that right now. All I care about is the need.

I sit up. Pull him with me. Open my door. Get out, turn back and look at him. "Come inside with me."

I wait at front of the truck as he slides out through the driver's side, closes the door behind him. I take his hand, hoping it's obvious what I mean, what I want. I should be nervous, should be terrified. It's been a long time since I've done this with anyone, let alone with anyone except—*no*. No thinking his name, not now. It's been a very, *very* long time since I've done this; that's enough truth for now.

But I'm not afraid and I don't know why.

I know I'm crazy for this. For Lock. For his hands, for his mouth, for how he makes me feel. For what I hope he will make me feel, once we get inside.

I'm up on the porch, unlocking the door.

But then Lock's hands are on my waist, spinning me in place. The screen door slams closed, and he presses me up against it. Cups his hand against my hip and palms my cheek. Feathers his lips against mine.

"Lock, come in with me." I whisper it again.

I reach up, grip his wrist.

Silver light from the full moon glints off my diamond. I see Lock's eyes flit from my eyes to the diamond, and just like that the spell is shattered.

"*Fuck.*" Lock grates the word, growls it. Backs away. "Fuck. I'm such a bastard."

He turns abruptly and jumps off the porch, jogging away.

"LOCK!" I shout his name. "Wait! Just…wait."

"I can't, Niall—I'm sorry. I'm sorry. I'm *so* sorry." He's in the yard, backing away, passing his hand through his hair, distraught, angry.

But not at me, I don't think. At himself?

"I can take them off, Lock. Just… come back."

He shakes his head. "You don't understand. You don't—you *can't. Fuck!*" With this last curse, he turns away again and starts running. Literally running away from me.

He's right—I don't understand.

The only thing I know right now is that I'm worked up, wild, horny, raging with need, turned on and left needing him. And he fucking *ran away from me.*

I'm so confused.

I let myself into the house, not bothering to lock

the front door behind me. I stumble mindlessly to my bedroom and flop onto my bed. My fingers find my lips; they're swollen from kissing. My nipples are so hard they ache. My core is throbbing. My stomach flutters. And god, my mind? It's manic. Crazed. I keep seeing him, feeling him. In those moments with Lock, before he bolted, I felt so…*alive*.

I felt his powerful hands on my ass, kneading and gripping. I felt his lips on mine. I felt his beard tickling and scratching my face, and I smelled the essence of pine he must oil it with—a heady, masculine smell.

And holy fucking hell, I felt his erection. It was a thick, steel-ridge presence between us. It felt so thick, so hard, and I could almost feel it in my palm. It'd be warm. Soft skin against my palm. I could feel every inch of it, and judging by what I felt in his jeans, there are a *lot* of inches.

I tug on the drawstring of my scrubs. I picture Lock naked. I start at his torso, bare, muscular. I picture him peeling his shirt off, crossing his arms in front of him and grabbing the hem of his T-shirt, dragging it off, flexing his pecs and abs in the process. In my fantasy, he swaggers toward me. Maybe we're out in a field, under the moonlight, like earlier. But alone. Miles from anyone. Shit, we could walk out my back door and be utterly alone within ten minutes; once we got past that stand of cottonwoods there'd be no one to see, no one to hear.

In my fantasy, I've got my back against a tree trunk, watching Lock. He tosses his shirt aside. Reaches down, unbuttons the fly of his jeans. Lowers the zipper. Stalks a little closer. Jeans ride low on his hips, the waistband of boxer briefs showing above. There's that bulge, thick against the material of his underwear. That V-cut, that sexy indentation of muscle leading down under to the Promised Land. His eyes would be blazing, like sunlight reflecting off seawater. He'd stop a few inches away from me, staring down at me, daring me.

And you bet I'd be up for the dare. I'd reach out, tug the jeans down. He'd step out of them, kick them aside. Nothing but his underwear. Big bulge begging for my touch. I imagine my own hands reaching out, slipping under the elastic, finding hot thick warmth. He'd moan a little, maybe shift his hips in a silent plea for me to touch him more. Shit, yeah, touch him more. Slide my fist down around him.

My fingers—in real life, in the sad reality of me alone in my room, lying on my bed fully clothed, my cat watching—slip under my panties, down to my core.

I imagine Lock with that underwear gone. Standing naked in front of me, his beautiful erection in my hand, and his eyes on me, desperate, pleading. He's at my mercy. He wants this.

But instead of giving him what he wants, I make him give me what I want, first. I'd guide his fingers to my aching core. He'd unburden me of my clothes, slowly, his gaze devouring me every step of the way. Maybe pepper me with kisses while he undresses me. And when I'm naked, he'd feather his fingers against me. But that's not what I want. If I wanted fingers, I'd use my own. I'm doing that now, in fact, touching myself, edging closer and closer to climax. But in the fantasy, I want more than his fingers. I reach up, put my hands on his shoulders, and push him down to his knees.

Worship me with your mouth, I'd tell him. Like in that book I just read.

And he would.

He'd have a nimble, expert tongue. Maybe use those thick fingers, too.

Tongue and fingers, faster and faster. Warm, wet, strong, skillful. Plying me higher and higher, taking me there without hurrying.

I'm totally gone for the fantasy. I can picture it, picture that thick blond mane of his between my thighs, can almost feel his fingers inside me instead of my own, can almost feel his tongue sliding against my clit.

Just like that—shit. Yeah. Yeah.

Oh god.

I hear a noise, somewhere, but I assume it must be the cat. I don't care.

I'm there, my hips bucking up off the bed, lightning zinging through me.

"Lock!" I cry out his name, because in my fantasy it's him giving me this orgasm, my first in well over a year.

"Niall, I—oh, holy *fuck*." I hear his voice.

My eyes fly open, and there he is.

In reality.

In my room.

Watching me get myself off. He for sure heard me call out his name. Watched me come thinking about him.

Fuck it: I stare him down, and finish myself off, finger the last few surges of fluttering heat out of myself while holding eye contact with him.

"Jesus." He rubs his face with both hands.

"What are you doing in my house, Lock?" I withdraw my hand, but don't tie my pants.

I don't sit up. I leave them loose and open and shoved down around my hips. My panties show, black briefs, nothing special or especially sexy. But his eyes go to them. My shirt has ridden up, baring my belly, a hint of purple bra.

Unconsciously, he adjusts himself—his erection.

"I—I couldn't just run away like that. Leave you thinking I didn't want—" He scrapes his hand through his hair, fist flexing, takes a step toward me. "It wasn't you. I wanted to explain. I knocked, I waited. I was worried about you."

"You spend a lot of time barging into the homes of single women you barely know?"

"No...I—no. I'm sorry." His gaze, though, isn't sorry. It's blazing with potency. Churning brine, storm-tossed waves. Eyes like the angry sea. "You called my name."

"You left me all worked up."

"I left myself all worked up." He's another step closer.

Chest heaving, eyes narrowed, brows drawn, jaw flexing, fists clenched. Scary, huge, primal masculinity embodied. Hair loose and wild, black T-shirt tight around brawny muscles. God, I can't get my fantasy-Lock out of my head.

I sit up, on the edge of the bed. "Why'd you run, Lock?"

"We shouldn't—" He's right here, now. Inches away.

My knees part, and his hips fit between them. I have to look straight up to find his eyes.

"Shouldn't what?" I ask, whispering for some reason.

"Do this." He's murmuring too, as if to speak too loud will ruin everything.

"Do what?" I'm not whispering, now, but breathless. Unable to speak any louder.

"This." He leans into me, presses me backward to the bed. He's on top of me.

God, this is even hotter than my fantasy. This kiss isn't desperate or soft, isn't hesitant or crazed. It's intentional. It's a promise. It's a kiss that tells me he knows how to kiss; he knows how to make me wild with just his tongue and lips. And god, does he ever. His tongue flicks and flits and teases, touches my lips, my teeth, my tongue. He breaks away, brushes a lock of hair out of the way.

"Really shouldn't do this, either." He curls the fingers of his right hand under the elastic of my panties and drags them down, my pants with them.

And just like that, I'm naked from the waist down.

"Or this." He shoves my shirt up. Tugs the underwire of my bra up and away to bare my breasts.

He kisses my lips, once, briefly. And then he's descending.

"Most definitely shouldn't do this to you." Kisses my breast, suckles my nipple into his mouth.

"Why—oh *fuck*—" I arch my hips off the bed as his fingers find my opening and slide in, one finger, a slick slide in and out, and then he adds a second, while his mouth pays lavish, ravenous attention to my breasts. "Why…why not?"

"Because there's so much you don't know about me." He says this, and then returns his mouth to my nipple.

"Would it—oh, oh, oh *Jesus Christ*…LOCK!" I'm right there, on the edge within seconds. And this edge? If the orgasm that I gave myself was me falling off a cliff, this, what Lock is giving me, it's me about to fall off the edge of the very world. "Would it change how much I want this with you?"

"It'd change things."

"Not what I asked."

He returns his mouth to mine, and now the kiss we share is hot and deep and slow. Intimate. Meant to go on and on and on. "I don't know."

"It would change—everything I don't—oh god, oh my god—everything I don't know about you?" I'm writhing under his touch, hips bucking, my breath coming in ragged gasps.

"Yes."

"Which means if you shouldn't be doing this to me—" I have to stop, have to suck in a breath, and focus on holding out, waiting, putting off the climax, so I can savor this, soak this up, memorize every sensation of what Lock is doing to me, the gift he's giving me.

I don't think he understands what he's giving me, what it means to me, how alive and how beautiful I feel, or how dead and lifeless and unbeautiful I felt until he came along. He doesn't have to understand. I don't care if he doesn't get it. I just need this. I don't care about anything but finally *feeling*. And, god, what feelings. He's every bit as good as I thought he'd be, and more.

And he's not even naked. Yet.

"Then I shouldn't—I *really* shouldn't—do *this*." I rip open the snap of his jeans, drag down the zipper.

I shove my hand between cotton and flesh. Reach down; grip a greedy, needy fistful of Lock. And god, there's so much to grip. My fingers don't meet, can't fully encircle him. I whimper as I get my hand around him. Groan in delight as I stroke him top to bottom.

"*No…*" he chokes out. "You really shouldn't."

"But I'm going to anyway." I use a moment—knowing this time together is limited, each second ticking away is one closer to when, according to him, everything is going to change—to jerk his pants down, use my feet to shove them to his ankles.

He kicks off his shoes and steps out of his pants, and then, just like in my fantasy, peels his shirt off. Exactly how I pictured. Leans back, crosses his arms in front of his body and yanks the shirt off. And fuck, he's even sexier than in my fantasy. Miles of muscle, lean, hard, bulging muscle. Corded forearms, thick biceps, razor-cut, grooved, ridged abs, that yummy V-cut I want to lick. He looks like a warrior from by-gone eras, even has scars on his torso and arms. Fairly recent scars on his chest, near his heart. Surgery scars.

I don't spend too long on that. Doesn't matter.

All that matters is that I've got him in my hand again, and he's kissing me, fingers moving in me, against my clit. I ache. Throb. I'm volatile. I take my time touching him, exploring him. Cup, curl, stroke, rub my thumb across the tip. God, I missed this. I need this so bad. I know I'll have a world of emo-tions to deal with later, probably including regret or remorse or guilt or shame. But right now, all I know is the power of the present. How beautiful this feels. How beautiful and desired I feel. His eyes are all over me. His mouth is all over me. His hands, his fingers. He can't stop. He knows he should, for whatever rea-sons he has that are so clearly eating away at him. But he can't.

And I *like* that he can't. I don't want him to be able to stop. It means he's as drunk on me as I am on him. It means I've still got something that can entice a man, when I thought I'd lost it. I'd barely subsisted for so long, dragging through each day, just existing, not feeling. Certainly not feeling like a woman who could ever be the subject of a man's desire again, let alone feel that desire for a man within myself.

I thought I'd died too, that day on the freeway.

But I didn't.

I feel Lock's hands lift me up, feel him unclasp my bra. Impatiently, I jerk my shirt off, tossing my bra with it. And being naked with Lock isn't weird, or awkward, or embarrassing. He's raking his gaze over me, devouring me, exactly as I'd fantasized.

"Niall, Jesus." He smooths a palm down my side, cups my hip. Nudges his knees between my thighs, towers above me. "You are..." He doesn't seem capable of finishing.

"What, Lock?" I stroke him. Touch his abs, rub my palm over his pectoral muscles, over his biceps, down to his waist, to the taut, hard, cool bubble of his ass. "What am I?"

"Fucking gorgeous." His palms are so rough, like sandpaper. It should hurt when he grips my breasts, but it doesn't. The rasp of his callused hands across my soft, sensitive skin is delicious, makes me tingle all over, makes me shiver. "The most beautiful thing I've ever seen. And I've seen some of the most beautiful things there are to see in this world."

My throat catches, a thick hot knot in my throat. "Don't stop there. You don't know how much I need to hear this. Especially if you mean it."

He laughs, white teeth flashing. "I mean it, Niall." His expression sobers. "But the truth is, we really—"

"I know," I say, cutting him off. "And I don't care. Whatever it is, don't tell me. Not yet. Just…just let me have this, okay? Please? I *want* this. I want *you*. Yeah, we just met, so we know basically nothing about each other. I don't care. Yeah, you're this drifter, and you're going to move on. Okay, fine. Just let me have this moment.

"I *need* it, Lock, I need it so fucking bad, and I'm not going to apologize for that, or for how desperate I know I must seem—I *am* desperate. And sure, maybe you have some earth-shaking thing to share with me. Maybe I'll hate you and never speak to you again, although I can't fathom what you could possibly have to tell me that could make me feel that way. I don't *care*. Not yet, not now. I will, probably. But right now, I just…I want to have sex with you. I want you to shut me up with a kiss, and not stop. I want you make me feel things I've not felt in—so long. Too long. And if you're gone in the morning—"

His mouth crashes against mine, shutting me up, as requested, with a kiss. His hands are all over me, roaming over my breasts, my hips, my face, my thighs. Delving in between my thighs, touching me there, bringing the wild heat back.

He dusts kisses down my jaw, on my throat, between my breasts. "I won't be gone in the morning," he says. "And I reserve the right to say I told you so, later."

I bury my fingers in his hair, let my knees fall apart, and hold on to his head as he settles between my legs, lips touching delicately to the insides of my thighs. Inward. Closer. And then, fuck yes, his tongue and lips are there where I want them, and it's infinitely better than I could ever have fantasized. He's so much more skillful at this than I ever thought possible. He's edging me, using his fingers now too, bringing me to the cusp of coming and then backing me off, bringing me closer yet, and then back, closer, and back. Again and again until I'm vicious with the need to let go.

"Enough, Lock," I gasp. "Let me have it."

He rumbles a laugh, and then does as I ask. Does this thing with his fingers and something else with his tongue, reaches up and tweaks my nipple, and then I'm screaming his name and thrashing and everything is white and hot and I'm dizzy and detonating, hips driving up off the bed, a live wire searing inside me.

He doesn't stop when I climax, though. He keeps going until I'm limp and then keeps going until I come *again*, harder, and then I feel him move up over me. I feel him on me. Feel his weight.

His beard tickles, and then he's kissing me.

And I feel him nudge against me. Hard, thick,

hot, soft. I reach between us, grip him. Stroke him and stroke him. Devour his kiss and lift my hips and slide him into me.

It feels so good I cry. Sob into his kiss, knot my fingers in his thick hair so he can't stop kissing me, and lock my heels around the backs of his thighs so he can't stop, so he can't get away.

He moves.

And it's heaven.

I bite his shoulder and claw my fingers down his spine and bury my nails in his butt cheeks, pulling him against me. I don't know this version of me. I'm a beast, thoughtless, feral, full of raging need for this, more of this, all of this. I hear myself making...*noises.* Desperate, erotic, wild noises. Loud shrieks, hoarse cries.

The way he moves, slow, deliberate, makes me even crazier because I need it harder. So then he gives it to me like that, hard and fast. But then he slows down again, fluttering soft and sweet and shallow. When I mewl in frustration, he pushes deep and increases the tempo.

Mastery. God, such mastery. He knows exactly what I want, exactly what I need, and he refuses to give it to me until I'm ready to vocally beg for it. He plays me like I'm an instrument, plucking the strings of my needs and desires. Mouth moving over my flesh, sucking, kissing, laving his tongue over and over and over.

Worshipping me.

I move with him, give in to his mastery, go where he goes, take what he gives. He feels me tense, feels me clench, hears my breath go short and ragged, and he moves faster and faster until I'm riding the edge, and now I'm falling over again, falling this time off the edge of the entire galaxy into the nova-hot epicenter of an orgasm so intense it steals my breath, my sense, any hold on any restraint I might have left.

I feel his motions stutter, feel his biceps flex. Feel his abs tighten.

"Niall, Jesus, I can't—I have to—fuck, I'm so close." He gasps this against my ear.

He pulls out, and I take hold of him with both hands and smear our mixed essences all over him and stroke him hard and fast and relentless until he growls like a lion, grunts, hips spasming, pushing his erection into my hand, his entire body going rigid, his face pressed between my breasts, breath coming in groans. I pump him hard and fast, feel him come, feel him unleash, feel it splash wet on my stomach, laying a hot wet line up to my diaphragm.

And then I give him what he gave me, soft slow endless touches until he softens in my hands.

Spent, Lock flops to his back beside me.

And immediately, grabs me, hauls me against his left side.

I move closer, throw my thigh intimately over his thigh. Hand on his belly. Not caring of the mess I'm making of both of us. I press my cheek to his chest, my ear over his heartbeat.

And now comes the fraught emotions.

It's the heartbeat in his chest that does it. Beating hard and fast, loud under my ear, slowing to a steady, rhythmic thump that is so familiar, so beautiful in its familiarity. This place, being held, cuddled in the shelter of a strong man's arms…is its own gorgeous brand of intoxicating. As much so as sex itself.

I look up at Lock, and I realize he's feeling his own maelstrom of emotions. And judging by the expression on his face, he's waging a war of some kind.

Losing, too, I think.

And, selfishly, I choose to wait. Choose to enjoy this for as long as I can.

Thump-thump…thump-thump…thump-thump…

Go all in just to lose again

SHE'S ASLEEP. SHEETS BUNCHED JUST BENEATH HER perfect, heart-shaped ass, lying on her side, one hand under her chin, the other thrown behind her. Curls springing awry, exploding everywhere, a bomb of brown ringlets. Long, thick black lashes dark against her cheeks. Innocent. Relaxed.

Perfect.

And my heart is hammering out of my chest, my gut is twisting. Guilt is a razor-sharp blade corkscrewing through me.

Confusion has my heart in a vise.

Panic is a serpent injecting poison into my veins.

And beneath all this is a complete and utter lack of regret for what we just did. Because that was…

I can't even articulate in my own mind what just happened. What it did to me.

My entire soul has been rocked off its axis.

I don't know which way is up. I'm not a crier. I'm not a pull my hair out, pacing back and forth type. I'm not a pensive, brooding sort.

Because I've never invested in anything, or in anyone. I've never let anyone mean anything to me.

I've known Niall for two fucking days, and what just happened, it was...

...I don't have any goddamn words for it.

It's just too much, too intense.

I am motherfucking *terrified*.

I have to get up. I have to move. I can't breathe in the same room with that woman, even if she is asleep.

And not just because she's so incredibly, indelibly beautiful I am compelled by some inexorable force to just *stare* at her when I'm near her. Not just because she's so sharp, so smart, so sweet. So eager. Jesus, not just eager, but fucking ravenous. She was a tiger, insatiable, literally snarling like an animal as she came apart beneath me. And I want that, I want to make her do that over and over and over, infinitely.

That, right there, is why I'm terrified.

That word, that concept: *infinitely.*

Forever, without end.

That smacks of commitment. It smacks of meaning, of investment, of purpose, of vulnerability and truth. And I have no experience with any of that.

I fucked her senseless, and she still doesn't know

the truth.

I came here to do who knows what, and for reasons I don't fully understand; yet here I am in a maelstrom of my own creation.

God, I'm a monster.

It's going to *gut* her. And that, in turn, is going to shred me.

I'm up, out of her room and out the back door. I'm still naked but I don't care. The nearest neighbor is a mile away and their house is tucked into a copse of oak and maple. There's no one around to see. And I wouldn't care even if they could see me; let 'em look.

Her back porch is a piece of shit. Literally nothing but half a dozen unpainted, unstained two-by-fours laid across some cinder blocks. No railing, no steps, nothing.

But, holy hell, what a view.

The moon is gargantuan. A silver-white disk in the sky, shining brilliant, bathing everything silver. The fields are endless, extending for miles and miles in every direction, waist-high grass waving in a gentle breeze, a thick stand of cottonwoods a ways out, limbs waving in the wind as if dancing to some unheard song.

It's peaceful.

Reminds me of the ocean, in a way. The rippling, the soughing of the wind, the utter calm, the stillness.

I breathe it in, try to soak up some of the peace, try to get it into my veins.

But I'm still panicking.

My flight reflex is going haywire, instructing me on an instinctual level to *run run run run run run*—

But I can't.

I *won't*.

I owe this woman…*something*.

I owe her the truth.

I told her I'd be here in the morning, and I fucking will be. I'll cut open the vein and spill the truth to her, and then I'll leave.

But the thought of telling her the truth makes everything inside me clench and constrict. I don't *want* to tell her. I don't want to leave. I like it here. The wide-open spaces remind me of the ocean, and they fill a similar void in me. I don't want to tell her because I don't want to give her up.

I want to lay her down on that bed and show her what it feels like to be properly worshipped, what it feels like to be paid homage as a goddess of her calibre deserves. I want to spend hours and hours kissing every inch of her, making her come apart again and again and again until she can't take it any more. I want to feel her lips on me. I want to watch her sink that lush mouth of hers down around me. I want to get her on her hands and knees and rut into her like a beast.

What we just shared was just the beginning. It was a tease of what we could have.

I want to cradle her against my chest and *love* her slow.

Fuck, that word really just went through my head.

God, Jeeee-sus.

I step off the porch and into the cool grass, feeling it tickle and prick and poke. I wade through the grass like I'm wading through the sea. I stare at the moon and deny, deny, deny all of the preceding.

What the hell have I gotten myself into?

I am not in any way equipped to deal with something like this, to handle a woman like her. She deserves so much more than I've got to give. Money doesn't mean shit to her. None of my crazy adventures will impress her. My well-rounded stocks portfolio—thanks to Mom's financial gurus rather than my doing—won't mean a damned thing.

Who I *am*—that's what will mean something to her.

And who am I?

I don't know.

Fuck, that hurts: I don't know who I am.

God, I need a fucking drink.

You put a new heartbeat inside of me

I WAKE ALONE. THE BED BESIDE ME IS EMPTY, THE SHEETS cool, long unslept in.

I'm a sticky mess, and that sends a grin spreading across my face. I'm sore, and that too has me grinning.

Before anything else I pee, rinse my mouth with mouthwash, hop in the shower and scrub my skin clean. Find Lock's T-shirt still on my bedroom floor, so he's around somewhere. I slip his T-shirt on, and you bet your ass I take a second to inhale the scent of it, to relish in the feel of a man's T-shirt on my body.

I find him in my kitchen, clad in nothing but his jeans, unbuttoned, unzipped, no underwear. Fucking sexiest thing I've seen, that look. Makes my insides quiver. Or is that the memory of what he did to me, how incredible he made me feel? Both, I think.

He's at my table, feet hooked toe-over-heel beneath the chair. There's my bottle of serious emergency, big-time breakdown whiskey on the table in front of him, one of my resale-shop juice glasses in his hand, half full of whiskey.

It's not even good whiskey, really. I rarely drink it, but sometimes, early on, when things were still fresh and I was liable to just completely lose my shit over nothing, over a tiny little thing like remembering the way Ollie would have done something, or said something, or the instinctual urge to go "Hey, Ollie—" and then realizing he's not there—sometimes, when that kind of thing would happen, I'd pound a shot or two of whiskey and breathe through the burn and refuse to cry.

Eventually, I got to the point where I didn't need the whiskey, and that was a hard-won victory in learning the fine art of emotional numbness.

I watch Lock from the hallway for a moment. I don't think he's seen me yet, so it's an opportunity to observe him unnoticed. He's got the glass in one hand, and it's obvious he's gripping it tightly; his knuckles are white. He lifts the glass to his nose and inhales deeply. The way a hungry person would inhale the scent of food—with relish, with anticipation. He touches the rim to his lips. Tips.

But then he lowers the glass—slowly, deliberately, as if each inch downward to the table is a battle fought and won.

He sets the glass with delicate care on the table-top. Lets go, and his hand is shaking.

Is he an alcoholic? That's what this is, a man fighting a demon.

And then, without warning, he bats the glass aside with a vicious swipe of his fist. "FUCK!" he shouts, and the glass smashes against the wall.

It's so suddenly violent and unexpected that I jump and squeal in fright, hand clapped to my chest.

I'm at his side in an instant, though. "Jesus Christ, Lock. What the hell?"

He slumps in the chair, head thunking against the chair back. "I'm sorry, I'm sorry. I'll clean it up."

He moves to get to his feet, but I press him back down. "No, it's fine. I've got it."

I sweep up the glass, dump it, wipe up the whiskey and spray down the wall and floor, then wipe it again. And then I sit in the chair kitty-corner to his, and pull the bottle of whiskey closer to me. Away from him.

"Lock, are you...are you an alcoholic?"

"I don't know." He scoops up the cap, twists it onto the bottle, slides the bottle away. "I'm not sup-posed to drink."

"Sounds like alcoholism to me." I touch his hand, cover his hand with mine. "I'm not—it's fine. It doesn't have to be a big deal."

He shakes his head, more in frustration than denial. "It's...more complicated than that. I used to drink a lot, yeah. But it was social drinking. I told you I sailed the world, right? That included a lot of partying. But then there'd be days and weeks where I'd be actively traveling, trying to make time to another port, and I wouldn't drink at all, or very little. I didn't drink to pass out. It wasn't a problem. It was part of my lifestyle, but if you talked to anyone who knew me, they wouldn't say I was an alcoholic or a problem drinker."

"Then I guess I'm lost."

A deep, deep sigh. "Like I said, it's complicated." He stares at the table, spends a solid minute in silence, clearly working through what he's going to say. I sense it's important, and I give him the time to think.

Finally, he shifts his gaze to mine. His sea-blue, sea-green eyes are full of pain, hesitancy, and misery. "You ready for this?"

I wobble my head side to side. "The way you're acting, I feel like maybe I'll never be ready."

"No, probably not." He blows out another breath. "Okay, here it goes."

But then he shakes his head, and doesn't say a word.

"Shit, why is this so fucking hard?" He shoots to

his feet, paces away.

Leans against the counter, both hands braced against the edge. Head hanging. Muscles flexing as if he's literally, physically, fighting a war with himself.

I have to stand up, have to go to him. He's in pain, and I hate seeing it. There's something in that thought that scares me, but I ignore it. I move to stand behind him. Run my palm over his back in soothing circles.

Straightening and pivoting to face me, Lock latches onto my wrist, pulls me against him. My ear is against his chest, and once again I hear his heartbeat.

"Hear that?" he murmurs.

I nod against his skin. "Yeah. It's your heartbeat."

"That heartbeat you're hearing…" A deep, shaky breath sucked in, even more shakily let out. "It's Oliver's."

I am rocked to my core. "Wh—what? What do you mean?"

"The heart in my chest, the heartbeat you're hearing right now, that's Oliver's heart." His voice is low, deep, as if he's pulling these words from the deepest chasm of his being. "His actual, physical heart, the organ, is in my chest."

"Lock, why—why the *fuck* would you say that?" My eyes burn. My heart is rabbiting. My lungs can't catch air. My knees shake. "What does that mean?"

His arm is around my waist, holding me against him. Too tight, almost. As if to keep me from escaping.

A prudent precaution, I think.

He's silent. I feel him shaking, as if a man of his stature, his strength, could be terrified into trembling.

"Lock? Talk to me. You can't say something like that and then clam up."

"I was born with a congenital heart defect. My great-grandfather had the same defect and he died at sixty. My grandfather at forty-five. My dad at thirty-eight. The doctors told me I'd likely not live past thirty."

"Oh my god, Lock."

"I made it to thirty-one. My heart gave out on my thirty-first birthday. I actually died on the operating table, but they were able to bring me back. Kept me on all those machines and whatever the fuck. I'd told my mom I didn't want to be kept alive, but she—you know what, that's not important right now. Point is, I have the rarest blood type in the world, plus an unusually large heart. The chances of finding a heart that my body would accept were…essentially nil."

I'm faint.

Shaking my head.

No. NO. *NO.*

It can't be possible.

He sucks in another of those shuddery breaths. "There was no hope. I was going to be kept alive on the fucking machines until my mom finally told them to pull the plug. And she should have. I'd signed a DNR saying I didn't want to be forced to exist that way. I should be dead right now. But then a miracle happened. That's what the goddamn doctors called it—a fucking miracle. A donor, against all odds. A heart big enough, and the same blood type. They put that heart in my chest, put me through all the rehab, the monitoring, and the months of tests. And then… sent me away. Told me I had 'a new lease on life'. Go, live, be free!" The bitterness, the sarcasm is venom-ous. "What the fuck was I supposed to do? I'd gone my whole life knowing I was going to die. Being told I was an extremely poor transplant candidate. Prepare for the worst, I heard them tell my parents more than once. Lived my whole life with a fucking deadline. That's what I called it. A deadline—some kind of ter-minally ill humor. Not really funny unless you're the terminally ill. And then, just like that, boom. Some-one died, and I got to live." He wipes his face with both hands. "Fuck, listen to me, making this about me. It's not about me. Forget all that bullshit I just said."

"Lock—I don't—I don't understand." I'm still leaning against his chest.

Listening to his heartbeat.

Oliver's heartbeat?

Could it be? That's what it sounds like he's saying.

"Oliver died in that car crash on the PCH. His organs were harvested and donated, and his heart...it was transplanted into my chest." He takes my hand, guides my fingers to those scars.

I shake my head. "You're lying."

"I wish I was."

I back away. Stare at him. Blinking hard against the flood of tears. "That's Oliver's heart? In your chest?"

He nods. "Yes."

"It was your heartbeat I fell asleep listening to last night?"

"Yes."

"After the most—the most earth-shaking sex I've ever had in my life?"

"It was for me, too." He says this quietly, as if the admission takes a lot of effort to get out.

I back up again, but then my legs give out and I collapse ungracefully to my butt, sitting on the kitchen floor. "And you knew? You've—you've known, this whole time?"

"It's why I'm in Oklahoma, Niall. I came looking for you."

"Then my truck dying, the way you rescued me—" Everything spins, a million thoughts and conjectures coruscate through me, take up my headspace, make me dizzy. "Everything, it was all—"

He kneels on the floor in front of me. "No, Niall, no. That was pure accident. Or fate, or…coincidence. I saw you trying to push that truck and I had to help. I didn't know it was…*you*…as in the woman I was looking for, until I went to have them fix it. I found your registration in the glove box, and that's when I realized it was you. I'd been looking, because I knew you were down here somewhere. But I had no idea how I'd actually find you. And then…" He shrugs. "You were there. And everything since was real. I haven't lied about anything."

I scoot backwards on my butt across the floor away from him, because I don't know what to think. I just don't. It's all too much and I'm sobbing, because *I heard Oliver's heartbeat.* I heard his actual heart beating. Just thinking about it slices me to pieces, and I collapse further, prone on the floor, roll to my side and curl up in the fetal position.

"Ollie—my Ollie…he died, and you lived."

"Yes."

I swallow hard against the knot. Breathe past the sobs, summon words past the hurt. "You knew. You kissed me, you…we made love…we fucked, or whatever you want to call it—and you knew the *whole time?*"

"Yes."

I can't fathom it. And looking at Lock right now, clearly neither can he.

"I'm sorry, Niall. I—" He shakes his head, as if he can't finish the rest, or as if there's nothing to finish. "If I could give it back—if I could give my heart so Oliver could live? I would. By all accounts, he was a better man than me in every way. I didn't...I never asked for this."

"Why didn't you tell me sooner?"

"I tried. I wanted to. But I just...couldn't. I mean, how do you come out with something like that? 'Oh, by the way, I know this might sound weird or whatever, but your dead husband's heart was transplanted into my chest.'" He barks a humorless laugh. "How do you think that would have gone down?"

"Better than this." I curl into an even tighter ball. "You need to leave. I need some time."

"I—yeah. Okay."

I watch through the bars of my fingers as he buttons his jeans. Zips. Trudges slowly into my room, finds his shoes, sits on the edge of the bed and tugs on his socks, stuffs his feet into the boots. Stuffs his underwear into his hip pocket. Moves, still shirtless—because I'm wearing his shirt—to the front door. Opens it. Stands in the opening.

Turns to look back at me. "I didn't mean for it to go this far. I never meant to cause you any more pain. I—" He closes his eyes slowly, as if summoning something from deep inside. "You took me by surprise."

"*I* took *you* by surprise?" My turn to laugh bitterly. "Got that backwards, pal." I force myself to my feet; force myself to move to him.

"I spent my whole life doing nothing, Niall. Avoiding anything and everything, because I felt like nothing mattered. Nothing I did mattered, because I was going to die soon." He looks at me intently, emotion boiling in his features—too much, too many, too intense to name. "You took me by surprise. I never expected to—to feel…" He trails off.

"Feel what?" I ask, my voice faint.

He waves a hand vaguely. "So…*much*. For one person. For the wrong person. It wouldn't have meant anything had I stopped to help anyone else in the entire fucking world. But it was…*you*." He lets out a sigh. I swear he's close to a breakdown himself. "It was you."

I shake my head. "Jesus, Lock. You can't do this. You can't do this to me." I could cry again. But I don't.

I move close enough to touch him. Put my hand on his chest. Feel his heart beat. Ollie's heartbeat. And now I do cry.

"You can't fucking do this to me, Lock. I can't take it."

"I know. And that's yet another reason why I hate myself. Not that I have any shortage of other reasons." He backs up, out of my touch, away from my reach. "Bye, Niall."

He turns and trots down the steps. Out to the dirt road, still shirtless.

I run out after him. I don't know why. I don't want him to go, but I need him gone so I can think. I stumble to a stop in front of him, pushing him to a halt. I stand in front of him. Stare into his eyes. I peel his shirt off myself, slowly. I reach up and gently tug it up over my head. I'm standing utterly naked in front of him, tears on my face, a turmoil of emotions raging inside me.

Even now I want him.

And, even now, his gaze rakes over me as if he can't get enough of looking at me. "Jesus fucking Christ, Niall. You should have just kept the goddamn shirt."

"Why?"

"Because you look the way you…you look at me the way you're looking at me and—" His hands are on me, he's yanking me against him, wrapping his fists in my curls and kissing the hell out of me. "Because I have to do this, when you look the way you do."

"It's just me. How I always look."

"Exactly."

I want so much. But inside, I'm a mess.

And he, clearly, is even worse off. I back away. "Where are you staying?"

"La Quinta." He digs a little envelope out of his back pocket, in which are two key cards. He hands me one. "Two-nineteen."

"Don't leave town, Lock. Please?"

He sighs. "If that's what you want."

"I don't know what I want. I just know I need time to figure it out. And I don't want you to leave until I do."

"Okay," he says, as if the word, the agreement, is a heavy burden. "I won't leave until you tell me to."

He grabs his shirt back and tugs it over my head. "That's my favorite shirt, so it's a kind of insurance."

He backs away from me—as if it physically hurts to do so—out of my reach. Backs away another few steps and then, with a heavy sigh, turns and jogs down the road. With an easy gait, he quickly approaches the main road.

I watch him until he's out of sight.

He wasn't lying, was he? When he told me he had

something to share, and that it would change every-thing. I should have let him tell me first.

But I'm also glad I didn't because, ho-ly shit, that was intense.

Best sex of my life.

And, god, that's hard to think about all by itself. There's so much all tangled up in this, so much to think about, so much to feel, so much to try to come to grips with.

I loved Ollie. I loved the shit out of that man. I *adored* him. I respected him. I fairly worshipped him. I *needed* him. And he loved me. Wanted me. Took care of me. Adored me. Sex with Ollie had been…well, it had always been about *love*. Sweet, sensual, envelop-ing, comforting, familiar, beautiful. I loved having sex with Ollie every bit as much as I loved being in love with him.

But what I just experienced with Lock…felt very different. It was out of this world. Shattering. Mind-erasing. And, really, it wasn't even as all-in as it could have been. He didn't finish inside me—he fin-ished *on* me. And fuck, was that hot. I *liked* that. God, I feel like a slut for it, but I liked it. Gripping him in my fist and feeling our essences sticky and slick on his hard flesh, pumping him and feeling him lose it, feel-ing him grunt and groan and shove against my hand as he came, shooting his hot seed all over my belly.

Fuck, I'm all in a tizzy again just thinking about it.

Several thoughts hit me at once.

He had the presence of mind to pull out, because he wasn't wearing a condom.

He seriously knew what he was doing, knew how to make me come hard and fast.

And he had impressive stamina.

I want him again. I want to roll a condom onto him and feel him inside me, feel him lose control again, only next time I want him inside me.

And, deep down, way deep down where you keep those thoughts that you shy away from admitting even to yourself, I want him bare. Like last night, but I want to take him all the way. Feel him release inside me with nothing between us. I want to feel that heat, that warm wetness inside me…god, I want that.

Sex with Lock wasn't necessarily *better* than sex with Ollie. It was just…*different*. Not as sweet, not as familiar, not flushed with that sense of soul-deep, hearts-entwined love. It was lust, between Lock and me. Primal, sensual, animal. So, so intense.

I can't stop thinking about sex with Lock, though. I want it too much. My libido had been woken up, after being dormant for so long. I have a more-than-healthy libido, a sex drive that drove Ollie to exhaustion trying to satiate. If I keep thinking about Lock,

I'll do one or both of two things: I'll finger myself again, thinking about him, or I'll get in my truck and go find him at his hotel.

I fantasize about what would happen if I did go find him.

I'd knock on his door and he'd open it, maybe freshly showered, wearing a towel, knotted loose around his waist. Hair wet and slicked back, beard damp, beads of water trickling down those broad, hard, round shoulders, down between his thick pecs, down, down, down. Maybe I'd untie his robe and follow that little bead of water down to his erection, where I'd lick it away. Lick him all over; lick him until he lost it, maybe down my throat.

I don't have a lot of experience going down on a guy. When I first started being active sexually, there was a lot of experimentation, the way you do when you're seventeen or eighteen. You're not really sure what you're doing. Trying things, clumsy but eager. Giving or receiving oral sex wasn't really on my radar: I wanted the real thing, so that's what I went after, all through high school and college. And then I met Ollie, and we were often too busy and too tired for more than slow lovemaking in the darkness, clutching each other close and kissing—making love, as husband and wife. There wasn't a lot of time or energy for much foreplay...for either of us. I never missed it, and I'm pretty sure Ollie didn't either.

But with Lock things are different. He went down on me like a pro. Made me come so hard I saw stars. Fucked me like I was all that existed in the whole world, as if my pleasure was his singular goal. Each thrust was for me, and me alone.

And…he's just gorgeous. Head to toe, he's a beautiful man, in a wild and rugged sense.

And I want things. I want to do things to *him*.

Naughty things.

Things I've never done, or haven't done in a long, long time. Since before Ollie, if ever. I was a little wild, before Ollie. A college girl, single and not prone to second-guessing myself, or being unsure about what I wanted. I drank a lot, and hooked up with hot college boys. And that's something you'll never hear me regret. It was a good time in my life. I had friends, I was good looking, I enjoyed my classes—as hard as they were—and I never had any trouble snagging a cutie after a party for some decent, if sloppy, sex. I don't regret it, and I will not apologize for it. Then there was Ollie, and that was a slightly different kind of sex. Similar to what I'd known, but better in every way, because it meant *so* much to us.

And now there's Lock, and it's something totally new, something I've never experienced.

Experienced. Uninhibited. Wild. Fierce. Pure unslakable lust.

I find myself on my couch, thinking of Lock. Thinking of the way he slammed me against the storm door and kissed me breathless. The way he warned me of things we shouldn't do.

I'm thinking of going to his hotel and doing all those things to him. Cutting loose, forgetting all my hang-ups and inhibitions, and taking everything I can from him. Getting him to show me the wild side of sex.

Shove him backward onto the couch. Rip off whatever stupid clothes he's wearing, and suck him off until he can't speak anymore. Suck the coherency right out of him.

My fingers have a mind of their own. Shit, my *mind* has a mind of its own—a will of its own, more accurately. I imagine Lock on the couch, in the darkness. Curtains drawn, a sliver of daylight is all that illuminates him. He is sitting on his butt on the couch, robe tossed open, baring himself for me. I'd be on my knees between his legs. He'd bury his hands in my hair, grip my curls in his fists and he'd struggle for control as I took his long, thick shaft between my lips.

As the fantasy develops my fingers are moving hard and fast, hitting my button just right. I'm gasping, mouth open, head back against my couch, eyes closed. Thinking of Lock. Of his gorgeous erection in my hands, in my mouth. Maybe I'd do my best porn star impression, giving him a blowjob he'd never, ever forget, for as long as he lives. I don't watch porn, never have, but that has no bearing on this fantasy. I imagine him protesting as he gets ready to come, being gallant and thoughtful and telling me he wants more, he doesn't want to come like this. The way those hot alphas in the romance books do. He'd try to pull me up, but I'd insist. I'd suck harder, tease and tantalize until he had no choice, he would have to let go. I'd make him lose control in a way he'd never felt before.

Oh god, I'm there, thinking of Lock groaning as he releases himself in my mouth, maybe some dripping on my chin as I pull out, dripping in a saliva-string line onto my tits. Oh—oh fuck. He'd be so hard, wet with my saliva, and I'd take him again, see if I can milk every last drop out of him, and then I'd let him go with a loud *pop* and sink back to sit on my heels. I'd have a sexy, self-satisfied look on my face. And then he'd grab me, not asking, not insisting, but grabbing me bodily off the floor, trading places. He'd be on his knees in front of me, and his tongue would go wild all over me, the way it did last night.

Oh god, oh fucking god, I come so hard I nearly slide off the couch, moaning and groaning all wanton and wild.

I come back to my senses on the floor in front of

my couch, Lock's T-shirt rucked up around my hips. I half-expect him to be there, watching me again. But he's not. He's at the La Quinta.

La Quinta? Really?

I sent him away.

I look at the whiskey bottle on the counter and it's—what time is it? I don't even know. Too early for whiskey, that's for sure.

I know why I want a drink.

Why I'm masturbating, thinking of Lock.

Because it's easier than thinking about why I made him leave.

I dissolve into sobs. It hits without warning, just a sudden blast of ugly crying, thinking of Ollie. Thinking of him dying. Remembering, feeling his loss all over again. Thinking of somebody cutting Ollie's organs out of his battered body and putting them in those special coolers, sending them out to be put into someone else. I wonder who else out there has one of Ollie's body parts?

Shit, shit, shit.

He has Ollie's *heart*. I heard Oliver's actual physical heart beating in Lock's chest. I felt it thumping under my ear, under my hand. That heart keeps Lock alive. That heart—my Ollie's heart—sends blood coursing through Lock's body.

I can't seem to stop crying, because it's all so

fucking confusing. I want Lock. I don't want to be lonely anymore. I want to *feel*. I want to be wanted. But how can I let that happen? How can I betray Ollie's memory that way, especially with Lock? The man who has my dead husband's heart in his chest. How can I do that?

There are no answers. Shit, I don't even know the questions.

I came to life when I first kissed you

I'M ALONE IN MY ROOM AT THE HOTEL. UTAH IS ASLEEP ON the floor, snuffing and huffing, legs moving in her sleep. I've got the curtains drawn, and I'm on my bed in just my jeans, idly flipping through the channels.

Bored.

Trying not to think about Niall.

Trying not to relive every last moment, over and over again. Trying to keep myself from jumping in my truck and hauling ass to her house, pinning her to the bed and fucking her until neither of us can see or think or breathe.

But fuck, it's hard.

So hard.

I'm hard—all it takes is a single stray thought, and I've got a raging hard-on.

I mean, Jesus. Like an idiot, I barged into her house, *again,* and caught her masturbating. Caught her in the act of giving herself a monster O...calling *my* name. She thought of me while she masturbat-ed. God, that's hot. So goddamn hot. See? I'm hard as a rock again, seeing her in my mind's eye, her hand in her pants, moving fast, hips flicking up and down, head tossed back, eyes closed, face in that beautiful, al-most-pained expression of orgasm. Calling *my* name.

And last night? I barely pulled out in time, and she wrapped that small, soft, perfect hand of hers around me and helped me finish. Helped me finish all over her belly.

In a fit of I-don't-know-what-possessed-me, I stopped at a drug store on the way home and bought some condoms, and—just to make myself feel bet-ter—some water and a jar of cashews. I was buying condoms because I was hoping like hell I'd get anoth-er taste of Niall James.

I'm trying so damn hard to keep my thoughts away from her, but it's impossible.

Those springy brown curls. Her hips, deliciously bell-shaped. That ass, so juicy, so plump and ripe for so many dirty things. Those goddamned perfect tits. D-cup—I happened to catch a glimpse of the tag on her bra. Pale, creamy skin. And her eyes? Light, light brown—the most expressive eyes I've ever had the pleasure of gazing into, streaked with shots of green. She can express wicked, biting sarcasm with just a look. Or she can beg me for more with a wild, hungry plea in those brown eyes. Almond-brown, that's the shade I'd say they were.

She's just…everything. All of her. I want all of her.

I fight it for hours. Even do some exercising. Pushups, mountain-climbers, planks, Bulgarian split-squats off the couch, until I'm trembling and sweaty and I stink to hell.

I shower, and all through the shower I have to fight myself, fight to keep my hand off my cock and my thoughts away from Niall. I can't jerk off thinking about her. I've done enough to her without using her like that.

But…fuck. Just fuck.

I get out of the shower, towel off, and wrap up in one of those thick terrycloth robes that hotels often provide. I pace around and fight my thoughts. I ignore the ache in my balls. The urge to go to her, take her mouth and use her hard until we're both spent.

I can't fucking help how my thoughts, when they go to her, turn dirty. The way I turned to her, and then had her beneath me. Her hand on me, stroking me. The way she yanked open my jeans with such ferocity, as if she needed me right then, couldn't wait. She knew exactly what she wanted and wasn't shy about going for it.

I picture all the things I want to do with her, and to her. Get her on her hands and knees, on this very bed. I'm sprawled out on my back on my bed, robe open, only sort of held closed by a loose knot. The TV is on, but I'm not paying any attention. I'm staring at the ceiling, fists clenched, jaw tensed, trying my damnedest to guide my thoughts away from Niall, and losing.

"Fuck," I snarl.

I give in. God, I hate myself for this, but I'm out of fight. I ache. I've been hard for hours, and I'm about to explode.

I wrap my fist around myself, close my eyes, and picture Niall. The way she was that first time I showed up at her house. Wearing nothing but a tiny tee. Big, beautiful breasts stretching the thin cotton. Nipples straining, hard and thick. Her tight core playing peekaboo under the hem, trimmed close. Not bare, no funny shapes, just well-trimmed and well-groomed fuzz. Perfect. All woman. Those thighs, brushing together but with a tiny little keyhole gap. If she took a deep breath, her tits would lift, and the shirt would go with them, and I'd have been able to see all of her core. Tight, taut, glistening with need. Shit, even better, wet with my saliva.

I'm stroking myself, thinking of her body, her core, the way she tasted, how sweet she tasted on my lips, how responsive she was, how her tits bounced as she writhed in my grip, the way she came apart so beautifully. God, I'm aching, throbbing.

I hear Utah snuffle in the other room, making a little sound in her throat, padding around and looking for a new spot to lie down. There are other sounds, but I'm not paying attention. I'm focused on imagining Niall, and getting myself there.

I happen to blink my eyes open, and for a moment I know I have to be lost in the throes of some kind of hallucination or exceptionally vivid fantasy, because I could swear Niall is here in my hotel room with me, watching me jerk off. Hand over her mouth, eyes wide, leaning against the doorframe.

I let go of myself, abruptly. I sit up. Blink hard. But the vision of Niall doesn't go away.

Her hair is loose around her shoulders, just the top part tied back out of her face. And she's wearing...god, holy fucking shit, she's wearing a shin-length sundress, tight and patterned red with white zig-zag stripes. Molded to her ass and thighs so tightly it's clear she's not wearing a damned thing underneath. No sleeves, just little straps over her shoulders. The top part is molded to her too, propping up her magnificent breasts. It's a casual dress, a summery thing. You see chicks wearing them all summer long. But on Niall? It's pure sin. Raw temptation.

She's got a little clutch purse in her hand, dangling at her side. She drops it, brows drawn, eyes wide, her expression one of torture, of need, of conflict.

"Don't stop," she whispers.

God, she's real.

She's real.

She's here.

I can't fathom it. Don't know what to do. I throb, my pulse hammering like a drum from nerves and need and from having been so close to coming and having stopped.

"Lock...don't stop. Keep going." Her voice is a dulcet whisper.

"What do you want me to do, honey?" My voice is a whisky-rasp, rough, gruff, low.

"Keep touching yourself." She takes a step closer, hips swaying sensuously. "You were thinking about me, weren't you?"

"Yeah," I grunt. "I was thinking about you."

I clutch myself in a shaky hand, my grip tight. I watch, enraptured, as Niall sashays like a ghost, a dream, a succubus toward me. She looks as conflicted as I feel about everything, but just as unable to stop this as I am.

"Touch yourself," she says in that slow, raw whisper, "and think about me. Like you were."

"I'd rather touch you."

"I know. Me too." She climbs onto the bed, and I'm aching in my hand. "But I want this, first. I want to watch you do this." She kneels on the edge of the bed near the foot end, out of reach. "The way you watched me."

I groan. "God, Niall. You're making me crazy."

"This whole thing is crazy. But I can't seem to stop myself." She inches closer. "Stroke yourself."

I glide my hand down, root to tip, once, slowly. "Like this?"

She moans, a tiny sound in the back of her throat. "God, yes. Like that." She puts her fingers over mine, holds me, but I can only feel my own hand on my erection, and her soft hand over mine—it's tantalizing and torturous. She shows me with gentle pressure how she wants me to move my hand. Slowly, in a smooth rhythm. "Like this."

I'm fighting the edge away, fighting for control. And losing. "Jesus, Niall. God…" My hips buck, and my stomach tenses, but I hold it back, fight it off, keep my eyes open.

She tugs the top of her dress down with one hand, lifting her breasts free. "Does that help?"

"God, Niall. You're so…"

"So what, Lock?"

I remember her telling me how badly she needed to hear me tell her how gorgeous she is. "Perfect,

Niall. You're utter perfection. So beautiful it hurts."
I groan and lift my ass off the bed, feeling my O rise
up inside me, making me shake and tingle and hum,
still fighting it off, now using muscle control to keep it
back. "God, I want to touch you. I want you to touch
me."

She lets her hand slide off mine. Her fingers
wrap around me, above my hand. Hers is small and
pale above my larger, tanned hand. We move in sync,
both of us stroking me, now.

"I want to watch, Lock." She inches closer. Biting
her lip, that conflicted expression of forbidden, irre-
pressible desire on her beautiful face. "You watched
me come, heard me say your name as I came. Now
it's my turn."

She finds my other hand, fisted beside me, and
lifts it, placing my palm on her breast. I take the heavy
globe in my hand, squeeze, knead; brush my thumb
across her nipple. She watches, rapt, as we pulse and
pump our hands on my erection. She doesn't take her
eyes off me as I get closer and closer to losing control.

But I never want this to end. I want to feel this
forever, her here with me, touching me, her soft
breast in my hand. Seeing the need in her eyes, knowing as soon as I'm done, I'll get to make her feel this
good, too. Or better.

She leans over me, breasts brushing my chest,

and kisses me. It's a soft, slow kiss. And all too brief. She pulls away, kisses the corner of my mouth, teasing me with the idea of another kiss, but then pulls her lips away from mine and kisses my chest. My stomach. Her hand above mine, still moving. Kisses my stomach. She glances up at me, hesitant. And then she lets go of me.

"Don't you dare stop, Lock," she says. "You're close. I can see it. Don't stop."

I keep my hand moving, jerking slowly up and down. I watch as she kisses her way down my body. Glances up at me, now and then. Reaches the tip of my erection. Glances up at me again, eyes full of need and trouble and so many emotions I don't know the names of them all. Places her palms on my thighs. Slides them up my body, and then back down. Surrounds my erection and my sac with her hands, touching, cupping, sliding back up my belly. Kisses one hipbone. Then the other.

God. Oh, god.

I can't help the words, now. "Jesus, Niall. I'm so close. I'm right there, I'm about to come."

"Yes, Lock, come for me. Let me watch. Let me see it." She whispers this against the taut skin of my erection.

I flex my hips into my hand, which now flashes up and down hard and fast.

She touches my wrist. "Go slow. Take your time. Make it last."

I slow down, but it's impossible to go slow when I'm so close. But she's got her hand on mine, as before, feeling me as I stroke myself to release as slowly as I can. Slowly, for her.

And then, fuck, fuck, *fuck*, she's got me in her mouth. Just a tiny taste. I nearly lose it, but hold it back. But then I can't hold back. Not when she does it again, taking me in her mouth, so wet, so warm, so soft, so fucking incredible. I groan her name in a drawn-out moan. Fist my fingers in her hair, involuntarily. Struggling for control. Her hand still on top of mine, guiding the pace of my strokes. Her tongue flicking and licking in circles against the tip.

I arch off the bed, fighting for enough control that I don't lose it in her mouth without warning, so I don't fuck into her mouth like the wild animal I feel like right now.

"NIALL—fuck, fuck, Niall, you have to stop. I'm—god, god, oh god, you have to stop or I'm— fuck, I'm coming. Right now, I'm coming, Niall—"

I feel it, can't stop it. No control anymore. She backs off at the very last second, letting me pop free with a loud noise, and then I'm jerking my erection into my hand, into hers wrapped around me. I spasm, and come all over myself. All over my hand, all over hers, all over my stomach. But after the first spasm, she knocks away my hand and buries me in between her lips, and takes the rest in her mouth, sucks it all out of me, moaning, and gliding her soft, strong hand all over me, up and down and up and down until I swear I come a second time, or more, or something, I don't even know what it is except another powerful, ripping, spastic explosion of gutting bliss.

I gasp and go limp. "God, Niall. Holy shit."

She's using the robe to wipe me clean, and then she's tugging at the terrycloth knot and jerking it out from beneath me, wiping her hand and mine, her mouth, and tossing the robe aside.

I watch this, gasping for breath.

I shake my head, rocked to speechlessness by the vision of her. Up on her knees, breasts bared over the top of her sundress, hair coming free of the tie at the back of her head, wisping around her face in ringlets, dress wrinkled and rucked around her thighs.

Lunging up and forward, I wrap my hands around the backs of her thighs, grip, feeling the muscular strength under the soft pale skin, and then slide my palms up to cup her ass. Tug her closer, closer, and she moves on her knees to straddle me, dress stretching across her thighs and then her hips. I brush the hem up, up, until it's bunched above her hips, baring her core for me. And yeah, she's not wearing any panties. She straddles me, moving over my thighs, my hips. Letting my slack manhood slide between her thighs, grinding on me, skin hot now, and softer than silk. I lay back, pulling her closer. Confused, she moves with my guiding touch, up over my stomach, my chest. Falls forward and grips the headboard, staring down at me in consternation.

"Lock?" Her voice is tremulous.

I have no words for her now. Only my tongue and lips all over her thighs and core. She rocks, groans. Tastes so sweet, so smoky, a taste I could lap up and never get enough of. I cup her ass with one hand, encouraging her to move. Encourage her to ride me. Slide two fingers inside her, spear them in and out. And god, she's so tight two fingers is all I can fit. She moans, rocks, moves.

"Lock, oh fuck, Lock. God, this feels amazing."

She lets go of the headboard with one hand and stabs her fingers into my hair, grips a handful and pulls my face against her, taking all she wants from me. Her hips are grinding in circles, and I feel her clenching around my fingers. She's moaning and whimpering, eyes open and staring down at me in an expression of wild, uninhibited need conflicting with amazement and bliss and the ever-present confusion as to what the fuck is going on between us. But she doesn't stop, continues to ride my tongue until her movements are stuttering and fluttering and her fingers are gripped painfully tight in my hair.

"Lock, Lock...*LOCK!*" She loses it, then, with my name shouted from her lips, shuddering, shaking, crying out wordlessly and grinding hard as I lick and slide my fingers in and out until she's limp and collapsing down, sliding down my body to lie on top of me, involuntarily shuddering as aftershocks rip through her.

"Shit, Lock. I haven't felt anything like that in—" She shakes her head against my chest, shrugging. "Ever, maybe." She lifts up, brows scrunched, eyes wide, lip quivering. "And that scares the hell out of me."

I smooth my hand in circles on her back. "I know what you mean."

"Do you?"

I nod. "Yeah. What I feel with you, what you make me feel?" I shrug, at a loss for words. "It's like nothing I've ever felt. I don't know what it means or how to deal with how intense I feel everything with you."

"Not the same, though." She traces idle patterns on my chest with a finger. "That's not the same as what I'm saying."

"What are you saying, then?"

A long pause, and then she sniffles. Flattens her left hand on my chest—she took her rings off. The skin is whiter where the rings used to be, indented slightly. "I had something amazing, with—with... with Oliver. And it really was amazing. *Really* amazing. Once in a lifetime beautiful. But...this?" She digs her fingertips into the muscle of my chest, sniffling yet again. "Whatever this crazy thing is between you and me, it's...*so* intense. I feel things, Lock...I feel things with you that I—that I've never...that I've never felt before. Such crazy, intense things I didn't even know were possible. And that hurts, and it's confusing, but it's so addictive."

"Niall, I—"

She's not done, though. "I want to tell you to leave. I don't know how to—how to deal with the fact that you've got—that you have—" she obviously can't even say it, placing her left hand over my heart, feeling it beat like a kick drum in my chest, but she continues in a ragged whisper, "...you have his heart. You're nothing like him. I don't mean that as a bad thing. You're just totally different people. But you have his...his heart. You have my...you have Ollie's... *heart.*" That last word is a broken sound.

I try again, even though I have no idea what's going to come out. "Shit, Niall. I'm sorry. I wish—"

"Don't!" she snaps. "Don't you *fucking dare* wish that. It's not going to bring him back, and I'm not going to wish you weren't alive. Because...because I'm finally *feeling* again, Lock. I was numb, ever since his death. All I felt was hurt and pain and anger and confusion and loss. And I couldn't keep feeling that, but I couldn't make it go away or get over it, so I just...I numbed myself. With wine, with whiskey, with work, with staying home and going to sleep however I could and going to work, and just...existing, until I was numb.

"Then you showed up—and I—I'm finally alive again, Lock. And the thing is, being alive again fucking *hurts*, it hurts so bad, Lock." Now she's crying, saying these words through tears. "It *hurts*. *Feelings* hurt. I don't know how to be without Ollie. I don't know how to...how to let myself feel good things without feeling guilty, because he's not here to feel those good things with me, and it's someone else making me feel those good things. How can I let that happen? He was the love of my life, and he's gone, and I shouldn't ever feel good things again, should I? But I—I want to feel them. I fucking—god, I can't get enough of how you make me feel. And I hate myself for that, but...I can't stop wanting more.

"I masturbated thinking about you too, right before I came here. I couldn't help it. I couldn't help masturbating to you, and I couldn't help coming here, knowing we'd do this, knowing how it would make me feel, both so good and so bad. Not good-bad, but confused bad. Guilty. Sick to my stomach and dizzy with anticipation and so eager for more I don't know how to contain it. I *need* this, Lock. I need what you make me feel. Because it means I'm *alive,* but I don't want to be alive, not without Ollie, but I know I have to be. I have to live. I have to…move on. I have to let him go. But how? *How,* Lock? How do I do that?"

"I don't know," I whisper. "I don't know."

I have so much going on inside me. Guilt. Need. Confusion. Fear. All layered above and in and around this other feeling, a new feeling I don't have words for. I can't even wrap my head around it. It's an immense, intense emotion centered around Niall, and it's not about sex, not really. It's not about her body. It's not even about my heart, the heart in my chest. It's…something more. Something deeper. Sharper. Bigger. It cuts. It rips. It swells so my chest feels like it's cracking open. It's the feeling of dizziness, right before you fall off a cliff.

I did that once, fell off a cliff by accident. I was climbing straight up a sheer cliff face in one of those remote Chinese fishing villages where the mountains are spires spiking out of the sea. I don't remember everything, just that I was a hundred feet up, no ropes, just my hands and feet and the stone. I reached for a handhold, felt the wind snatch me right off the cliff face and toss me like a doll out into space, free-wheeling, arms flying, pinwheeling. I just barely missed being smashed on the rocks, and I hit the water like a ton of bricks, so hard I couldn't breathe. Only instinct saved me, kept me fighting for the surface, fighting for breath, even though I was in agony, wondering if maybe I'd crushed all my bones on the impact of my fall.

I feel like that now. I'm drowning. Free-wheeling, pinwheeling through space, stomach in my throat, no up, no down, no surface to hold on to, only something sharp and hard beneath, waiting to smash me to pieces.

And here she is, pouring her heart out to me. Spilling everything, braver than I could ever hope to be.

I can't speak. My tongue might as well have been ripped out of my head for all that I'm capable of speaking.

Fear is a serpent in my chest, pumping venom in my veins. I want to run. But I can't. I can't. But I also don't want to run, because she's in my arms and nothing has ever felt so good, nothing has ever felt like this, like her. God, there's never been anything like her in my life, and I've got her in my arms and I don't dare let go. Don't fucking dare.

But, god, I'm so paralyzed it's painful. I'm not even breathing.

And then she lifts up, forearm braced on my chest, hair a loose wild fall of curls on my skin, eyes the color and shape of almonds streaked with green, fingers tapping unconsciously along with the rhythm of my heartbeat, her eyes on mine. Piercing, seeing so much, too much.

"Lock?" She's searching me with those eyes. Seeing all, or seeing nothing, I don't know. "Say something."

"I—" I shake my head, as if to shake words loose. "Niall…"

What do I say? How do I put into words what I can't even put into thoughts in my own head?

All I can do is kiss her.

I roll over with her, cup her face in my hands and kiss her, trying to show through the kiss the ineffable, unfathomable feelings I can't express. Through the kiss, I hope she'll begin to understand what I sure as fuck don't.

At the risk of sounding like a fuckboy douchebag…I've kissed a lot of girls. I've had an uncountable number of hot-and-heavy makeout sessions, so I know how to kiss. I know how to turn a woman on just with kisses.

Nothing in my life, no woman, no encounter, no kiss could have ever prepared me for the next sixty seconds. I know it's exactly sixty seconds because right before I kiss her the clock on the bedside table flicks from 11:31 p.m. to 11:32 p.m. I watch the red lines forming the numeral change and then I lean in and our lips are fused, and my life is irrevocably altered.

We kiss.

Not for the first time, but it's a minute of my life that I know will always be indelibly imprinted on my mind as the most important kiss, the most important minute of my life.

And then I open my eyes just in time to see the clock change from 11:32 p.m. to 11:33 p.m.

I don't really have words for the kiss.

It's so much more than the meeting of lips. So much more than tongues tangling. It's...

See? I don't even know.

It's the feeling of my heart being ripped open, the long-fallow soil of my soul churned and tilled. It's a feeling of belonging, a sensation utterly alien to someone like me. It's a wanting to belong. Needing something I've never wanted. Something, as Niall said, I didn't even know existed. Except for her, she's talking about physical sensation, and for me this is... deeper. Something...more.

And yes, the way she makes me feel, the way everything with her feels is so much *more*. We're not doing anything I've never done before, nor do I think any of this is new for her. But something about the way it is between us is…different. *More,* for the lack of a better word. More, in the way the heat of the sun is *more* than the flames of a bonfire.

That one kiss, and I knew what it was I was feeling; it's an emotion I am simply unprepared to accept. Unable to accept. Incapable of comprehending. I can't even think it. This isn't denial, it's the sheer incapacity to wrap my head around a concept so unutterably, inconceivably massive and strange.

I just can't.

Cannot.

All this in the space of sixty seconds. One minute of kissing a woman, and I am a man turned inside out and spun in circles so I can't find up, can't stand on my own two feet. I'm shattered.

By a kiss.

I break away from her, roll off and slide off the bed, stagger backward, rubbing my wrist across my mouth as if to wipe away the stain of change. As if I could wipe away the effect of that kiss.

As if I could ever go back to the person I was before that kiss.

The word thuds and thunders through my mind, it sears across my soul in lightning-white letters:

L

   O

      V

         E

The word arrives in my brain unbidden, with no context, no surrounding thoughts. It might as well be a neon sign, so brilliantly clear is this epiphany.

And how do I handle it?

I freak the fuck out.

The worst me is just
a long gone memory

I'LL NEVER FORGET THE LOOK ON HIS FACE AS HE LURCHES off the bed and stumbles away from me. It's an expression of stunned and fearful befuddlement. He doesn't know what's hit him. He doesn't know what it is, what to say, what to feel. Or how to handle it. I don't know what he's feeling, or what he's thinking, or what he's afraid of, or what's confusing him. I just know he's totally overwhelmed.

I get it. That kiss was one of the most intense kisses of my life. Maybe *the* most. I get it. I don't say this, because I can't help him through this. Either he's man enough to handle this, or he's not. I see it in him, the war, the fear, and the panic.

I sense what he's afraid of, and I don't dare examine it too closely myself, because I'll panic, too. Surely it can't be *that*. That word, that feeling, that emotion.

But what if it is?

If he were to be man enough, strong enough, brave enough to be what I need to get through the pain, it could be beautiful, between us. But it all rests on him.

And I sense he's not used to putting effort into anything. He's coasted through life. Never had anyone depend on him; never had anyone expect anything of him. This, what's building here? It would demand a lot of him. *I* would expect a lot of him.

"Lock," I whisper, because I feel like a normal speaking voice could spook him. "Lock, just... breathe. It's okay."

"I don't know how to do this." He doesn't whisper, he speaks in a low rumble from across the bedroom.

Naked, and so gorgeous. All hard planes in the moonlight, thick muscles and tan skin and taut curves, grooves of definition and slabs of bulk. Thick, shaggy, wild hair loose around his shoulders, his beard a tangle. All man, masculine, rugged, sensual, sexual.

"You don't have to know," I tell him. "Not right off the bat. We can figure this out."

"I don't know what *this* is."

"Hell, neither do I."

I move off the bed and stand a couple of feet away from him. My dress is a mess, the top tugged down under my breasts, the hem shoved up around my hips. I stare at him, wanting him, not wanting to deal with these emotions right now. I want the physical. I want his hands, his mouth, his manhood. I want to forget all this intensity and just feel like a...*woman*, again. I forgot, for a while, what that means. How it feels.

It's a need.

Sultry, sensual, sexuality. Knowing myself, knowing what I want, and not being afraid to go after it.

I let out a breath, because I came here for him, wanting him, wanting something I'm not sure I should have, wanting something so bad I can taste it. It's not forbidden, but it still feels wrong, somehow. We're two consenting adults, neither of us committed to anyone else. And that's the problem, for me. I *am* committed to someone, but he's dead. And his heart beats inside the chest of the man I want.

Dammit, it's too confusing.

It's just easier to not think about it. It's easier to let my hormones drown out my thoughts. Easier to stare at Lock's beautiful body, easier to think about those big, talented hands on my skin, that nimble tongue slippery and firm and tasting every erogenous zone I have, and some I didn't know I had. It's easier to tell myself that *later* will be soon enough to think things through, *later* is soon enough to sort out my heart and mind and body.

I've lived outside my own head for so long, shutting out the world, shutting out emotions, shutting out needs and desires and hormones. I've floated through life over this last while, more a presence than a person.

And now?

I'm fully here, fully present in my mind and heart and body.

And right now, I only want to pay attention to the present.

I don't know how long we stand there, neither of us moving.

I know the moment my tenuous hold on restraint snaps, though.

I peel my dress off, toss it aside. Glide toward him. He groans, a tortured sound. I move closer to him, until there are mere inches between us, and then centimeters, and then our bodies are touching, my breasts against his chest, our hips brushing, his manhood nudging me. I slide my palms over his chest, over his shoulders, down his sides. Cup his taut, hard backside, his trim, narrow hips. Reach between us. Stroke him.

"This doesn't solve anything," he whispers.

"No, it doesn't," I agree.

God, he's so perfect in my hands. Hard as steel,

so thick my fingertips don't meet when I wrap my hand around him, skin like velvet. He's breathing hard, hands at his sides, fists clenching and unclenching. Fighting for control. Fighting himself.

His gaze is a maze I can't navigate, a wild, blue-green labyrinth, and I don't have a ball of yarn to find my way. I dive in anyway.

Slide my fist up and down his length until he's grinding involuntarily into my touch.

"Niall, shit…" he murmurs.

And then he's got my wrists in his hand and I'm flying through the air, his arm under my butt carrying me across the room, settling me on my back on the mattress. His mouth is on mine, and this time the kiss isn't the subsuming tsunami of intensity and tenderness and meaning it was before, this time the kiss is furious and hungry and utterly sexual, teeth clashing and lips slamming, devouring and demanding. His hands pin my wrists above my head, and his mouth slides away from mine, descends to my breasts, and I writhe in his touch, fight his grip, needing to touch him, to hold him, to encourage him. But he doesn't let go. He laves at my nipples, flicks them to hypersensitivity, erect and hard and begging for more. My hips lift, my core throbs, screaming for attention. And god, does he give it. Fingers find me wet and waiting, and I moan my relief as he manipulates me to a writhing fervor, whips me into a frenzy with kisses to my lips and licks to my nipples, his fingers moving in quickening circles.

He's levered over me, kissing me, touching me, and his hand is gone for a brief moment. I hear something crackle, and my eyes fly open to see him ripping open a condom with his teeth, rolling the rubber down around his shaft with one hand in a smooth motion. He tosses the wrapper aside, knocks my thighs apart with his knees. He still has my wrists pinned over my head. I fight him, but he's unrelenting. He bites my lower lip, tugs it away with sharp but gentle teeth, and glides his erection against my opening.

"Lock…" I don't know what I'm saying or what I'm asking for.

"You want it?" he whispers into my ear, his breath hot.

"Yes, *god* yes." I do know what I'm asking for.

"Say it, Niall."

"I want it. Give it to me. Please, Lock. I need you." Wrong thing to say.

He tenses, and his eyes narrow, his chest inflates with an inrush of breath. Jaw tenses, flexes. He searches me with that gaze as turbulent as a storm-tossed sea.

He slams into me, and I whimper as he fills me to stretching. I could cry from the bliss of it, how he feels inside me, and I'm straining against his grip on my wrists, gyrating my hips against his, leaning up to nip at his skin with lips and teeth wherever I can reach. Chin, cheeks, lips, neck, shoulders, kissing and nipping and sipping at his skin. His mouth is begging, pleading silently for more.

"Oh, fuck…" His voice is ragged. As if he's giving in. "God, Niall. You feel—"

I slam my mouth up against his, mash my lips over his. To shut him up the way he shut me up. I move my hips in a silent plea for motion. He pulls away from my kiss, rooted as deep as he can go and stilled, holding there, hips flush, my wrists pinned up over my head. My breath comes in gasps of need, making my tits shake and sway. I arch my back, pushing them into him. Toward him, needing his mouth on them again.

I don't understand why he won't let me touch him. But he won't. He doesn't let go. He holds my gaze, unblinking, and begins to thrust. Slowly. Gently. Sinuously.

I begin to understand, now, as he moves, holding my touch at bay.

If I touch him, he'll be lost.

He thinks he can control this. Stop this.

By making sure I'm not touching him, he's trying to hold off what's building between us—and I'm not talking about orgasms.

Boy, have I got news for him.

I can touch him with *so* much more than just my hands.

I don't know why I'm doing this, because what's building is every bit as confusing and terrifying for me.

I trace up his calf with my toes, a light, tickling touch, and I move in sync with him, finding the perfect, slow, sensual rhythm, slow as taking deep breaths, in….and….out, unhurried. He's setting the pace, and I'm going with it. But this is perfect. It's so perfect. I trace his calf. Up to his knee, flatten the arch of my foot against the back of his leg and caress downward, curling my foot in around his so our legs are tangled. Glide my other foot up his leg, hook it around the back of his knee, and now, both of my legs are snaked sinuously, intimately, around his. I pull him closer to me. Arch my back, pushing up against him, rubbing my breasts against his chest, turning each motion into a thrust of my hips against his and a brush of my nipples against his body all at once. I lean close and murmur in his ear, let the raw ecstasy of feeling him like this escape my lips. Give voice to the pleasure I'm feeling. I moan in his ear. Soft breaths, whimpers, whispering his name as he slides in and out, and in and out, so slowly we're both made wild and crazed with it.

He knows my game, and his expression becomes ever more tortured as he feels the intimacy wrapping us up together, closer and closer and closer.

"Fuck…" he groans, and lets his forehead rest between my breasts. His hand releases my wrists, and I'm quick to cling to him, to stroke the broad cliff of his rippling, undulating back, to cup the bubble of his ass, to pull at him.

"Niall…god, Niall."

I don't have any words for him. I only have moans against his neck, whimpered gasps against the shell of his ear. My hands sliding all over him, wherever I can reach, tracing the bulges of every muscle, every vein. He's above me, but he's not in control anymore.

I am.

I move us faster. Writhe my hips against his and cling to him and breathe faster and moan louder, and bring him with me.

"Niall—" He's losing it, now. Back arching, hips slamming, breath coming in ragged, rushing gasps, hands scouring my skin, hands on my hips, pulling hard at me. Face buried in my breasts.

I palm his cheeks and bring his face up to mine. "Kiss me, Lock."

"Goddamn it, Niall." He tries to pull away, tries to fight it.

"Kiss me when you come, Lock." I snare his beard and demand his lips.

He gives over to me, kisses me, shivering and shuddering as he comes.

I reach between us and touch myself, bringing myself to shuddering orgasm with him, writhe with him, cling to him, kiss him as I come.

We tremble together in silence.

"Goddamn it, Niall," he gasps, his voice ragged and broken. "What the fuck are you doing to me?"

I wish I knew.

A burned out star in a galaxy

HOLY SHIT. HOLY MOTHERFUCKING SHIT.

Niall James just rocked my world. Knocked me off my axis. She's left me breathless and dizzy and overwhelmed and panicking. That, what we just did together? That wasn't sex. It wasn't fucking.

It was…

God, I don't even know.

I *felt* her.

I felt her *soul*.

She just gave me a gift, a precious glimpse at the depths of who she is. She left herself vulnerable, showed me the inside of her heart. She's as scared of this as I am, but she's willing to go for it anyway. She sees what I'm feeling, and I think she understands it better than I do. She's had it, had something greater than I could ever fathom. And she lost it. The reminder of what she had and lost is thumping so hard in my chest I feel it in my throat and against my ribcage. She surely must hear it, right now. Feel it, under her cheek.

I'm lying on my back, holding her. Her face is on my chest, her hand on my stomach, her knee across my thigh. This intimacy, it's so powerful it leaves me unable to draw a breath. This feeling of tenderness, this sensation of *belonging,* right here, in this moment, with this woman, it's so goddamned all-consuming and so heady I can't see straight. I could be drunk, I'm so off-kilter and dizzy. But my heart—my metaphysical heart, I mean—is a shredded, raw, bloody mess. Calcified. Ossified. So long unused, so long accustomed to emptiness, nothingness. And now I'm feeling things, and my poor heart can't take it.

I've never held anyone this way.

Never. Not once.

All the sex I've had, and yet I've never held a woman this way. It never occurred to me, nor to the women I was with, I don't think. Even Leanne, the only woman I've ever fucked more than a handful of times, we never stayed in bed together afterward. She'd get out of my bed, go clean up, and would return to her cabin. We would meet in the saloon afterward sometimes, for drinks, and conversation.

I never even thought about doing something like that with Niall. We finished, and I rolled to my back and she went with me, pressed her cheek to my chest, resting in the cradle of my arm. And it feels so fucking right to hold her this way, so utterly perfect. Better than catching a long wind and feeling the lines tauten and the sail belly out, better than lying in the bow at midnight and staring up at an endless sky full of stars. It's a rush, too, a jolt of pure adrenaline rocketing through me, stronger than any rush I've ever gotten from all the crazy, dangerous shit I've ever done. Skydiving? Got nothing on this. Racing a motorcycle around winding Italian two-lane roads? No comparison. Free-climbing a sheer cliff face, hundreds of feet up, nothing but churning surf below? Not even in the same league.

Dying, and being brought back to life? Not even *that*.

Several minutes have passed, and neither of us has spoken a word. After an experience like that, what do you *say*?

I feel it when she falls asleep. Her breathing shifts, slows, softens. Her fingers twitch on my stomach. She nuzzles closer. My heart cracks. Bleeds. I breathe in her scent, tighten my arms around her.

Tighten them, because I'm *this* close to running.

I need a drink.

I need to leave.

She deserves better than me.

I don't deserve her.

I don't know how to do this.

I've never wept in my life, but I'm close to it now. Thinking about her. Trying to understand what I'm feeling. How can one person engender so much inside me? How can I talk myself into staying, talk myself out of bolting into the night like the coward I am?

I try to simply breathe, and hold her through the night. I know I can't sleep so I don't even try.

I just stare at her in the moonlight, watching her sleep, and feel everything coming apart inside me.

I don't know how to do this.

I don't know how to love someone.

Especially not someone who's been through so much. She's so strong, so beautiful.

At some point in the early hours of the morning, she rolls away from me, shows me the curve of her back and the bell of her hip, curly brown hair falling around her face and spilling onto the pillow. Her fingers are curled under her chin, and her lips are pouted slightly. And god, god, god, she's snoring ever so softly. That sound is what does it. It's the straw that breaks me. Her snoring, a sound so slight and sweet and cute it makes my heart thump and thunder and twist in my chest. A sound so sweet I want to kiss her while she sleeps.

I slide off the bed, unable to catch a decent breath, unable to swallow. I dress quietly. I don't have anything to pack, I just need to grab my backpack and Utah's food and her bowls.

Like Lot's wife, I make the deadly mistake of turning to look back. She's a goddess at rest, the blanket and sheet at her waist. Fuck. Fuck. How can I walk away from a woman like her?

Because it's what I do. I can't do this. I thought I could but I can't. I'm not what she needs. I just don't know how to be that man.

There's a desk near the window with a pad of paper and some hotel pens. I scribble her a note.

Niall,

I'm so sorry. For everything. For showing up. For so many things, I guess. I'm not the kind of man that's ever been there in the morning, and I don't know how to do it now. You deserve better.

I wish I were better with this sort of thing. I wish I knew the words to express to you how incredible it was to know you. The time I had with you was…the best thing I've ever known. Ever will know, probably. And you? You're the most beautiful woman I've ever known, and ever will know.

Goodbye.

And I'm sorry.

Lock.

I hustle Utah quietly out the door. We're in the truck and out of Ardmore before dawn breaks over the horizon.

Just lost in the sky wondering why

GODDAMN IT, LOCK.

I promised myself I wasn't going to cry about this, but I know I'm going to. Just as soon as I get home.

But, apparently, life or fate or whatever has other plans.

It's early morning. Six, maybe? I shower before I leave the hotel room, wash my hair and scour my skin clean, trying vainly to scrub away so much more than just a night of lovemaking. I slip my dress on, regretting the decision to come here commando. No bra, no panties, not a damn thing but the dress, which is a whole lot of not much. It felt sexy on the way here last night, but now? Not so much.

God, I feel like such an idiot for thinking a guy like Lock could change his ways.

I wanted him to. I dared to hope he could.

And that note? What the fuck, Lock? That's the best you can do? If you're going to leave a note, at least make it a good one. That shit you wrote sucks. A complete cop-out.

I make it home, slip on some clean clothes. I realize I'm in no shape to work, so I call in sick and decide to just drive. I need time to sort myself out. I pick a direction, and just drive. And think. About Ollie. About Lock. About loss, about death, about myself. My thoughts are a maelstrom, whirling a million miles an hour, going haywire like an Oklahoma tornado: unstoppable.

I roll the windows down and crank up the radio. I turn the dial until I find anything *but* country. Modern pop, something new and peppy and upbeat.

God, Ollie. Why'd you have to die? Why couldn't I have saved you?

Why'd Lock have to come crashing into my life? Why did I give in? Because now I want more. I want him back. I want him to be the man I think he could be, if he'd dare to try.

I drive so long, so far, I lose myself. I have no idea where I am. I'm so lost in my thoughts that when I finally shake out of my trance I realize the weather has taken a rather dramatic turn. It dawned clear and promised to be sunny, but as I drove it clouded over—low, heavy cloud cover. And now, as I drive, I realize those clouds aren't just gray, they aren't just cloud cover. Those are storm clouds. Low, heavy, dark, threatening thunderheads.

I keep driving, but now I'm keeping a nervous eye on the sky.

Rain patters on the windshield. A few drops, here and there, at first. Then harder. I close the windows and lower the volume on the radio. Mile after mile I drive, and the rain beats harder and harder, and the skies darken, going leaden and then nearly black, so even though it's nearly midday, it could very well be past sunset. It's like nightfall, after dark.

Out the window, I can see smaller trees bent sideways in the driving wind.

Something in my gut stirs, clenches. I slow down, scanning the horizon. Wind buffets the truck, rocking it on its suspension. Even with the windows closed, the wind howls deafeningly. I should turn around, go back home. But then I realize I'm far enough away from home that I wouldn't make it before this storm breaks. And something in me says I shouldn't be on the road when it does.

I accelerate, seeing a sign on the highway announcing the nearest town is less than ten miles away. Rain batters and splatters on the windshield, thick, fat hammering drops in a deluge so blinding the wipers make no difference even on full blast. The wind is screaming now and hitting the truck side-on, rocking it, knocking the rear end sideways, pushing me toward the ditch. My heart is in my throat, my pulse hammering, both fists gripping the steering wheel for dear life.

I can't see shit. It's pitch black outside, with only the occasional flash of lightning in the distance to illuminate the storm-wracked world.

Finally, ahead of me, civilization appears: a single main drag with a gas station, a diner, a drug store, and a liquor store on one side, and an auto garage, a hardware store, a supermarket, and a car parts place on the other. There is also a church with a wide corona of grassy yard and a small cemetery. I can tell there are a few square miles of residential streets on either side of the main street, as well as a strip mall with a doctor's office, a video rental place and another bar. I pull into the gas station, just to get off the road and out of the truck. I park near the front door of the gas station market, exit the truck and jog into the store, soaked to the bone in the few steps it takes to get from my truck to the store. The wind is a roar, twisting street signs on their poles, blowing trash down the street, sending traffic lights swinging on the power lines.

There are a few other trucks parked out front, and an ancient Buick parked at a gas pump. One of the trucks looks familiar, but I barely have time to notice it. I manage to make it into the store itself where a group of men are clustered around the coffee station, clutching Styrofoam cups of coffee and talking about the storm.

"Powerful shit comin'," one old, white-haired man says, in a thick twang. "Powerful, I'm tellin' ya. Ya'll best get home, down in'ta a basement, if you got one. This here is the makin's of a tornado. Big'un, 'less I miss my guess. This here town is gonna get flattened, I do believe."

The next voice to speak sends shivers down my spine, and ripples into my core. "You're sure?" It's Lock. Of all the people, in all the places in the state, he has to be here, standing inside this gas station.

"Son, I lived my entire life in these parts. I been through more twisters'n I can count. This here is shapin' up to be an F-4, at least. Probably an F-5. You got any brains in that big, bearded head of yours, you'll get to safety."

"I'm just passing through. Nowhere to go."

I'm standing by the door, dripping wet, frozen in place just by his voice.

"Well, son, I've got a shelter and you're welcome to it. Take this here main street coupla miles east a ways. I'm the big red barn with the little white house. Shelter's around the back of the house. Just go on down and hunker it out."

"Where will you be?"

The old man waves a gnarled hand. "Out there. Folk's'll need a hand after she blows herself out."

"Think I'll stick with you, in that case."

"You ever sit through a twister?"

Lock sounds to me like he's trying to suppress amusement. "No sir, but—"

"It ain't no fuckin' hayride, boy. Get to the shelter."

"I haven't been through a tornado, but I've sailed through more than my share of hurricanes and typhoons. Nearly capsized twice, lost my mainsail once, and had my dinghy ripped away another time. I think I can handle a tornado. Besides, maybe I can help when it's over."

The old man shrugs a shoulder. "All right, then. Your funeral. Just stay clear of her path, and when she's gone, smell for natural gas. Leaks happen, and that's a quick way to get blowed up if you set off a spark in the wrong place."

"Got it."

The old man finally sees me. "You lost, sweetheart?"

I shake my head. "No, I just…I was going to wait out the storm here, too."

Lock hears my voice, pivots sharply, eyes like lasers fixing on me. "Niall." He takes a step toward me.

"What are you doing here?"

I don't know how to answer that. If I open my mouth, venom will flow, I just know it. I'm pissed at him, and now that he's in front of me, I want to lay into him. Rip him a new asshole for being a coward.

I take a deep breath, letting it out slowly. "I went for a drive."

"Two hours from home?"

I narrow my eyes at him, keep my voice sharp and cold. "Yes, two hours from home. Which makes it kind of funny, running into *you* all the way out here, two hours away from home."

"Niall—"

"Save it, Lock. Not the place, not the time."

As if to punctuate my statement, a loud siren cranks up to a deafening, shrieking wail. The old man slaps a cover on his coffee and heads for the door.

"There she is," he says. "She's made touch-down." He climbs into an old, battered, but well-loved F-150, cranks the engine and backs out.

He pauses at the main road and then turns right, heading for who knows what. Chasing the storm, maybe.

Lock's gaze returns to mine. "It's not safe here."

"It's not safe anywhere, right now."

"We should go for that guy's shelter," Lock says. "North two miles, big red—"

"I have ears."

The siren is still howling, and now the sound of the wind is loud enough to drown out even that. Outside, rain is driving in sideways sheets, the traffic light isn't just swaying or twisting now, but is suspended sideways by the wind force. A blue plastic wading pool tumbles down the road, and then a trampoline, a stop sign, and various other debris. The other men in the store are standing stock-still, clutching coffees and staring outside, brows wrinkled, trying to be stoic but clearly afraid.

And if *they're* afraid, tough old farmers and cowboys born and raised in tornado alley? Shit. This is *bad*.

Lock stares at me, then glances outside, then back to me. Jaw flexing, fists clenching and unclenching, tension in his shoulders. I recognize the signs: he's fighting a war with himself, and losing.

"Fuck," he growls. "Come on."

He grabs me by the hand and drags me into a stumbling run out of the gas station toward his truck. He rounds the front bumper with me in tow, hauls open the passenger seat, and physically lifts me up and into the cab.

"Lock, I'm not—"

"You're going with me. End of story." His voice is hard and irritated as he reaches past me to click the seatbelt into place.

He shuts the passenger door after me, so abruptly it bumps my knee. As soon as I'm in, Utah is trying to lick me from the backseat. Lock trots over to my truck, retrieves my purse and keys, and then jumps into the driver's seat of his truck, smelling wet and looking delicious…and pissed off. What did *I* do to *him?* I'm the one who's pissed.

He twists the key in the ignition savagely, jerking the shifter into reverse, peeling out in a wide arc, and then we're lurching forward, back wheels skidding and fishtailing on the wet cement as Lock guns it. He twists the transfer case knob, activating the four-by-four. We head onto the main road, turning right. The engine roars, and we bolt forward as the turbodiesel spools up and unleashes power. I hear the wind, ever-present, wild, powerful, terrifying. I twist in my seat and scan the horizon.

Clouds, low, thick, curling, black. Whipped into a churning froth by the wind. I feel the truck swaying as the wind batters us, and glance over to see Lock white-knuckling the steering wheel with both hands, jaw tensed, body hunched forward, scanning the horizon, looking for the twister, same as me.

"Fuck. Jesus—" His voice is shocked, stunned breathless. "Fucking hell, that thing is…*huge.*" He points to two o'clock out the windshield.

I follow his outstretched finger, and my breath leaves my body in a horrified whoosh.

We're heading north—to our right, from the east, sunlight is visible through a break in the clouds, shedding a thin stream of weak orange light. To the left is a hell-scape. Lit by the sun, the anchor-shaped wall cloud is an impenetrable fortress of thick, angry, violent black, a frenzied maelstrom of wind and rain and hail.

The funnel?

A massive wedge easily a mile wide, hundreds of feet high, visibly rotating even from this distance. We're traveling parallel to it, following its path...and losing pace. And then it abruptly veers east, directly toward us.

The sound? I've heard the usual descriptors before, of course: freight train, jet engine, et cetera.

Words don't do it justice.

The twister is easily half a mile away from us, and even with the windows closed the roar is...beyond deafening. It's as if the skies themselves have given voice to some colossal, superhuman rage. Screaming, howling, roaring, so loud that conversation is utterly impossible and my ears ache from the sheer decibel force.

My heart is hammering in my chest, just watching the thing, mesmerized, unable to look away.

Hail bounces violently off the hood of the truck, off the roof in staccato drumming thunder, cracking off the windshield, huge golf balls of ice. Rain blasts at us in sheets and horizontal waves.

Lock is hauling ass, going at least seventy on the two-lane highway, trying to outrun the tornado—which I remember reading somewhere is the worst thing you can do.

He rolls down his window.

My ears ring from the violent assault of a wall of sound, as if I was standing two feet away from the screaming engine of a 787 without ear protection. I'm gripping the oh-shit bar with both hands, trying not to hyperventilate, trying not to scream.

Utah is on the floor of the backseat, cowering, whining in her throat, tail tucked, eyes fearful. I know how she feels.

We're in its path, now. It didn't just veer, it pulled a ninety-degree shift in course, spearing toward us like a mile-wide ICBM. It's right outside my window, blocking out the world, black as night, the destructive finger of a vengeful god. I can see debris caught by the up-rushing vortex—not just sticks and rocks and bits of lawn detritus, I'm talking entire house roofs, car doors, barn doors. I watch it rip a hundred-foot-tall oak tree clean out of the ground, lift it, hurl it skyward, and then the massive tree is lost in the wild, whirling cyclonic demon.

The tip of the wedge scrapes across the ground and engulfs a house. I see the roof sucked off, tossed heavenward, lost.

I'm screaming now, trying not to, but losing it completely.

Terror is a fist in my throat, demanding release.

A car whips past our hood, airborne. Twisting. Tumbling. Hurtling.

I saw a face in that vehicle, a snatched glimpse as the airborne missile seared past.

Lock has the gas pedal floored. I feel our velocity as a reckless rush through the storm, pushed back in my seat as he accelerates. Thrown to the side as he jerks the wheel around something in the road—an entire cow, lifted, tossed, and slammed down in the center of the road, turned into a pile of meat and gore. I scream as we fishtail, rock onto two wheels, wind battering at us, trying to push us over. Somehow, impossibly, Lock spins the wheel just right, we crash down onto four wheels, and then he guns the engine, sending us jolting forward, the twisting wall of hell shredding trees and houses and fences and livestock a mere thousand feet away. I can't hear anything except the deafening. The chunk of a house, a corner, a bit of roof, and torn stubs of studs, crashes into the road twenty feet in front of us, shattering into splinters, and then the two-hundred-plus miles per hour winds hurls those studs and spars and shingles at us like baseballs from a pitcher's hand. A two-by-four flies directly at us end over end. There's nothing we can do to stop it, or avoid it. Lock slams on the brakes, throwing us forward into the dashboard, and then we shrink against our respective doors, ducking and covering our faces as the two-by-four spears through the windshield directly between us.

I can't breathe, can't cry, can't scream. Can't even hyperventilate. The two-by-four would have smashed my skull into fragments if I'd ducked a split second later. Lock has us moving again, slewing around the remnants of the house.

The twister is on an intercept course with us. Moving faster than belief can credit. Slinging debris in every direction and sucking up more as it swallows a barn, and then the farmhouse, and then flattens and shreds a thousand acres of wheat in minutes.

The twister veers again, and now Lock jerks the wheel around again, sending us skidding and stuttering sideways on the highway, then down the ditch and into a field. The seatbelt goes taut, nearly crushing my chest as it tightens, and we jounce and crunch and lurch across the field, hillocks sending us skyward, wheat slapping the hood.

I crane my head to watch our rear end: the twister seems to be following us with a sentience, matching our every move, determined to catch us and swallow us. We're angling across the field, nowhere to go now except further across the field, thousands of acres of wheat extending away from us in all directions. I keep watching, and maybe it's my imagination, but the funnel seems smaller, narrower, thinner. Still deadly and following us, but getting ready to rope out, hopefully.

We've gained some distance, finally. Debris is no longer falling and crashing all around us, but the noise is still a painfully loud roar, and the rain and hail is still torrential.

I can breathe, now, but it hurts. Something hurts. I don't want to look to see why, or what. Not yet.

I swivel in my seat and see the twister spinning and skirling, half its original size now, more of a true funnel than a wedge. It jumps and hops, leaping half a mile at a time, slamming down to send dirt and sod and debris flying in an explosion, carving this way and that erratically, thinning with every passing second.

And then, abruptly, it's gone.

Lock is utterly focused, so he doesn't notice. Just keeps driving across the field, both fists white-knuckled on the wheel, brow furrowed.

I touch his arm. "Lock. Stop. It's gone." My voice is hoarse, quiet.

"It's gone?" He slows, scans the horizon behind us.

"It roped out finally."

He stops the truck. There's a moment of silence as Lock sits upright, still gripping the wheel, sucking in deep, gusting breaths, and then he slowly peels his hands off the wheel, one finger at a time. They're shaking, trembling.

There's a two-by-four between us. Lock shoves it back through the hole in the windshield, and it falls onto the hood with a loud thump. And then he unbuckles his seatbelt, unbuckles mine, and hauls me bodily across the console to sit on his lap, wedged between his big, hard, hot, wet body and the steering wheel. He cradles my head against his chest, breathing hard.

I stiffen, fighting how right this feels, how comforting his arms feel. But I can't help giving in to it. I just can't help it.

"Jesus." Lock's voice is a stunned rumble. "Just... *Jesus.*"

"Yeah."

"I've been through hurricanes and typhoons. I've jumped out of airplanes. I've jumped off cliffs. I've climbed Kilimanjaro and Everest. I swam with sharks once, not on purpose, and not in a cage. They just... appeared, swimming around me. And *that*...was easily the scariest fucking thing I've ever experienced."

"I've been shot at. I watched a truck full of soldiers meant to be protecting our crew of doctors get blown up by an RPG. I was on ground zero of the Haiti earthquake. And this was easily the scariest thing *I've* ever experienced."

Lock finally releases me from the crushing death grip. Slings open his door and helps us both out of the truck and onto our feet, lets Utah hop out and trot off to do her business. We stand in the wheat field, staring back at what had been a thriving small-town farm community. There is nothing left.

Ruins.

Trees lying across the road. Cars on their roofs in the fields, or standing on end against crumbling walls. Two-by-fours speared into concrete. Smoke skirls and whips skyward, a thick black column, something burning.

"Jesus," Lock says again. "There's just...nothing left."

"We have to go help." I hate the feeling in my gut: Fear. Loathing. Dread. I know what I have to do, and I'm terrified to do it. "There's going to be hurt people. I have to go help them."

Lock nods, a grim expression on his face. "Yeah. Let's go."

"What are you going to do?"

He frowns at me. "Whatever I can. Whatever I have to."

I want to spew venom at him, because for some reason my anger at him chooses this moment to rise up in my gorge like vomit, hot and acidic. But I don't say anything. I choke it down, turn away, skirt the hood and climb into the cab. I have to work to hide the pain as I do so, because that two-by-four didn't entirely miss me. It grazed my ribs. I can feel the damage, and I know I'm bleeding, but not badly. Nothing's broken or bruised. I got lucky. And I don't have the will to deal with Lock trying to macho me out of doing what I know I have to do.

He must see something in my expression, though, because when he climbs back behind the wheel, he glances at me. "You seem surprised that I'd be willing to help."

"Seems to me you're better at running away than sticking around to do what needs doing." Well damn, there goes my plan to keep my vitriol to myself.

"Wow. Okay." He rubs his forehead with the knuckle of his forefinger as he trundles us back across the field to the main road. "I guess I deserved that."

"Guess you did."

"Niall—"

I hold up a hand. "I can't have this conversation with you right now. I need to focus on the job, now. I'll give you a chance to explain yourself later, if there's anything to explain. But I can't deal with you right now. I just can't. I need supplies, and I need to find a place to set up triage."

Lock doesn't answer right away. Or at all, really. He drives carefully around debris, going off road as much as he stays on the road. Pulls into the parking lot of the strip mall and stops in front of the doctor's office. The main door is ripped off its hinges, the glass smashed across the sidewalk. Papers are scattered in the hallway, tumbling across the parking lot, drifting like absurd flakes of snow. Part of the roof of the strip mall is gone, nowhere to be seen. We both get out of the truck and make our way carefully into the office. The power is off, obviously, for the whole town most likely. But with the roof gone, we can still see. Desks have been hurled against the walls, blocking doorways. A rolling desk chair is lodged in the drywall, up near the roofline.

"Hello?" Lock calls out. "Anybody here?"

"H-hello?" a small, tentative female voice calls out. "In here. The door is jammed."

Lock locates the source of the voice—it's coming from a closet of some kind. The doorframe itself is twisted, wedging the door shut. "Get back as far as you can. I'm going to try and break it down."

"We're all sort of wedged in here," the voice responds, "so we can't go very far."

Lock throws his shoulder against the door, and it cracks, but holds. He kicks underneath the handle, once, twice, three times, and the door finally splinters enough near the latch mechanism that he can jerk it back toward himself. He gets it open enough to be able to grab the edge of the door and yank it off. Half a dozen women are huddled in the janitor's closet with the brooms and mops and cleaning supplies, tear tracks on their faces, clinging to each other.

"Is anyone hurt?" I ask, as they file out.

They all shake their heads. "No," one woman says. "We're all fine. Shaken up, but fine."

Once they emerge from the closet, they all sort of just stumble to a stop, stunned at the damage.

"God, would you look at this?" a nurse says, shaking her head, staring around, her voice thick, tearing up. "It's just...ruined."

"The whole town is like this," Lock says. "You're lucky this building is standing at all. Some are just gone."

"God...it just came out of nowhere," the same woman says.

Another woman, wearing business casual underneath a lab coat—making her the doctor or PA—straightens, clears her throat. "We should go out there and start helping."

"That's why we're here," I say. "I'm a triage nurse. I need some supplies. Bandages, forceps, needles, stuff like that. I need to set up somewhere."

"We'll stick with you, then," she says. "Let's gather supplies. Melanie, get all the bandages, tape, and packing gauze you can find. Lucy, pain killers. I don't think we have any morphine, but see what else you can find. Elle, suturing supplies. Clear this office out, ladies. I have a feeling we're going to need everything we can get."

The nurses scatter, and begin digging through the wreckage to find the necessary supplies.

"There's not going to be enough," I say. "I used to work with Doctors Without Borders. I've seen plenty of natural disasters. And this one…this is bad."

"I have a feeling you're right," she says, and then extends her hand. "I'm Greta, by the way, the physician's assistant."

I shake her hand. "Niall."

"I'm Lock." He gestures outside. "I'm going to back the truck up to the door. We can load up and I'll help you guys find a good spot."

It doesn't take long to strip the wrecked office of medical gear. It's not much, not enough, but it's a start. Hopefully we'll have backup in the form of FEMA or something before long. Lock carts the full boxes and crates to the truck, stacks them in the bed, and then helps the nurses up into the bed, one by one. Utah has her head hanging out her window, which Lock must have opened at some point. Now that the storm is gone, it's heating up, and quick.

Once we're all loaded, Lock heads toward town. The main street is strewn with rubble, impassable after a certain point. One entire building, what had once been the diner, is completely gone, while the building next to it seems relatively untouched. The gas station and drug stores are still standing, but the auto garage, supermarket, and liquor stores are all flattened. The residential areas and the farms beyond, however, seem to have been the hardest hit. Houses are gone. Trees are torn away at the roots, toppled over. Cars are smashed, tossed, crushed. Smoke flutters skyward. The scent of leaking natural gas fills the air.

I point at the churchyard. "There. The church." I glance at Lock. "I'll need tents. Makeshift, if necessary, just tarps and poles. Whatever you can manage."

"How many and how big?" he asks.

I shrug. "Probably...three? Intake, surgery, and recovery. A fourth, for supplies, water, food. Let's make this the hub of the recovery efforts. Somewhere for people to gather. In situations like this people need to feel like someone is in charge, like there's a headquarters."

He nods. "Got it." He jolts up over the curb, not bothering with the parking lot, and pulls to a stop in the center of the yard. The nurses immediately set to work unloading the supplies from the truck, and I work with them, sorting what we have and doing an inventory. Lock hops into his truck, leaves the churchyard, and drives down the street to the hardware store. I focus on the job at hand. People will be arriving soon.

My stomach is in my throat. I'm not ready for this. I don't want to do this. I'm going to be looking for Ollie the entire time, and he won't be there.

I have to do this.

Ollie is gone.

This is what I do, and I'm good at it.

I can do this.

Lock is here. Lock is capable.

I stifle a sob, though, because my pep talk can only do so much.

Lock is still in the hardware store when the first person arrives, an older woman with a nasty gash on her forehead and a shard of wood through her bicep. Greta helps her sit down on the grass. I untie my hair from the ponytail, shake it free, braid it behind my head as quickly as I can, then I tug on a pair of rubber gloves. I pull a wad of the gloves out of the box and shove as many as I can into my back pockets.

I kneel over the woman, stanch the bleeding on her head first, and then get a bandage on it. I examine the wound on her bicep. The shard of wood is a good foot or so long, a couple inches thick, jagged, as sharply pointed as a knife. Straight through her arm, protruding from her tricep.

Greta does her best to soothe the woman as I remove the shard. We don't have any morphine, so the process is slow and excruciating. She screams, writhes off the grass as I pull the shard free. That, unfortunately, was the easy part. Now I have to search the interior of the wound for splinters.

I feel shade go up overhead, providing relief from the heat, but I don't spare a glance. It's Lock, I know, erecting a tent. More of an awning, really, just a tarp and some poles staked into the ground, kept taut with some lines. He has it up quickly, efficiently.

I can't breathe for the tension. For the desire to glance around me, looking for Ollie. He should be here, tending to victims.

But he's not.

It's just me.

I feel Lock behind me. When I finish with the woman, I rise to my feet and turn to face him. He hands me a bottle of water.

"You'll need tables, probably," he says. "I spoke to the pastor of the church here, and he's going to bring some out."

"How bad is it out there?"

He winces. "It's bad. Really bad. Some of the older fellas are going to take over setting up the tents here. I'm going to start looking for people."

"Be careful," I say, because I can't help myself.

I'm still mad at him, but beneath that lies a thick, undeniable layer of need and affection, and tenderness.

He wipes the sweat off his face, nods at me. "I'll be okay. I'll be checking in when I bring people up here. Let me know if you need anything."

A four-wheeler arrives just then, towing a slab of corrugated tin, on which are several bodies, all of which are injured. There's no more time for talk, then. Lock, looking pale and shaken, helps the driver of the four-wheeler lift a victim off the piece of tin and onto a table, which the pastor just finished setting up. Another pair of women arrive from the church, carrying a long folding table between them. They plop it into place, rack open the legs, and tip it upright. Immediately, another injured person is set onto it.

The nurses scurry into motion, assessing, bandaging the more minor wounds.

I see Lock lurch to his truck, pull open the door, lean into the opening, bracing himself. Heaving.

The man I'm working on doesn't look good. I

don't think he'll make it. A wall fell on him, crushing his chest, turning his torso into a gory, mangled mess. He's barely breathing, and those breaths are labored and whistling. It's not pretty, so it's unsurprising Lock would vomit at the sight.

He's got blood on his shirt. On his hands.

He glances back at me, and I try to give him an encouraging look—he can do this; it will be okay.

He nods, straightens. He visibly strengthens himself. Hops into his truck, and then he's gone, heading into the residential section.

I lose track of time after that.

Someone brings in another few crates of supplies at some point, flats of water bottles, more bandages, more medical tape, thread, needles, hemostats, even some morphine ampoules. I see Lock every now and then, but only in passing. Every time I see him, he's dirtier. Blood is caked on his shirt, making it dark and stiff. Same thing with his shorts. He's wearing yellow leather work gloves, has a green and white bandana tied around his neck, which he can tug up over his mouth and nose if need be.

People are pouring in, brought in by truck and off-road vehicle, carried, walking on foot, however they can get here. There's a fire truck somewhere, ambulances finally. A swarm of cop cars.

The paramedics find me. Somehow, I've been left

in charge, because everyone seems to find me and ask for directions. It's too much, too much. But I can't stop. I can't shirk it off.

I keep seeing Ollie. A tall man with black hair going gray at the temples...he looks just like Ollie from behind. And then he turns, and it's not him. Not my Ollie. And my heart breaks all over again.

Ollie...god, Oliver. How do I do this without you? I don't know how. But I have to.

No thoughts. No feelings.

I try to shut it all down, push it all down. Numb. Efficient. Wound to wound, patient to patient. Assess, treat, move on—assess, treat, move on. Repeat, and repeat, and repeat.

Repeat.

Hours go by and I have no idea what time it is.

Someone sets up klieg lights, citronella torches against the mosquitos.

I'm exhausted. My hands ache from suturing and bandaging and compressing.

I've lost count of how many I've lost.

Lost count of how many I've saved.

They just keep pouring in.

I heard talk between treating one victim and another that the tornado hit another town a few miles away first, before hitting this one. Apparently, it was flattened even more completely, so those residents are being brought here.

I have no knowledge of anything beyond the tent. I see Lock a few times. Dirtier and dirtier. His face above the bandana is nearly black with dirt and grime. His eyes find me, and we exchange a long look.

I feel tears boiling inside me, deep down. But I shove them away. No time for that.

Lock sees it, though. He nudges the bottom of his chin, tipping his head up. A gesture to me: *keep your chin up.*

I'm trying. Fuck, I'm trying.

Everyone else shines out but me

I DON'T KNOW WHICH FUCKING WAY IS UP ANYMORE.

I'm beyond exhausted, but I have a new appreciation for the work that disaster relief professionals like Niall do on a regular basis. There's no way to describe it, and there's no way to describe how utterly done I am. I've set up tents, transported the injured and the dying, jury-rigged plumbing and electrical systems, and about a million other things. I've been around this town so much I know it like the back of my hand.

But I'm not done.

That much is obvious.

There are still houses and buildings to be cleared, but at least there are plenty of emergency personnel on site now, professionals. Firefighters with gear. The electrical company is busy re-wiring the power lines. A wrecking crew showed up, hauling cars out of the way. An old farmer named Earl showed up with a bulldozer to push and haul heavy wreckage out of the way. Plenty of good ol' boys with pickups and tow chains. We move in teams from building to building, house to house, pick through it all, looking for bodies, dead or alive.

And there are a lot of both. I've never encountered this many dead bodies before, and I don't know how to handle it except to stay numb and do the job. Numb is easier said than achieved, though. When you see people crushed under walls and impaled by limbs of trees, you lose the capacity to stay numb after a while. Many, if not most, had shelters. And there was enough advance notice that the storm was coming that a lot made it into their shelters. But there's always the stubborn, the ignorant, the unlucky. The ones who couldn't, or wouldn't, take shelter.

Right now we're nearing the end of a street, on the second to last house. We've cleared the other side already, so when we're done on this side we'll turn the corner and start all over again.

We are trying to pull down a wall. I've managed to yank part of it away and a guy named Bill, on the other side, is pushing against it for all he's worth. I've been working with Bill for hours, now. Big dude, a few years younger than me. Faded green John Deere ball cap on, dirty blue jeans, Budweiser T-shirt, shaggy blond goatee. Strong as an ox, and just as silent. Utah is with us. She trots around, sniffing. Sometimes she'll paw at a spot, and usually there's someone under the rubble. Smart dog, she is. Not trained for this, but good at it nonetheless. We let the wall fall away with a crash, pull chunks of drywall away and toss them aside. Cinderblocks, bricks, and two-by-fours. Siding. This house is flooding, a water pipe having burst somewhere we can't find or reach yet. We clear the entryway to a bedroom, or what was a bedroom less than twenty-four hours ago. Shreds of posters, ripped bedding, a mattress lolling halfway over the destroyed portion of exterior wall. A dresser, clothes hanging out of the drawers, is toppled onto its side. Smashed TV.

Water trickles and pools and laps cold around my ankles. Fortunately, hours ago, I was able to borrow a pair of rugged, waterproof CAT workboots and some thick Carhartt socks from the ruins of the hardware store, so my feet are staying dry and warm for now. I've got a portable headlamp around my forehead, the kind of thing nighttime cyclists use to light their way.

The bedroom seems empty. The closet is just one of those shallow things with bi-fold doors. I peek inside, just to be sure.

We look through the kitchen. Bathroom. Another bedroom.

I hear shouts and then some banging. Utah barks, a high, sharp yip, scrabbles with her paws at a heap of bricks, shingles, and two-by-fours in front of a door to the basement. I call for Bill who lumbers over to where I'm standing. The door is completely blocked by rubble. Chunks of roof, piles of cinder-block. There's too much here to move by hand.

"I'll go find Earl with the 'dozer," I say.

Bill just nods, grabbing cinderblocks in each hand and tossing them aside, grunting—which is the most I've heard from him since we started working together. I run off and find Earl with his bulldozer just a few doors down, condensing a pile of rubble between what had been two houses.

"Earl! Need a hand over here," I shout.

Earl just waves, finishes what he's doing, and then swivels the big machine in a circle and trundles noisily toward me. I hop up onto the tread as he stops next to me.

"Got a blocked basement doorway. Big piece of roof I need you to move so we can get down there. I hear voices."

Earl gestures behind his seat with a jerk of his thumb. "Get that there chain around the piece you need moved. Get it fixed on there good."

"Got it."

I grab the chain, which is long and heavy as hell, and it's got a thick hook on the end. It's grimy with grease, brown with age. I loop the chain around a large chunk of the roof, secure the hook back around onto the chain, and then secure the end of it to the plow of the 'dozer.

I yell for Bill to stand clear, and then give Earl the go-ahead. The machine beeps loudly as it reverses, and the massive engine groans as Earl applies the throttle. The piece of roof grinds and scrapes and shudders, and then slowly drops down as Earl hauls it backward. As soon as it's clear of the footprint of the home, I unhook the chain, coil it, and pile it back in place behind Earl's seat.

By this time, Bill is breathing heavily and has the pile of cinderblock mostly cleared. I lend a hand and we can finally get the door open. It almost comes free with a good yank, but it is still stuck shut. Bill, impatient, rips the hinges right out of the frame with one big heave, and tosses the door aside.

We shout down the stairs, hear voices call back, panicked, terrified, screaming. Utah is barking like mad.

"We've got 'em, girl. Good job. Good girl, Utah." I pat her head, and then tell her to sit. She immediately quiets, sits on her haunches and watches us.

I've got a pocket LED flashlight, which I shine

down into the darkness of the basement; the beam reflects off rippling water, and then illuminates a woman's face, a man, two children who are no more than ten or twelve years old, a boy and a girl. Huddling on the steps, holding onto ceiling beams and exposed pipes, running out of air and out of space as the basement fills with water from the burst pipe.

"Jesus," I breathe, and then call out to them. "Swim this way. We've got you!"

They haul themselves toward the doorway. I grab a hand and pull hard. It's the mother, sputtering, whimpering, her arm locked in a death-grip around her daughter. She pushes her daughter up to me first, splashing as she fights to find the stair treads in the frigid, murky water. I hook an arm around the girl's middle and haul her bodily up and out. Bill takes her and sets her on her feet. Someone, Earl probably, has caught on that we've found survivors, and now there's someone here to take the girl, wrap a towel around her and speak to her in soothing tones. I pull the mom up and out, and repeat the process for the dad and son.

As all four are piled into the bed of a pickup they slump back with relief, shivering and huddling together, weeping, clinging to each other. The pickup flashes its brights as a signal, and then bumps down the curb to the street and away to HQ.

Bill and I are trudging heavily to the next house when a two-ton truck, painted in brown and green camo, full of National Guardsmen, squeals to a noisy stop. The rear gate slams open, and young, fresh-faced Guardsmen disgorge and spread out. A middle-aged man emerges from the passenger side of the cab, sees Bill and me, and makes a beeline for us.

"Lieutenant Brian Markson," he announces, warily eyeing Utah, who is standing at my side. "National Guard. You boys part of the recovery effort?"

Bill and I exchange glances. No shit, bro. We're both filthy, obviously exhausted, wearing work gloves and headlamps and face masks—hours ago someone handed us proper surgical face masks, the sort surgeons wear, and I got rid of my bandana. So...what else would we be?

Neither of us answers. We're too damned tired.

The lieutenant doesn't seem to notice our lack of response, or else he assumes it's an affirmative. "We'll take over from here, gentlemen. You looked peaked. Hit the HQ and get some grub, there's a food station set up."

Yeah, I know—I helped set it up. Back when it was still broad daylight and it didn't hurt to be awake.

"Which way is it?" I ask. "I'm not from around here, and I'm so tired I can't remember."

Bill nudges me with an elbow, grunts and gestures—the klieg lights around the HQ are visible from here, a clear beacon.

"Oh. Right." I try to laugh it off, but nothing's funny anymore. I try to take a step, but I trip and almost fall.

Bill's massive hand closes around my elbow, and he keeps me upright.

"Thanks," I mumble.

I get another grunt in reply. Dude is seriously taking taciturn to a whole new level, in that he has literally not spoken a single word in something like six hours. But he's a workhorse, tireless, and powerful. A good man to have at your side in this kind of situation. Or any, really, except those that might require even a minimal level of verbosity.

It's not far from where we are to the HQ, a mile at most, maybe a mile and a half. But getting there feels like running a marathon, each step requiring concentration and determination, and the distance never seems to get any shorter. Even Bill seems to be dragging, his big, heavy feet plodding even more loudly against the asphalt of the road. We're almost out of the residential area. Passing between the ruins of two houses, which have already been cleared. Or so we thought.

Bill halts abruptly and flings his huge arm against my chest, barring my way. He holds a finger to his lips, cocks his head, listening. I strain to hear. It's not silent, not by a long shot. The 'dozer groans and beeps in the distance, voices shout, rubble and wreckage crunches and grinds. But I hear it, too. A nearly inaudible mewling sound. A little girl, maybe, buried somewhere.

Despite our fatigue, we strain, trying to locate where the sound is coming from.

"Hello?" I call out. "We hear you. Where are you?"

The mewling gets louder, but there are no words. Just...louder whimpers. My gut sinks. Utah goes into a mad barking frenzy again, the high sharp bark she uses when she's trying to communicate something. She trots to a pile of wreckage, the ruins of an out-building of some kind, a barn or a shed. Tin and wood and old bricks, all jumbled together in a jagged heap. The sound is coming from deep inside the pile. Bill, suddenly energized, attacks the rubble with renewed zeal, tossing bricks and two-by-fours aside like so many handfuls of confetti. Utah is barking like crazy and I go to work beside Bill, and soon we have the top of the heap exposed, the start of a hole. The mewling is louder, now. I angle my headlamp, shine my flashlight down the hole. This was a sizable structure—the heap of rubble is a good twenty or thirty feet across, piled some eight or ten feet high. I'm up on top, peering down. The LED beam slides across a little leg. A scrap of blue fabric. A jelly shoe, the kind little girls have worn for decades.

"Hey there, honey," I call down, trying to sound comforting. Not my strongest suit, being tender and comforting. "I'm coming down, okay?"

A low, coughing moan echoes in response. I tug my face mask into place against the swirling dust and examine the hole. Decent sized pocket created by the way the wreckage fell, just enough space for a little body. I won't fit, but I've got to find a way to get down there. I grip the edges of the opening, a jagged two-by-four, some cinderblocks, a scrap of tin roof, and lower myself down carefully. My feet touch something relatively solid, and I slowly let my weight down, making sure the heap won't shift or give. I have to crouch, as the space is maybe four feet high and less than three feet across. By a sheer miracle of luck, the tiny space protected this little girl. She's young. Five? Six? Fine blond hair, matted with blood, pale skin. Blue sundress with white flowers on it. Torn, dirty, bloody. One foot bare, one foot with a pink jelly shoe on. She's curled up, pinned under a slab of tin roof, the whole weight on her right arm and part of her right leg.

She's facing me. Curled oddly.

I crouch and shuffle closer to her, and brush the

hair out of her eyes. Blue eyes, terrified, agonized, weak. Fluttering. Searching me.

"Hey, I'm Lock. I'm gonna get you out of here, okay?"

"Unnnhhh." She blinks hard, a tear trickles out. "Stuck...." She's so weak she can barely get the word out.

"I know. But I'm gonna get you free, okay? You'll be okay." I examine her more closely, looking closely at the rubble pinning her. "Can you wiggle your toes and fingers okay?"

She moves her fingers, and I watch her toes. No damage to her spine that I can see. I'm worried if I shift the pieces pinning the girl, the whole pile will shift with it. Burying us both, maybe. But she's fading fast so I have no choice.

I yell up to Bill who's standing at the opening looking down, helpless. With tacit understanding, I know he will stay there to assist any way he can. Not much for him to do, yet, though. This hole barely accommodates me.

I crouch over the girl, put my back against the tin, widen my stance, angle my toes out, rock back on my heels, spine straight—like I'm going to do a deadlift.

PUSH.

The heap on my back groans and grinds. It shifts

slightly…but holds. The girl moans in agony as the weight eases off her, and she tries to move, but she's too weak. She can't move, and I can't hold the pile and grab her at the same time. I can't hold this for long, it's hundreds of pounds, probably more. I try to reach and stretch, while keeping the load steady on my back. Teeth clenched, I grunt as I manage to snag her sleeve, and get a grip on the fabric. I tug and, at the same time, push up as hard as I can to further reduce the load off her. She seems to understand what I'm trying to do, and using all her strength, she wiggles, scrabbles, crying, her right arm limp and mangled. God, my throat clenches. She's so little. But she's moving. Inch by inch.

"That's it, honey. A little more. Just a few more inches, okay? You can make it." I'm shaking with the effort of maintaining my stance and supporting the rubble. I hurt like hell.

She's got something clutched to her chest, but I can't see what it is. It looks like something she's protecting. I'm close to giving out, but then the girl is finally out far enough. I sink slowly to my knees, letting the load settle. I'm gasping for air, and the sweat is pouring off me in the darkness. But I can't allow myself to rest for long.

"Come on, sweetheart. Let's get you out of here."

I scoop her up in my arms, mindful of her injuries. She wiggles in my hold. "Miss Molly!"

I glance down to where she'd been lying, and instead of what I expect to see—a doll or stuffed animal or something—there's a tiny ball of fur, a little calico kitten. Jesus. Cats. Fucking hate cats. But the girl is whining, reaching, and I need to get her out of here.

"I'll get Miss Molly," I promise the girl. "But I need to get you out of here right now. You need to see a doctor, okay? You're gonna go see my friend, Mr. Bill, okay?"

She nods weakly against my chest, going limp now that she's assured I'll rescue her kitten, too. Bill is at the hole opening, reaching down with both hands. He wraps his big paws around the little girl's waist and lifts her free. I hear and feel his weight sliding slowly down the pile outside. I scoop the kitten in my hands—still warm, thank god. It's shaking, curled into a tight ball, but she doesn't fight me, lets me set her outside the hole so I can climb free myself, and then I descend the heap with the kitten tucked under my arm.

Bill has the girl in his arms. She's tinier than belief can credit, especially in Bill's burly, brawny embrace. She's blinking, fighting to stay conscious. There's blood caked on her temple, and I'm worried about a concussion, or worse.

"Hey, look who I have." I lift the kitten in front of the girl's face. "Miss Molly, safe and sound."

"Molly…" Shit, her voice is so weak. So weak. My gut is twisting. I glance at Bill, whose expression is tight, pinched.

"What's your name, honey? Can you stay awake and tell me?" I nod at Bill, and we move as fast as we dare toward the klieg lights.

"T-Tori," she murmurs.

"We've got doctors real close, okay? I just need you to keep your eyes open for me. Just stay awake a little longer. Can you do that for me?"

"I'm tired."

"I know. You'll get to rest soon, I promise. You're gonna be okay. You're gonna be just fine."

"Hurts." She says this with tears in her eyes. "It hurts lots."

"I know, sweetie. We'll fix that, too."

Bill is nearly running, now. Long strides across lawns and parking lots, and over parking pylons and between heaps of rubble. I keep pace, and keep a running dialogue with the girl, asking questions, trying to keep her talking but only getting weak, monosyllabic answers. The kitten is curled in the crook of my arm like a tiny, furry football.

And then we're on the main road, Bill, Utah, and me, crossing the street, jogging toward the welter of activity and the glare of lights that is the HQ. There are half a dozen tents, now. Generators clatter with the rumble of diesel motors. Voices shout, orders are called out. It's controlled pandemonium. There are moans of pain. People in camo, civilians in jeans and T-shirts, nurses in scrubs, doctors in aprons.

Utah peels away from me, finds my truck where it's parked in the grass, hops up into the bed, curls up, head on her paws, and falls asleep immediately. She's earned it, that dog has.

It takes me less than ten seconds to find Niall in the midst of the madness. Her hair is tied back in a thick braid, but many wisps have escaped to paste against her cheek and temple. She's still wearing her cut-off jean shorts, the ends frayed into white strings and the orange tank top she'd been wearing when she stumbled into the gas station. At some point she found or was given a pair of white Keds. Once-white Keds, that is. They're now filthy from the churned-up grass and dirt under foot, and stained reddish-brown. She's got an apron on, the kind line cooks wear, looped over her neck and tied around her waist. It's covered in red, layers of shades of red ranging from dark old rust to bright new crimson. Her forearms are stained red, as well. Her hands are clean, but I see she's pulling a new pair of rubber gloves from her back pocket, snapping them on with expert, experienced speed. She's bend-ing over a table, speaking in low, quick tones to the paramedic beside her. They're hovering over an older man with white hair. He's bleeding from the stomach, and a gash to his thigh.

Niall presses a wadded-up bed sheet against the man's stomach, and the white cloth quickly soaks up the gore and turns red. The paramedic is suturing the man's thigh wound with unbelievable speed. Niall pulls the sheet away, tosses it to the ground at her feet. The paramedic jabs an ampoule into the patient's uninjured thigh, quieting his screams of pain. I'd barely registered the screams, honestly. There's so much noise, so many cries of pain and groans of agony that one more sound didn't register.

But now it does.

And it's gut-wrenching.

We move through the crowd, dodging people.

A paramedic stops us. "Over there. There's an open table." He points to the other side of the tent.

We get the girl onto the table and lay her down carefully. The paramedic is already at work, shining a penlight into her eyes, examining her head wound, her leg, her arm. He raises a hand without looking away from the girl.

"ASSIST!" he shouts, and another man, this one dressed in the camo of a National Guard corpsman, jogs over.

We're shoved aside, Bill and I, as the medics go to work.

Neither of us seems inclined to move away. We just watch as the two men converse while dressing wounds, spitting medical terminology and orders at each other, working in practiced concert. Someone appears beside the table with an IV line and a bag of clear fluid. The corpsman inserts the needle in Tori's left arm, tapes it in place, holds the bag up, but seems to need both hands, looking around for someone to take the bag. I step in, take the bag, hold it up, and the corpsman goes back to working on Tori's right leg.

"She's lost too much blood," the paramedic says.

I want to argue, but don't.

I just hold the bag and meet Tori's glazed gaze. "Tori, honey. How old is Miss Molly?"

"T-t-t-ten....weeks."

The corpsman eyes me. "Keep her talkin', man. Keep her fightin'."

I stand there, asking any question I can think of—except questions about her family. I don't know the situation there; don't know if I want to know.

Then, I feel her. Niall. Moving in beside the paramedic standing at Tori's head. She examines the head wound. Glancing at me. Calling for an IV pole. Ignoring me as she looks over Tori's leg and arm. They aren't good. I know that much. I haven't looked too closely, but I know there are breaks in the bones.

I don't know how long Niall, the corpsman, and the paramedic work, or how long I remain, even after the IV pole arrives and I don't need to stand there anymore. I pulled Tori out of the wreckage. I know her name. I know she loves kitties and puppies, but kitties even more. I know she's six years old, and in first grade. Her favorite color is pink. Her favorite show is something called *P.J. Masks.* She likes macaroni and cheese, and PB and J. I know she knows how to ride a bike, but only with training wheels.

My throat is thick. My chest aches. My eyes burn.

I feel a hand on my arm. I look away from Tori and find Niall staring up at me.

"We've done all we can," she murmurs. "Now she has to do the rest on her own."

"Will she…will she be okay?" I hear myself ask.

Niall nods. "I think so. The wound to her head is pretty bad, but you kept her awake, so I'm not as worried about the concussion. She's lost a lot of blood, that's what's most worrying. But I think she'll make it."

"Good," I manage. But that's all I can get out.

Embarrassingly, I feel close to a nervous, weepy breakdown. I'm about to start bawling like a little baby.

I clear my throat, blink hard—against both the

tears and the visions of the bodies I've seen today. "Good work. I—shit."

I have to turn away, and get out of the tent, out from under the blaze of the kliegs. Into the shadows. Find some wreckage, shelter in the lee of a still-standing wall. Sit on a pile of rubble and shake. Tremble. Feel vomit surge against my teeth, hot, bitter, acidic. My eyes burn, leaking hot salty tears. Fucking crying. Jesus. But I can't stop it. My shoulders heave, and I'm fighting the breakdown with everything I have. I can't keep the bile back, and I bend at the waist, head between my knees, and let it stream out between my lips into the dirt at my feet. I spit. Gasp for air.

I feel her again. Sitting beside me, hand on my back. "Quit fighting it, Lock. After a day like today, you've earned it. Nothing wrong with letting it out. No one will think less of you for it, I swear. Least of all me."

I can't fight it. My shoulders shake, and I'm crying silently. Niall just smooths her hand in circles on my back, pulls my hair loose of the ponytail and strokes her fingers through it. She doesn't say anything, because she knows from experience there's nothing to say.

When I'm finally able to exert some control, able to breathe and sit up and wipe my eyes, I turn to look at Niall. She's filthy. Still wearing the blood-covered apron. Clean hands, rubber gloves abandoned. Pale. Circles under her eyes, staring skyward at the stars. Into the distance, into memory.

"You used to do this every day, didn't you?" I ask.

She has her knees drawn up, arms crossed on her kneecaps. She drops her head between her arms, nodding sluggishly. "Worse than this."

I can't even fathom what could be worse. "How could it get worse than this?"

She looks up and laughs a bitter bark. "This was a natural disaster. No one *did* this. It was quick, a few minutes of Mother Nature's violence, and then it's over and you clean up. Tend to the wounded, sort the dead, and start organizing the mess. Not minimizing the horror of this, but...compared to what I've seen? This was..." She shakes her head, trailing off, hangs her head once more. Raises her head, passes a hand over her face.

"I was stationed in Africa. The Central African Republic. There was a civil war. One tribe against another. Nothing new, but messy as hell all the same. That was...god...so fucking awful. We'd get trucks full of bodies. Two-tons, like those the guardsmen came in, but piled with bodies. Missing limbs, stomachs ripped open, guts falling out. Brains leaking out of bullet holes. Just...bodies. And it's not just the bodies that's so terrible, it's knowing people are doing this to each other... *on purpose*. Over a difference in beliefs. Gunning each other down. Setting off car bombs. Pipe bombs. Leveling entire villages. Killing pregnant women and children. Raping and slaughtering everyone. Just...massacre. And we'd get them all, half-dead, already dead, dying. We'd spend thirty, forty hours at a time, tending to them. Truckload after truckload of bodies to fix."

"Jesus Christ, Niall." I'm speechless, trying and failing to understand what she's witnessed.

A shrug. "It's what I was good at. I never froze, never panicked, never puked. It helped that I was an ER nurse in LA first. I had experience with that kind of scenario. But nothing can really prepare you for dealing with the massacre of an entire village." A deep breath. "I had Ollie. He was my rock. No matter how gnarly it got, he was there. He was strong. I could just...look at him, and know it was going to be okay. Even when it wasn't okay, it'd be okay. As long as Ollie was there." She sniffles. Coughs. Breathes in deeply, lets it out with a shudder. "Today was...the hardest thing I've ever done. Doing it without Ollie...I kept looking for him. I kept *seeing* him. It's the first time since he died that I've done trauma work."

The only thing I can do is wrap my arm around her waist and pull her closer to me. She hisses as I tug at her, wincing away from my hand. It's not as if she doesn't want me to touch her, but more as if she's hurting.

"What's wrong?" I ask. "Are you hurt?"

She seems to realize for the first time that she's still wearing the apron. She unties it, tosses it aside. Then she lifts her shirt up, revealing her ribs, baring the bottom edge of her bra...and a wicked bruise along her side, along with a wide, deep cut across the edge of her ribcage, crusted over with dried, scabbing blood.

"Holy shit, Niall! When the hell did that happen?"

She drops the shirt, twists, rotates, stretches. "When the two-by-four went through the windshield, it didn't entirely miss me."

I feel faint with...a complicated mix of emotions. Don't know what they are, or what their names are, but they are unpleasant, and powerful. "Why the hell didn't you say something?"

I get a glare from Niall. "What could you have done? I'm a trained medical professional, Lock. I knew I was fine. It hurt, but I was fine, and there's not much to be done for this kind of thing anyway. And if I'd told you about it, you'd have gotten all macho-overprotective and tried to make me stay in the truck or some shit. I didn't have time to be hurt. I had a job to do, so I did it. That's why I didn't tell you."

I waver, hesitate. She's right. I would have…well, done exactly what she said. And now, looking back, I'm realizing how incredibly tough she is. She worked, god, I don't even know how many hours nonstop, on her feet, with a nasty injury. Never said a word, just dealt with it, and got the job done.

I feel so inadequate around her, sometimes. She's just so damn…*tough*.

"Fuck." I wipe my face with both hands. "You're something else, Niall."

"Not really."

I take her hand. Squeeze. "Yes, you are. You never hesitated. Even hurt, you dove in and took charge. Fixed everyone who came through that tent. You're amazing."

She eyes me. "You did the same thing, Lock. You stepped up. You saved that little girl. I heard about what you did. Went into that hole after her, got her free, and even saved her cat."

"I just did what had to be done."

"That's all heroism is, Lock. Doing what has to be done."

I shake my head forcefully. "Don't say that. Not about me. I'm not…that. I don't even want to say the word. You're a hero. Oliver was a hero. Me? I'm…not. Don't know what I am, but I'm not…that."

She turns toward me, her knees bumping mine.

"You don't give yourself enough credit, Lock. You're a better, stronger man than you think you are."

I don't know how to answer that. "I don't feel like it. I just…don't see it. At no point in my life have I ever been strong. Or courageous. I was selfish. Afraid. Not of dying, because that was inevitable. Or maybe I *was* afraid. I don't know. Maybe I was afraid of dying, even if I'd accepted it. But I wasn't strong or courageous about it. I ran from it. Lived on my sailboat and drank to get away from it. Did crazy shit, because I didn't care if I died in the process. I was gonna die anyway, so why not go skydiving or cliff diving? Why not race motorcycles and…all the crazy shit I did."

"Lock—"

"And then I got…" I tap my chest, over my heart…Oliver's heart— "this. And now I have a life to live all over again. And I don't know what the fuck to do with it."

"You live." Her eyes meet mine, blazing, piercing. Seeing into me, seeing my weakness, my fear. "You love. You do what needs doing."

"You make it sound so easy. Like, oh just do it! Life isn't a goddamn Nike commercial."

Niall shoots to her feet, paces away a few steps, then stops and turns to speak to me from where she is standing. "It's *not* easy, Lock. I mean, shit, if it was easy, I wouldn't be hiding out way the hell down here in fucking Ardmore, Oklahoma, taking temperatures and blood pressure, would I?"

I stand up now, too. Close two of the steps between us. "Niall—"

She stabs a finger at me, angry now. "You think you're the only one who doesn't know what to do with their life? You think you're the only one afraid of letting someone in? I lost my *husband*...I lost *myself*, Lock. He was—Ollie was—" She tips her head back, blinks hard, pinches at her tear ducts as if to physically prevent the tears from falling. "He was *everything* to me, Lock. He was all I had in this whole world. He died, and I couldn't cope with being alive and alone. I still don't know how to cope, but I want to *try*. I want to live again. *You* make me want to try." She says the last sentence so quietly I almost miss it.

She's closer, somehow. Her breasts are brushing against my chest, and she's staring up at me, eyes wide and the exact shade of green moss on brown tree bark. She's not blinking now, just breathing deeply, her tits swelling in that tight orange tank top. God, I just cannot help checking her out. Old habits die hard, I think. But fuck, is she beautiful. And the way she's looking at me? It hurts so goddamn bad, cuts me right to the bone, to the marrow, to my very soul, because there's...hope in her eyes. Belief. Desire.

All directed at me.

Hope that I can…what? Be the kind of man that could deserve a class act, tough-as-nails, hot as hell, hardworking, talented woman like Niall James?

Can I be that man?

Shit, I want to be. So bad, I want to be.

But am I? Can I become that?

Hell if I know.

"Me?" I ask, the word a whisper, a breath, disbelieving.

"You, Lachlan Montgomery. You."

"Why?" I scrape my hands through my hair and fight the onslaught of emotions, but they come out of my mouth anyway. "I'm empty, Niall. I'm no one. I have no career. No marketable skills. I walked away from you, shit, I *ran* away from the best thing I've ever experienced, from the most amazing woman I've ever met, because I'm afraid of my own emotions. Why would I of all people make you—make *you* want to live again? It doesn't make any sense, Niall."

"Because you're…*alive*, Lock. I don't know how else to put it. You're…vibrant. Vital. Larger than life. You're just so…*much*."

We are faced off, now. As if we've both run out of words, momentarily. And then Niall sways in place, blinking, as if she's been struck by sudden dizziness. I grab her; hold her close, mindful of her side.

"When was the last time you ate?" I ask her.

She shrugs in my embrace. "I have no idea. It's been a while."

I steady her and we walk back across the street, to a long tent erected over several picnic tables. There's a food and drink station set up on one end, with repurposed livestock water troughs full of ice, soda, and water, and another small table piled high with handmade, plastic-wrapped sandwiches and little bags of chips. I guide Niall to a bench, fetch us food, three sandwiches each, soda, and some chips. We dig in with gusto. I honestly don't remember the last time I ate either. Probably yesterday, sometime. I left in a hurry, stopped in this town for gas, and was planning on hitting the diner when both Niall and the tornado hit town. And that was hours ago. I don't know what time it is, either. Past midnight. Nearer to dawn, maybe? The sky beyond the jagged horizon is tinged with lighter shades of black and gray, the precursor to impending dawn.

Apropos of nothing Niall glances at me over her sandwich, alarm on her face. "Where's Utah?"

I jerk a thumb at my truck, parked in the grass beyond the cluster of HQ tents. "Asleep in the back of the truck."

"I heard talk about her, people saying she was helping find people in the rubble."

I nod. "She's amazing. She'd sniff around, listen,

and if she found someone, she'd go crazy, pawing and digging. She never ceases to amaze me. I've never had a pet before her."

Niall stares at me in shock. "You...*what?* You've never had a pet before? Never?"

I shake my head. "Not so much as a goldfish. My dad was allergic to cats, my mom didn't want a dog, and they never allowed anything else in the house. Then after high school I moved onto my boat, and it never occurred to me to get one." I smile.

"Utah sort of adopted me. I've never done a single thing to train her. She just...does what she wants. She was neglected when I found her, though, had a rope tied around her neck, but it was so tight her fur was staring to grow around it. I didn't know what else to do with her, after I'd cut the rope off, and she just... took to me. I washed her, cleaned her up, brushed her fur, all that. And then, somehow, the thought of her not being around just didn't make any sense."

"So you adopted her, too."

I shrug. "She's the only thing I've ever bothered to take care of. And she doesn't need much. Food, water, and some love."

"Imagine that." Her voice is low, amused, laced with meaning.

I hang my head; eat the crust of my last sandwich. "Niall, about how I left—"

"You're an idiot," she says, around a big bite of ham sandwich. "We've established that."

"It's just—"

"It fucking hurt, Lock." She looks at me now, chewing slowly. "It hurt so bad I don't...I don't even have words. I thought it meant something, what we shared last night. Or the night before, or whenever it was. It hurt. I expected you to be there. I thought we'd...I dunno. Have breakfast. I thought—"

"You thought I could be someone I'm not." I hate how bitter I sound. "I've never been that guy. I've never been there the next morning."

"So I'm gathering."

Her words burn like acid. I feel sick to my stomach with what I'm about to say. Heat fills me. My pulse hammers in my veins, like drums in the depths. "Doesn't mean I—um. That I don't want to try. If you...if you're willing."

She eyes me, her expression carefully blank. "If you can't figure *that* out, you're more of an idiot than I thought."

Always landing on a lost bet

Lock doesn't seem to know what to do with that. To hell with it—I'm not going to hand-feed him every answer, or make it too easy on him.

"I'm falling asleep right here at the table," I say. "I need to lie down somewhere."

He stands up, offers me his hand. I take it, but warily. He leads me to his truck. I can hear Utah snuffling and snoring in the bed, and as we round the tailgate, I see that Lock found a mattress at some point and shoved it into the bed of the truck. He tugs open the rear driver's side door, pulls a rolled-up sleeping bag out of the backseat. He unzips it to turn it into a blanket and tosses it into the back. I'm too tired to care about the assumption that I'll sleep with him—I totally will. Sleep, that is. Nothing else, not even if we had privacy. He hasn't earned that back, yet. He has to own up to his feelings enough that I'll trust him.

We fucked, and it was good. But that was just fucking, because I was horny and he's hot.

Then we had sex that bordered on making love, and it was the most amazing thing I've ever experienced.

And then his stupid, cave-man ass ran off on me, because he's too sissy to handle his own emotions.

So now he has to man up, and I'm not waiting around too long for him to get his act together. So, in the meantime, I plan to sleep on this scavenged mattress in the back of a pickup truck, under the stars, between a dog and a man for whom I have complicated feelings.

I'm about to hop up onto the tailgate when I feel his hands on my hips, and he spins me in place. He lifts me effortlessly, sets me on my butt on the tailgate. And damn him, because my knees just sort of slide open all on their own, admitting him, letting him wedge his trim waist between my thighs. He cups my jaw in his hand.

I'm not doing this with him, I tell myself.

Yeah…that's a one hundred percent big fat lie.

He's inches away. His chest is a cliff-face blocking out the world beyond him. I hear sounds, but they're faint, distant, and irrelevant. He has my face in his big, rough hands. He's staring down at me. Sea blue-green eyes lit by the moon and the stars, and by the klieg lights behind us. He sucks in a deep breath, lets it out slowly, brows furrowed, as if searching deep within himself for something.

Feints for a kiss, teases me with it. I can't help letting my lips part, can't help lifting my chin to seek the kiss. Damn him, and damn me.

I wasn't going to do this, I wasn't going to let him pull me under the hypnotic vortex of his hotness, his charm, his magnetism. When he gets close like this, I lose all sense, all reason. I've always had extreme distaste for storybook heroines in the romance novels I read, the tittering numbskulls who go all breathy and stupid when some sexy hunk gets close, and then they'd let him do whatever he wanted.

I get that, now.

And it's not fake; it's real.

I'm turning into a tittering numbskull, I'm breathy and stupid, and I'm seconds from compromising myself, right here and now.

Just because some sexy hunk swaggered up close to me, staring at me with big beautiful eyes and holding me with big beautiful hands, surrounding me with big, hard muscles.

"Lock...don't—" I manage to breathe out. "Please don't."

"Don't what?"

"Try to distract me by kissing me."

"I'm not."

"You are too. You can't kiss me out of dealing with your emotions. It might work temporarily, but not long-term. Not on me."

"Damn." He rests his forehead against mine. "You know all my tricks."

I laugh, and taste his breath. "Yes, Lock. I do. Problem is, you're only tricking yourself."

"I know, Niall. Just...give me time. I'm working up to it."

He releases me, and I'm finally able to breathe properly. A hop puts him on the tailgate beside me, and then he's scooting us backward, onto the mattress. Which is dry, but not precisely clean. Beggars can't be choosers, though, I suppose, and it's better than a reclined truck seat. Utah is stretched out on one side, and Lock positions me in the middle, up against Utah, and then settles in behind me. He drapes the opened sleeping bag over us. Utah is warm, soft, and smells like dog, obviously, a pleasant, earthy aroma. I dig my fingers into her fur; rest my head on my arm, my forehead against her back. She snuffles, and her tail thumps a few times.

And then I feel Lock behind me, wriggling to press up close against me. His arm is around my waist, cradling me just beneath my breasts. His hips are against mine. His chest to my back.

I'm bone tired, the kind of exhausted that leaves your eyes burning, your limbs heavy, and your head foggy. But this? This is too perfect, too warm, too right, and I don't want to fall asleep just yet. I just want to enjoy it, and relish it.

Between a dog and a man is a good place to sleep, I think. Warm, safe.

I slide under the edge of sleep slowly, deliriously, happily. Hoping that when I wake up things will still be this simple and perfect between Lock and me.

I wake to warmth, to a burly arm draped over me, a slack hand possessively cupping one of my breasts. Horndog, even when he's asleep. The problem with me is that I don't mind—even in the slightest. I like the feel of his hand on me. I like the hard presence of his body behind me. Speaking of hard...I feel his morning wood through his shorts, huge and thick against my butt.

God, I want him.

If I didn't hear voices nearby from the HQ tents, I'd probably be doing something about his erection, right now. Something about the throb between my thighs.

I can't, though. And I won't. Not until or unless

he owns up to his feelings for me. I know he has them. I just need him to be open enough, and vulnerable enough, and man enough to own them.

And what about my own feelings? They're damned potent. Scary. It's impossible, in some ways, because I know every time I lay my head on his chest and hear his heart beating, I'll think of Ollie. I'll never not be able to think about Ollie, and I'm worried that'll mean I won't ever truly heal. Is that fair to me? Is that fair to Lock? Could we have a successful relationship if I'm reminded of Ollie every time I feel or hear Lock's pulse?

I mean, it's so crazy. My husband dying meant that Lock lived.

As I wake up I'm reminded about the tornado and the subsequent hours of trauma. That all reminds me that life is short. That you never know what's going to happen. Even losing Ollie didn't show me that. Rather, Ollie's death only put me into denial, forcing me into a shell, deep down behind mile-high walls. It made me afraid of life. Afraid of myself. Afraid of the future. Afraid of doing the job I'm best at. Afraid of my body, of my desires, of my heart and its needs.

I could have died yesterday. If that two-by-four had hit the windshield a few scant inches to the right, I *would* be dead.

That knowledge changed my thinking in an

instant. I don't want to waste any more time being afraid. I don't want to live alone, shut down, going through the motions, empty, listless. A becalmed ship on a glassy sea.

There's a radio playing somewhere. Low, but just loud enough that I can hear it.

It's a country song. A man's voice, singing with guitar and piano accompaniment.

I can just make out the words. And they...wreck me:

> *I was a boat stuck in a bottle*
> *That never got the chance to touch the sea*
> *Just forgot on the shelf*
> *No wind in the sails*
> *Going no where with no one but me*
>
> *I was one in one hundred billion*
> *A burned out star in a galaxy*
> *Just lost in the sky wondering why*
> *Everyone else shines out but me*
>
> *But...*
> *I came to life when I first kissed you*
> *The best me has his arms around you*
> *You make me better than I was before*
> *Thank God I'm yours*

I was a worn out set of shoes
Wandering the city street
Another face in the crowd
Head looking down
Lost in the sound of a lonely melody
Empty pockets at a roulette
Always landing on a lost bet
Just live for the spin and hope for the win
Go all in just to lose again

But...
I came to life when I first kissed you
The best me has his arms around you
You make me better than I was before
Thank God I'm yours
The worst me is just a long gone memory
You put a new heartbeat inside of me
You make me better than I was before
Thank God I'm yours

I was a boat stuck in a bottle
That never got the chance to touch the sea

I came to life when I first kissed you
The best me has his arms around you
You make me better than I was before
Thank God I'm yours

The worst me is just a long gone memory
You put a new heart beat inside of me
You make me better than I was before
Thank God I'm yours
Thank God I'm yours
Thank God I'm yours
Thank God I'm yours

"*No wind in the sails, going nowhere with no one but me...*" That's it, that was my life exactly. I find myself crying as I listen to the song, and the repeated refrain.

I'm so thankful I had Ollie.

But he's gone, and I can't bring him back.

I can't pretend he's coming back, and I can't keep hiding from my own life.

"God, that fucking song," I hear Lock say behind me.

"I didn't know you were awake," I say.

"I felt you wake up." His hand flexes, and then freezes as he realizes how he's holding me. But he doesn't let go, and I don't make him. Instead, he clutches my breast more tightly.

"You heard that song, then?"

He nods against the back of my shoulder. "Yeah. I heard it while I was driving yesterday, and I..." He trails off, shaking his head. "I had to pull over to listen to it."

"I've never heard it before. It could be describing me."

"Yeah, me too." His voice is quiet, a low murmur. "You know, I never really believed in the other part of what that song is about."

I try to wrap my head around his convoluted statement. "What? Love?"

"Yeah."

"You can't even say the word?"

"The word is just a word. The meaning behind it is what I've always been skeptical about."

"What about your parents? Didn't they love each other?"

A long silence. "Eh. I mean, they liked each other okay, I guess. My dad died young, and my mother never remarried. I don't think she's ever even been on a date since. She just doesn't...care. She's not like that. She's all about business. She and my father were more business partners than anything, I think. They weren't openly affectionate, and I never heard them say they loved each other. When Dad died, she didn't cry that I ever saw, didn't really mourn. She just... took over the business, and that was it."

"That's...sad."

"What's the story with your family?"

I hate talking about my family, because it's one of those subjects better left in the past. I'm not really bitter about it, and I don't think I have any lasting hang-ups about it, I just...don't like talking about it. But I guess I have to with Lock at some point.

I shrug. "Not much to tell. My father ran off with the nanny when I was eleven, and Mom wasn't...she couldn't hack it as a single mother of two, I guess you could say. She relinquished custody of my younger brother and me to my grandparents and then she left. I haven't seen her since. Don't know where she is, and I don't care anymore. My grandparents died when I was in nursing school, and my brother is a drug addict living somewhere in the bowels of LA." I roll in his arms, face him. "My dad abandoned me. My mom abandoned me. My brother abandoned me. My husband died. So I guess my point is, if anyone has a right to be cynical and bitter about love it's me."

"But you're not?"

I shake my head. "No, Lock, I'm not. I'm afraid, yes. I'm worried—"

"Worried about what?"

It's hard to vocalize everything I've been thinking. I close my eyes and think it through. "The thing with your heart, Ollie's heart. I don't know what to do with that. If that wasn't between us, there'd be no problem at all. I really like you. I enjoy your presence. I feel alive when I'm with you. I feel like...like life is worth living when I'm around you, and before I met you, I didn't exactly feel that way. But…you have his *heart*, Lock. He died, you lived. How am I supposed to wrap my head around that? I feel it, I think about it—about *him*—every time I lay my head on your chest. It's fucked up, and I'm messed up about it."

"Then where does that leave us?" He rolls away from me, onto his back, staring up at the sky.

It's a few hours past dawn, but still early, and it's very quiet, especially after the chaos of yesterday. Even Utah is quiet. It's cool, dew beading on the outside of the truck. The sky is gray-blue, and getting lighter every moment to deeper shades of clear, cloudless azure.

"I don't know, Lock."

"Yeah, me neither." He sits up, rubs his eyes. "I have to piss."

And then he's sliding out from under the sleeping bag and hopping down from the truck bed. Utah goes after him, bounds off a few paces, stops, shakes herself, stretches, and then squats to do her business. I watch Lock beeline for the port-a-potties, baffled by his abrupt departure.

Just like that? That's it? Really?

God.

I want to go home. I have to call the office and give them an update. I need to feed Pep. And I need to be away from Lock, especially if he's just going to shut down again, or puss out on me. I thought I wanted this with him, I thought for a moment that maybe I was willing to put myself out there with him, to give it a shot.

But if he's so out of touch with himself, then maybe I'm better off without him.

The thought hurts, though, strangely.

I leave the truck bed, too. I pay a visit to the port-a-potties, and then quickly check in at HQ where, thank god, things are under control. All the people who needed medical care have either been taken care of or they've been airlifted to a hospital.

I head toward the gas station where I left my truck, intending to leave before Lock can leave me hanging again. But when I get to the gas station, there's nothing left of the place. The building is a pile of rubble and boards and shattered glass. Any vehicles parked when the twister hit have been tossed around like LEGOs, and any still standing have had the windows sucked out. And my truck? It is somewhere in the rubble. I can see hints of rust-red paint under the heap of twisted metal. The gas station sign was ripped from its framework and has slammed down across what I assume is the cab of my truck.

Shit.

Shit.

Shit.

That was my ride home.

It was my last connection to Oliver.

It was my means of escape from Lock.

Suddenly, I feel him beside me. "Well, that sucks," he says.

"No shit."

"You were just gonna take off?" His voice is quiet, but sharp.

"Yeah. Taking a page out of your book." I suppress a shuddering sigh. "Or that was the plan, at any rate."

"I'll take you back."

"No." I shake my head and wrap my arms around my middle.

"No?" He sounds baffled.

"I think it's best we part ways, Lock. I can't keep going back and forth with you." I'm barely whispering, because this is hard. It hurts.

He groans, tips his head back. "Niall, c'mon. How are you going to get home?"

"I don't know. I'll figure something out."

"Why is it best if we part ways?"

I spin to face him. "One minute you're all over me, the next you're shutting down. You don't know what you want. Or if you do, you're too scared to admit it, much less act on it. And I'm just starting to find my feet. I feel…fragile. Like a little colt, you know?

Wobbly. And you keep jerking me around. I can't take it, Lock."

"Let me take you home. Please. Give me that much time with you."

"YOU left ME, Lock. You *ran away*. A hint of emotional connection, and you took off like a fuck-boy pussy."

"Jesus, Niall, tell me how you really feel. Damn."

I shove at his chest, but the big bastard barely moves. "I'm not going to mince words to spare your feelings. Whatever I feel about you is irrelevant if it's not reciprocated. I'm not interested in casual sex any-more. I don't have the time, and I honestly feel like I'm worth more than that. I had a good time with you. I could have seen more happening. I still do. But you're...even now, you're not giving anything back. You want more time with me? You could have all the time you wanted, you just...you have to work for it."

"I don't even know what to say. I'm trying. This whole thing is new to me. All of this. I don't know what I'm doing. You say I have to work for it, but I don't even know what that means."

I turn away, groaning in frustration. "Have you ever had to work for anything in your life?"

He laughs, a bitter sound. "Nope." But then he steps in front of me. "I'm willing to learn, though. Willing to try. Just...give me a chance."

I stare at him, because I'm at a complete loss for words. His eyes, god, those fucking eyes of his speak to the veracity of his words. They emote, those green-blue orbs of his. They speak of the feelings inside him he doesn't know how to deal with, doesn't know how to express.

Men. Ugh.

It's not that hard, is it? I mean, really? Is it?

"This whole thing is just so confusing, Niall. There are so many layers to it. There's my heart, and how that all came about. There's the fact that I..." He swallows hard. "The fact that I'm feeling things for you, when all I came down here to do was...I don't even know! I still don't know why I did this. I drove from fucking California to find you, and I have no idea why. I needed something. I was looking for something. Closure, maybe? Answers? But I don't even...I don't even know what the questions are. And you—you're...I've never met anyone like you, Niall. And I don't think I ever will. Plus there's the fact that I have no idea what to fucking do with my life, but you make me want there to be...*something*. I don't know. Make me want to be somebody you could—love." He halts after that last word. As if he can't believe he just said it. "Because right now, I don't feel like I am that man."

I'm about to respond—although I have no idea

what I'm going to say—when we're interrupted by a medic from the National Guard.

"Dr. James?" He's young, fresh-faced. Barely needs to shave.

"I'm not a doctor. Just a nurse."

"Sorry, ma'am. I just thought you'd like to know, the little girl that was brought in last night?"

My heart sinks. "Oh god. What happened? Is she okay?"

"Oh, yes ma'am! Sorry, I didn't mean to worry you. It's just that her parents showed up. I thought you'd like to know."

"Her parents?"

He nods. "Yes ma'am." A shrug. "Apparently she was with a sitter when the twister hit. They were out of town, I guess, and they just made it back. No sign of the babysitter, though. So either she didn't make it out, or she took off. No way to know just now, I guess."

Lock speaks up. "That house was cleared. I know it was. I was working on the one next door. They checked it. There were no bodies there."

The medic seems troubled by this information. "Which could mean the sitter just left a six-year-old girl alone in the middle of a tornado? Who does that?"

"That's messed up." Lock shakes his head. "Can we see her?"

The medic shrugs. "Don't see why not. She's doing as well as can be expected under the circumstances. She'll heal."

Lock takes my hand. "Come on, let's go say hi to Tori."

I go with him, and we find little towheaded Tori sitting up in her cot, her mother and father on either side of her. Everyone is crying, the mom, the dad, Tori, a nurse nearby. I stand back and watch as Lock approaches hesitantly. When Tori sees him she lights up, sniffles, wipes her nose on her arm.

"It's you!" She reaches down between her knees with her uninjured hand, lifts a tiny calico kitten out of the blankets covering her up to the waist. "Look, Miss Molly! It's Mr. Lock. He saved us."

Utah leans in close to Tori, sniffs delicately at the kitten, who is staring at big old Utah as if she were an alien.

"Utah here is the one who found you. Her and Bill. I just got you out."

Tori scrunches up her nose. "Are you an angel, Mr. Lock?"

Lock stifles a laugh. "No, sweetheart. I'm the farthest thing from an angel you could imagine."

Tori seems enamored with Lock, understandably. Shit, even Tori's mom is having trouble not staring at him.

"Well you're a hero, at least," Tori says.

He shakes his head again. "Nope. You wanna know who the real hero is?" Tori nods, and Lock points at me. "That woman right there. You see all these people in these beds? All the boo-boos they have that are all fixed up? She did that."

Tori looks at me, and then back to Lock. "She's pretty. Are you gonna marry her?"

He's saved from having to answer that knotty little question by Tori's mother. "Mr. Lock, I don't even know how to thank you." She sniffles, tries to smile. "You saved our little girl."

Lock shakes his head, uncomfortable. "You need to thank Niall, and the other medics who worked here yesterday, not me."

"But you went in after her."

"Anyone would have done the same thing."

"But you did it, Mr. Lock."

He tries to shrug it off. "She's a beautiful little girl. I'm just glad she's going to be okay."

"So are we."

After hugging Tori, Lock stands up and turns away. The HQ area we set up yesterday is a bustling hive of activity now, with Guardsmen in camo hustling in a million different directions, unloading cases of water from a semi, tending to the wounded, handing out food, directing traffic. The groan of heavy equipment fills the air as the real work of cleaning away the wreckage begins. There are enough medics and EMS's here now that I feel comfortable leaving, knowing the situation is well in hand.

I turn to Lock. "If the offer to drive me home still stands, I'll take you up on it. I really don't know how I'll get home otherwise. My truck is a goner, I'm afraid."

He nods. "Let's go."

The ride back to Ardmore is a quiet one. Lock tells me to play whatever music I want, so I spend most of the two-hour drive scanning stations, listening to a dizzying variety of music. Lock is mostly silent, one hand on the wheel, the other tugging at his beard under his chin, brow furrowed, eyes narrowed. Lost in thought, I think.

Let him think. God knows I don't mind the time to reflect, as well.

I feel off. Unsettled. Antsy. I already miss Lock, and he's not even gone yet. I'm already lonely again, yet I'm still sitting in the truck with him.

At long last, sometime past noon, we pull to a crunching stop in my driveway.

Lock jabs his thumb at the volume knob, turning

off the radio. "Niall, I—"

I eye him, taking in his drawn, pinched expression and the heaviness in his eyes. "Don't, Lock. I can see it on your face plain as day." I reach back, ruffle Utah's ear. Shove open the door. "Goodbye. And... thank you."

He pinches the bridge of his nose. "For what, Niall?"

"You woke me up. I'm alive. I was asleep—no, more than that, I was...half-dead. And now? I feel like maybe I can start over."

"What are you gonna do?"

I shrug and shake my head, trying to smile past a sob caught in my throat. "I have no idea." Wave a hand at the world at large. "Maybe I'll buy a boat and sail the world."

He laughs in disbelief, closing his eyes and shaking his head. "If you do, don't start in the Caribbean. You'll never leave if you start there."

I shoulder my purse; hop down out of the cab. I walk slowly, hoping he'll change his mind. He rolls down the passenger window, as if to say something. My heart lurches in my throat, but he shakes his head again. I hear the shifter jam into reverse, and then he's backing out. Utah's head hangs out the back window, her tongue lolling happily.

And yeah, just like that, he drives away. Not a

backward glance, not a word of goodbye.

Bastard.

Fucking *bastard*.

You make me better
than I was before

I DRIVE IN A DAZE. I DON'T KNOW FOR HOW LONG, OR HOW far. I managed to get my windshield fixed, and somewhere past the Oklahoma state line, I stop for gas, pumping it in a stupor.

I don't dare let myself think.

Because I know I'm an idiot. I'm driving away, *again,* from the best thing that's ever happened to me.

But I'm doing it on purpose. For her.

And for me.

I need a purpose. I need…to find myself. I fucking hate that cliché, but it's true. Sometimes clichés become a cliché because they're so damn true, you know?

Niall James deserves more than the man I am right now.

Too bad I don't know how to explain that to her.

I can barely make sense of it myself.

Fortunately, I had the presence of mind to leave myself a sliver of an opening with her, just in case. She left her purse in my truck while she was tending to the wounded. She had her phone in there, so I programmed my number in it, and then called myself from her phone, so I'd have her number. Maybe someday I'll feel ready to re-connect with her.

Leaving like this feels wrong, but it also feels right. I'm falling for her. Shit, I've already fallen. I know she feels the same way. But I also know that's not necessarily enough.

So I have to find that elusive *something*. The hell if I know what it might be, but I have to find it.

I read a quote somewhere, in some book, or maybe it was from a movie, I don't know, but it said, *"Not all who wander are lost."* It might possibly be from *The Lord of the Rings.*

But, regardless, that sentiment may be true for some people, just not for me.

I'm lost as fuck.

I mean, I have GPS, so geographically, I know where I am. I really don't know how I ended up here, or what my subconscious is trying to pull on me, but

I just crossed the border from Nevada into California. Apart from stopping for gas and brief layovers at motels along the way, Utah and I have been driving for five days straight. Five days with nothing to think about except what the fuck I can do to find that elusive something I'm searching for.

I've got an inkling of something, but that's about it. It's not even really a full-fledged idea, really, more... the general *shape* of a possible idea. An idea of an idea. Basically, I know now that I've never felt so alive and appreciated and useful and...*fulfilled*...as when I was in Oklahoma, helping out after the tornado. I want to do that. I want that feeling again. I don't really know how to describe it—that feeling that comes when you're helping people, when you know you're changing lives for the better. The sharp swelling ache in your gut, in your heart. I *want* that.

But I'm not a doctor. I'm not a nurse. Hell, I'm not even really a hard laborer, used to running machinery or hauling rubble around.

So how do I get that feeling? What are my skills? What are my resources?

I'm not sure about my skills, other than those I learned at sea, but I know I do have resources, a shitload of resources in the form of millions of dollars at my disposal. A fortune that's been sitting around collecting interest, piling up on itself as Mom continues to expand the family businesses.

Driving down the highway my mind begins to spin, weaving ideas and dreams, pushing me outside my comfort zone and into the realm of *what if*, into the realm of doing something valuable and useful with your life.

The only true measure of a person is what they do with their lives.

Astrid was right. Damn me, but she was right. And I want to do something with my life. Niall germinated that seed, and I know that if I ever want to feel like I deserve her, like I'm a man worthy of a woman like her, I have to do something worthwhile.

Also, I just want to do it, for me. To finally *do* something real in this life, to be a man others can respect. And maybe, just maybe, I can find a way to use my financial resources to get into disaster relief.

Problem number one? I don't have a single fucking clue about where to start.

Problem number two? You know who does know where to start? Mom.

Which is why, I suppose, after more long hours of thinking and driving, I find myself passing the iconic Beverly Hills sign, and then driving through the security gates at Mom's house.

"You want to do *what?*" Mom is, understandably, incredulous.

"Disaster relief. I want to start a non-profit corporation that supplies funds and resources to international disaster relief organizations like the Red Cross and MSF."

"MSF? What's that?" She idly traces a pattern in the sweat on her glass of rosé.

We're outside in the garden again, where Mom prefers to have her serious conversations.

"Doctors Without Borders."

"Oh. And you want to give them money? Why not just make a donation, in that case? We could always use the tax write-off from a hefty charity donation."

"No, Mom, not a single donation. I'm talking about starting a *business*. A corporation."

She scrutinizes me. "You mean...you want to *work?*"

I frown at her. "Jesus, Mom, tell me how you really feel."

"I'm sorry, Lachlan, but we're past pulling punches at this point." She examines her jade-green manicured fingernails studiously, pretentiously. "You've never worked. Never even shown a hint of interest in anything but booze and women and chasing the next adrenaline rush."

I nod and stare down at my sweating glass of Pellegrino. "I know. But...I'm starting to want more."

"What's changed?"

I shrug. "You told me not to waste it. Getting a second chance, I mean. I experienced some things out there—" I wave a hand vaguely, indicating the world at large, "—that changed me. For the better, I hope. Made me want to...I don't know. Do something worthwhile."

Mom is quiet for a long time, staring at me, searching my face, thinking. "She must be pretty incredible."

"Who?" My heart pounds, aches, hurts.

"Don't bullshit me, Lachlan. The only force in this world that has the power to truly change a man is a woman. You *died*, and that was the spark, because you physically *had* to change the way you were living. But it didn't really change who you were deep down." She reaches out, takes my hand in both of hers; I don't think she's ever hugged me, not since I was a little boy, and she's certainly never held my hand. So this physical contact between us? It's huge. "So, if you've changed so much that you not only want to go into business, start working...but start a non-profit disaster relief corporation? The only way something like this happens to a man like you is through a truly amazing woman. So, who is she?"

I swallow hard. Keep my eyes on the table, hoping to hide the uncontainable wealth of emotion even thinking about Niall brings up inside me. "Niall. Her name is Niall. She—she's a nurse. With MSF. I met her...well, it's a long story." I blink, focus on breathing, and consider how to tell my story. "Actually, it's not a long story, just a hard one to tell. She and her husband both worked for MSF—Doctors Without Borders. They were here in California between assignments, and they got in a car wreck. Niall's husband died. He—he was an organ donor."

Mom's face pales, and she sets down her glass. "Oh no. Lachlan, you don't mean—"

I nod. Tap my heart over my chest. "Yep. His heart is in here. Keeping me alive."

"How did you meet?"

I don't answer right away. "I had Larry find her. I—I'm still not sure why, honestly. I didn't know what to do with myself. I was just...fucking lost. I was looking for any kind of direction, anything. I don't know. Larry tracked her down in a little place called Ardmore, in Oklahoma. After Oliver died, she sort of...went into hiding, I guess you could say. Lost her drive, her will, or whatever. Her husband had gotten her into MSF, and she couldn't do the work without him. I went down there to find her. I don't know what I was hoping to accomplish, or what I thought I'd find, but what happened was…well, something I could never have predicted. I met her completely by accident, and—" I don't know how to say the rest.

"Fell in love." Mom cuts to the chase, as always.

"I guess so, yeah. She's amazing. A seriously talented nurse, hard working, easy to talk to, and just… beyond beautiful. She's everything good in this life."

Mom's eyes are soft and a little damp, hearing me. "Well, when do I get to meet her?"

I choke. "I don't—I don't know." I stand up, pace away. Clench my hands into fists to disguise the way they shake. Stare out at the view of Los Angeles spread out beneath us. "I ended things. I walked away."

"It sounds like you really care about her, Lock. I've never heard you talk about any woman this way. They've always seemed rather disposable to you, if I'm being honest. So why walk away, if you feel that strongly?"

"Women were never disposable to me, Mom." I speak quietly, keeping my voice under tight control. "I acted that way on purpose. There were several women I really cared about, but I never let them get close because I knew I was going to die. Why let them get attached to a man with an expiration date? It wouldn't have been fair to them."

Mom is silent, hearing this. I hear her chair scrape, hear her heels on the flagstones, feel her behind me. "I never knew, Lachlan."

"That's the point. If I'd told them, oh, don't bother falling in love with me because I'm gonna die, how many of them do you think would have tried to stick it out anyway, or prove some kind of point? It was my burden to bear." I laugh. "Quite a burden, getting to spend that time with all those beautiful women."

"Don't gloss over it, Lachlan." Mom touches my shoulder tentatively. "You were protecting them."

"And sometimes the only way to make sure they left on their own was to play the part, act like they really were disposable to me. They weren't, but they couldn't know that."

Her hand remains on my shoulder and, oddly, I don't mind it. "So what about this woman from Oklahoma…Niall, you said her name is?"

I let out a shuddering breath. "Niall, yeah…I've never felt anything like what she makes me feel. Including…inferior. Which is why I walked away."

"You're not inferior—"

"Fucking *bullshit*, Mom! Yes, I am! Or, at least, I was. I'm working on changing that, which is the point of all this. You, my own mother, were stunned speechless when I suggested I go into business, let alone start a non-profit. I was a playboy, Mom. I did nothing. I had no value as a man. No way to measure my own self-worth. Everything I have came from you and Dad. I didn't work for it, never earned it. Thirty-one years old, and I've accomplished precisely dick. No skills, no talents, no passions. Nothing. I can't even drink anymore, which was the one thing I *was* good at! That and fucking, and now that I've met Niall, she's all I want, all I can think about. So that's out too. Makes me pretty damn inferior, I'd say."

"Lachlan, you—"

"Just *listen*, Mom." I turn around to face her. "I walked away because I have to *become* someone worthy of a woman like her. She's back with MSF, finally, out there doing what she does best, what she loves— saving lives. She literally saves lives for a living, Mom. I watched her work, too. There was a tornado—"

Mom gasps, cutting me off. "My god, you mean that F-4 in Oklahoma? You were there?"

I nod. "We were smack dab in the middle of it. Ground zero. Saw the damn funnel with my own eyes, a few hundred yards away. And she didn't—she never hesitated. She got to work, just automatically. Started a triage center for the injured and ran it by herself until the authorities showed up. And for the first time in my life, I felt useful. I pulled people out of the wreckage. Dug them out, in some cases. Went house-to-house, looking for survivors and bringing the wounded to Niall. It was…terrible, but amazing. Doing something *good*. Selfless.

"But once we left, went back to Ardmore, I knew I couldn't be with her. She was going to go back to MSF—I knew it then, even if she didn't. And what was I going to do? Follow her around? She deserves better. And I needed to—figure myself out, I suppose. I really do care about her. Love her, even. But it won't work until I get my shit squared away. Until I do something worthwhile. Not for her, but for me. So I can feel worthy of her. That's what this is about. I may never get her back, I realize that. Like I said, this is for me. But if I do ever get a second chance with her, I want to know I deserve her."

Mom is crying. Quietly, elegantly, but crying. "I don't know what to say, Lachlan."

"Say you'll help me." I put my hands around her thin biceps, hold her. "I need your help. I can't do this without you."

She leans into me, runs a knuckle carefully underneath her eye to wipe away a tear without smudging her makeup. "Of course. I would love nothing more."

The next few months are a whirlwind. Lawyers, shareholders, investors, clients, donors, Mom sets up meetings with all of them and lets me outline my plan for them. A plan which she helped me shape and articulate: we set up a non-profit corporation—which we name Beyond Thirty-One, for obvious reasons—dedicated to raising money, gathering supplies, and recruiting volunteers and skilled tradespeople, all for disaster relief efforts.

Mom meeting Utah was pretty funny. I fully expected Mom to hate the big hairy dog, but they seem to have bonded. Mom takes Utah to doggy salons for pampering, and takes her for walks around her glitzy neighborhood. Mom, in four-thousand-dollar heels, walking a mammoth beast like Utah who, in turn, is wearing a Swarovksi crystal-encrusted harness, pulling my elegant mother along, tongue lolling, sniffing, pissing. It's hysterical. But it's also helpful, because it lets me work without having to put Utah in doggy daycare or hire a professional dog walker.

And yes, for the interim, I'm living with my mother. Nearly thirty-two, and I'm living with Mommy. But honestly? It's great. Her house is so large that we both have our own privacy, and I'm not ready to be alone just yet.

We found a floor for lease in an office building in LA where we'll headquarter Beyond Thirty-One, and

Mom lines up about a thousand interviews for interns and office staff. But then, instead of helping me with those interviews, she hands me a printout with a few sample interview questions, and tells me she has her own businesses to run, so I'll have to handle this part myself.

The first dozen interviews are a mess. I'm nervous, have no idea what to say, or what to ask, or what I'm looking for. But by the time I've interviewed the hundredth person, I've got the hang of it.

A week of interviews, and I've got my staff, a couple dozen young, talented, passionate kids with fire in their bellies for the work we're going to do.

Now I've just got to get the financial structure in place, and that's where Mom comes in. I'm not planning on doing this small. This isn't going to be a handful of college kids raising a few thousand bucks to install some wells. This is going to be on an epic scale, with major money for major impact. I'm going to need a board of directors, as well as serious investors and donors.

But they can't be idle ghost partners, or uninterested, invisible, never present investors. They have to be involved. They have to understand.

Mom has to understand.

And that's when I come up with another idea.

Uganda
One month later

"You look ridiculous, Mom." I grab her arm and direct her back into the hotel. "You can't wear that. This isn't Beverly Hills."

She balks. "Clearly, Lachlan. But I will not comprise my appearance simply because we—"

"Your appearance will not matter. And you'll be miserable wearing that out there. Trust me on this."

This being Africa, it's a little hot outside, and Mom is wearing a Chanel pantsuit, Louboutin heels, and a massive straw hat, à la Audrey Hepburn. Pearls. Jesus, the woman is wearing pearls. We're in Uganda to help out with relief efforts connected to the ongoing civil wars in the north. We're not going to the front lines by any stretch of the imagination, but we'll be close enough for Mom and the other potential investors to get an impression of the kind of relief work I want to do.

All the board members and major investors are here as part of what I'm calling, as CEO, an "operational awareness exercise". Meaning, get the rich, sheltered assholes out of their cushy Malibu Barbie lives and make them see what they're investing in, what we're doing. So far, I'm no one's favorite person. When these people travel, especially on a long trip like this, there are five-star accommodations waiting, limos and helicopters and massages and Mai Tais and cool pools and white sand beaches. But not on this trip. Here, there's dust, dirt, brutal baking heat, smelly, broken-down buses, tiny, cramped, hot rooms in ramshackle, run-down, roach-infested hotels. Languages they don't understand, food they don't understand, cultures they don't understand. They're no more than ignorant white foreigners here, and no one cares how much money they have.

And Mom is the worst complainer of all of them.

And we haven't even gotten to the relief station, yet.

It's another two and half hours of jouncing, jolting, and sweating in a pair of thirty-year-old Land Cruisers. Everyone is wilted, cranky, and glaring daggers at me.

We finally arrive at a rearward aid station, primarily used for dispersing supplies and volunteers to the stations closer to the worst of the fighting. When the vehicle is parked, we all hop out and stretch, working the kinks out of our backs.

A tall black man approaches, dressed in faded khakis and a blue and white striped collared shirt, head shaved, sweating, with a clipboard in one hand.

"You are Lock Montgomery, I think, yes?"

I extend my hand, try not to wince from the pressure of his crushing grip. "Yeah, I'm Lock. You're Peter?"

He nods vigorously. "Yes, yes. Peter Obote. Thank you for coming, we very much need your assistance today. There was a bomb set off in Gulu, many dead, many more injured. Now the fighting has got worse than ever, and all the aid stations are past full. We are a small place here, and there are not many of us to do the work." He eyes my companions, none of them under fifty, all of them inappropriately dressed for the location, the work, and the weather, and all of them looking frightened and out of place, especially when a truck full of UN peacekeeping forces rumbles past, hauling soldiers carrying fully automatic weapons. "You are sure about this, Mr. Lock? You, maybe this is good work. Them? I am not so sure."

"I'm sure, Peter. Lead the way. We're here to help."

He leads the way into a low cinderblock building covered by a corrugated tin roof. Inside is a jumbled, chaotic mess of crates and boxes, cases of water, canned goods, medicine, food, and medical supplies.

Peter points with his clipboard. "We have convoys of supplies coming and going all the time, and we do not have enough manpower to even organize this. It is a mess, and when they come to get supplies for other stations, it is most impossible to find anything."

"You need it organized?"

"I would be most grateful, yes. I have a group of children coming as well, to help with this work."

And then Peter is gone, and I'm left with nine rich old white people who have never lifted anything heavier than a bottle of wine, and a mountain of supplies to organize.

I clap my hands. "Well, folks, this is why we're here. Let's get this party started. Milton, Henry, Vic, why don't you start piling those cases of water by the wall near the door? Jane, Mom, Amy, Martha, get these medical supplies sorted and stacked—like with like, as much as possible. Bob, Thierry, Elaine, we'll work on the food supplies, get them stacked and organized in the back. And...don't hurt yourselves, but don't wimp out on me. Yeah?"

The next two hours are brutal. Everyone complains and no one wants to put their back into anything; this is probably the first time most of them have done hard physical labor in their lives. And then, all at once, a huge gaggle of Ugandan children arrive, everyone shouting and chattering in their native language, a good twenty of them all shepherded by two older women wearing headscarves and severe expressions. The kids don't bat an eye when they see us. The women in charge of them immediately size up the work we're doing and divide their charges into several groups and instruct them to help us.

Those kids put us adults to shame, even me. They work like dogs, scrambling as if their lives depended on it, working in effortless unison when something is too heavy for one person.

This is the first breakthrough.

The second comes the next day when Peter sends us with a convoy carrying supplies to a nearby village. More hours by truck, in the dust and heat. And then we're in among the straw huts, surrounded by curious faces and strange voices, hands reaching out desperately. The convoy helpers push back the crowd, and now I can see why Peter sent us here; I think he understood my purpose in bringing the board members here rather well. This village was obviously hit hard by a recent battle of some kind, and one that wasn't localized to organized adult male fighters.

Nearly everyone is sporting a bandage of some kind. Faces are still bloody and bruised and swollen. Limbs are missing. Agony and desperation is on every face. Thirst. Starvation. There are very few adult men, and the few I see are crippled by injury. Women, children, the elderly. All battered and cut and wounded.

I watch the faces of my board members; they are horrified. Shocked. Distraught.

They move on autopilot, following the instructions of the aid workers. Handing out food and water, helping set up a medical tent, assisting the medics in re-wrapping bandages, checking wounds, dispersing medicine. I see tears. Vomiting. Shaking.

I see Mom with a male aid worker, who seems to be translating for the woman Mom is helping. The woman has a bandage wrapped around her head, speaking rapidly, gesturing. The more she speaks, the more upset I watch my mother become. If I'm reading the woman's gestures correctly, she's telling my mother about being struck on the head, thrown to the ground, and likely raped. When the medical aid worker finishes re-wrapping the woman's bandage, Mom leans in and hugs her. Mom, who is the single most standoffish and least physically affectionate human being I've ever known, is hugging a perfect stranger.

We spend the day in that little village, helping. We don't leave until well past sundown, and the ride back is utterly silent, everyone staring off into space, lost in thought.

I don't give the board members a chance to think too hard; we spend an entire week living in that aid station, helping Peter and his people. By the time the week is over, pretty much everyone has picked up a few useful words and phrases, has learned to jump into situations and help out without being told.

They're not bad people, these board members, just sheltered. Privileged.

When the week is up, we make our way back to Kampala and the international airport, and we board a private jet bound, not for Los Angeles, but for Monaco.

You can't put people like this to work like I did and not reward them at the end, after all.

I give them forty-eight hours to unwind, catch up on sleep, relax by the pool, sip some champagne, and then I gather them in a meeting room.

When everyone is seated around the table I stand up, move to the front of the room, and wait until the silence has grown uncomfortable.

Mom breaks the silence. "Your point is well-taken, Lachlan." Her voice is soft, containing a note of what I would normally call humility, if I didn't know any better. "Thank you for this trip. I know I balked at the beginning, and…honestly, I feel a bit foolish, setting out wearing Chanel and pearls. But then we went to that village, and I met that woman. Oh—look at me. I'm a mess just thinking about her." Mom is crying again, which sets everyone else on edge, makes them shift in their chairs, clear throats and look away, remembering their own similar experiences, most likely. "Seeing the things we saw last week…I get it now, Lachlan. I get it. So…thank you."

Milton stands up. Shifts on his feet. Clears his throat. "I have a motion for the board. I know this isn't how things usually work, but we're all here, and I want to pass the motion while it's fresh in our minds. I propose we do this again. Once a year, at least, as a board. Uganda, somewhere else, anywhere. Wherever Lachlan sends us. We'll put our feet on the ground in the places we've spent the year sending supplies. We'll get down there and meet the people. I've always prided myself on staying in touch with every part of my companies. I visit the mailrooms and the break rooms, attend company picnics, visit employees in the hospital, things like that. Stay connected."

Milton clears his throat again. He's the oldest, stodgiest, most cantankerous of the lot, so this is immensely surprising to me, to everyone. "But this… this is different. You all know, you felt it. Those people have nothing, literally *nothing*, and then the fighting breaks out and they get hurt or killed, and for what? Tribal differences? I don't even know. This is not just making a donation. It's not like sitting in my office, writing a check and patting myself on the back. What you're doing here, Lachlan, with this company is phe-

nomenal. I signed on because your mother is a pira-
nha with balls of steel, and she left me with no choice
but to contribute. I signed on for the tax deduction,
and to appease your mother. But like your mother
said, I get it now. So, the motion: every member of
the board must attend a minimum of a once yearly
trip to a location of the CEO's choosing, to experience an operational awareness exercise. All in favor
say 'aye'."

There's a chorus of aye's, and not a single dissen-
sion.

I think I've won over the board.

I'm sitting in an office in Geneva, wearing a suit and
tie, waiting for the meeting to start.

The office is that of the International Federation
of Red Cross and Red Crescent Societies, and the
meeting is to negotiate an arrangement between Beyond Thirty-One and the Federation.

Our corporation is in place, funded, and staffed.
We have warehouses full of supplies and a distribution network. We have teams of volunteers on stand-
by, from general labor to skilled trades, doctors, lawyers, building contractors, anything and everything I
could think of, and a bunch more suggested by our

staff and board members. Now we just need places to send it all. I contacted the Federation and obtained this meeting, and now I just have to sell my services. I have another similar meeting with MSF next week.

An older man wearing a sleek gray pinstripe suit walks into the office, sorting through a file folder full of papers. "So, Mr. Montgomery. You run a non-profit, and you wish to help, is that right? I confess I only skimmed your email."

It doesn't take long for me to get his undivided attention, as I explain what Beyond Thirty-One is all about, and what we have at our disposal. Within fifteen minutes, he's practically glowing.

"It's rather remarkable, what you have set up, I must say. I could use a dozen non-profits like yours, and we'd still never be able to reach all the people that need help. But what you're offering, it will go a long way, and help a great many people." He leans back in his chair, twirling a pen between his fingers. "I can have a list of contacts for you by the end of the day. That should get you started."

Manila, Philippines
One year later

A typhoon swept through here a week ago, wiping away huge swaths of slum housing, leaving flooding in its wake on a huge scale. We were boots down the day after the typhoon subsided, building shelters, distributing food, water, medical care.

I've been running Beyond Thirty-One for a solid year, now. The LA office runs itself, setting up fundraisers—which I attend as much as possible, whenever I'm stateside—finding suppliers and distribution networks, connecting our resources to those in need. I'm not just the CEO and chairman of the board, though. I'm the public face. I'm the frontman. I go with the supplies, go with the volunteer teams. Hit the ground first, and go to work.

My first inclination was to keep this private; to make sure no one ever knew anything about me, keeping the whole thing on the down low, but Mom had other plans. A quiet blog post about a former playboy turned philanthropist, combined with the fact that I'm not exactly bad looking, and that I'm on location several times a month, getting dirty and meeting people, handing out supplies and building houses and tending to the sick…well, the story caught. I wouldn't say I'm famous, but our donations have skyrocketed, as did the number of volunteers.

I don't do it for any of that, however.

I could easily stay in LA in my cushy air-conditioned office, hit the fundraiser party circuit, and play it easy. But that's not why I started this company. I did it to be involved. To be physically present. To make a difference. I won't do any of that, sitting in LA.

Plus, Niall is out there somewhere.

I finally got up the courage to call her one day, late at night, from Thailand. My heart was pounding as I heard the phone ring, but then I got a recorded message saying her number had been disconnected.

That hurt.

She's moved on, I suppose. Good for her.

I get a call from a woman with MSF, asking if I have any resources to spare for relief efforts in Nepal, after a nasty earthquake. The woman has a pronounced French accent, says her name is Dominique.

She's about to hang up when a thought strikes me. "Dominique, wait. I have a strange question for you."

She hesitates. "*Oui?*"

"Do you know anyone named Niall James?"

Another long pause. "*Oui.* I do. She is a very good

friend of mine." A pregnant silence. "You are he, *non*? She has spoken of you. You hurt her, you know."

I sigh. "I know. Is she in Nepal?"

"That is not my place to say. If she wanted to find you, she would have, I think."

"Look, I'll send everything I can to Nepal, regardless. You have my word on that. I just want...I don't know. An opportunity. I just want to see her, talk to her. Even once. That's it."

"Send your supplies to Nepal. If you happen to be with the shipment, you may get your opportunity. That's all I will say."

"Thank you, Dominique."

"She has finally started to find peace. Please, if you wish to thank me, do not disturb that for her."

"I love her."

"Sometimes, the fact of love is not enough. It is what that love looks like that truly matters. Step carefully, and think of her before yourself, if you do love her as you say."

Wise words from a stranger.

A few days later, I'm in the back of a cargo plane full of supplies and volunteers, headed for Nepal.

I'm trying not to hope too much.

The best me has his arms around you

Basantpur, Nepal

DR. VAN EICK HAS A PAIR OF HEMOSTATS CLIPPED TO the young woman's femoral artery, pinching off the blood flow. She doesn't have long. She's lost so much blood, too much, probably. But if he can get that artery reconnected she might have a chance, that along with a shitload of plasma infusions. I'm the only nurse in this tent, which is crazy, because the wounded are coming through faster than we can deal with them. Right now, for example, Dr. Van Eick needs me to hand him utensils, but there's two incoming who need immediate triage care, and a third whose bandages need changing, a fourth who needs more pain meds…the list goes on and on.

We've both been up for more than forty-eight hours, and it looks like another forty-eight are on the books. Another earthquake rocked Nepal three days ago, leaving the whole valley in a shambles. My MSF team was sent here directly from our last assignment, a dengue fever outbreak in Malaysia. We literally packed up, hopped on a plane, and got to work. I don't think I've showered in a week.

The earthquake, though...god—7.8 on the scale, razed entire cities. Every humanitarian organization in the world is represented here, and it's still not enough.

Erik—Dr. Van Eick—finally finishes the trickiest part of the surgery and brusquely waves me away. He's an asshole, but he's a damn good surgeon.

I'm on autopilot, doing what needs to be done. Hours, hours, hours. Night falls, dawn breaks. Dominique finally finds me, forces me to find a bed and sleep, which I do.

No dreams, fortunately. Usually, I dream of Lock. Sometimes of Ollie. Sometimes it's not clear who it is. Just...someone. Beside me, with me, kissing me, whispering to me. I hate the dreams, because I always wake up alone.

At least I have my MSF team.

I sleep for a good six hours before I'm shaken awake by Dominique, whom I don't think ever sleeps, even though she's always making sure we all do.

Another two days of non-stop work.

Three more.

It just doesn't end.

I lose track of time, of hours and days.

I'm sitting in the mess tent, shoveling down some food between surgeries when I feel it. The shaking. It starts slow, but then picks up. A rumble, at first. Then a roar. Then everything is heaving, the ground under my feet is bucking like a wild bronco. I'm tossed in the air, and hit the edge of a table on the way down, which topples beside me. The tent is collapsing. Everyone is screaming, including me. I feel a hand grab me; hauling me upright, out from underneath the collapsing mess tent.

The hand on my arm is ripped away, but I don't see by what, or how. I can't see—I'm dizzy and disoriented from the blow I took to the head when I hit the table. I see an already-ruined building crumbling a dozen feet away, chunks of rubble flying like missiles. I feel an impact to my shoulder like a ton of bricks, hot searing pain slamming through me, and then I'm airborne again, hitting the ground.

Can't breathe.

The quake is still roaring, insane, impossible, endless, a rumbling underfoot loud enough to crack the sky. I hear and feel a building collapsing nearby, but I can't move, can't breathe. I feel something massive hit the ground a few feet away, and I know this is it.

This is where I die.

I moan in pain, and try to find my feet. I'm at the foot of a wall, and it's swaying. But I'm paralyzed with pain and the air has been knocked out of me, I can't breathe, can't move. I try, but I can't.

And then I see him.

I must have died—that's the only explanation for what I see.

Or it's my imagination, or a guardian angel.

Problem is, the guardian angel looks a hell of a lot like Lock.

Same build, tall, broad, muscular, thick, shaggy blond beard, long blond hair tied low on his nape. Wearing a white T-shirt with the red crescent of the IFRC, and a pair of tactical khakis. He just…appears in front of me. Scoops me up in his arms.

He doesn't speak, just clutches me in his arms and runs flat out as the wall where I was lying collapses. Dust rises, billows, and settles.

The quake and the aftershocks are fading in fits and starts.

He stops running.

God, those eyes. I blink. Breathe, finally, in painful gasps.

"Lock?" My voice is raspy, my throat on fire from inhaling dust.

"Niall." He searches me with his eyes. "Are you okay?"

I cough. "Yes. No. I don't know." I reach up, touch his jaw, stroke his beard. "Is it really you?"

"Yeah, babe, it's me." His fingers touch the side of my head, come away wet and red. "You need a doctor."

I shake my head. "No, I need to find my team. I need to—"

"You need to relax a minute. This is a nasty wound. You need help. You can't help others until you're seen to."

"How are you here?"

"I do some work for a relief agency."

He's walking with me in his arms across the rubble-strewn hellscape that was once the city of Basantpur, and then I feel him duck, and we're in a tent. There's shouting, in French and English and half a dozen other languages, but I hear Erik's voice above it all, shouting orders in that gruff Dutch accent of his, organizing. I hear him shout my name, needing me at his side.

"Erik!" I call out, but I'm so weak that my voice goes unheard.

"Hush, Niall." Lock touches my lips with his finger.

I feel myself being lowered onto a cot, and then

Erik's face is above me, and his fingers are probing. He gives me a local anaesthetic, begins stitching.

"Not so bad," he says when he's done. "You were lucky."

I sit up on the cot, swoon, sway, and two pair of hands steady me. I wave them off. "I just need to catch my breath. I'll be fine. I need to help."

"You need to rest. No helping for you."

"We just got hit by another quake. You need me."

"I need you, yes, but I need you healthy." Erik holds up a hand over my attempt to argue. "No. No. You rest."

He walks away, and then Lock is kneeling beside me. Hands on my shoulders, urging me to lie down. I fight it, but my head is swimming and it hurts to breathe and everything hurts, and—

Lock.

Lock is here.

I force my eyes open. "I'm still mad at you."

He chuckles. "I know. I deserve it."

"You just…left."

He shushes me. "Later, Niall. Rest now."

I fade. Slip under.

I wake and his eyes meet mine. He looks like Lock but

there is something different about him. There's a quietness, a sense of calmness, a level of self-assuredness that wasn't there before. A confidence.

"Why'd you leave?" It's the only question that really matters.

A sigh. "I had to." He stares at me unblinking, truth in his eyes. "It wasn't just about not being able to admit that I was in love with you, it was…knowing I needed to be okay with myself before that could go anywhere."

His words rock me. I stare at him for a long, long time. "You—you were in love with me?"

A small, tired smile. "I still am."

"Still?"

A tired nod.

"I didn't think I'd ever see you again," I say.

"Me too. I called you, a few months ago."

I frown. "I don't have a phone anymore, Lock. I got rid of it when I re-joined MSF."

A wry grin. "So I discovered."

"What would you have said to me if you had reached me?"

His eyes are closed, an arm draped across his face. "That I love you. That I…miss you. That I'd like to see you."

I finally manage a glimpse past him, at the devastation beyond the tent. I lift my chin in gesture. "How bad is it out there?"

A long sigh. "Really bad. Really, really bad. We were pretty far from the epicenter, though, so we got off easy compared to the areas hit hardest."

I gasp. "It must have been a huge one, then."

"Eight point two."

"Oh my god."

"And they just finished rebuilding from the last series of quakes a few years ago. It's unbelievable." He moves his arm, glances at me. "How are you feeling?"

"Dizzy, thirsty, achy. But better."

"Good. You slept for thirteen hours. I was getting worried."

"Thirteen hours?" I try to sit up. "Holy shit, Dr. Van Eick must be—"

"'When you're ready, not before'—his words."

A silence, then. Long, and profound. Our eyes on each other, unwavering.

"I missed you, too," I admit, finally.

He holds out an arm. "Come here."

Slowly, gingerly, I sit up, totter the few steps to his cot. Lie down in his arms, and sigh a deep sense of contentment. The world beyond this cot is a hellish nightmare landscape of ruin and rubble, but here? In his arms? None of that matters. Not right now.

He turns his face toward me, buries his nose in

my hair. "God, Niall." His voice shudders, shakes. "I fucking missed you. So goddamned bad."

"You *left*." I hate how angry I sound, even still. "You just…left. Didn't even say goodbye."

His voice is so quiet I have to strain to hear. "I couldn't—if I'd hesitated, I wouldn't have had the balls to go. I had to become a man worth loving, Niall. You'd have loved me as I was, but…I had to feel like a man worthy of your love."

"So….what? You joined the Red Cross?"

"Not…exactly. "

I sense that he's withholding the truth. "Lock." His eyes meet mine. "What is it you're not telling me?"

He sighs. "A lot, I suppose. Does the name Beyond Thirty-One mean anything to you?"

I think for a moment. "I do remember hearing rumors of a new company donating a lot of money and supplies to relief efforts. From what I remember hearing, it's a new non-profit, run by some jet-setting playboy."

He fidgets, glances away. "I…that's me."

I frown. "What? What do you mean?"

"Beyond Thirty-One is my company."

"But they were saying the guy who runs it is a millionaire or something. Like, stupid rich. There were a lot of rumors floating around about him, but I haven't had time to look into it."

He nods. "The rumors are mostly true. I come from a wealthy family. My grandfather made a fortune in both oil and real estate, and my dad expanded the family business quite a lot before he died, and then my mom took over and streamlined it all and turned an already sizeable fortune into one several times larger. As the only heir, I was always supposed to take over, but I never cared. I was going to die, so why fucking bother, right? So, I prefer the distinction that my *family* is wealthy; I personally am not. I didn't do a damn thing to earn a single penny of my inheritance."

I nod. "I guess I understand the distinction." A pause, a breath. "When you say your family is wealthy…?"

A casual shrug. "I've never really paid too much attention to the exact numbers. I think Mom is worth somewhere in the neighborhood of…several hundred million. Maybe more."

I'm a little dizzy, suddenly. "And you personally?"

Another of those lazy shrugs that say it doesn't really matter. "My shares put me at, I dunno…quite a few million."

"And you were staying at fucking La Quinta?"

He laughs. "They allowed pets," he says with a shrug.

I try to sort through my thoughts and feelings. "So you started Beyond Thirty-One?"

He nods, more willing to meet my eyes now. "After the tornado, I knew I wanted to help people. To do what you do, but...my way. I've never had the slightest interest in the family businesses, sitting in some office crunching numbers and analyzing contracts or whatever the fuck. That day in Oklahoma... it changed me. *You* changed me, and then the tornado, helping with the recovery...it *meant* something. *I* meant something. I did something *good*. Something for someone else. My whole life had always been about me, about making myself feel good, about forgetting that I was going to die sooner rather than later. I never did anything that had any value or significance. I got a taste of that in Oklahoma. I'm not a doctor. I'm not a skilled tradesman. I have no skills at all, really. What I do have is time and money. So that's what I'm using."

"So when you said you left to become a man worthy of my love...?"

"That's not the only reason. Maybe it started out that way, to some degree. But I *love* doing this. It's a mission. A purpose."

"So...do you feel like a man worth my love, now?" I sound...I don't even know. Desperate, and hopeful all at once.

"Yes." He's looking at me, those blue-green eyes searing and tender at once. "I'm not letting go, this time."

"You better not."

"You know it's going to be weeks before we get any privacy, right?"

I sigh. "That crossed my mind, yes. I've waited this long, I can wait a little longer. Besides, there are a lot of people that need our help."

"What if I can't wait?"

"Then we'll figure something out. You're a creative guy, you'll think of something, I'm sure."

He's fading, I can tell. I let him get some sleep. I bury my face against his chest. Feel his heart beating. Resting on his chest, I listen to his heartbeat and let myself miss Oliver for a few moments.

Thump-thump…thump-thump…thump-thump.

That's Oliver's heart. Beating. Alive. A reminder. It hurts, even still, and I know it always will. But then Lock's hand squeezes my waist, and I feel his breathing even out, and the heartbeat is steady, reassuring, and strong, and I don't mind the pain so much.

Sometimes I think you need a little pain to remind you of the good things in life.

I spent so long avoiding everything because I couldn't handle the pain. But when you face the impossible, when you let yourself feel the pain, when you let it pass through you, when you refuse to let pain and fear keep you prisoner, you discover that life is always worth living. You discover your own strength. You rediscover beauty.

Love is always a risk. Sometimes you lose, as I did. But I'd still not trade a single moment of my time with Oliver, not for anything, even if it meant experiencing the agony of losing him again. I had something amazing, and yes, I lost it. It hurt. It still hurts. It will always hurt. But the pain isn't the only thing that exists in the world. There's more. There's beauty.

I don't sleep right away, even with Lock snoring beneath me. I hold him; let myself be held by him. Feel that heartbeat, count the thrums, and I'm thankful for each one.

Lock and I barely see each other for the next month. He's busy with the recovery efforts, and I'm busy with the endless stream of injured and sick. We find each other now and then; share a meal, a couple hours of conversation.

And honestly, as hard as it is, as much as we both want more, want privacy, this time spent simply getting to know each other feels…necessary. We learn each other. We find comfort in just being near each other. Sometimes we'll share a kiss in the midnight hours, but we always stop before we get carried away. We both know a single touch is all it will take for either of us. Touch is a lit match in a room full of gunpowder. A single spark will set off an explosion we won't be able to prevent. So we're careful. Quiet, slow, brief kisses as we share a meal, sit under the Nepali stars and bright silver moon. Hold hands, walk between mounds of rubble and wreckage.

What a place for romance.

But that's what this is: a bizarre courtship. Dating in the ruins of an earthquake-flattened city, in a far-flung corner of the Earth.

My MSF team has been reassigned to a malaria outbreak in South Sudan, but we've been given a week off, first. Lock needs to get back to California eventually, so we're unsure what's next for us.

He'll head to wherever, and I'll head somewhere else. When will we see each other? Is there a future for us, if we're never able to be together?

I'm packing my things as I think about this.

I feel him, as I always do, before I see him.

He's behind me, silent, watching. We haven't spoken much about what our reassignments mean for any possibility of an "us", because I don't want to bring it up, and neither does he, and it's easier to put it off as long as possible. But I'm supposed to be on a truck out of Basantpur later this afternoon, and he's on a flight tomorrow, and we're running out of time.

"Niall," he says, his voice hesitant.

I keep packing, don't turn around. "Yeah?"

"You have some time off, yeah?"

I nod. "Yeah. A week."

"So…what if we spent that week together? Just you and me. I was thinking Madagascar. Not too far away, and it's supposed to be a great place to visit."

"And then what?"

"We'll figure that out along the way. Niall, there's no way in hell I'm letting you get away. I walked away once, to find myself. Well, I found myself, and now I've found you. I'm never letting go again. The details are things we can work out, together."

His hands rise. One cups the back of my head, the other cradles my cheek. He tips my head back, and his lips find mine. Slant across my mouth, teasing a kiss. I fist my hands in his shirt, pulling him closer. I wrap my arms around his burly shoulders, cling to his neck. Leap up, curl my legs around his waist.

Delve my tongue into his mouth and taste him.

I begin to lose myself in his kiss.

But then a knock on my door interrupts us, and I

slide off Lock, straighten my shirt, my hair. It's Dominique. "Hi, um...hi."

She grins. "It seems you and *Monsieur* Lachlan have resolved your differences." Her eyes twinkle, but they betray a sharpness. "May I have a moment with Niall?" she says to Lock.

He nods. "I gotta go talk to Federico anyway." A wink to me. "Save me a seat on the bus?"

When he's gone, Dominique moves to sit cross-legged on my bed, toying with the zipper on my bag. "He is a fascinating man."

I nod. "Yes, he is."

She eyes me. "Is he good for you? After what happened, I worried for you, you know. I still do."

I smile. "He's good for me. I'm good. I wasn't, for a long time. But I am, now, and that's thanks in large part to him."

Dominique stands, moves past me. "Well, that's good then. Just don't let your personal life interfere with your job."

"Have I ever?"

"I must say it, to be clear. You know this." She taps her watch face. "If you are coming with us, the truck to the airport leaves in two hours."

Thank God I'm yours

WE DIDN'T GET THE WEEK IN MADAGASCAR. IN FACT, we don't get any time off until three months later. I also never got back to the LA office, because there's just so much to do out in the field. I've got the team at Beyond Thirty-One working closely with MSF, both for professional and personal reasons, and things are running smoothly.

So as soon as Dominique gives the word for Niall to have some time off, I've got us on the first plane out of here. I literally just bought tickets for the first commercial jet leaving town.

Turns out Johannesburg, South Africa is a damn nice city. I find us a hotel, based on the recommendation of my office manager back in Cali. My only request was a suite with a view, and something special.

We go up to our room. I tip the bellman and close the door.

Niall glances around at the room, which, admittedly, is pretty fucking nice.

"Damn, Lock. This place is…amazing. Like, wow."

I shrug. "Yeah, it's not exactly the La Quinta."

A moment of humor, and then the tension of the moment takes over.

It's a strange moment, finally being alone together. Two years have passed since I drove away from her in Ardmore, Oklahoma.

I'm a different person.

And she…is the same.

So beautiful she leaves me breathless.

Suddenly, I don't even know where to start. We're alone. In private. I've been dreaming about this for months. Long, lonely months. For *years,* in fact. There's been no one else in that time, because there *is* no one else. Not in the whole world. I thought about it, but I couldn't follow through. I kept hoping, somehow, someday, I'd find her, and I didn't want anyone between us when that day finally arrived.

I'm glad for those years of abstinence, now.

Because the need is…a wild, hungry presence inside me, a nearly sentient being in and of itself, dwelling within me.

I stand and stare at her for long, tense moments.

Thick, curly brown hair tied back out of her face.

Eyes brown with flecks and streaks of green, wide and bright and fixed on me. Tiny khaki shorts molded to her amazing ass. A forest-green spaghetti strap tank top, the shade of which makes her eyes appear more green than brown. She was wearing flip-flops, but she's kicked them off. Had a purse on her shoulder, but she dropped it to the floor by our bags.

"Is it weird to be nervous?" she asks.

I shake my head. "I am too."

"It's not like we've never done this before."

"Not like this we haven't."

I take a step closer to her. Another. She remains motionless, her gaze tilting up to mine as I get closer and closer with each step. Her breathing deepens, swelling her breasts in her shirt. Finally, I have her in my hands. Cup her waist. Slide a palm down over her hip. Up her side, around to her spine. Pull her closer to me. Flush. Body against body.

I want this to be perfect. But the ravening part of me wants to rip the clothes from her body, shove her down to all fours and bury myself in her. Take her hard and wild.

I have an image of Niall, naked, on her hands and knees, hair loose in a curly brown explosion, spine arched as she thrusts back into me.

Something of my thoughts must show on my face, because Niall sucks in a sharp breath. "Whatever it is, Lock, don't just think it. Do it."

I gently tug the elastic out of her hair, freeing it to blossom around her face. "How do you know what I was thinking?"

She frees the bottom button of my short-sleeve button-down shirt. "I don't know what you're thinking, but I know that look, so I can guess."

"What if I thought something crazy?"

Another button. "Then feel free to muffle me if need be."

Holy shit. I stand stone still, collecting the shreds of my restraint. Letting her undo the rest of the buttons, slide the shirt off my shoulders. I just breathe, and focus on not ravaging her like some kind of god-damn caveman.

"I've been missing you for two years, Niall. You have no idea how crazy I feel right now." I tug open the fly of her shorts.

She meets my eyes. "You're saying this whole time you haven't—"

"There's been no one. I've barely had time or privacy for my own hand."

Her eyes narrow. "Damn, Lock."

"You sound surprised."

She shrugs. "You used to be—"

"I used to be a lot of things. You made me want to change. So I did." I slide my palms up under her shirt, find the clasps of her bra and unhook them. "I always hoped I'd figure out a way to find you. Turns out fate or whatever had a different plan. You're it."

"I'm it?" She's barely breathing, working at the button of my shorts, gazing up at me, eyes glittering with need.

"You're it for me." I push up her shirt and bra at the same time, strip them both off her. Toss them aside. Take in the lush wonder of her big, beautiful, bare breasts. "I'm yours, Niall."

Her breath hitches in her throat as I cup a breast in my palm. "Lock…"

I lean in, close my mouth over her nipple.

"Oh, thank god, thank god," she whispers, arching her spine, pushing more of her soft skin into my mouth. "I'm yours, too."

Her fingers, even as she revels in my mouth on her tits, are not idle. They're unzipping me. Tugging shorts and underwear off. Fisting her fingers around my erection, sliding her hand up and down my length, stroking swiftly, eagerly, greedily.

I pull out of her touch, abruptly. "God, Niall. It's been so long, I'm—I won't last long if you keep doing that."

She reclaims her grip on my shaft. "I don't care how long you last. I need to touch you. I need to feel you. If you come too soon, I'll just make you eat me out."

"That's happening anyway," I say, gasping as she closes both hands around me, now.

"Then shut up and let me touch you."

We're still standing in the middle of the living area of our suite. Curtains wide open, sun shining bright. Bathing Niall's skin golden. Gleaming off her hair. I want so many things. I want her touch. I want her mouth. I want to pin her to the wall and fuck her senseless. I want to kiss her breathless and love her delirious.

But I'm helpless to do any of that. She's got me in her thrall, hypnotized by her touch. Struck dumb, paralyzed by the ecstasy of her hands on my skin. Her mouth on my chest, her lips on my stomach. Her hair tickling and sliding lower. Her kisses to my belly, to my thighs. Her tongue gliding up the underside of my erection. Her lips closing around me.

Suction.

Wet warmth enveloping me.

Her fingers sliding and her hands gripping, stroking, plunging. Her moans humming around me.

"Niall, shit. Shit...oh Jesus. I'm—I can't hold back, Niall. It feels too good."

She doesn't respond. Doesn't say anything. Just moves faster. Strokes harder. Works her mouth on me relentlessly. I can't help burying my hands in her hair and guiding her motions.

When I come, it's a heady rush of bliss pouring out of me, erotic visions of her mouth sliding around my erection, hair obscuring her features, breasts swaying.

When she releases me, I stagger backward. Sink to my knees, dizzy. She's in front of me, staring down at me. Bare from the waist up, shorts unbuttoned and low around her hips. I clutch her ass and haul her toward me. Tug those stupid, useless shorts off. Bare her completely for me.

Stare up at her.

Sink two fingers into her opening, watch her gaze go glazed and vacant as I slide those fingers in and out, smear her own essence everywhere. Pull her to my mouth.

Keep those fingers moving, lap at her. Feel her hips begin to grind. Feel her hands in my hair, as mine were in hers. She shows me how she wants it, as I showed her. Hard and fast. Relentless. Tongue swiping and flicking until she's mad with the impending orgasm.

When she comes, it's with a breathless scream, clutching my hair in clawed fingers, grinding against my mouth, calling my name over and over.

Hair in her face, panting, staring down at me. "Take me to bed, Lock."

I stand up, take her in my arms. Carry her to bed. She wipes at my face and beard with her hands, cleaning her juices away.

I lay her down gently, press my body against hers and kiss her.

Slowly and gently at first.

So she knows, so she feels it.

She breaks the kiss first, breathless. "Need you, Lock." Reaches between our bodies.

Strokes me to readiness. Pulls me to her.

"I don't have—"

"It's fine," she cuts in over me. "We're covered."

"They're out there with my things."

"I said we're covered, okay?" She arches, guides me to her opening. "I don't want that." Works her hips, sliding me deep, sliding me home. "I want this. Just this. Just us."

I rest my forehead against hers, struggling for breath, for thought, for sense. This is so intensely, deliriously perfect it hurts.

She clings to my ass, pulls at me with each thrust, as if to make sure I don't try to escape. God, I couldn't. We move together in silence, watching each other, eyes wide, breath coming hard and fast as we meet each other with each thrust. I cup her face, my other fist pressing against the mattress. I refuse to look away or even to blink.

Her face takes on that lovely, wild, almost pained expression of a nascent orgasm. "Lock...god, Lock. I missed this so much. I missed this with you more than I can...oh god, oh god...more than I can say."

I'm incapable of speech right then, focusing on holding out until she's at the edge, until she's falling over, until she's writhing beneath me, crying my name, weeping with the intensity washing through her, hips bucking against me.

When I feel her clench around me, I'm lost. I can't hold it back when she does that, when she clamps down around me, writhing, moaning.

"Niall, Niall...god, oh....oh god." I feel three words on my lips as I come.

I kiss her as my orgasm fades to shudders and I taste them on her tongue.

And then, in the brief, trembling moments after we've both emerged from post-orgasm stupor, she rolls us so she's on top.

Pins my shoulders with her hands, all her weight on me. Leans down, leans close.

"You told me you were in love with me, but I haven't really heard you say the words." Her voice is a hoarse, vulnerable rasp. "Fucking *say* it, Lachlan."

I had it all planned out.

Romantic date. Strolling down some secluded avenue, my arm around her waist. Press her up against a wall and kiss her and say those words I've never said to anyone.

But she's demanding them now.

Thank God I'm yours

Is he panicking?

God no. Please, no, Lock. Not after everything we've been through.

He carves his hands up the backs of my thighs, over my ass, along my spine and up to comb into my hair. Tugging my face down, slanting his lips across mine, kissing me with such fragile tenderness that my heart beats fit to burst in my throat.

"I love you." He whispers it. As if stunned to hear such a thing emerge from his lips.

I, meanwhile, revel in those words.

"I love you, Niall James." He says it again.

I'm overwhelmed, then. Collapse onto him, and of course his heartbeat thunders under my ear.

"I keep thinking about that song," he says. "The one we heard that night in Oklahoma? After the tornado?"

I nod against his chest. "I remember."

"There's a line… 'You put a new heartbeat inside of me.' Not many people can say—" His voice catches, and he has to start over. "Not many people can say that and mean it literally. But you did. Literally, and metaphorically."

"I love you." I murmur it to his chest. To his heartbeat.

And I think I'm speaking twofold. To Lock, of course, but also to Oliver. To the memory of Oliver, that is. The Oliver that will live on in the deep, secret portions of my heart. Not secret, perhaps, but private. Deeply, intensely private. Totally mine. Something I'll never talk about, because they belong only to me.

But it's also for Lock. The start of something new. Something different, and beautiful. Something wild and primal, yet also domestic and comforting.

"I never believed in love," he says. "I never…I never thought I'd hear anyone say that to me. Never thought I'd say it. Because…even though I didn't believe in it, I refused to say it if I didn't mean it. Because I think…I think I always *wanted* to believe in it."

"Believe in it now." I roll off him, curl up with my back to his front, tuck his arm around me.

"I do."

We wake in the same position that we fell asleep—his arm around my waist, palm against my stomach beneath my breasts. The sun is still shining, but now it is the red-gold of evening. I feel him stir behind me. Feel him stir between the globes of my buttocks, going thick and hard. He stretches, pushing against me. Groans with the stretch, flexes his palm.

Cups my breast.

Kisses my shoulder. Brushes my hair aside, kisses my neck.

"Hi," he says.

I flex my hips, wiggling my butt against him. "Hi."

I reach behind me, seeking somewhere, anywhere, to touch him. Find his neck. The back of his head. Groan as he slides his palm down from my breast to the juncture of my thighs. I spread them open for him, admitting his touch. And holy shit, it doesn't take long to get me ready, for him to bring me to a helpless climax, holding onto the nape of his neck and writhing against him.

While I'm still spasming and whimpering, he rolls to his knees. Hooks his hands in the crease of my hips, hauls me up onto my knees. I'm gasping, still shuddering, but I know what he wants, and fuck, do I want that too. I'm just too shaken by the orgasm to do much but let him position me as he wants. I think it's better this way. I like it this way. Helpless to his touch.

He's behind me, one hand at my core, the other gripping his erection. Touching the crown to my opening, pushing in gently.

Fuck gently; I want it hard.

I snicker at my own pun.

"What's funny, Niall?" Lock's voice rumbles behind me.

"You're being all gentle and stuff," I murmur. "And I thought, 'fuck gently, I want it hard.'"

He flutters his hips, teasing me with not enough of him. And then, without warning, he slams deep. Hard. "Like this?"

I'm rocked forward, gasping. "God, yes. *Fuck* yes."

His hand buries in my hair, gathers my curls and uses that grip as leverage. Not gently, exactly. Roughly, beautifully. I push against his thrusts, moan his name—"*Lock! Lock!*" He loses control quickly. Hand on my hip, pulling back into his thrusts, grip on my hair keeping me pinned in place. Hips pistoning. Slamming his thick shaft into me, over and over, until I'm blasted into a frenzy by wave after wave of climax, and he's still going, driving into me, grunting, groaning, chanting my name like a prayer.

"Niall—Niall—Niall...oh god, Niall..."

And then he's unleashing, not with a shout, but collapsing forward onto me, burying his face into my hair, against my ear, thrusting deep and shuddering there, gasping my name too many times to count.

That's all there is to the whole world, then. Just Lock and me, shivering together in the crimson gloaming.

"God, I love you, Niall."

And—that's *all* there is.

Hearing it. Feeling it.

Owning it.

"Thank god I'm yours," he murmurs, a smile in his voice. Referring to that song. To that moment, in the calm after the storm.

"Thank god I'm yours," I murmur back to him.

The End

PLAYLIST

"Yours" by Russel Dickerson

Snapback—album by Old Dominion

"Stay a Little Longer" by Brothers Osbourne

"Rum" by Brothers Osbourne

Southernality—album by A Thousand Horses

"Whiskey on My Breath" by Love & Theft

Just Feels Good—album by Thompson Square

Three—album by Gloriana

Jekyll + Hyde—album by Zaz Brown Band

Fuse—album by Keith Urban

Pioneer—album by The Band Perry

Platinum—album by Miranda Lambert

747—album by Lady Antebellum

Kill the Lights—album by Luke Bryan

Just As I Am (Platinum Edition)—album by Brantley Gilbert

High Noon—album by Jerrod Nieman

Riser—album by Dierks Bentley

The Outsiders—album by Eric Church

"Live Like You're Dying" by Tim McGraw

Pageant Material—album by Kacey Musgraves

Annie Up—album by the Pistol Annies

Dustin Lynch—album by Dustin Lynch

Days of Gold—album by Jake Owen

Summer Forever—album by Billy Currington

Fly—album by Maddie + Tae

Chasing Down the Wind—album by Green River Ordinance

Remedy—album by Old Crow Medicine Show

No Man's Mama—album by Carolina Chocolate Drops

Build Me Up From Bones—album by Sarah Jarosz

Wide Awake—album by Joy Kills Sorrow

The Phosphorescent Blues—album by Punch Brothers

Untamed—album by Cam

Between the Pines (Acoustic Mixtape)—album by Sam Hunt

Tangled Up—album by Thomas Rhett

Illinois—album by Brett Eldridge

"Whiskey Lullaby" by Brad Paisley and Allison Krauss

Ignite the Night (Party Edition)—album by Chase Rice

The Driver—album by Charles Kelley

New City Blues—album by Aubrie Sellers

Front Row Seat—album by Josh Abbot Band

"Yours"
By Russell Dickerson

I was a boat stuck in a bottle
That never got the chance to touch the sea
Just forgot on the shelf
No wind in the sails
Going no where with no one but me

I was one in one-hundred billion
A burned out star in a galaxy
Just lost in the sky wondering why
Everyone else shines out but me

But…
I came to life when I first kissed you
The best me has his arms around you
You make me better than I was before
Thank God I'm yours

I was a worn out set of shoes
Wandering the city street
Another face in the crowd
Head looking down
Lost in the sound of a lonely melody
Empty pockets at a roulette
Always landing on a lost bet
Just live for the spin and hope for the win
Go all in just to lose again

But…
I came to life when I first kissed you
The best me has his arms around you
You make me better than I was before
Thank God I'm yours
The worst me is just a long gone memory
You put a new heartbeat inside of me
You make me better than I was before
Thank God I'm yours

I was a boat stuck in a bottle
That never got the chance to touch the sea

I came to life when I first kissed you
The best me has his arms around you
You make me better than I was before
Thank God I'm yours

The worst me is just a long gone memory
You put a new heartbeat inside of me
You make me better than I was before
Thank God I'm yours
Thank God I'm yours
Thank God I'm yours
Thank God I'm yours

Jasinda Wilder

Visit me at my website: **www.jasindawilder.com**
Email me: **jasindawilder@gmail.com**

If you enjoyed this book, you can help others enjoy it as well by recommending it to friends and family, or by mentioning it in reading and discussion groups and online forums. You can also review it on the site from which you purchased it. But, whether you recommend it to anyone else or not, thank you *so much* for taking the time to read my book! Your support means the world to me!

My other titles:

The Preacher's Son:
Unbound
Unleashed
Unbroken

Biker Billionaire:
Wild Ride

Big Girls Do It:
Better (#1), Wetter (#2), Wilder (#3), On Top (#4)
Married (#5)
On Christmas (#5.5)
Pregnant (#6)
Boxed Set

Rock Stars Do It:
Harder
Dirty
Forever
Boxed Set

From the world of *Big Girls* **and** *Rock Stars***:**
Big Love Abroad

Delilah's Diary:
A Sexy Journey
La Vita Sexy
A Sexy Surrender

The Falling Series:
Falling Into You
Falling Into Us
Falling Under
Falling Away
Falling for Colton

Jack Wilder Titles:

The Missionary

To be informed of new releases, special offers, and other Jasinda news, sign up for Jasinda's email newsletter at http://eepurl.com/qW87T.

Made in the USA
Middletown, DE
19 July 2016

33602756R00257